Chladni's Euphon

DAVID HARRY
TANNENBAUM

Cover art copyright (C) 2022 Ana (Kat) Gally Zelaya

Library of Congress Control Number: 2022940640

ISBN: 978-1-943267-96-5 Trade Paperback

Printed in the United States

Red Engine Press

# Lee County Acronyms

CIA    Criminal Investigation Assistant

ASA    Assistant State Attorney

DFU    Digital Forensics Unit

SOU    Special Operations Unit (SWAT)

ROR    Release on Own Recognizance

RTIC    Real Time Intelligence Center

COD    Cause Of Death

# THE SEMINAL SOCIETY

| Edison | Chladni | Newton |
|---|---|---|
| Phonograph | Acoustics | Scientist |
| 1847 - 1931 | 1756 - 1827 | 1643 - 1727 |

| Galileo | da Vinci | Wolkenstein |
|---|---|---|
| Science | Artist | Composer |
| 1564 - 1642 | 1452 - 1519 | 1376 - 1445 |

# ERNST CHLADNI

WHO, YOU MIGHT ASK, IS this guy Chladni? I, for one, can't recall ever hearing his name mentioned in high school or college in any context. And yet, he is credited with being the 'the father of acoustics', whatever that means. According to Wikipedia, Ernst Florens Friedrich Chladni was a German physicist and musician in the late eighteenth and early nineteenth centuries. His acoustic accolade stems from his research on vibrations, sound and different materials, which led to his patterns and "plates" for each material. These observations are still used today in the design and construction of guitars and other vibrating instruments. Moreover, his work paved the way for the discovery of mathematical solutions in quantum mechanics leading to the understanding of electron orbits. No wonder the fictional Seminal Society is so interested in him!

What is even less well-known is that Chladni also invented a musical instrument he called the euphon which was custom-built to his specifications using a series of parallel glass rods to produce pleasing sounds. Using wet fingers, the glass rods are stroked causing vibrations, which in turn produce a mesmerizing musical sound. Chladni traveled Europe giving scientific lectures by day and holding euphon concerts by night.

At his death his euphon disappeared. That much is fact. It is fair to assume everything else in this story about Chladni and his euphon is fictional.

*Euphon*

# ONE

ELEVEN DAYS INTO 2021, ALMOST three months after their sensational arrests of the perps in the Scotty McDermitt homicide case, Lee County, Florida, rookie-detective Leslie Hodges and her partner, Daryl Fischer, remained buried in paperwork. It was just past nine in the morning, and she had been working the case files for two hours already. This was Leslie's first involvement in preparation for a murder trial, and she was determined to be at the top of her game. Pulling her computer closed, she exclaimed to no one in particular, "I hope it's not always like this!"

"You talking to me, Hodges?" Fischer called, still several steps from her cubby of an office in the Pit area of the Sheriff's office. "If so, I didn't catch a word you said."

"Oh, it's nothing. I just need to be back working the street," Leslie answered, not apologizing for the outburst. "The never-ending questions from the prosecutor's office almost make me wish I never solve another homicide. Is it always this bad?"

"You get accustomed. Those that don't, find other employment. Seriously, you think this is bad, see what crap they pile on you when you stop closing cases. This'll feel like a day at the beach."

"Three months at the beach's more like it."

"Came to give you some good news," Fischer said, his voice upbeat.

"I can use good news."

"That interview you did with our perp the night of his arrest, where you asked about previous art heists, he might have insider knowledge of. Remember his answer?"

"Sure do," Leslie quickly answered. "Matter of fact, I was just reviewing that file. He gave us information on an oil-on-wood da Vinci in possession of the National Gallery in Washington. We had to look it up, remember? Ginevra de' Benci. The only painting by da Vinci on public view in America. I never heard of it."

"Right. Turns out Homeland Security's been following up and found a connection between the guy who created the fake replacement and a billionaire art collector. By the name of…"

"Stratis," Leslie blurted. "Morris Dexter Stratis up in Pittsburgh." Leslie remembered all too well her uncomfortable off-the-record meeting with Stratis while sitting in a private jet parked at the Pittsburgh airport.

"Wrong! Not your buddy Stratis. Turns out they have a clear trail leading to an electronics wizard named Sanjay Kumar. Another one of the Seminal Society collectors — a husband-and-wife team. Sanjay and Riya Kumar. From what I hear, she's the force behind their collecting."

"Homeland Security? What the hell's DHS doing chasing missing da Vincis?" Suddenly impatient with Fischer dancing around the subject, Leslie challenged, "More to the point, why the hell should I — or we — care?"

Ignoring his partner's outburst, Fischer continued evenly, "The Kumars supply state-of-the-art satellite tracking data to the military. They both hold high level clearances. When their names popped up in the database, the Kumars became fair game for several agencies."

"A wealthy businessperson buys art. What's the big deal Fish? What aren't you telling me?"

"Another art collector—possibly a Seminal Society Collector, possibly acting alone—a man named Alexandre Colton, having a link to the Russian foreign service, is poking around valuable art collections. With international money movement under such heavy scrutiny, art and other collectibles are perfect vehicles for financing terrorism. I assume DHS is concerned about the Kumars getting involved with the Russians."

Leslie, realizing matters pertaining to Homeland Security were never just passed around for the fun of it, said, "Okay, I'll bite. What am I missing here?"

"Captain Stetson has contacts over at DHS. Someone's tipped her to something." Fischer checked his watch for the second time in as many minutes. "We're due in the captain's office in five."

"You buried the lead! Should have led off with that tidbit. What's going on?"

"I got nothing more, except to say I don't know of any ongoing DHS security operation here in Lee County at the moment."

"So, what's this about?"

"There's a Chladni euphon, a one of a kind, on tour in the U.S. From what I gather, the last exhibition starts this week up in Pittsburgh at the Carnegie Science Center."

"A what?"

"Euphon. Musical instrument. A Chladni first."

"Chladni! One of the Seminal Society soulmates? His soul is the one that went to Newton—or so the Society believes. That Chladni?"

"Nailed it!" Fischer again checked his watch. "Show time!"

The upcoming meeting with Captain Karen Stetson would be only the fourth time that she and Leslie had met, other than nods in the hall

3

the few times they had passed each other. The last time they had spoken was when the captain had personally congratulated Leslie on the arrest in the McDermitt homicide investigation. Leslie was the least-experienced detective to head-up — and solve — a homicide in Florida. As such, it made a great PR story. Leslie doubted the accuracy of the premise, but if her boss believed it true there was no need for corrections. Legends, as Leslie well knew, were not always founded on factual accuracy.

———◆———

"Close the door, please," Stetson called when Hodges and Fischer walked into her office at precisely 9:15. "Glad you both could come. Leslie, I've been reading your reports in the McDermitt file and I must say you're thorough. I'm impressed. Wish all the deputies would take the time you do. As I told you at the time, that was a nice piece of work. Fish, I assume you concur."

"For sure, Captain," Fischer replied. In fact, he had worked on the file at the insistence of the sheriff because of his seniority. But it had been Leslie who had put the pieces together. "Hodges led in every aspect."

"Couldn't have done it without Fish's support and ideas," Leslie chimed in. "We worked as a team."

"Fish may have told you," Stetson went on, ignoring Leslie's accolade, "Homeland Security has word of a possible art theft that may happen soon. You interested in working it?"

Leslie looked from Stetson to Fischer hoping to discern what was really being asked of her. Normally, her assignments came from her direct boss, Sergeant Hudson Oakmore. Being asked by the captain was…well it just didn't feel right. "Why should I have qualms about an assignment?" Leslie replied, confused as to why she was being asked and not commanded. "I suppose I don't understand the question."

"The question is simple," Stetson replied. "Do you or don't you? But frankly, I must confess I'm puzzled why DHS suggested you. I assume it's because of your experience with the Seminal Society collectors and their penchant for possessing valuable artifact Firsts."

"I did meet one of the collectors. Man by the name of Morris Dexter Stratis. The Edison phonograph is a First, that's true. But otherwise, I have no expertise in art crime."

"No matter. This is not a Lee County matter, so unless you have an objection, I'm assigning you two to the task force."

"If it's not Lee County, then where?"

"Pittsburgh, best I can tell."

"Pittsburgh?" Leslie said, thinking of her brief time in that city working on the Edison phonograph case with Detective Pete Jakowski.

"Truth is, Hodges, I doubt you'll ever leave Lee County. Sheriff won't approve the funds. I doubt the folks up north will either. That leaves DHS and whoever knows about them? These things always come down to budgets. If this moves forward, I want direct reports from you. DHS will pressure you to play it close. Tell them yes, but report to me. Is that clear?"

"It is, Captain."

"Good. Fish, work with Hodges on this and be sure to set up a secure link that only I can access. Anyone gives you problems, send them to me. You got that?"

"Yup. Loud and clear."

"Fish, as you well know, these alerts usually play themselves out. Lotta agitation, little action." Stetson waited for Fischer to nod in agreement,

5

then added, "Hodges, as I said, these inter-juris-
dictional investigations almost always break down
over money. They try to use our travel and expense
budget for trips and things they themselves can't
get authorized. Sheriff'll have none of that. I'll
authorize travel costs one time for you up and back
to Pittsburgh should that be necessary. We'll cover
overtime for hours worked. All other costs are on
whatever agency authorizes it. Make certain you
work that all out before incurring the expense."

"Does that mean you don't know who I'll be
working for?"

"That's exactly what it means. I won't know
before you know. Frankly, right now it appears this
is only hypothetical. DHS doesn't see things the way
you and I do. We see a pregnant woman and smile.
They see a suicide bomber. Different missions, different visions — different results. God bless them.
Couldn't do their job. Any more questions?"

A million questions swirled in Leslie's mind,
but not one of them made it to her mouth.
"Okay, then," Stetson intoned, as the pair
turned to leave, "one more thing. Pete Jakowski's name came up. He's apparently well-
versed on the Society collectors and an asset for
the government. He and I worked some cases
years back. If it works out, partner with him
on this and you have my permission to follow
his lead."

"Jak was certainly helpful on the McDermitt
case. I'll say that much."

"I would expect nothing less from him. He
might work for that tiny Borough of Verona, but
he's well thought of across Western Pennsylvania.
That's all I have. Carry on."

"Lucky you," Fischer chided on their way back
to the Pit. "I have no idea what you just fell into, or

how I'll be able to help. But I'm here if and when you need me."

"Appreciate the support, Fish. Have no idea where to begin unpacking this."

"It'll unpack itself. Until then, keep your head down on the McDermitt file."

"Kind of advice you give someone in a bunker."

"Same thing."

"What do you mean, it'll unpack itself?"

"Boots might seem to be downplaying this, but she wouldn't have briefed us if nothing was on the plate. That's not how she works. Right now, she's confirming to someone somewhere that you're on board. You'd be well served to pack your bags for a trip north where the frost is on the pumpkins."

"What would you know from frost and pumpkins?"

"Not a bloody thing! Never been north in winter and never plan to be. Dress warm."

# TWO

FISCHER WAS SPOT ON. WITHIN an hour after leaving the captain's office, Leslie's phone rang and the letters JAK displayed on the screen. She knew the ex-Steeler as being friendly to a fault. More importantly, Captain Stetson had confirmed that his reputation extended beyond the Borough of Verona, a small, sleepy town just north of Pittsburgh along the Allegheny River.

"I suppose Boots briefed you on why I'm calling," Jakowski said, after exchanging greetings and invoking the captain's widely used nickname. "Does the name Chladni ring a bell?"

"Twenty questions is not my strong suit," Leslie parried. "How about filling me in?"

"Sparse as it may be, here's the skinny. First, the reason you're involved is because someone at DHS read your report speculating that the da Vinci piece in the National Gallery might have been tampered with. I believe your report said, 'replaced by a forgery'. Apparently, one thing led to another, and the Seminal Society came to the surface. As you may remember from the Edison phonograph theft, the Society holds that the soul link between Newton and Edison is one Ernst Chladni. Father Of Acoustics is Chladni's claim to fame. He invented a musical instrument called a euphon."

"Youphone? Never heard of it. Spell that?"

"E-U-P-H-O-N. Euphon."

"What the hell's a euphon?"

"Looks like a small piano, but instead of having strings and keys it has glass rods that vibrate when you stroke them with wet fingers. Guy by the name of Alexandre Colton is trying to buy the euphon. Colton is known to DHS as a Russian intelligence agent. SVR."

"Hold on a moment," Leslie said, struggling to follow. "Lost you. Even assuming this Colton character works for Russian foreign intelligence, what's that have to do with you? For that matter, with me?"

"You because of your McDermitt report and the fact you know at least some of the Society collectors. Colton is believed to be a new Seminal Society collector."

"One to be exact," Leslie said. "I know only one collector. I'm hardly an expert."

"One's enough. More than most. Me, I'm involved because I know the same collector as you do, Morris Dexter Stratis. I'm also involved because I work closely with a Pittsburgh art dealer. She's tight with DHS — and with Treasury. Understand that to mean IRS."

"I still don't..."

"Coming to it. A husband-and-wife team, Riya and Sanjay Kumar, came up on DHS's radar as also being interested in the Chladni. The Kumars have a tax problem. That brought in the IRS. Hence my phone rang. And now yours is ringing."

To Leslie, this had all the traits of shit rolling downhill. "What do they want from me?" she demanded, looking for cover. "I'm no art expert."

"They're not interested in art experts. They need cops versed in the Society. You and I fit the bill. We're it, I'm afraid."

"Sounds like slicker time, you ask me," Leslie said, hearing Junior, her deceased husband, say, 'They call it foul weather gear for a reason. When shit comes down from above, you pull the slicker tight around you and pray it's sealed."

"Hope you have one big enough for the both of us, Leslie," Jakowski replied. "We're both directly in the path."

This conversation with Jakowski brought back pleasant memories of a delightful dinner he had treated her to when she had flown up to Pittsburgh. She had been working on the McDermitt case and was in Pittsburgh to interview the daughter-in-law of the deceased, Scotty McDermitt. The Edison original phonograph was found missing after Scotty's death and Leslie had reason to believe the missing phonograph had ended up in the hands of Seminal Society collector Morris Dexter Stratis.

"Like I said to you, Jak, I don't subscribe to the idea of souls moving from one person to another. That said, if I were a believer, then I suppose it's as likely as not that Chladni's soul would have passed to Edison who was born twenty years after Chladni died. They both were obsessed with sound."

"I won't argue one way or the other about their souls being shared. Among other things, Chladni's the guy who determined the speed of sound in various mediums. Of course, Edison is known for his sound genius as well."

"Circumstantial evidence, at best," Leslie replied, wondering where this was going.

"You and Stratis are on the same wavelength, pardon the pun. I've heard him comment that it was a shame Edison hadn't lived before Chladni so that euphon's music could have been preserved forever."

"Other than some chatter on a couple of obscure sites, I can't find anything online even mentioning the Seminal Society. What more do you know about Chladni and this...this euphon?"

"Only that Chladni toured Europe giving engineering seminars at universities by day and performing euphon concerts at night. Concerts had standing room only as I understand. I won't comment on how full his science lectures were. He died while on tour and the euphon vanished."

"And you're about to tell me Chladni's euphon was recently located and the Seminal Society collectors are going after it because it's a First."

"Bingo! And from what I gather, bidding already exceeds a hundred million."

"How the hell do they, whoever they are, even know the damn thing's authentic? Could be a scam."

"That's how we know about this at all. Before that much money changes hands the damn thing, as you call it, was authenticated by supposedly the world's expert in stuff like this. A Dr. Sigmund Fuller."

"How the hell do you authenticate something no one's seen or heard played for almost two hundred years?" Leslie asked, her natural curiosity piqued.

"If they can do it with thousand-year-old mummies and things, they can do it with a two-hundred-year-old musical instrument," Jakowski quipped. "Seriously, Dr. Fuller lives in your neck of the woods and is the world's expert on 18th century furniture and art. In fact, he's the one who located the euphon after years of forensic detective work. Wrote a detailed report analyzing wood samples, the veneers used in construction, the glass rod lengths and whatever all else there is in a euphon, all based on extensive research conducted in consultation with curators at the Polish National Museum. A few months ago, the government of Poland accepted Sig's report. Chladni's euphon is now in the permanent custody of the Polish National Museum."

Leslie thought about her conversations with Stratis and with the insurance guy, Jack Silver, the CEO of Great Southern Insurance Company. She recalled her own research when she was investigating the homicide linked to the missing Edison phonograph. "If the euphon is in the Polish National Museum then why are we even discussing it?"

"Dexter Stratis made a large grant to the Polish Museum to allow the euphon to be displayed in the United States to, as he put it, create international interest in the piece. Stratis has paid all expenses for a six-city tour that is finishing up here in Pittsburgh at the Carnegie Science Center. Exhibition opens tomorrow."

"Now I'm confused," Leslie said, her instinct screaming that the big detective knew more than he was letting on. "I was told there might be a theft. I'm certain the Science Center has adequate security and doesn't require the assistance of a rookie Florida cop. Care to explain just why you called?"

"It's not the Science Center who is concerned. It's DHS." Jakowski went on to explain that yesterday DHS intercepted international communications vaguely suggesting an imminent theft of the Chladni.

"Let me guess. Those communications identified Seminal Society collectors."

"Bingo! It's nice working with bright people. A guy by the name of Alexandre Colton was one. The Kumars another."

"What aren't you telling me?"

"A third communication was addressed to Stratis."

"I suppose I should have guessed that as well! What else should I know? Or should I just keep guessing?"

"Hey! Don't shoot the messenger. I'm just reporting what I know."

"Let me understand this," Leslie said, now more confused than when she walked out of Stetson's office, "DHS is going on high alert based on a vague intercepted message or two." Thinking of Stetson's example of DHS seeing a pregnant woman and sounding a bomb alert, Leslie added, "Even for the DHS, that's a tad over the top."

"Except that all three recipients immediately changed their plans and are on their way to Pittsburgh. Something's going down — if it hasn't already."

"Proves nothing! Can you spell paranoia?"

"DHS is paranoid for sure. But, hey, just remember, even paranoids are right every now and again."

# THREE

WITHIN HOURS OF LESLIE'S HEADS-UP
from Jakowski, and while she was researching
the three Seminal Society collectors identified by
Jakowski, namely Dexter Morris Stratis, Riya and
Sanjay Kumar, and Alexandre Colton, a private
cargo plane landed at the Greater Pittsburgh International Airport and taxied to a remote hanger. Once inside the hanger, a door just aft of the
pilot compartment opened and stairs lowered.
The lone passenger, Gonzalez Whitacre, a tall,
well-maintained man with intense eyes, and longtime head of security for Gables International
Protective Services, stepped out. Before descend-
ing the steps, he studied his surroundings long
enough to satisfy himself that nothing was amiss.
Whitacre then proceeded down to the spotless
hanger floor and walked directly to the jet's main
cargo door. At the security chief's nod, a man in
jeans and a blue work shirt opened the door and
slid out a wooden crate measuring thirty inches
wide, eighteen inches deep and twelve inches tall,
and placed it at his feet.

Whitacre carefully examined each of the several seals he had placed on the lid crate to ensure
it couldn't be opened without his knowledge. He
then motioned for a portable scale, lifted the crate
onto the scale bed, and proceeded to enter the
readings into his electronic logbook. "Right on,"
he said, motioning in the direction of an armed
guard wearing a blue-gray uniform bearing a GIPS
logo. The guard was standing beside an armored

van which bore the Gables International Protective Services name and logo.

An overweight man wearing a suit and sporting a tipped sideways bow tie, stepped down from the van's passenger seat and together with the guard walked across the hanger toward Whitacre. Whitacre, using his cell phone, snapped photos of the guard and the passenger. Satisfied that the two men approaching him were properly vetted, Whitacre introduced himself.

"Mr. Whitacre," the passenger said, "as I'm positive you already know, my name's Grover Hendricks, Chief of Security for the Carnegie Science Center. We've never had the pleasure of meeting, but I must admit you look exactly like your picture. On behalf of the Science Center, welcome to Pittsburgh. Trust you had an uneventful flight."

"Other than weather delay, uneventful," Whitacre answered. "The way I like it to go. Sign and it's all yours. I'll be on my way back home to Miami."

Hendricks, suddenly alert, said, "Thought this plane came in from Fort Myers. Not Miami. You were due in hours ago." He examined the crate, eyeing Whitacre suspiciously. "I see no markings. This crate's for the Carnegie Science Center, is it not?"

"It is."

"In your custody since leaving the possession of Dr. Sigmund Fuller in Fort Myers? Correct?"

Whitacre studied the pudgy security man before saying, "The euphon in there was dismantled in my presence and placed in two leather bags inside that crate. Sealed the crate myself and personally drove it from Fuller's place to the airport, watched it onto the plane. Other than being in the hold, it's been in my sight the entire time. Seal's not been tampered with. Weight's spot on. Sealed and delivered. What more can I do?"

"Suits me fine," Hendricks said, breaking into a smile for the first time. "Just wanted to hear it directly. I've been assured your company can be trusted."

"Company prides itself on trust worldwide. Have a reputation to maintain."

"I read Dr. Fuller's authenticity report. Thorough, I must say."

"He started to demonstrate the sound to me, weird it was. He took sick and his lady friend and I dismantled it and packed it for shipping."

"Weird in what way? What's that mean?"

"Sound. It sounded like...well, I don't know. Maybe something from outer space? He only played it a few minutes before Selma, that's his lady friend, had to help him to bed."

"So, you and this Selma dismantled the euphon and packed it for transport?"

"Took a while. The bags are inside the wooden crate. Everything sealed. Want to open the crate and check the seals on the bags?"

"No need. The crate seals seem to be in place. I'll check the bag seals at the Center. Did I hear correctly? You're going to Miami. Not Fort Myers?"

"I'm based in Miami. Going home to momma. Got me a few days off."

"Doing anything special?"

"This and that. Wife's got it all mapped out. Paint the kitchen and bathrooms."

"So, tell me about the delay?" Hendricks probed, his natural curiosity surfacing. "Expected you several hours ago? Had a problem?"

"Mostly weather related. Some was because of the extra time it took to disassemble and pack it."

"From the picture I've seen I can't believe it's all in there."

"It's all there all right. Miniature piano with glass rods instead of piano keys. Neat how it breaks down and all. Wouldn't have thought it possible."

"All appears to be in order," Hendricks said, satisfying himself he had asked all the right questions, but still nervous. In keeping with museum policy, he had scheduled a confirming forensic check of the euphon at the Science Center. The lateness of the hour had forced him to reluctantly postpone the inspection until morning "Have a good flight home," he called to Whitacre who was already halfway up the stairs. "Enjoy painting."

# FOUR

LESLIE SPENT MOST OF TUESDAY answering even more questions from the lawyers on the Mc-Dermitt case. She also investigated a missing six-year-old female who happily turned up following an 'Amber Alert' tip. The child was at the home of her divorced father who told Leslie he got the days mixed up. He believed it was his weekend with his daughter. The explanation he had given for not answering his phone didn't sit right. A detailed background check was now on her desk. "Leave it alone," one of the other detectives had advised her. "You'll drive yourself crazy trying to resolve domestic disputes. No one was hurt. The little girl's safe."

"He ought to be arrested for stupidity at the very least," Leslie had responded.

"If that were the case, we'd have no jail space."

"If that had been your daughter, would you say the same thing?" Leslie had pressed her colleague.

"That been my daughter, I'da shot the bastard!"

"Now who's over the top? You still think I should back off?"

———

On Wednesday morning Leslie had a phone interview with two homeowners who filed burglary charges when TVs went missing from their homes. Same MO in both cases. Digging through the database she found five more home invasions that fit the same pattern. She flagged all the similar files in preparation for consolidating the investigations. "Catch one, close seven," she commented to Fischer.

"Good luck with that," Fischer responded. "Most likely it'll be solved when the perp is caught on camera. We'll see."

At 11:15 she thought about lunch and her standing Wednesday noon date with her significant other, Assistant Prosecutor Allen Smith. Not normally one to spend time thinking about lunch, Leslie now looked forward to her lunches with Allen, and listening to his latest adventures in court. Today was no exception.

Allen had been a cop before going to law school. That gave them a similar foundation. But that is where the similarity ended. Leslie had been born and raised into a middle-class white family in Gulfport, Mississippi. Allen was the son of black Florida tenant farmers. On the surface, it would appear that they could not have been born further apart. Yet, here they were, comfortable and perfectly compatible with each other. Maybe not yet in total unconditional love, but close to it.

"Lobster rolls on the pier?" Leslie asked when Allen came on the line. "Or do you have something else in mind?"

"I definitely have something else on my mind," he replied. "I'm afraid it's going to be hotdogs at my desk. Unless you want a raincheck."

"Hot dogs'll work. Except I'll pick them up on the way over. The ones in the courthouse didn't start life out all that well and whatever they do to them makes them even worse."

"Careful what you say. That's my go-to lunch. Not many other choices."

"What about bringing your own? You like peanut butter. Hard to mess that up."

"Trust me. Anything's possible when I'm let loose in the kitchen."

"Don't sell yourself short. I've tasted enough of your perfectly done steaks to know you're good with the grill."

"You suggesting I bring a grill to the office? Charcoal or propane?"

"You know what I mean. See you in twenty. Hey, steaks for dinner works. Your place or mine?"

"Mine," Allen responded, "but let's hold the steaks. I heard of a great place to check out. Fancy's over on Salrose. And bring your toothbrush."

"Looking forward to it. Love you".

"See you soon. Bye."

———————

Walking into Allen's office, Leslie placed two hot dogs in front of him and cleared a space on his small corner table for hers. "Be back in a moment with drinks," she called, disappearing into the reception area heading for the staff break-room. Returning to the office, she asked, "Where's everyone? Place is empty."

"Staff lunch meeting. More discussion on handling protestors. Mandatory."

"And you?"

"Excused. I need to finish preparing the latest installment of Mr. Smith cross-examines the defendant. Cross is scheduled to begin right after the afternoon recess."

"What's the case about?"

"It's a humdinger. The defendant..."

"Sorry, wait," Leslie held up her hand. "Fish's calling."

"Hey, what's up?" she answered.

Fish got right to it. "Man you flagged was found DOA at home in Miromar Lakes ten minutes ago.

Possible homicide. Thought you'd be interested. I'm on my way over there."

"I flagged him? What's that..."

"You entered him in the database after your call with Jakowski. Name's Fuller."

"No kidding! The antiques expert? Fuller?"

"One and the same. Or so it would appear."

"On my way," Leslie exclaimed, mechanically sweeping her hot dog back into its paper sack.

"Looks like a definite case of eat and run," Allen observed wryly. "What's going on?"

"Long story short. Seminal Society collectors have their wallets in a tizzy chasing a long-lost artifact. Something called a euphon."

"A what?"

"Euphon. It's a musical instrument."

"And the big rush is?"

"A guy by the name of Fuller who certified its authenticity was just found dead."

Leslie scampered around to Allen's side of the desk, kissed him, tasted mustard, and kissed him again. "See you later. And...break a leg on cross." She tossed her barely eaten lunch in the trash basket on her way out of Allen's office.

Even with lights and siren, it took her twenty minutes to arrive at the gated community just off Ben Hill Griffin Parkway several miles north of the Miromar Outlet Mall. It was obvious which house held the dead body. Several Lee County Sheriff cars sent blue flashing lights reflecting from windows, making the scene appear more like a circus than a death.

A white pickup with a Miromar Lakes logo on the driver's door was parked along the narrow roadway and a COVID-masked man in an orange workman's vest was busy trying to disperse onlookers. He was losing that battle.

Leslie maneuvered as close as she could, got out and walked past several houses, her badge held high as she went. Noting that the medical examiner's van had not yet arrived, she approached the nearest uniformed sheriff's deputy, a woman Leslie's age. "How about clearing a path for the ME techs. And move these people back at least two houses. I want the names of everyone who saw anybody coming or going from the Fuller home today. Note down what they saw, the time they saw it. Get copies of any video or pics they may have taken."

"Sure thing, Detective," came the deputy's' reply, happy to have something to do.

"Sign in, please, Detective," instructed another uniformed deputy as Leslie was about to enter the house.

"Doing this the right way. That's good," Leslie said, as she wrote her name and badge number in the logbook directly under Daryl Fischer's entry. He was seven minutes ahead of her. Seven minutes, she knew, was an eternity at a crime scene, allowing opportunity for contamination. She felt better knowing her partner, a senior investigator and, by consensus, one of the best, wasn't likely to cause problems. She also knew that as a rookie she still had a lot to learn from him. To his credit, Fischer, in the McDermitt case, had been an excellent mentor, giving her as much rope as she was willing to take, all the while pointing out the landmines.

The only other person in the house, according to the logbook, was a woman named Selma Fritz. On her drive from Allen's office, Leslie had requested that the 9-1-1 call be replayed for her. She heard the anguish in Fritz's voice as she identified herself and struggled to describe her friend hanging in the garage. The woman was choking back sobs, struggling to breathe, as she begged the operator to hurry. The time stamp on the call was 12:05 PM.

Leslie took one step into the house, pausing to take in the scene. She imagined people living here as she absorbed the feel of the home. She then proceeded across the living room toward the back of the house, continuing her observation of the contents, the pictures hanging on the walls, the knick-knacks on the shelves, the fan hanging from the great-room ceiling slowly rotating. Leslie labeled the scene as middle-aged comfortable. What she almost overlooked and would have had there not been motion in the lanai at the back of the house, was a well-dressed slender woman standing along the back edge of the pool peering into space. Selma Fritz. Leslie judged the woman to be in her sixties.

Retracing her steps back toward the front of the house, Leslie paused in the doorway to the garage, again gathering a first impression. Her eyes went immediately to the man hanging from the ceiling, his feet less than a foot above the tiled floor, a belt looped around his neck and tied to a rope extending from a pulley bolted to the ceiling. The agony frozen into his life-less face made it difficult to immediately guess age, other than to say over sixty, possibly in his early seventies.

"Leslie," Fischer called from behind her, "let me introduce you to Dr. Sigmund Fuller."

Leslie's mind immediately went to her crime-scene instructor's lecture on hangings. "Hangings," the instructor had said, "are usually suicides. Of course, there's always the possibility they're homicides in disguise, staged to appear self-inflicted. Once in a while it works the other way. A suicide made to look like a homicide. In all hanging cases, just as in cases that are unquestionably homicides, an investigator should determine if there was life insurance. If there was, the perp is often the insurance beneficiary."

"You calling this murder? Suicide? What's your gut say?" Leslie asked Fischer, anticipating a non-committal response from her seasoned partner.

"Too soon. Briefly spoke to Selma Fritz back there in the lanai. She's the one who found him. Poor woman. I thought I'd wait for you before questioning her. She keeps repeating, 'I can't believe he did this. He had so much to live for'. It's almost a mantra."

"Give me a moment in here and I'll join you."

Using her cell phone, Leslie photographed the garage, noting the hoist structure in the ceiling, the tall ladder leaning against the near wall, the tool bag on a work bench, numerous tools hanging on a pegboard, a blue, recent model Audi parked to one side, a man's mountain bike leaning against the workbench. Next to the workbench along the far side wall a small, perhaps 3-foot by 4-foot, closet jutted out into the garage. Next to the closet sat a professional looking radial arm saw. A shop vac was in the corner. The floor was tiled and immaculate. Leslie couldn't help but thinking that her kitchen floor should be so clean.

"Dr. Fuller," Leslie said, looking up into his tortured face, "I don't know if your death had anything to do with Chladni and the euphon, but one way or another I promise you we'll get to the bottom of it."

# FIVE

LESLIE WASN'T YET READY TO speak with the Fritz woman, opting instead to remain in the garage thinking through the steps necessary to hang oneself. The mechanism up in the ceiling was most likely used to lift the bike for overhead storage. She made a mental note to determine when it was installed and by whom. She also wanted to be certain she knew how the pulleys worked and their weight limit.

"Leslie," Fischer's voice interrupted her thought progression. "Need to interview the witness. Like to get it behind us before the van arrives. They're a half-hour out. I ran a quick check on Fuller. His wife died little over seven years ago. No record of remarriage."

Leslie quietly followed her partner into the living room where Selma Fritz was now seated, head down, shoulders slumped. Her brown hair, despite her apparent grief, remained perfectly coiffured, but her makeup was smudged. Vinyl gloves, matching the kind Leslie and Fischer were wearing, covered both hands.

"Selma Fritz," Fischer began, "this is my partner, Detective Leslie Hodges. Detective, this is Ms. Fritz. As I understand it, you and Dr. Fuller were engaged to be married."

"I'm so very sorry for the loss of your fiancé." Leslie said. "Please let me assure you we're here to help in any way we can."

The woman turned her tear-stained face toward Leslie. "How can you just leave him there hanging like that?" she demanded. "It isn't right! I wanted to get him down, but the 9-1-1 lady told me not to touch anything. I shouldn't have listened!" Tears began to flow again. "I thought the cops would help me, but they refused, made me put on these awful gloves. They won't let me back in the garage!"

"I believe you told the operator he was...gone," Leslie began, trying to make her questioning feel more like friends talking than an interrogation.

"Yes, he was."

"How were you so certain?"

"I could see from the angle of his head. No movement. No sound. Just nothing! Just hanging there like...like a side of beef."

"After you called, what did you do?"

"Went out to the pool. Tried to sit, but I couldn't. Oh, my God! He's gone!" A new cascade of tears streamed down her face, and she made no move to staunch the flow.

"Take your time," Leslie coached. "Can I get you a tissue?"

Selma opened her bag and pulled a Kleenex from a small packet and dabbed at her face. The sleeve of her blouse pulled back revealing what appeared to be a nasty burn on the side of her right arm just above the wrist. Judging from the angry redness, it appeared to be recent.

"What brought you to Dr. Fuller's house today?" Leslie asked, when the woman finally looked up.

"We had planned to go to lunch. Sig said we'd be celebrating."

"Celebrating what? Your engagement?"

"No. Did that several days ago. Something else. He didn't tell me."

"Any guess?"

Fritz resumed wiping her cheeks. She started to speak, her lips quivered, but no words came.

The two detectives remained silent giving Fritz all the time she required. Another swipe with the tissue and she said, "We were celebrating the successful conclusion of the American tour of the Chladni euphon before it went back to Poland. Do you know about the euphon?"

"A bit," Leslie acknowledged, not wanting to show her hand. "You should assume we know nothing."

"The euphon is a musical instrument invented by Ernst Friedrich Chladni around 1790. It was lost when he died. Sig found it buried in a wall. His client is a distant relative of Chladni, a man by the name of Ernie Chlad. Lives not far from here. When the euphon was found the Polish government declared it a national treasure and insisted it remain in Poland as a tourist attraction. A benefactor arranged a one-time tour of the U.S., in theory, to create excitement. The agreement with the Polish government was that after each exhibition in the States, the Chladni was to return to Sig for verification before it went to its next location."

"How did that work?" Leslie asked, trying to visualize the logistics.

"Pretty smoothly, actually. A security company was hired to transport the euphon and it came here to Sig's house for his inspection after each exhibition just like the agreement specified."

"What's the name of the security company? I assume it was the same company each time."

"Gables International Protective Services."

"When was this euphon here last?"

"It left Monday night for Pittsburgh, its last stop. From there it was to come back for one last inspection before being returned directly to Poland." Fritz stopped talking. The tears broke free, accompanied by deep and uncontrollable gasps.

Again, the detectives waited patiently, knowing there was precious little they could do or say for the grieving woman. When she again brought herself under control, Fischer said, "Why not start with when you arrived here today and walk us through it."

"Is this necessary?"

"It is," Leslie answered gently. "Just take your time and tell us in your own words everything you can."

"Like I said, we had a lunch date. We were planning to celebrate by..." Fritz began to sob once again.

The two detectives remained silent, waiting for her to continue.

When Fritz again spoke, it was with a sad smile. "Sig called around 8:30 or so all agitated. He had received a call that something had happened at Pittsburgh Science Center to question its authenticity. I asked him how that could happen. He said it had to be a big mistake. He said that unless he fixed it, he was ruined."

"Did he say how he planned to fix it?" Leslie asked.

"Not exactly. But he did say we had to move our lunch celebration back an hour. He said he had to meet with Ernie Chlad to prove he hadn't lied about the authenticity of the piece."

Fischer leaned forward. "Is that the same man you said owned the euphon?"

"That's correct."

"Did Dr. Fuller tell you how he planned to prove he had been right?"

"He said something about a rod being substituted. Nothing more specific."

Sensing Fritz was uncomfortable talking about Fuller and his work, Leslie decided to refocus the interview. "What time was your original lunch?"

"Noon. He told me to come to his house at 12:30. That would give us time to drive to the restaurant by 1:00." Again, she paused. Her lips tightened, but no tears came. "This was important to Sig, so I spent extra time getting my hair and makeup just right. Dressed a bit fancier than I would for a normal lunch." Fritz glanced down at her skirt and low-heeled shoes, then continued. "I decided to stop at Target and pick up a card to cheer him up."

"What time was that?" Leslie inquired.

"I left my condo at 11:15 to give myself plenty of time. I found the exact right card almost immediately, so I called Sig to tell him I was running early, and to see if that would be a problem. If so, I was planning on spending time browsing the store. He didn't answer. It's not like him not to take my call. So I hurried over here."

Fischer asked, "How did you get into the house? Your own key or what?"

"I pulled into the driveway and used the button on my mirror, the one he programmed for me, that opens the garage door."

"Did you drive in, or..."

"Oh, heavens no. He's meticulous about his garage. You might have noticed; his car tires are on pads. No, I walked in and my eyes were on his bike that was against the workbench. Sig would never leave his bike down. He always had it up on..." Tears again streamed down her cheeks. Sniffling, she continued, "Oh, God! I almost bumped into him! That part of the garage had a shadow or something, so I didn't see him until..."

"Anyway," she continued," I guess I was concentrating on my phone, but I saw him just before it was too late! I jumped and screamed!"

"Then what did you do?"

"Called 9-1-1."

"What time was that?"

"Let's see, I think it was just around noon. I remember telling myself I had three quarters of an hour to dither at Target. When Sig didn't answer I cut my shopping short and drove straight here."

Leslie, visualizing Fritz's movements, asked, "Did you call Dr. Fuller from your cell? I mean when you were at the shopping center."

"Yes."

"Then the time will be on there. Can you please check it for me?"

"Here it is," Fritz announced, after fumbling with her phone a moment. "It was 11:29."

"Did you call him again after that?" Leslie pressed.

"I tried."

"At what time?"

"Says here, 11:49."

"And what time did you call 9-1-1?"

"Don't know the exact time."

"It'll be on your cell."

Fritz again studied her phone. "12:05," she quietly said.

Fischer nodded to Leslie that the times matched the official call log. "Did you touch him?" she asked.

"As I said, I was told not to!"

"Good. Did you touch or move anything else in the garage?"

"Don't think so. I was... beside myself. I may have. I don't remember."

"When you called Dr. Fuller, at 11:49 you were in your car driving here. Do I have that right?"

"That's right."

"Did you leave a message?"

"I asked him to call back."

"And did he?"

"No. Not like him."

"Did you notice anything unusual in the house while you were waiting for the police to arrive?"

Leslie asked. "I presume you've been here several times and might notice if something was out of place."

"I don't think so," Selma replied, squeezing her eyes shut as if trying to form an image in her mind. And then "No wait. Not something in the house, but when I was standing in the lanai out by the pool, I thought I saw something — or someone — move out there. Can't be certain now. I was so...so upset."

"Can you visualize what you saw?"

"Not even certain it was anything."

"Could it have been an animal? Or larger?"

"Movement is all I can remember."

"Inside the lanai — or outside?"

"Sorry, it must have been nothing."

"Did you go straight out there?"

"Yes, and I didn't touch anything, if that's your question! Oh, wait. I closed the garage door first. I didn't...didn't want the neighbors seeing him hanging that way. Oh, God that's awful!" Tears again streamed freely.

Leslie patiently waited for Fritz to compose herself. "Were you in the main part of the house or in the lanai, by the pool, when the deputy arrived?"

"By the pool."

"How long was it from your 9-1-1 call until the deputy showed up?"

"Seemed like forever. But I suppose about ten minutes."

The logs showed a four-minute response. This discrepancy, both detectives knew, was understandable.

"How long have you...you known Dr. Fuller."

"Please call him Sig. That's what he prefers. I've known him going on six years this month."

"How'd you two meet?"

"Sig is a historian and expert on European artifacts. He specializes in 17th — and 18th — century artifacts. I have a doctorate in medieval history and collect European furniture. We met in the town of Bamberg."

"Never heard of it," Leslie said, turning to her partner for help. Receiving none, she turned back to Selma. "Where's Bamberg?

"In Upper Franconia. That's in Germany. We were…jockeying for the same estate furniture. He won. His client had a bigger wallet than I did. He bought me dinner afterward. His wife had died not too long before. We hit it off and one thing led to another. Sig convinced me to sell my place in Miami and move closer to him. I bought a condo not far from here and things progressed from there." Tears flowed again, seemingly uncontrollable.

The conversation was interrupted when Leslie saw out of a window that the Medical Examiner's van had just pulled up. "I see the ME's techs have arrived," she told Selma. "How about I have them take your fingerprints and then you can go home. We can arrange for a deputy to drive you and your car home if you don't feel up to driving."

"I don't really want to leave, but I suppose I'll just be in the way here." Fritz stood, grabbed the chair arm, quickly sitting back down. "And you're right, I don't think I should drive."

"We'll be happy to see you home safely. Wait right here and I'll get it all set up."

"I'll be fine," Fritz quietly said, "just give me a moment."

"That looks like a nasty burn on your arm. Do you need it looked after?"

"Cooking accident. My wrist hit the oven when I was basting a chicken. Unfortunately, that's been happening a lot lately. Eyesight going, I guess."

"Please let us know if you need medical assistance or anything else."

Leslie's attention turned to her buzzing phone. "Detective Jak," she greeted, "what's on your mind?"

"Information update on the euphon. It arrived at the Science Center several hours late Monday night from Fort Myers. Exhibition opened on schedule yesterday morning at ten for VIPs and at noon to the general public."

"You didn't call to give me the morning art critic review. What's up?"

"Apparently, Colton planned to steal the euphon early Tuesday morning before the exhibit opened. Didn't work as planned. DHS is pissed!"

Jakowski seemed to love guessing games. "Why in the world is DHS upset about a heist that didn't occur?" Leslie asked, sensing she'd get more information by playing along than she would if she forced him to cut to the chase.

"DHS planned to take Colton into custody the moment he laid hands on the euphon. The guard he had bribed was working for them"

"I take it the theft never occurred." Leslie thought about what she had just said, then added, "Wait! Don't tell me Colton got away with the euphon!"

"The euphon came in so late, the time frames were thrown off. Colton postponed the heist by a day."

This was moving too fast for Leslie. "Hold on, Jak. Let's see. If the heist was postponed a day that would make it...this morning. So, did DHS capture Colton in the act? You're calling to tell me I won't be needed in Pittsburgh."

"You're ahead of the story," Jakowski replied. "When the exhibit closed last night, the museum released a statement saying the authenticity of the euphon had been called into question and the exhibit would be closed for reevaluation. The dimensions of one of the glass rods didn't match the written documentation provided by Dr. Fuller."

Not letting on she already knew about the forgery from Fritz, Leslie asked, "What the hell does that mean? Didn't you tell me yourself that the euphon had been authenticated here in Florida by Dr. Fuller before it even arrived in Pittsburgh. The glass rods had to match! What happened?"

"Mystery of the day. Fuller certified the euphon to a security guard, a man by the name of Gonzalez Whitacre. He works for the security firm hired to transport the euphon."

"What do we know of this Whitacre character?"

"One of the best in the business. I'd stake my reputation on him with no worry."

"Same question about Fuller. What do you know of him?"

"Guy's world class! Wrote several books on the subject. I've known him for years as well. His reputation is stellar around the world."

"Yet, something happened from the time Dr. Fuller certified the euphon and the time it was examined in Pittsburgh. That much is obvious."

"The head security guy for the Science Center is being questioned now, but I doubt he'll shed any light on this. The seals were intact when the crate arrived at the Center. That much is known."

"Is it customary for an incoming exhibit to undergo such scrutiny? I mean, we have Fuller in Florida certifying it. Then it's sealed for delivery and delivered to Pittsburgh by a private security service—seals unbroken. Why'd they do another check? Overkill I'd say."

"Great question! Apparently, the museum received a tip telling them to check the glass rod dimensions. As I said, a glass rod was wrong."

"Go on," Leslie said, not yet ready to inform the Pittsburgh detective of Fuller's death, "you have my full attention."

"Colton called the heist off and flew down to Florida. DHS had Colton in their cross hairs and lost him. They're most unhappy."

"I understand why DHS is pissed! Doesn't explain who changed the rods or why. And who — and why — tip off the Science Center?" A thought struck Leslie. "Where's Dexter Stratis in all this? He arranged the exhibition. I'd assume he's upset."

"I suppose so. Only thing we know at this point relative to our friend Stratis is that he was one of the VIPs who viewed the euphon yesterday morning."

"Thanks for the update, Jak. Something for you in return. I'm currently working a crime scene where your Dr. Sigmund Fuller was found hanging in his garage. TOD was around noon today."

Silence. Followed by, "Now, that's something." More silence. Then, almost as an afterthought, "Suicide or..."

"Too early for that. Forensics team just arrived."

"Your gut?

Same question she had asked Fischer. Demanded the same answer. "Frankly, I'm too new at this to have an intuition one way or another. Can't even speculate."

"Fair enough. Keep me in the loop."

"Do my best," Leslie replied.

"Along that vein," Jakowski said, "the instant the euphon was pronounced suspect, the Science Center, under the terms of the exhibition agreement, notified Poland. I'm told the Polish authorities demanded that it be sent directly back to Fuller for his opinion. Then it was to be returned immediately to the Polish National Museum."

"Anything more for me? I need to return my attention to the crime scene."

"Only that the Kumars, as well as Colton as I said, left for Florida. Both planes landed before midnight last night."

"What about Stratis?"

"What about Stratis?"

"Did he also come down here last night?"

"Can't answer that."

# SIX

ALLEN SMITH WAS WORKING ON his second beer when Leslie walked up, kissed him on the cheek, and plopped down across the elegantly set table. A glass of wine was waiting for her.

"Sorry, Honey," she apologized. "Took longer than I thought to put my report to bed." It hadn't been the actual writing that had taken so long. It had been Leslie's desire to review and understand every element of the crime scene. The exam of the victim would not even begin until morning, except for the basics, such as air and body temperature, skin color, obvious wounds, observed blood loss. "I was looking at the fish."

"You were what?" Allen said, setting his glass down to study his friend. "Say again."

"Oh, sorry. That's an expression Junior used when he had a case he didn't exactly understand. A story one of his mentors told."

"What's it mean?"

"It's a long story told by an entomologist about his professor. A guy named Agassiz."

"I heard that name. Museum named after him at Harvard if I'm not mistaken." Allen emptied his glass before continuing. "Love a good story. Tell me about the fish. That's what Agassiz was known for."

"I'll cut it down for you. You want the long version, look it up. When the student indicated he wanted to study zoology the professor dug into a jar and handed him a foul-smelling fish. He was to put the fish in a metal pan and was to use no instrument in its study. Walking from the room, Agassiz said, 'By and by I will return to ask what you have seen.' After ten minutes the student believed he had learned all there was to learn about the fish. He sat back and waited for the professor to return, which he did after a few hours. Needless to say, Agassiz wasn't impressed, and the student ended up examining that fish for several days, periodically sprinkling yellow alcohol on it as instructed. The professor returned often to quiz the student, each time leaving disappointed. The student found a pencil and drew the fish from every angle, cataloged its fins, put his fingers down its throat to count its teeth, examined its scales, reciting all that he had observed to the professor. When the student finished his recitation, the professor simply said, 'You must look at your fish,' again leaving the student with the odorous fish. All the next day the student dutifully examined the fish, seeing very little more than he had already reported. At the end of the day the professor inquired, 'Have you seen it yet?' The student listed all he had learned to a frowning professor who again sent him home to contemplate the fish. The student was instructed to report back in the morning." Leslie paused, draining her own glass. "Want me to continue?"

"Love listening to you. Go on."

"Don't think I want to know what that means. The next morning, after spending a sleepless night mentally studying the fish and feeling sorry for himself, the student returned and confessed, 'the only additional thing I can report is that the fish has symmetrical sides with paired organs.'

A large smile appeared on Agassiz's face and the professor said, 'Now you're ready to learn. Remember to always look at your fish.' "

"So," Allen asked, "what did you learn by looking at your fish?"

"Only that I know nothing."

"You must know the time of death. That's a start."

"That's akin to learning the fish has scales. All we know for certain is death occurred before 12:03 because that's when the good doctor was found by his lady friend. Fiancée is more accurate." Leslie went on to describe the crime scene and her interview of Selma Fritz. She forced herself not to compare Selma's reaction to her own emotional freefall when she had been informed by the Police Chief of Junior's death one month shy of their 7th wedding anniversary. The only real difference was that crying came easily to Selma Fritz while Leslie could not. Moist eyes at the funeral, but no real tears. Leslie had refused to discuss that aspect of her grieving with the Tampa police psychiatrist when the topic had come up.

Sensing her distress, Allen placed his hand over hers. "This is close to home for you, Les. Maybe you should pass on this one. Just saying."

"Every death is a loss to someone," Leslie replied, taking comfort from Allen's warm hand. "Wife, husband, child, parent. The agony of loss is there. If anything, my pain pushes me in a way I can't describe."

"What do you think of the wine?" the waitress asked, stopping at their table.

"Excellent!" Leslie replied, happy to be interrupted. "What is it?"

"Chardonnay. It's from a little vineyard up near Orlando. For our anniversary my husband surprised me. We spent two nights there. Place called Lakeridge Winery. They make great wines and their food is excellent. You guys ready to order? Or do you need more time?"

To Leslie's surprise, Allen asked the waitress for a recommendation. Never once in the four plus months she had known him had he ever ordered anything a waiter suggested. She had asked him about that quirk a few weeks back. His reply had surprised her. "I suppose," he had begun tentatively, "it has to do with me being black and growing up in Florida. Nothing overt. Sure, there were times when I couldn't get service, or had to wait exceptionally long for a table. But I'm not talking about those times. When I went somewhere, even with my mother, I heard waiters tell other people about exotic sounding specials, like scallops Florentine, or chicken cacciatore. For us, they recommended fried chicken. On a good day it'd be pork ribs."

Leslie thought about her own childhood in Mississippi and visualized the restaurants she had eaten in as a child. To her embarrassment, she couldn't recall ever having seen a black person eating together with whites. "I'm sorry," she said, "How'd you cope?"

Allen's eyes clouded for an instant before he responded. "Became a cop, didn't I? Went to law school and graduated, didn't I? Passed the Florida frick'n bar exam, didn't I? Became an assistant prosecutor, didn't I? That's how I've coped. That's the only way to cope."

She affectionately squeezed his hand. "And that's a hell of a lot more than I've accomplished," she said, admiring his achievements while feeling his well-controlled anger, perhaps for the first time glimpsing life through the eyes of a non-Caucasian.

"Hardly," Allen replied, "You had a distinguished career as a Tampa cop, now a Lee County detective. Youngest rookie to solve a homicide. Within four months of joining the force. That's not exactly sitting still."

"Five months, but who's counting," she laughed.

"I had an idea this morning," he said. "Let's get away from business, enjoy some time together. Been excited all day thinking about it. That winery sounds like a perfect place. Not too far. Not too close."

"Love it!" Leslie surprised herself at how good the idea felt. Then reality set in. "Got a feeling work life's about to go in the tank."

"What's that mean?"

"Means with this new case my life's not going to be my own for a while. Gotta be available."

"As long as you're not trying to tell me something."

"Goodness, no. Love the idea. Work's all."

"One last question? What the hell's a euphon?"

"It's a musical instrument based on vibrating glass rods."

"What's it sound like?"

"Have no idea. Someone said it's like music from another world — outer space."

"Aren't you curious? You of all people, I'd think..."

"Just haven't gotten that far yet. Spent the day at the Fuller crime scene and studying the case file. I understand I can go on YouTube and listen to music created by something called a Cristal Baschet."

"Cristal Baschet? Never heard of it."

"Invented in the 1950's I believe. Uses glass rods like the euphon, but that's where the similarity stops. In the Baschet, the rods are vertical, and the sound plays off a wooden baffle. In the euphon, the rods are horizontal and directly vibrate the wooden sound board. At least that's what I believe I've learned."

While Leslie was explaining the euphon's operation, Allen punched YouTube and crystal baschet into his cell phone browser and a moment later said, "Here it is! Crystal spelled with an 'i' and not a 'y'. It's classified in the multi-timbre percussion category." As he spoke, surreal music, seemingly coming out of the atmosphere, filled the area around them.

"Turn that off!" Leslie instructed. "Sounds like it came from outer space." Indeed, several diners had stopped what they were doing to listen.

"You're right on about outer space," Allen said, heeding Leslie's instruction on turning off his phone. "Wikipedia says the Cristal Baschet was used to create the soundtrack for the science fiction movie, *Interstellar*."

"'Haunting', is the word that comes to mind," Leslie said, "No wonder Chladni played to packed houses. Enough of this. Tell me about the cases you're working on."

Allen's face lit up as he ran through the matters he was preparing for trial. Mostly domestic relations, husband hits wife, wife hits husband, everybody sorry—until next time. Three liquor store robberies, all caught on surveillance video. Two with knives, one with a gun.

Dinner was served and eaten while Allen related stories centering around judges. Some evidenced the inexperience of a young lawyer, Allen. Some highlighted the arrogance of the judge. All were entertaining.

"Okay, no more shop talk," Leslie insisted once the busboy cleared the table. "I like your idea of taking some time off and going up to that winery. Our visit to the circus museum in Sarasota was great fun."

"Should we set a date so I can book something?" Allen asked. "Or is this one of those, it'll be nice to do someday, thing?"

"If I hadn't just caught the Fuller case, I would say book it. But now, it'll have to wait until we sort out the case, sooner rather than later I hope."

"I vote for sooner. You know, Leslie, I don't think I've ever known anyone like you. I mean..."

"Just what exactly do you mean?" she teased. "Explain yourself, counselor."

"For one thing, when you get focused it's hard to break your concentration. For another, you need everything to be in order, everything to make sense, every statement to be accurate."

"Junior used to call that my OCD. That's why he encouraged me to be a detective. Said I was the second coming of Monk."

"Who?"

"TV show. Detective Adrian Monk saw anything out of place, any sound that was off, anything at all not exactly as it should be. Didn't understand people but knew what wasn't right. He was on the spectrum. Asperger's, I think it was. On TV for many years, starting, I'd say about fifteen years ago."

"I'll have to watch that. Be fun. I can see traces of the OCD."

"Like what traces?" Leslie asked, trying to discern the message Allen was sending.

"On Mondays you wear red. Wednesdays, like today, tan. Let's see, green, I believe, for Tuesdays. Gray means it's Thursday. How'd I do?"

"I suppose I should be happy you pay attention. It just makes it easy to know what to wear each morning No decisions involved."

"I know Sunday is yellow. And Saturday is... don't tell me. Blue."

"Left out Friday."

"You make it sound like school. Need I take notes?"

"Depends on your memory and how you learn. Me, I'm a kinetic learner, so notes don't help as much as movement. There will be a test, however."

"The reason you don't need to take notes, dear Leslie, is that total recall memory of yours. Do you forget anything?"

"It's not so much a good memory, but my mind works on pictures, images. If I see it, or even picture it, I can call up the image and see what's there."

"What a great gift."

"I don't claim to recall everything I've seen. But if I can conjure up the image, I can read it or see it anew. Comes in handy."

"I'll bet. So, do you have an image in your mind of a gray blouse in your car?"

"Is that your way of asking if I'm spending the night?"

"Not very subtle, I admit."

"Along with a toothbrush and a few other things."

"What are we doing hanging around here, then?"

She again squeezed his hand. "I was wondering that myself."

# SEVEN

LESLIE'S PHONE ALARM SOUNDED AT seven and the last thing she wanted was to get out of Allen's bed. Unlike Junior, who had tossed and turned and generally fidgeted all night, Allen slept peacefully, either on his back or on his right side facing away from her. The first several times she and Allen had spent the night together that had bothered her. His response when she finally said something, was, "Never thought much of it. I mean, how I sleep. I suppose I'm uncomfortable facing inward. You're reading way too much into my body position when I'm in La-La land."

"In La-La land?"

"Ya, that's where you put me after we've made love. I'm down for the count."

Looking over at him now, Allen appeared to still be down for the count. She considered waking him. Time, however, was short. She was scheduled to meet her partner at the home of Ernst Chlad, owner of the euphon, at eight-thirty. The forty-five-minute drive, preceded by a ten-minute shower, and fifteen minutes to dress and brush her hair, allowed very little time for what she had in mind. One final glance in his direction and she reluctantly threw her legs over the side of the bed. Allen's arm clamped onto her shoulder before her feet hit the floor, causing her to fall backward, her head landing on his naked chest.

"Thought you'd never ask," she said, rolling over to face him.

———————

The dashboard clock read 8:28 as Leslie turned off Ben Hill Griffin Parkway. She silently congratulated herself for arriving at the Chlad house on time. She asked herself if it was coincidence that Ernst Chlad, owner of the Chladni euphon, lived in the same Miromar Lakes development as had Scotty McDermitt, owner of the Edison phonograph. Scotty had died in a single-vehicle accident and the phonograph that she had owned disappeared. Leslie had reason to believe the missing Edison phonograph was now in the hands of Morris Dexter Stratis, one of the Seminal Society collectors.

The similarities of neighborhood ended at the main gate. Leslie recalled the McDermitt residence being valued in the half-million-to-million-dollar range. The Chlad house she was now approaching was on a cul-de-sac, its back facing a lake, not far from a bocce court where several men were gathering for a game. This house, Leslie guessed, would easily fetch several million.

Her partner was waiting for her when she stepped onto the sidewalk. "Spend the night with Allen?" he asked, a large smile spread across his face.

"Daryl Fischer! How the hell..."

"Wouldn't be much of a detective if I didn't realize you're always fifteen minutes early for an interview, especially for first-thing-in-the-morning appointments. Today, you barely made it."

"You say anything more on that subject, Fish, so help me I'll file a grievance."

"Sensitive, are we?" Fischer shot back.

"You heard me. Now ring the bell and let's get to work."

Fischer mumbled, "My, my, my. Wonder why so sensitive?"

She ignored the taunt — for now.

An attractive brunette answered the door, dressed for a fashion runway — or so it seemed. As Leslie knew from her research, Carol Chlad was fifty-nine years old and married to Ernst for thirty-eight years. Ernst himself was sixty-two, a graduate of Miami University, and a retired math teacher.

"Do I know you?" the woman asked Fischer, seemingly unaware of Leslie standing behind him.

Fischer held up his identification. "I'm Detective Daryl Fischer. I called yesterday. We have an appointment. This is my partner, Detective Leslie Hodges."

"You must be here for my husband. He's busy getting ready for a visitor — or something."

"Are you Mrs. Chlad? Carol Chlad?" Fischer asked gently.

"Your badge says sheriff. Are you the sheriff?"

"Deputy sheriff," Fischer patiently responded.

"And the girl behind you? Is she a sheriff too?"

"I'm a deputy as well," Leslie answered, moving beside her partner. "Can we come inside please?"

"You look too young to be a sheriff. And girls are not sheriffs."

"We're sheriff deputies," Leslie replied, forcing her eyes soft and trying to maintain her smile. "You are Carol Chlad, right? We do need to speak with your husband. As Detective Fischer said, we have an appointment."

"How do you know my name? This sounds ominous. Is my Ernie in trouble?"

"He's not in trouble," Leslie explained, convinced something was off with the woman across from her. "Would you please tell him we're here."

"Am I in trouble?"

"No one's in trouble. Please, are you Mrs. Chlad?"

"My name is Carol Chlad. What do you want?"

"We just need to talk with your husband. Ernst Chlad."

"Oh, my! Where are my manners? Come into the living room. I'll go fetch Ernie."

The detectives followed Carol to an expansive living room at the back of the house. Leslie was more than impressed by the art hanging everywhere and displayed on stands and shelves. The living room opened out onto a lanai dominated by a magnificent infinity pool, the water blending seamlessly with the horizon. The lanai seemed to Leslie larger than some people's entire homes. A semi-circular bar stood in the corner opposite a professional-looking grill. A lake with a small sandy beach area was visible just beyond.

"He's just finishing up something," Carol said, returning a moment later. "Said it will be a few minutes. Can I fetch you something to drink? Coffee. Tea. Water? If you haven't eaten, I can have Bekka put something together for you. Eggs? Nice pancakes?"

It all sounded good to Leslie, especially the coffee, which she hadn't had time for. Following Fischer's lead, she declined the offer, instead asking, "Ernst is your husband. Am I correct?" Leslie was mindful of how often deputies, for one reason or another, went to the wrong address, or arrested the wrong person, all with horrible consequences. She wasn't about to allow a mistaken identity to interfere with this case.

"Yes. My husband is Ernie."

"While we're waiting for him," Leslie said, "maybe you can help us with some details?"

Carol slipped into a seat, staring at Leslie, her brows furrowed but saying nothing.

"We're investigating a death. Dr. Sigmund Fuller. Does that name, Fuller, mean anything to you?"

"Some doctor died? What's that have to do with me...us?"

"Is it fair for us to assume you don't know Dr. Fuller?"

"Dr. Fuller? You say he died? He's not my doctor." The twitching increased. "Oh, I suppose he could be. I have so many, I don't remember them all." Carol stood and placed her hands on the back of the chair as if for support.

Fischer produced a picture of the deceased. "Please, Mrs. Chlad, if you will, take a look at this picture and tell us if you have ever seen this man."

"Oh!" Carol sucked in her breath and let it out slowly. She did it again. Then finally said, "That man lives here in Miromar Lakes. I've seen him at the pool and the grill. Sometimes he comes to our weekly special dinners, but not every week."

"Has he been to this house?" Leslie asked, again looking around and taking in the fabulous art all around her.

"I don't remember. Ernie brings friends here I don't always know." Carol sat back down, her hands now folded in her lap.

"Do you know the name of the man in the picture?" Fischer asked, adjusting the screen so that Carol could see the image clearly.

"I don't remember." Suddenly her face came alive. "Oh, it starts with an 'S'. Sam...or, oh, now I know! Sig!" A big smile appeared on her face. "Yes, Ernie called him Sig."

"Does your husband work?"

"Retired."

"When he worked," Leslie asked, as a new friend might, "what did he do?".

"Teacher. Taught math at Fort Myers High School."

Teacher, huh? Leslie said to herself, again glancing around and taking in the sumptuous surroundings.

"Oh, I know what you're thinking," Carol advanced. "Everybody asks. How did a school-teacher get all this?"

Leslie responded by raising her eyebrows.

"My daddy had a...a...." Carol's eyes narrowed, as if struggling to recall something. Her lips moved without sound. Then she said, "My daddy, he delivered packages between Tampa and...and... around. Big company paid him a lot of money, plus stock. I'm an only child and the stock's mine. Even with all this," she waved her hand in a circle, "the stock's still worth more than when I got it."

Leslie thought about her own family back when she grew up in Gulfport. Grandfather had a farm and delivered milk with a horse-drawn wagon. Her father inherited the business and within a few years trucks had replaced the horses. Then convenience stores replaced the trucks and her father had to take a job in the local grocery to make ends meet. But for a quirk of fate, some conglomerate could have bought the milk business, and this could be her life. "Just the two of you live here?" Leslie asked, shaking off the unsettling thoughts of what could have been.

"Mostly. We have two sons. Keri in Tampa. Amos over on...I forget where he lives. We're here alone. They visit, mostly on holidays."

"Could you please describe your day yesterday, if you don't mind," Leslie said, trying to picture Carol's life.

"Yesterday was Wednesday, was it not?"

"Yes. Wednesday."

"Our group has lunch on Wednesday at the grill. On the lake with the white sand beach. Good food."

"What time was lunch?" Leslie prodded.

"Noon. Like always."

"Were you there?"

"Of course. I never miss it."

"Before you went to lunch, what did you do?"

"I took a swim." Carol pointed in the general direction of the pool, "Then got ready. At my age, dear, takes time."

Leslie wouldn't know about makeup, having not worn any, except for special occasions, since joining the force back in Mississippi almost twelve years ago. "And after the lunch?" Leslie asked, "you came home?"

"We went over to the card room. Then a drink. Ernie and I had planned on going out to celebrate."

"Celebrate? A birthday? Anniversary?" Leslie was angry with herself for not noticing from the file that yesterday had been a special day in their lives.

"Oh, nothing like that. No. Ernie's been working on something special for months, years, even. He said everything was finally in place. We were going to celebrate."

"Where'd you go?" Leslie wanted the name of a good place to take Allen for special times.

"Our plans were canceled. Ernie wasn't feeling well. Went to bed early. I was so worried about him. It's just not like him to do that."

"Is your husband sick? Maybe we should come back when..."

"No, dear, he's better now. But he's been acting...strange for a while."

"Strange in what way?"

"Always on the phone. Lots of meetings. Things like that."

"Do you know who he's on the phone with?"

"Mostly that guy we talked about before. Sig. Sometimes Sig's friend."

"You know the name of the friend?"

"Girlfriend. Sig's girlfriend."

"Selma Fritz?"

"Never heard that name. I don't know."

Fischer pulled up Fritz's picture on his cell phone and turned the screen to face Carol. "Ever see her?"

"I think that's her. I don't remember."

"What time did you leave for lunch yesterday?"

"Around noon. Give or take."

"When you left for lunch was your husband here?"

"After my swim I was in a hurry getting ready and all. I suppose he was in his office working where he always is." At the sound of approaching footsteps, Carol looked up. "Oh, there you are, dear." She stood. "These people have been waiting to talk with you about a doctor who died."

Chlad held his hand out in greeting. Realizing the recent COVID protocols made shaking hands questionable, he lowered his and said, "Hi, I'm Ernie Chlad. And your names are?"

"I'm Detective Hodges and my partner here is Detective Fischer. I believe you know we're here to talk about Dr. Fuller." Leslie turned toward Carol. "You're free to stay if you wish or not."

"Honey," Chlad said, addressing his wife, "how about coffee for all of us."

"That would be nice," Leslie replied changing her mind. "Black for me."

"Likewise," Fischer said. Then to Chlad, he said, "Your wife indicated you didn't feel well last night. Better now? Or should we come back another time?"

Uncomfortable with allowing any more time to escape before the interview, Leslie nonetheless remained silent.

"I'm feeling better," Chlad replied. "Must have been something I ate for lunch."

Seizing on the opening, Leslie jumped in. "What did you have? And where? I want to avoid that place."

"Hot dog at some stand over on Bonita Beach."

"That where you had lunch yesterday?"

"Yes."

"Were you over there fishing? Surfing?"

"At my age walking the shoreline is enough for me."

"Alone?"

"I was."

"Is that something you do often? I mean walk the beach."

"When I need time to think, that's where I go. Something about water rushing the shore calms me."

"And me as well," Leslie said, trying to build a bond. "I'm thinking that when it comes to relaxing influences, there are water people and mountain people."

"So, you're here to talk about Sig. Dr. Fuller. What do you want to know?"

"We'd like to understand your relationship with Dr. Fuller," Fischer answered, his face now all business.

"Yesterday is a blur to me. I wasn't feeling well. That hot dog really got me."

"Can you recall the name of the place? I agree with my partner. Want to stay away."

"One of those pop-up things. Moves from place to place is all I know about it. So, what can I tell you about Sig?"

"Let's begin with your relationship."

Before Chlad could answer, a woman, Leslie guessed Cuban, entered the room with a tray. She placed brightly colored coasters and small monogramed cocktail napkins on tables beside each person. She set a cup on top of each coaster. Carol then followed and poured coffee. She added a spoonful of sugar and a drop of what appeared to be cream into her husband's cup. The maid laid a small biscuit beside each setting.

"I forgot the question," Chlad said when Carol followed the maid out of the room.

"Your relationship with Fuller," Fischer said, taking a sip of coffee.

"What makes you believe I have any relationship with him?"

"You're the owner of the original Chladni euphon, are you not?"

"How do you…"

"It's on display up in Pittsburgh at the Carnegie Science Center. We also know Dr. Fuller specializes in authentication of art and old objects and was the last person in Florida to have had possession of it. We also believe he certified the authenticity of the artifact."

"As a matter of fact, he's an 18th century expert on European art and furniture. And yes, he authenticated the euphon as the one invented by my ancestor."

"How long have you known Dr. Fuller?"

"Let's see. We moved to Miromar Lakes little over six years back. Met him about five years ago at the main pool. Got to talking."

"Did you own the euphon back then?"

"Did not. Could not."

Leslie leaned toward Chlad. "What's that mean? Could not?"

"It didn't exist."

"Didn't exist?" Fischer pressed. "Please explain."

"Well, it existed, but nobody knew it did."

"Please fill us in," Fischer continued. "Assume we know nothing about the euphon."

"Do you know anything about its history?"

"As I said, assume we don't."

Chlad launched into a long discussion about Chladni being the father of acoustics and about his research into the speed of sound through various substances. He spoke about Chladni's figures which were depictions of sound waves at different frequencies. Winding down, he asked, "Can you believe those figures are still used to assist in the design of musical instruments, such as the guitar, violin and cello?"

"Figures? What do you mean by figures?" Leslie's curiosity had been piqued.

"You can go online and see it for yourself. He put salt on a plate and vibrated the plate. The salt moves around to form lines of vibration and those lines are frequency dependent. It's the figures they use to tune musical instruments when they're being built. My ancestor, Friedrich Ernst Chladni, was a genius, particularly where sound is concerned. They call him the 'father of acoustics' for that reason."

"What about the euphon? How does that work?"

Chlad's eyes came alive as he explained how in England in 1738 an instrument called a Verillion was created to produce church music by using beer glasses filled to different levels. "Can you imagine," Chlad playfully asked, "the church relying on beer glasses? That's a good one, don't you think? Wonder if the clergy was ever sober." He laughed nervously at his own humor.

"Churches have been known to do much worse," Fischer responded, sounding as if he would rather be somewhere other than here.

"Anyway, Ben Franklin heard the English church music, came back to Philadelphia and invented the glass armonica in 1782. Franklin brought his armonica back to Europe and upon hearing it, Chladni, not to be outdone, invented the euphon as the first instrument to make musical sounds by vibrating glass rods. I'm told he based the dimensions and the exact glass composition of his rods on the speed of sound through glass, using the salt figures to make the calculations."

"What did the euphon sound like?" Leslie asked.

"It was unlike anything ever heard before. Sig believes no other euphons were ever made."

Fischer's interest came alive. "If you've never heard the euphon played then I wonder..."

"Oh, I've heard it played all right. Here," he said, pulling out his cell phone, "is a recording we made just before it went on tour." He proceeded to play music that sounded as if it came from an outer space movie, the sounds gently hanging in the air, emulating several percussion instruments all being played simultaneously.

"I'm no musical expert by any means," Leslie said, "but if I didn't know any better, I'd think someone was blowing into something making it vibrate. It sounds like a high-pitched guitar and violin rolled into one." Leslie noted to herself that the sound she was now hearing was smoother than the sound of the Cristal Baschet Allen had played the previous night.

"I was thinking cello," Fischer added. "But certainly, other worldly. How about sending us a copy of that recording?"

"Not prepared to release it just yet." Chlad replied. "We didn't want it out yet for fear it would promote fakes if they had access to the actual original sound."

"For now, we'll respect that, but please be certain to save it."

"Oh, no worries on that front. It's too valuable. If you care to listen to similar music, I refer you to the Cristal Baschet. There are several online recordings. The euphon is purer and a bit softer in transition. Overall, the sound is the same, generated by moist fingers running along the length of each glass rod. In the euphon, the vibrations of the glass are picked up by metal rods and transmitted to a wooden sound board. In the Cristal Baschet the metal rods deliver the sound to cones sized for the different octaves."

Leslie, finishing her biscuit and washing it down with the last of her coffee, asked, "What happened to Chladni's euphon when he died? I'm under the impression it was lost."

"As I assume you already know, Detective, Chladni died in 1827, in Breslau, which is now Wrocław, Poland. The euphon was located by Sig after a long, and might I add, expensive, hunt he conducted on my behalf."

"Let's see, that's at least seven, maybe ten, generations back. There could be hundreds, maybe even over a thousand possible heirs. How do you know you're the rightful owner?"

"Sig traced it back. You're right, Chladni is ten generations back. He died without children and his cousin, a guy by the name of Chaldenius, Otto Chaldenius, took possession of his few things. But they never found the euphon. I'm a direct descendant of dear old Otto. When Chladni's first name was used at all, it was Friedrich. However, records show his full name to be Ernst Florens Friedrich Chladni."

"And you have full title? You don't share it with your...your many, many cousins?"

"Fuller took care of all that. I have a deed, I believe they call it Letters Patent, signed by the governor of Wroclaw, proclaiming me as sole heir to the Chladni euphon."

Leslie wondered how much that had cost but said nothing. Title to the euphon was not her concern. "Is it your plan to display the Chladni publicly, say in a museum? Or keep it for yourself in this beautiful home of yours? Or..."

"Much more complicated than that, I'm afraid. Polish government declared it a national treasure. After this brief tour, it goes back to Poland for display in the National Museum."

"How does that work?" Fischer asked. "I mean you said you put up the money to locate it, and now you can't even keep it?"

"Oh, they've reimbursed me for out-of-pocket expenses. As soon as it returns from this exhibition, I'll be paid a finder's fee, as they call it. Sig worked all that out. I'll do okay on this." Chlad looked away, his eyes lost in a distant universe.

The detectives both remained silent allowing their host time to come to grips with whatever was troubling him.

"Or at least I thought I'd do okay," Chlad finally continued. "It would have been a nice return on my investment. Now that it's been...then yesterday it all fell apart!"

"In what way?" Leslie probed, knowing the answer, but wanting to hear it from Chlad.

"One of the potential private buyers, I mean before the arrangement was signed with Poland, called to ask about the forgery. Naturally, I had no idea what he was talking about. He told me about the public announcement Carnegie had made about their findings of a discrepancy with one of the rods."

"Who called you, exactly?"

"Alexandre Colton. Met him several times in Poland. He's very interested in the euphon."

"I'm confused," Leslie said, "If Poland declared the euphon a national treasure, then how could there be private buyers? And why pay you anything? All they had to do is keep it."

"I'm certainly no expert in these things," Chlad answered, "but as Sig explained it, I would have filed suit and it would be years before it was resolved. He said ten or fifteen years was not out of the question. Another man, name of Dexter Stratis, donated a lot of money so the euphon could tour the United States. I believe it was this guy Stratis who negotiated the agreement for the government to reimburse me for expenses. Once the euphon got back to Poland they were to pay me a million dollars a year for ten years."

"What does this Stratis person get out of the deal?"

"Don't really know. He's an art collector. He's also a large donor to museums around the world. You'd have to ask him."

"Has he called you about the euphon since the Science Center released its statement?"

"No."

"Anyone else call?"

"Sig called to tell me about the forgery. He was upset, to say the least."

"What time was that? The call from Dr. Fuller?"

"Nine. Yesterday."

"What did he say, exactly?"

"Said the Carnegie believes the rod lengths are wrong. I asked him how that could be since he's the one who authenticated them in the first place." Chlad's voice was steadily rising and his face turning red. He reached for his coffee and drained it. Replacing the empty cup, he sat back, seemingly lost in thought.

Leslie, after a moment, asked, "What did Dr. Fuller say in answer to your question about the euphon being…being non-authentic?"

"He said it was perfectly authentic when he handed it over to the security service who transported it to Pittsburgh. I said that didn't seem possible. Then...then he...he well, he got angry. Said I was ungrateful for all he had done. Said without him I'd have nothing. Said he was the one who was the victim, not me."

"What'd he mean by, he was the victim?"

"I suppose," Chlad replied, "he was referring to...I suppose...his reputation."

"What else could he have meant?" Fischer pressed, picking up on Chlad's hesitation.

"Well, the deal was, like I said, that once the euphon is returned to the Polish National Museum I receive a million dollars a year. Sig gets a commission of fifteen percent."

"Okay," Leslie replied, sensing they had pushed Chlad to his limit. "How did you leave it with Dr. Fuller when you last spoke to him?"

"He told me to come over to his house. He said he had planned a special lunch with his friend, Selma Fritz, but given the situation his plans had changed."

"In what way had they changed?"

"Don't know exactly, but he said Colton had called him and would be there as well as one other interested party. Said he would show us documentation proving he had shipped the original euphon up to Pittsburgh with the proper rods."

"Do you know who that other party was?"

"I don't"

"Did he tell you what that documentation was?"

"Just said it would be convincing."

"And what time were you to meet him?"

"At 11:45."

"Did you go to his house at that time?" Leslie asked.

"Around that time. Rang the bell. Knocked on the door. When he didn't answer the door, I called his phone. Got no answer."

"So, you didn't see Dr. Fuller at any time yesterday?" Fischer asked, wanting to have Chlad clearly on record.

"That's right. He didn't answer the door or the phone. I then drove over to the beach to think. He was dead when I got home."

"How did you know he was dead when you returned home?" Leslie asked.

"Police cars all over the neighborhood. Couldn't get close to his house."

"If you couldn't get close, how did you know it was his house?"

"One of the guys I play bocce with told me."

"Guy's name?"

"I know him only as Gino."

"Did anyone overhear that conversation?"

"A guy by the name ot Ed. Another guy also might have heard. Name's Steve."

Leslie, thinking about the entire timeline, from back before Chlad even knew about the euphon until now, took a moment to sort it out. "Help me here," she finally said. "You moved into the neighborhood you said about six years ago."

"That's right."

"You met Fuller soon after?"

"Correct."

"From what I understand, the euphon was located less than a year ago."

"Where you going with all this?" Chlad demanded, clearly agitated.

"Just making certain I understand the full picture. Am I correct, the euphon was located about a year ago?"

"It was. Sig found it hidden in a wall in a boarding house in Wroclaw where Chladni had been staying. That's where my ancestor died. Sig's theory was that when Chladni died, the proprietor of the boarding house realized the value of the euphon and hid it in a secret area behind a wooden wall. According to Sig, most houses of 16<sup>th</sup> and 17<sup>th</sup> century construction were stone. Aristocrats covered the stone with ornate wood. To keep thieves — and tax collectors — away from their valuables they constructed intricate hiding spaces in the walls. Sig found an old registry in the Wroclaw town hall archives showing the two lodgings where Chladni stayed when he was in Wroclaw. It was then called Breslau, Kingdom of Prussia. My understanding is Sig used something he called a millimeter wave imaging tool to locate it."

Visualizing the scene, Leslie said, "Then I suppose the owner of the boarding house died without having told his family or anyone else where he had hidden the euphon. So, no one ever knew it was there."

"That was Sig's theory," Chlad replied. "Or something like that."

"Okay, so when did you first learn about the euphon? Was it a family thing talked about over the years? Stories passed down generation to generation. What?"

"Frankly, never heard of it before...before Fuller mentioned it to me."

"When was that?"

"About five years ago."

"In what context?"

"I don't recall how it came up. My memory is one day at the main pool we got to talking. Sig mentioned that my unusual name, Chlad, was very similar to that of a famous scientist in history. He asked me if I knew about the euphon. When I said I didn't, he dropped the subject. Sometime later he gave me information about Chladni and the euphon."

"What happened then?"

"He said he was going to Poland to search for it and invited Carol and me to join him. We declined."

"Declined why? Sounds like a great adventure."

"It was winter and Carol dislikes traveling in cold weather. Anyway, he called, maybe six months later, all excited. He had come back from Poland with a long list of names of people. Said he had a good idea on how to locate the lost euphon. He got me and Carol excited."

"Carol knew Fuller?"

"They met a few times."

"What made you believe you were the owner of the euphon, assuming Fuller could locate it? After all, as you said, it was ten generations ago."

"Sig produced an elaborate family tree based on church and government records. It showed I was the only one that had direct right to it."

"Then what?"

"He convinced us that if he were to find the euphon, he could find a buyer who would pay tens of millions of dollars for it. Maybe even hundreds of millions. He, Sig, would get a finder's fee in the form of a sales commission once he had found the euphon and it had been sold." Chlad's eyes narrowed, his face again flushed. His jaw clenched.

"Mr. Chlad," Leslie said, "I know this is difficult for you, losing your business partner and all. Just a few more questions and we'll be out of here."

"Thank you, Detective. It's a trying time. What more can I tell you?"

"When Dr. Fuller suggested he could find the euphon, did you believe him?"

"Not in the least. Not in the beginning. It was really an incredible longshot. Sig's theory about the euphon having been hidden in a wall by an innkeeper had no real basis in probability. It was only Sig's hunch. And even if his hunch was right, Sig had to hope that the city archives might have old visitor registries or at least the locations of the inns in Wroclaw at that time. He had to hope also that Chladni would have been staying at one of those inns in town, that the inn where Chladni stayed was still standing, and that the current owners would allow Sig to do the millimeter wave scan of their walls."

"Not to mention the possibility that someone had already found the euphon in the course of a renovation and did who knows what with it," Leslie added. "That's an awful lot of ifs."

"A lot of ifs for sure," Chlad agreed. "But in the end, Sig was very convincing."

"But convincing to what end? Why would Dr. Fuller need to convince you of anything?"

"Because he wanted us — well, Carol really — to underwrite the cost of his investigation, including what he had already spent out of his own pocket on the first trip."

"And it seems that Carol was, in fact, convinced that it was all worth a shot."

"She did. And she turned out to be right."

"Before you, or your wife, gave him the money, did Sig — Dr. Fuller — mention the Polish Government? Or the National Museum?" Leslie asked, struggling to fit the timeline together.

"He may have. I don't recall. I do recall him at one point talking about a private sale."

"No doubt the proceeds of a private sale would have been higher than the amount that the Polish Government would have been willing to pay you in order to keep the euphon in Poland, assuming that they could be convinced that you were the rightful owner."

"That was Sig's theory of things, for sure."

Chlad focused his attention on something in the distance out through the lanai screening. Without looking at either detective, his voice barely audible, he said, "You would probably want to know that, all told, we paid Sig close to three-and-a half million."

# EIGHT

BACK AT HER DESK, LESLIE brought up the Fuller forensics file. The techs had spent seven hours cataloging the house. She began with the garage, paying particular attention to the pulley system attached to the ceiling. The report confirmed her initial thought — that the pulley system was designed as a bike hoist. The tech's diagram showed that the far end of the rope was tied to a cleat mounted on the back garage wall. The rope extended up from the cleat to a pulley attached to the ceiling and then ran over to a second pulley spaced three feet from the first pulley. The victim was found directly below the second pulley. Pulling down on the rope end by the cleat caused the rope hanging down over Fuller's head to go up. A simple mechanism used for storing two-wheeled bikes against the ceiling.

A second diagram showed a stick-figure body, a belt looped around its neck with the end of the belt tied to a hook on the cord hanging down from the second pulley. According to the hoist specifications, each pulley had a weight limit of fifty pounds. Fuller weighed one-ninety-five. His body had moved upward only a few feet before a bearing in the pulley directly above his head shattered and seized.

The inventory of Fuller's wallet, found in his pants pocket, listed Visa and Texaco credit cards, Social Security and Medicare cards, Florida driver's license, Miromar Lakes card, and a Chase Bank

ATM card. The report was signed by Langston Williams, Senior Crime Scene Analyst.

"Hey Langston," Leslie said into her cell, "This is Detective Leslie Hodges, I'm working the..."

"I remember you. Slender, wild green eyes. The garage hanging. How can I help you?"

"How about I buy you lunch, we can chat."

"I'd love to score a free lunch, Detective. But you need to know I won't tell you one blessed thing more over lunch than I would on the phone, or at my desk."

"I wouldn't expect otherwise. It's just that while we're eating there's less chance of us being interrupted."

"Fair enough. Where and when?"

"Now's fine with me. You pick the place."

"How about Fat Katz at twelve forty-five? We can eat outside."

"That's a plan. See you there."

---

Leslie stood to greet the senior crime scene analyst when he arrived ten minutes late. Williams nodded to a guy sitting by himself at the edge of the patio as he made his way to where she was seated. "So much for a quiet day," he said, starting to reach out his hand in greeting and quickly pulling it back remembering the COVID protocol. He slipped gracefully into the seat opposite her at the small table. "Friends call me Lang. Well, they call me other things as well, but Lang will do. Hey, look. I bought us forty-five minutes. Guy just found in the Preserve off Corkscrew. First responder believes COD was a bear. Game warden's not so certain. Team's on the way. I have some time."

"Keeping you busy it seems."

"On and off. Mixed thoughts on it. I like to be busy, the more the merrier. But when I'm busy that means some poor slob's dead, most likely on the wrong end of a slug That's not good. But, hey, I take solace knowing what I do helps ease the pain for the victim's family. I suppose that works for you as well."

Leslie nodded. "That's what we do," she agreed. "You plan to eat, we better order." She hadn't been around anyone this chatty in a while. It was refreshing in its own way.

"You ready? I know what I'm ordering. A turkey burger. They're the best here. Send all my friends over here. Helps I know the owner."

"Friend of yours?"

"Married to his daughter's all."

She looked at him as though with new eyes.

"What's the matter? I can't be married? Or a black man can't be married to a white woman?"

"Nothing of the kind," Leslie quickly responded, caught off-guard by his obvious sensitivity. After all, she, herself a woman from the deep south, was seeing a black man and thought nothing of it. His reaction reminded her that bringing Allen home to meet her parents could be problematic. "I didn't see a ring. Didn't know you were married."

"With what I do, rings get in the way. Not trying to hide anything, promise. Have two great kids. Need to have you and Allen over sometime for a cookout."

"How do you know about…Allen?"

"County's a small place. Everything criminal filters through the Criminal Investigation Office. Allen works as a criminal prosecutor. You do the math."

"So why bust my ass?"

"Sorry. Goes with the territory. My bad."

Uncomfortable with this line of conversation, Leslie said, "Let's order. I'll do the same as you. Sounds good."

Lang raised his hand and almost instantly a young woman appeared. "Nice seeing you, Lang," she said. "Been hiding or what?"

"Been busy. Make this fast, please Liddy. Two turkey burgers, mine with fries. A coke."

"I'll take mine without the fries. Coke's fine," Leslie said. Looking down at the table, she noted Langston had a file folder open. "What's this?" she asked.

"Talk about that in a moment. What I'm about to say needs to remain between just us. If you're recording me, turn it off."

"Wouldn't record you without permission. But in fairness, I owe it to my partner to tell him what I know."

"Orally—for now. Not in the file."

"Deal," Leslie replied.

"Preliminary COD is strangulation, with no evidence of assistance."

"Suicide, in other words. Saw that in the file."

"For now," Lang said, sitting back to allow the waitress to place the burgers in front of them. He devoured half his sandwich while Leslie thought about what she had just been told.

"I take it you have an alternate theory?" she finally queried.

"Still off the record."

Leslie nodded.

"Me? I'm calling it homicide. I'm pretty sure the final ME report will reflect my view. Doc's just not there yet I'm afraid."

Leslie nibbled at her sandwich, saying nothing.

"Think about the logistics," Lang said after brushing a napkin across his lips. "Guy using a bike-lift pulley system to hoist himself up. I suppose it's possible, but frankly even with the mechanical advantage the pulley system provides, I don't think it can be done. But, hey, that's the ME's call."

While Lang was talking, Leslie recalled how far the body was from the rope end which had been tied neatly around the cleat.

"The horizontal distance," Lang continued, consulting the file as he spoke, "from the cleat on the back wall to the centerline of the body is thirty-eight inches. Deceased's arm has a thirty-four-and-a-half-inch extension, again measured from the centerline. Even assuming he pulled himself up, he would have had to tie the end off?"

"That's three and a half inches short you're saying."

"If it was that simple, the medical examiner would negate homicide. No, Detective. There is the possibility the deceased could have walked over to the cleat, jerked himself up a foot or two, looped the rope around the cleat and allowed himself to swing back under the pulley."

"Not very likely. But, I suppose, possible. So, why's the ME leaning toward suicide?"

"No evidence of a second person in the garage. Not yet anyway."

"You think otherwise?"

"Several smudged fingerprints are not back yet. One on the wall beside the cleat, others on the door into the house from the garage. My take is a guy bent on suicide would not rely on looping the rope on a cleat he could barely reach with a noose around his neck. No, he would have pre-tied the rope around the cleat with the hook up near the ceiling. He would then have climbed a ladder, or stood on a box, and jumped off."

"Inconclusive, at best," Leslie responded, nodding in agreement. "What else should I know?"

"It's all in the report. I'll say this, again off the record. Certain tools were cleaner than we ever see them. The table saw, for example, was spotless. No wood chips or fibers on the blades. I'm thinking that someone wiped the tools clean."

"Any guess as to why? Or when?"

"My guess is as good as yours. I'm thinking the tools were used to cut a material someone didn't want anyone knowing they were cutting. The only thing I can add is that we did find a few spruce chips and traces of a veneer on the floor behind a worktable leg. It's a long shot, but we may be able to source the spruce. But forget the veneer."

"Spruce? Veneer? What do you make of that?"

"Couldn't begin to speculate how long they were there. Or where they came from? Sorry."

"Anything else?"

"Never seen a soundproof room — booth — in a garage before. Thing's built like Fort Knox. When the door's closed you can only hear what's electronically piped into the booth. Eerie feeling being in there with no sound."

# NINE

FISCHER WAS WAITING FOR LESLIE when she returned from lunch. "Learn anything of interest from Lang?"

"He convinced me it's a homicide."

"Not what the preliminary report calls it."

Leslie proceeded to brief her partner on what she had been told, then said, "Add to that the fact there was no note, and the fact Fuller had asked Chlad to come to his house. That doesn't feel like a suicide."

"Until the ME report officially changes, we need to treat Fuller's death as a suicide."

Leslie held her ground. "I'm still not buying suicide. And, unless I miss my guess, neither are you."

"Fuller had reason to kill himself. The euphon he certified proved to be a fake. His reputation was gone. His living most likely gone as well."

"Can't argue with the physics. Suicide would have been hard to pull off the way he did it. Imagine trying to tie a rope onto a cleat after you've hung yourself. Not likely."

"You planning on reporting to Boots it's a homicide?"

"Isn't that what senior partners are for?" Leslie quipped, knowing full well this was hers to argue.

"She asks my opinion; I have your back. Brass trusted you on the Edison case, see no reason for her to take her money off the table."

Thinking about the possible suspects, Leslie said, "With the Edison phonograph, we only had

Stratis sniffing around. Now, as you know, there are three. I found a bit about the Kumars, but it had to do with their business, something called Sat Inquest. Best I can tell, they exclusively lease the data from a series of satellites. They use that data to provide tracking information to the military. Top secret, highly sophisticated data. Internet rumor has it they have at least one government contract worth in excess of five hundred million a year. Needless to say, they're well connected."

"Didn't your friend Jak alert you that the Kumars, as well as that guy Colton, were down here the night before Fuller's death?"

"They both were. I suppose we should interview them."

"I suggest briefing Boots first. There may be blowback if they're so well connected."

"The good news," Leslie reminded her partner, "is Boots already approved us working on the case."

"But that was to help with a Pittsburgh investigation having tentacles reaching into Florida. Now it's a Florida homicide with Pittsburgh flavor. Horse of a different color, you ask me. Better brief Oakmore at least. He's more skittish than Boots."

"Your wish is my command," Leslie said, having already come to the same conclusion that Hud had to be in the loop. "You want to join…"

Her partner had turned away, answering his cell in the process. Leslie flipped open her computer and entered euphon into the search engine.

Fischer interrupted, "I think you should hear this. One of the IRS team's on the line." Into his cell he said, "Hold a moment. I'm putting you on speaker so my partner can hear what you're saying."

Fischer listened to the response, then said, "No, I won't say your name out loud."

He listened further, before saying, "Agreed. Give us a moment to step into an interrogation room." Fischer motioned Leslie to follow him.

Pulling the door to the room closed behind them, Fischer said into his phone, "We're in a secure room and you're now on speaker. My partner, Detective Leslie Hodges, is here with me. Other than her, we're alone. Please repeat for Hodges what you told me."

The voice filling the room was female, deep and coarse, suggesting a life-long heavy smoker. "I was saying, one of the bidders on the euphon is a man named Alexandre Colton. He was hours away from snatching the euphon from the Science Center when their security, working with ICMS and with the Polish National Museum, declared the authenticity of the euphon suspect. The Polish authorities demanded that the instrument be sent to Dr. Fuller for re-certification and then immediately returned to Poland. Needless to say, Colton's pissed. Frankly, the team was as well. We were ready for him."

"Never heard of IC whatever," Fischer said. "What is...?"

"International Committee on Museum Security. It's part of the International Council of Museums, ICOM. When the euphon arrived at the Science Center it was examined by a museum forensics expert who called in an ICMS specialist when the measurement of the one of the glass rods did not match the specifications found in Fuller's report. They compared the euphon with sound recordings taken in Poland and found a mismatch."

"Seems to be a Pittsburgh problem," Fischer said. "Don't understand why the IRS is briefing Florida cops."

"Colton immediately decamped and is in your neck of the woods, ostensibly to sell a piece of art unrelated to the euphon. He's trying to make it look as if he's raising money to buy the euphon. It's all a smokescreen. The guy's a foreign agent. That man'll stop at nothing to obtain the euphon."

"If the euphon is not authentic, why continue to raise money?" Leslie asked, puzzled where this was going.

"Good question. If you assume the piece at the Science Center is a fake, and if you assume the original forensics was accurate, one could conclude the original euphon is somewhere in the vicinity of Dr. Fuller, since he is the one who last had the original."

"Are you implying," Leslie asked, "that Dr. Fuller substituted a fake euphon for the original?"

"I'm not implying anything. Just providing facts and letting you know Colton has his mind set on possessing that euphon. If the thought of a substitution crossed your mind Detective, then one can imagine it crossed Colton's mind as well. You have your hands full down there."

"What's that mean?"

"As you might know, there are at least two other bidders. Guy named Stratis. And a husband-wife team, Sanjay and Riya Kumar. I suppose there are plenty more."

"You started to say something about surveillance," Fischer reminded the speaker, signaling Leslie to hold her questions. "Please continue."

"We have surveillance video showing Colton presenting a stolen artifact to Dr. Norman Vesquez, the world's premier Peruvian art expert. If authenticity of the artifact holds, then Vesquez is authorized to broker a sale. This guy Vesquez is known for his...let's just say...his ability to overlook Interpol's Stolen Works of Art Database. The piece Colton has in his possession is the Blue Footed Golden Booby. Check the database and you'll see what I'm talking about. Current value may be well over three hundred million. Given the right buyer, perhaps even higher. If you catch Colton with the Booby, it'll be a simple arrest. Simple conviction."

"Do I understand," Leslie clarified, "the IRS is handing this stolen Booby thing over to us. Why?"

"I made it even easier for you," the voice continued without answering the question. "I've included a copy of the Golden Booby listing from Interpol's Stolen Works of Art Database. Slam dunk case. Simple possession and Colton'll do prison time. They don't come any easier than this. Please, Detective, just watch the video and chalk up an easy collar."

Out of deference to Fischer, Leslie refrained from snapping, "Or what?"

Fischer compliantly said, "We'll take a look, see what you got."

The line went dead.

"Who the hell was that?" Leslie demanded, thinking this was the same source Jakowski had received his earlier information from.

"Keep it out of the file?"

"To the extent possible. But I can't promise categorically."

"Fair enough. Carmella Schenley. Lives in Pittsburgh. An art dealer."

"Fish, spare me! I may be a newly minted detective, but I've been a cop long enough to know that wasn't an art dealer. If I'm wrong, hell, I'll turn in my shield."

Fischer reached out his hand, as if to accept her credentials. "Be careful with your pronouncements." He dropped his hand and smiled broadly. "As it turns out, you're not entirely wrong. She is an art dealer in Pittsburgh, but the dealer business is a front. She's IRS and has made it her life's mission to bring down the Seminal Society collectors."

"Why them?"

"On the surface, I suppose it's because they collect Firsts. When they succeed, like with the Edison phonograph or the Chladni euphon, the artifact is taken away from the public for private pleasure. Falls in the category of cultural heritage crime, a category of white-collar crime. Make that starched white-collar crime."

"And under the surface?" Leslie probed.

"I've had dealings with Schenley a few times, and each time I came away feeling…well, unsettled. I don't know her real agenda. Something personal I presume."

"Time to brief Hud?"

"First, let's review the files Schenley sent, satisfy ourselves all's in order for an arrest. Good chance there's already a court order for a much larger operation and we're only a small piece of what's going down. Knowing Schenley, she'll include the existing order, but redact anything of real value."

Within fifteen minutes it was clear they had enough evidence to arrest Colton for possession of an antiquity clearly shown in Interpol's Stolen Works of Art Database. As Fischer had suggested, a heavily redacted United States Foreign Intelligence Surveillance Court Order was also attached in support of audio and video surveillance.

"Seen enough?" Fischer asked, stretching his back.

"That Blue Footed Golden Booby certainly is gorgeous. He's clearly transporting it in our jurisdiction. Let's do it."

Fischer led the way across the Pit to the boss's office. Hud's admin informed them Oakmore was out for the remainder of the day. "Boots is covering."

"Great timing, you two," Captain Stetson said when the two detectives appeared in her doorway a few minutes later. "I just reviewed the Fuller forensics report. Inconclusive, at best."

"Have more information on that, Captain," Leslie said, proceeding to detail her lunch meeting with lab tech Williams, concluding with, "I agree with his assessment of homicide."

"And you, Fish," Stetson asked, turning to the senior detective, "do you concur?"

"I do," Fischer promptly replied, fulfilling his promise of having his partner's back.

Addressing Leslie, Stetson asked, "I'm assuming the Fuller homicide's linked to the Pittsburgh matter we discussed? I take it you didn't go north."

"Working it from here, Cap. The Chladni euphon, the one on display up there, turns out to be suspect. The problem is, Dr. Fuller, the deceased, vouched for its authenticity just before the instrument was shipped north. There's speculation that…"

"You think Fuller had something to do with a substitution?"

"We're working it," Leslie replied, not yet willing to commit. When her captain remained silent, Leslie continued, "The reason we came to see you is a call we received from an IRS agent by the name of Schenley." Leslie proceeded to outline their conversation with Schenley, ending with, "The video we received from Schenley shows Colton in possession of a gold statue with blue feet identical to the antiquities listing. Before we arrest Colton, we wanted to run it by Oakmore, see how he wanted us to proceed."

"This your contact Fish?" the captain asked. "I've heard Schenley's name a few times over the years. Can't imagine her reaching out to a rookie like Hodges."

"It is. Worked with her once or twice."

"Standup?"

"Yes — and no. As I told Leslie, the woman makes me edgy. In a previous tip from her, yes, we arrested a guy on gun possession charges. My instinct told me the gun we seized was a plant, but we were already committed, so we got a warrant for his home and office. Guess what? In his house we found a vase stolen from Persia. The vase was on the antiquities list. All very neat and orderly. Worked out well — too well in fact. I felt we had been manipulated. Can't really explain it any better than that."

"Had the gun been planted?" Stetson asked.

"Never did find that out. With the antiquities arrest, the gun charge was dropped."

"Tell you what," Stetson said, "You two stay out of this Colton matter. Don't need either of you tainted if there's blow back. I'll have Cox run it to ground. He's..."

"But..." Leslie interrupted, wanting to say that since Colton was chasing after the euphon it would be best if she made the arrest. It would allow her to interrogate a potential antiquities buyer — murderer.

Before Leslie could plead her case, Stetson said, "Cox is sitting surveillance downtown. This will be a nice break for him."

———◆———

"Mind telling me what you know about Interpol's Stolen Art list?" Allen asked Leslie several hours later. They were seated across from each other in the small dining area of his apartment having drinks before dinner. "The file Detective Cox sent over has your name in the chain of custody of a Foreign Intelligence Surveillance Order. I assume that's because it involves stolen art."

"You know what they say about assume. So be careful."

"You saying you know nothing about the Booby bird on that list"

"I'm telling you to be careful, is all."

"You're sending me a message. Only problem: I'm not receiving what you're sending."

Leslie, unsure of exactly what ethical obligations she was bound by, decided the less said the better. "Best to drop this line of conversation."

"Not fair of you to..." Seeing Leslie's green eyes go almost black, Allen changed his question. "Just tell me how you came upon the file?"

"Allen, frankly, I'm not sure what all I can tell you. Some of what we have came from a source who we promised to keep confidential."

"Okay, I'll drop it. You still working on that fake musical instrument matter?"

"I'm working the Fuller hanging, if that's your question?"

"That must be how you came into possession of the Alexandre Colton tipoff? I drew the short straw on prosecution for possession of solen property."

"Can't say much more on that subject. Sorry, my love."

"A lawyer from IRS is pressing for a search warrant for Colton's hotel, rental car — and private jet parked over at Page Field. Hearing's at nine in the morning."

Cox, Leslie knew, had picked up Colton a few hours ago. "I'm surprised Colton's not already bonded out."

"He is. Court has Colton's passport. Lawyer guaranteed the judge he'll show for the hearing in the morning."

"Who'd he hire?"

"Susan Morehouse."

"Makes sense. Since she represents the Edison and Ford Winter Estates and knows about cultural heritage art."

"Here's the thing," Allen said, leaning across the table and lowering his voice even though he was in his own apartment, "Lee County has already searched his rental car and the hotel and found nothing. Searching the jet makes me uncomfortable. Nothing more in Florida we know about. They really want access to his home in New Jersey and who knows where else, but they don't have probable cause. They're hoping we find something in his plane that'll help them. There's a game being played here. Only I don't know what it is."

"Makes two of us," Leslie replied, keenly aware of Allen's agitation. "If you think I'm part of that game, think again."

"I confess. Thought crossed my mind."

"Allen!" Leslie exclaimed, pulling her hands back and sitting upright in her chair.

"Tell me you're not working me on this, and I'll drop it."

Leslie was angry with Allen for even thinking she would play him. But she knew that if the tables were reversed, she would confront Allen. Readjusting her chair, she calmly replied, "I'm not working on the Colton file. Period. And I'm certainly not working you either." Which was true, but not exactly the full story. "Now where's that famous roasted chicken you promised? Been hankering for it all day."

# TEN

IT WAS UNUSUAL FOR LESLIE to dwell on the past, focused as she was on her several criminal investigations. Yet here she was at 7:10 in the morning driving on the now familiar route from Allen's home to her office. She continued to tell herself that Allen's questioning of her about the Colton matter was not distrust so much as it was him trying to be thorough — and perhaps build confidence in her as a trusted partner. The bottom line was that she now spent her life questioning people, using small inconsistencies to build criminal cases. She bristled when the tactic was used on her. Overly sensitive? Maybe. But still...

The word Fish flashed onto her phone.

"We caught a burglary," her partner announced without introduction when she answered. "Over on Metro Parkway. Pawn shop. Quick Cash. Need to take a statement. Meet me there, no code."

"Roger that. Hey, while I got you, I'm thinking I need to brief Jak up in Pittsburgh on the homicide — and on Colton. Thoughts?"

"Go for it. Just keep the agent's name off the record."

———————

Pete Jakowski answered on the first ring. "Great minds think alike," he said in greeting. "Just about to call you."

"About what?"

"Your dime. Go first."

"Off the record, we're treating the Fuller death — at least for now — as a homicide," Leslie replied. "Strangulation by hanging. Second, Alexandre Colton was arrested late yesterday for possession of stolen property." Jakowski remained silent. "Your turn," Leslie said, "that's all I got for now."

"As you said, we're still off the record. Please keep..."

"I understand," Leslie snapped.

Jakowski, ignoring Leslie's agitation, responded, "Any idea how The Carnegie Science Center determined the euphon was fake?"

"Why do I have the feeling you're about to tell me?"

"Someone called with a tip to check the glass rod lengths."

"That's in keeping with my information as well," Leslie confirmed.

The sign for the Easy Cash pawn shop came into view and Leslie pulled into the small lot, rolling to a stop beside Fischer's car. The parking area served a gym on the corner nearest the entry, a beauty shop at the far end, with the pawnshop next to the gym. "Gotta go," she said to the Pittsburgh detective. "Talk later."

———◆———

Leslie was reminded of her early years on the Gulfport police force as she approached the plate glass windows of the pawnshop, its name etched in bold letters. The rows of cell phones, calculators, electric guitars, microphones, a collection of hammers, saws, drills brought back memories of her early years working with a partner, a veteran of forty-two years, and perhaps the only man who had consented to partner with a woman barely older than his granddaughter. When Leslie left for Tampa to marry Junior, he retired.

Fish fell in beside her. "Easy way to start the day. Take a report, get it over with. These things never add up to much."

Leslie pulled the door open. "Showing the flag never hurts," she responded. "Community policing at its best."

A woman looking to be in her mid-fifties with yellowish gray hair was leaning on a counter beside an ancient cash register, a newspaper spread open in front of her. "I'm Deputy Fischer. This is Deputy Hodges. You call in a burglary? So, what's missing?" He made no move to pull out his notepad.

Leslie clicked on her cell phone's recorder and held it up so the proprietor could see they were taking her seriously.

"A cell phone and an iPad's all," the manager responded without emotion.

"Value?"

"Loaned $75 on the phone and $125 on the pad."

"So, $200 in all. Time, if you know it, of the burglary?"

"Less than two hours ago," the woman immediately responded. "Five-fifty-three to be exact."

"You know the time how?" Fischer asked.

"Silent alarm."

"Have video?" Leslie interrupted.

"Threw a towel over the lens. Found it when I arrived."

"You know the perp was a male because?"

"Because before the camera was covered, I could see his hand. A male hand with a burning bush tat. Guy goes by Jackson Hils." She retrieved a paper from behind the register and handed it to Fischer. "Here's his address. Wouldn't be surprised to learn it's fake — just like his name."

"Are you're positive, its..."

"When personal electronics are stolen it's always the owner. They pawn the stuff to buy drugs, expecting to round up enough cash in a few days to buy it back. When that fails, they panic. Without the phone, they can't reach the dealer. That's when they come looking for their phone. Guy was in yesterday trying to trade a rusty scooter he most likely snitched somewhere for his phone. That kid's in bad shape."

Ten minutes later, having gathered everything they needed, Leslie opened the front door of the pawnshop, pausing to allow her partner to proceed her into the bright sunlight. Instead of going out, Fischer stopped. "Meet you at the office," he said, "forgot to leave a card."

Leslie continued through the door and turned left toward her car. She paused, thinking she should also leave a card, thought better of it and turned back to her car. Slipping her cell phone into her pocket with her left hand, she reached for her keys with her right.

POP! POP!

It took less than a second for Leslie to process the sound of gun shots. In that brief interval, she, by instinct, performed several tasks almost simultaneously. Dropping her keys, her hand went toward her Glock, her eyes focusing first on the woman at the far end of the sidewalk, and then shifting to the shooter; a man standing beside a pickup truck in front of the beauty shop, holding a gun pointed at the woman. Leslie's eyes locked onto the shooter, while her brain processed the vision of the woman's head exploding.

Reaching for her weapon initially proved futile. The belt holster she had worn on her right hip for eleven years was now positioned under her left arm. Her weapon belatedly drawn, she yelled, "Stop! Police! Drop your..."

The man abruptly turned to face her, his weapon rotating to line up with her chest. "Police!" She repeated. "Drop..."

The gun moved slightly upward. Leslie dove sideways to her right just as she heard another POP, POP, her body glancing off Fischer's front bumper before hitting the pavement. Landing awkwardly, her gun barrel hard against her ribs, she was immediately thankful that she hadn't released the safety.

A male voice from the direction of the shooter shouted, "Christ! I'm hit! Help..."

Leslie slowly got to her knees and peered over the hood of the car. The shooter was nowhere in sight. "Deputy Badge 21301. Code zero," she barked into her mic. "Active shooter! One dead! One possibly shot! Location: Easy Cash. Metro Parkway. Plain clothes officers, male and female, on scene!"

Leslie, still crouching, ran toward where she had last seen the shooter, listening intently for any sound of movement. She heard nothing and saw no one inside the truck. Carefully peering around the front of a parked car, she saw the shooter on the ground, blood spurting from his upper chest between his shoulder and heart, his pistol several inches from his fingers.

Running toward him, she kicked the weapon further out of reach and immediately ripped open his blood-stained shirt. Blood was spurting freely. She pressed her hand hard against the entry hole just below his shoulder and waited for the blood to slow. It seemingly took forever before what had been a constant stream became a trickle. In that time, she mentally recreated what had transpired from the instant she walked out of the pawn shop.

She had seen a woman walking briskly from the parking area toward the beauty salon. Two gunshots were fired from a gun held by the man who was now beneath her. That same man had then turned the gun toward her. She watched as the gun rose slightly allowing her time to dive to the ground, glancing off the front fender of her partner's car as she fell. One — possibly two — gunshots reverberated from the store fronts. It was all vivid, and in slow motion.

Fischer suddenly appeared over her. "Keep him alive," he commanded, his voice barely above a whisper. He backed away.

When she looked again, Fischer was sitting on the ground beside the fallen woman, slumping over as if he had fallen. She suppressed the desire to leave the shooter and assist her partner, knowing that if she removed her hand, the shooter would bleed to death within minutes.

"Fish! You all right?" she yelled.

"Doin' my best," came the feeble reply.

A paramedic suddenly appeared over her. "Ease up, Detective. I'll take over."

A second paramedic called, "His breathing's shallow, but steady." Turning to Leslie, the second paramedic said, "And you are?"

"Detective Leslie Hodges."

"If this man lives it's only because of you, Detective. Lost a lot of blood as it is."

Leslie hadn't heard the sirens, but several Lee County Sheriff cars were now in the lot along with two EMT teams.

After the hand-off to the paramedic, Leslie leaned against the truck to steady herself. Fischer, she saw, was now lying on his back, uniformed deputies kneeling on either side of him. She tried to run toward him, but her legs were wobbly. Struggling to keep herself upright, she fell against the truck's hood, her vision moving in and out of focus. It was all she could do to keep from vomiting.

Stumbling toward her partner required concentration. Remaining upright was difficult. Then the sidewalk began spinning. She toppled forward.

"Hodges," one of the deputies yelled, grabbing Leslie's shoulders and easing her to the ground. "Stay down, Detective," the deputy instructed. "You're in no condition..."

Ignoring the warning, Leslie tried to stand, only to feel the ground rotate around her. She fell back to her knees, her pulse beating fast and struggling to breathe. She was shivering from cold even though the outside temperature was in the eighties.

The deputy stood between her and Fischer, blocking her path. Every time Leslie tried to move, she was overcome with dizziness and nausea. She was losing the battle to avoid heaving.

One of the EMTs bent down, examined her, and declared, "This one's in shock. How's that one?"

"Stable," came the reply. "Need to get them both to the hospital."

"Fish!" Leslie managed. "You okay?"

"He'll be fine," the calm voice of the paramedic said. "What's your name?"

"Detective Leslie Hodges," she replied, annoyed with the woman for blocking her view of Fischer. "Let me..."

"What day of the week is this?"

"What the hell business..."

"Do you know what day it is?"

Leslie drew a blank on the day.

"I'm going to ask you to lie back. Put your head on this." The EMT slipped a folded blanket under Leslie's head and placed another over her. "Please remain calm. You're in shock."

"Fischer," Leslie called, "what happened? Did you..."

"I can't allow you two to talk," the Sheriff Deputy who was now kneeling beside Leslie said. "Internal Affairs is on the way to take statements."

The paramedic slipped an oxygen mask over Leslie's mouth and nose. "Better tell them to meet her at the hospital," he said. "Time's not our friend here."

"Transport them in separate vehicles, then," replied the deputy. "They need to be separated until their statements are taken."

"Can't do. We only have two vans available. That guy over there only has minutes left on his clock. Can't wait to load this one. They're preparing an operating room for him as we speak." Indeed, while the EMT was talking, the backdoor of one of the medical transport vans slammed closed and the vehicle began gathering speed. "With the amount of blood lost it'll be a miracle if he survives even to the hospital."

"Then how 'bout I take Hodges in my car," the deputy suggested. "Will sitting up harm her?"

"Only if you don't mind cleaning up a mess. From the looks of things, she could let go any moment." Turning to Leslie, the EMT said, "Detective, before you heave, you best get that mask off your face. Hear me? Don't need you drowning on us."

Leslie nodded, wanted to ask about her partner, but it was all she could do to keep from vomiting.

"Give me a barf bag," the deputy replied, "we'll do just fine. Lee Memorial?"

"The sooner the better. We'll let them know you're coming. Keep the blanket on her. She'll need the warmth."

"How's Fish?" Leslie finally asked, trying to put the pieces together and failing miserably.

"Through and through. Doesn't appear to have hit a vital organ. Bleeding's under control. Don't know about tissue or bone damage. You didn't hear that from me."

The deputy helped Leslie up, stabilized her and aimed her toward her car, one of a dozen with flashing lights now occupying the entire parking area, some spilling into the street, with still more arriving.

Progress toward the vehicle was slow. It was as if Leslie had forgotten how to walk. The blue and red flashing lights sent another wave of nausea through her body, this time she lost control and emptied her stomach onto the asphalt parking lot, some of it catching the front tire of the deputy's car.

"Sister," the deputy said, "I'm sure happy you managed to get that there oxygen mask off in time. You need to get all that outta your system out here. I don't care to spend all day cleaning the car. Inside, better use the bag."

Leslie nodded, opened the car door and climbed in. Before the door was closed the dashboard began to spin. She leaned to her side, pushed the door wide open, and emptied whatever remained inside her onto the ground.

# ELEVEN

LESLIE'S NAUSEA HAD SLOWLY FADED. A nurse was checking her vital signs in preparation for removing the IV drip from her arm. "Okay now, let's see you walk," the nurse instructed.

Twice around the small room and Leslie said, "I got this. Good to go."

"Not exactly," came the terse reply. "I can remove the drip. Doctor will have to sign the discharge orders. May take a while."

All of her electronics, including the TV remote, had been confiscated. She had no way of knowing if Allen was aware of what had happened. If he knew, had he been trying to reach her?

No sooner had the nurse left than in marched a woman trailed by a much shorter man. The woman said, "I'm glad to see you out of bed, Detective Hodges. You don't appear to have suffered any major damage. Thank God for that." The woman, smiled just enough to erase the otherwise permanent harshness from her face. "I'm Lieutenant Carol Maxwell. This is Sergeant Wilber Cakecroft. We're with Internal Affairs as you probably already guessed. We're here to take your statement. When we're finished, you'll be free to leave. I suppose that is if you're not too...unsteady."

"If you want," Cakecroft began, his deep voice belying the fact he was barely five foot four and not a pound over 130, "we can hold this up if you want to consult counsel first."

Leslie had heard stories of Internal Affairs and how they could twist the facts. She started to ask for counsel, then thought better of it. "My answers won't change before or after, so get on with it."

Cakecroft took the lead. "We are here to talk about the incident you were involved in earlier today in front of the Quick Cash pawn shop on Metro Parkway. Do you remember the facts surrounding that incident?"

"I believe I do. Yes."

"Since that incident, have you spoken to anyone about the events that occurred?"

"No."

"Not to Deputy Brownwell?"

"Who?"

"The officer who drove you here."

"Not that I'm aware."

"What about TV?" Cakecroft glanced at the TV above her head. "You watch or hear anything?"

"Not been on."

"And you haven't spoken to your partner?"

"Not since I left the pawn shop. How is he?"

"He's okay. Before we get to that, how about detailing everything that happened from the moment you entered the pawn shop until Deputy Brownwell arrived. We're recording this interview. Do you have a problem with that?"

"Record away."

"Begin from when you were first called to the scene. You know the drill. Tell us what you saw. Heard. Felt. What you did. What anyone else did."

Leslie began with Fischer's call, their interview with the woman in the pawn shop and how, when they were about to leave the store, Fischer turned back to leave his card. She then described walking outside and turning toward her parked car just as two pistol shots were fired in rapid succession. Leslie, the image indelibly burned into her brain of the woman's head disintegrating, went on to describe the scene that had played out in front of her. She described the man who had pulled the trigger; how she had fumbled for her weapon; what she yelled to the man with the weapon; how he pointed the firearm directly at her chest; his gun being raised ever so slightly; her diving to the side just as his gun fired. She recounted hearing the shooter yell that he was hit and how she then ran to him and applied pressure to his wound.

"How many shots were fired at the woman?" Maxwell asked, her tone challenging.

"I heard two. I believe they both hit her. But I can't swear to it."

"You yelled at him. What exactly did you yell?"

"Police! Drop your gun!" Leslie thought a moment, then added, "I might have said more, I don't recall. I was concentrating on drawing my weapon."

"When you yelled 'police', what was the shooter's reaction?"

"He turned in my direction and pointed his weapon at my chest."

"Then what?"

"As I said, his gun moved upward toward my head, and I knew he was about to fire. I dove to the side and heard a third shot."

"In that order? Dove first, heard the shot second? Or the other way around?

Leslie closed her eyes, causing the lieutenant to grab her arm.

"What the hell?" Leslie demanded, yanking herself free.

"Thought you were about to fall. Sorry."

"You said you heard a third shot," Cakecroft repeated. "Was that before or after you dove to the side?"

"Simultaneously, I suppose."

"Did you draw your weapon at any point?" he asked.

"As I said, when I heard the first shots I reached for my weapon. Trouble is, I wore it on my gun belt on my right for all the years I worked the streets. That's where my hand went. I was slow, but yes, my weapon was in my hand when I yelled for him to drop his weapon. That's when I saw his arm go up."

Sergeant Cakecroft leaned in close. "Here's the thing, Detective. You said you had your weapon out when the third round was fired. You also said you found yourself on the ground between your and your partner's cars. You said you never fired. Are you positive that's how it went?"

"When I saw his gun level at me, I knew I didn't have time to fire. Everything was happening so fast. His arm moved. I dropped to my right hoping to take the slug in my left side and not dead on. I know I didn't fire because the safety was still on when I hit the ground."

"You never fired?"

"No time."

"Did you hear a fourth round?"

Leslie again thought a moment, replaying everything from memory. She recalled the sound of the gunshot — or shots — and tried to put everything in context with her own movements. "Might have been a fourth. If there was, it was essentially simultaneous with the third. Thought the sound was a single shot reverberating off the glass. But it could have been two."

"Describe the woman who was shot."

"White, mid-forties, weight in the neighborhood of 125, brunette, short cut, green blouse."

"The shooter?"

"Weapon was a six-shot Ruger 1705," Leslie began before drawing a blank on his face and what he was wearing. How many hours of training had she sat through mastering the art of detail recognition in times of stress, only to fail miserably when she was called on to perform. "I'm blanking out on the rest."

"You know the weapon down to the model, yet you can't tell us if he's white, black, Hispanic."

"I know the model number because I dealt with so many of them on the streets of Gulfport and some in Tampa."

"What did you do after you dove to the side?"

"Shooter yelled for help. Poked my head up, didn't see him. I crouched my way to where I had last seen him. He was down beside his truck bleeding. I ripped his shirt open and pressed my hand over the wound."

"Did you call it in?'

"Don't recall it. How's the shooter? Did he..."

"In intensive care. Doctors don't give him much chance. They say he's only alive because of your quick action. Take a guess. How long was it from the time you went down until the time you applied that pressure?"

"A good twenty, maybe thirty seconds."

"Try six," Maxwell said, a momentary twinkle in her eyes. "Bullet hit the right subclavian artery. He'd be long gone if he had bled uncontrolled for twenty seconds."

"Bullet from where? I never shot. Who the hell shot him?"

"Your partner, who else?" Cakecroft said, now also smiling

"So, there was a fourth shot!" Leslie replied, confused.

Maxwell clicked the recorder off. "Came from Fischer. The way we see it, shooter had you in his sight. Fischer came out of the pawn shop, weapon drawn. He saw the shooter's gun pointed at you and he fired."

"Never really heard it."

"Preliminary ballistics suggest," Maxwell began, her eyes continuing to soften, "based on where the shooter's slug hit the door behind you, it would have hit you in your upper chest if you hadn't moved. You'd be the one in that operating room — if you were lucky. Fischer most likely caused the shooter to delay a fraction of a second. Maybe even change his aim slightly. In any event, you're alive because of Fischer's quick action."

"I hope he's not being suspended for the shooting."

"He'll be on medical leave for a while, and I can't discuss our findings. If I was a betting woman," Maxwell winked, "I'd bet he'll be back on the job by the time the doctor clears him for duty. That bullet hole in the building behind you speaks volumes for this being a justified discharge. Keep that between the three of us would you please."

"And the fact I'm alive because of his action?" Leslie said, processing what she had just learned. "Doesn't that exonerate Fish?"

"That as well. By the way, you have a visitor. One of the newer prosecutors. Guy's pacing like an expectant father. I'll send him in. Get some rest. Don't forget to file your incident report and be as thorough as you can."

"I see you're excited to see me," Captain Stetson said coming through the door. She was in uniform, her hat under her arm. Her tired eyes a mismatch for the broad smile on her face. "Perhaps your excitement is for your friend Smith, who graciously allowed me to jump ahead in line. Hope you don't mind."

"Of course not, Captain. How's Fish?"

"No permanent damage I'm told. Muscle involvement, that type of thing. He'll be here a few more days. I think our PR folks want him away from the press. God, those press folks can

be annoying. Shit'll hit the fan when the scum-
bag dies."

"Is that likely?"

"More so than not at this point. Anything you
want to tell me that you didn't tell IA?"

"Told them everything I know."

"Mind repeating for me. I won't have access
to their report for a while, if then. But I did get
a thumbs up from Carol just now. She and I were
partners for a few years back in the day. She's as
straight as they make 'em. Lucky you drew her.
Cakecroft goes along to get along. He'll add nothing to the investigation."

Leslie repeated her narrative for her boss who
remained silent until she finished.

"So, as I understand what you just said, you
didn't hear the fourth shot. That means you don't
know if Fish shot before or after Terrig."

"Terrig?"

"The shooter. Wallace Terrig. Shot Amelia
Bishop, his former girlfriend. Preliminary investigation is she left him for another man."

"I'm uncertain about the fourth shot," Leslie
answered. "Sorry."

"Not uncommon. We believe Terrig and Fish
fired at substantially the same instant. Bet you
know every detail of Terrig's gun. Amazing how
your whole mind focuses on what's about to kill
you. Since you've already given your statement,
I'm cleared to discuss this with you. And I'm positive several others will be along to get it from
you firsthand. Here's what we believe happened.
Terrig fired two rounds into the back of Bishop's
head within a second of each other with extreme
accuracy. This guy practiced. You must have called
out because..."

"I did. Don't recall the exact words."

"...because as we see it, he heard you and turned in your direction. Hesitated, we believe, because he thought you were a civilian. His focus was on getting out of there and disappearing. License plate was smeared with mud. When he realized it was you who had yelled 'police', and saw your weapon, he pulled the trigger. Sound right so far?"

"Yes."

"Here's where the timeline gets a little squirrelly. Fish appears behind you, weapon in hand because he heard the shots. Terrig paused trying to decide which of you presented the most danger to him. He decides on Fish and moves his aim slightly upward. You interpret his slight motion as him pulling the trigger and dive to your right. Your head moved out of Fish's firing line and he and Terrig shot essentially at the same time. Terrig's slug passed through Fish's left arm and embedded in the door behind him. You know where Fish's round went."

Leslie again visualized the scene, quickly realizing she was alive because her partner is left-handed. Had he been holding the gun in his right hand her head would have been blocking his line of fire.

"Good job all around," Stetson said. "Good job! This is Friday. You're scheduled off for the weekend. I want you to take Monday off as well. After that, take whatever time you need." Stetson's smile broadened. She shook Leslie's hand and quipped, "I'm just thankful Fish isn't right-handed. Saved me from preparing a eulogy." With that she turned and left the hospital room.

A moment later a disheveled looking Allen appeared in the doorway. Without thinking, Leslie ran to him and was about to throw her arms around him when she stopped. "I almost just screwed up by hugging you," she said in explanation of her action.

"Screwed up?"

"I thought we were keeping our...our relationship private for now."

"Half your damn office is out there! If they can't figure it out, then take away their detective shields and assign them to guarding the soda machines at the bus station."

The image caused Leslie to burst out laughing. She hugged him tightly. "Thanks for coming. What the hell do I need to do to get out of here?"

"Doctor's signed off. You're free to go."

"My blouse and jacket are covered in blood. And besides, they took them as evidence. I'm sure as hell not going out in this God-awful gown!"

"Today's your lucky day." Allen retrieved the bag he had dropped on his way in. "Ta da!" he announced, unfolding a Red Sox jersey with a matching warm-up jacket. "Hope you're a Sox fan."

"I am now! Give me a minute and we're outta here."

"I suggest washing the blood from your neck. It's a better look. The jersey'll cover your slacks."

# TWELVE

"SARGE! I THOUGHT YOU WERE on vacation!" Leslie exclaimed when she emerged from her room and spotted her immediate supervisor, Sergeant Hudson Oakmore.

"Fishing can wait. It's not every day we have two deputies in the hospital. Thank God it's not the morgue! They tell me you had a bout with shock. Gone now?"

"Other than extreme hunger, I'm feeling fine. Thanks for stopping by. Oh, this is my friend, Allen. Allen Smith."

"I met Allen a while ago. Had a nice chat. By the way, nice piece of work saving that asshole's life."

"Hear he's in critical condition. Any update?"

"One way or another, he's critical all right. Survives the bullet, he'll die by lethal injection. Premeditated all the way."

"I understand the victim was his girlfriend," Leslie said, hoping for more information from her boss.

"Former girlfriend. Broke up with him several months back. He and his Ruger have spent countless hours at a shooting range. You're lucky to be alive."

"Fish saved me."

"Speaking of your partner, he's been asking after you. Up in 568. Stop by and show him you're okay."

"I'll do that."

When Oakmore walked away, Leslie turned to Allen and asked, "You okay with me saying hello to Fish before we leave?"

"Why shouldn't I be? I'm just relieved you're walking out of here on your own."

"Just checking, is all."

———◆———

Room 568 was at the far end of the hall. It seemed to Leslie that every detective, investigator, technician, and secretary from the Sheriff's office was in the corridor, all wearing masks, some with vinyl gloves as well. Some elbow bumping her, others flipping a salute, all congratulating her on a job well done. Leslie wondered if the good job accolades came from the fact she hadn't been killed, or from what to her was the more important aspect—saving Wallace Terrig's life.

"Hey partner," she called, finally making her way into Fischer's room. His bed was slanted upward into the sitting position, his eyes closed, head tipped to the side. A woman, presumably his wife, sat in a chair between him and the far window reading from a Kindle. "Oh, I'm sorry to disturb," Leslie said, stage whispering, and backing toward the door.

"Oh, no. That's alright," the woman said. "You must be Leslie! Please come on in." Standing, she added. "He's been asking about you. I'm his wife, Jessica."

"I'm his partner, Leslie. He's sleeping. I'll come..."

"No. He wants to see you." Moving close to the bed and taking Fischer's hand, Jessica said, "Honey, your partner's here to see you." Turning to Leslie, she continued, "He's having a hard time throwing off the anesthetic. Doctors say it could be hours yet."

"Nice to meet you, Jessica. Your husband saved my life today. I came by to thank him."

"Call me Jess. He credits you with saving his life. Claims that man's gun was pointed directly at him when you shouted. You diving to the ground distracted the shooter and Daryl says that's what allowed him to get a shot off."

Jess's account differed slightly from her own and from the way Stetson told of the incident. Leslie had every faith that the experts would sort out the time frames and correctly piece it all together. She studied her partner a moment, thinking he was about to say something. When Fischer remained motionless, she said to his wife, "He doesn't seem to be waking up. How's he doing?"

"Nothing permanent, thank God," Jess replied, a worried expression crossing her face. "Tore a muscle is what the surgeon said. They're concerned about infection."

"Best if he sleeps," Leslie replied. "I'll catch him in the morning. Besides, I need to get something to eat."

"Thank you for coming by. I'll tell Daryl you're okay. He's worried. By the way, your coworkers took over the visitor's room at the end of the hall. Pizza and sandwiches. Hospital security took away the beer."

"Sounds good. Think I'll join them." Leslie turned to leave.

"Is that you, Les?" a weak voice called from behind her. "Come closer." Leslie approached the bed and with a barely audible voice, Fischer asked, "Were you hurt?"

"A few scrapes, nothing serious."

"I saw you go down. Thought you were hit. They say you saved the perp's life."

"He's not out of the woods yet. If I'd known you were down, I'd have come for you. I'm sorry."

"You did exactly what you were trained to do. I'm alive because you challenged him."

"You give me way too much credit."

Fischer's eyes closed for a moment. When they opened again, his voice was even weaker. "This is my wife, Jess."

"We met a moment ago," Leslie said, concerned for her partner. "You need to rest now."

"I'm tired," he said, his voice tailing off. His eyes closed.

"I'll come by tomorrow," she said to the seemingly sleeping form. "Jess, let me know if there is anything I can do to help."

In the doorway, Leslie turned back. "He's the best partner I've ever had."

"He says the same about you," Jess replied, deep concern in her eyes. "See you tomorrow."

Allen followed Leslie to the waiting room where several large pizzas, still in their boxes, were spread on a table. A half dozen empty boxes were piled on the floor. The only person in the room was Simeon Cox, the detective who had been assigned to arrest Colton. Leslie had met him once, briefly, at Stetson's last all-hands briefing. He was tall and lanky, in his mid-forties with a good-ol'-boy Tennessee twang and unruly ash-blond hair. Seeing Cox, Allen turned to Leslie. "I assume you and Simeon know each other."

Leslie glanced around looking for the person named Simeon. Seeing only Cox, she realized they were one and the same. "We do. Only I hadn't known his first name until just now."

"Cox is how everyone knows me," the detective said, reaching out to bump fists, his eyes running up and down her slender body. "Congratulations on today. Good show."

"Thank you," Leslie responded, taking a step back. "Allen told me he's working on the Colton arrest with you. How's that going?"

"Not as well as it should be," Allen answered. "Your buddy up in Pittsburgh saved my ass! Turns out the court hearing down here on the search warrant was a diversion. A ploy to keep Colton pinned down while they got a warrant in Maryland that covered the plane. They've already gone through his home up there. Plane's next."

"How did that save your ass?" Leslie asked, failing to make the connection.

"First off, as I told you, Colton hired Susan Morehouse. I believe you're dealing with her in the Edison matter. Frankly, she's a real pain. I got the call from your friend Jak thirty minutes before the hearing informing me of the Maryland warrant. Judge would have reamed me a new one if it would have come out that I hadn't informed him of all the facts."

"What'd you do?"

"Took the deal Morehouse had offered. We get the phone records for the time Colton was in Florida in exchange for dropping the warrant for his airplane."

"Sleeves off your vest, seems to me," Leslie said, swallowing a bite of pizza.

"Yeah," Cox interrupted, "and there's something for you, Leslie. Found it in the cell phone metadata. Colton called Fuller's phone number around midnight on Tuesday the twelfth. Then again at 7:33 Wednesday morning. Fuller returned the call at 8:40. That conversation lasted seven minutes."

"Phone call times don't give us much," Leslie said, helping herself to a second slice of the cold pizza.

"Agreed. But the phone location services app does. Shows him at Fuller's house at 11:12."

"Now that we can use," Leslie agreed. "Half hour to forty-five minutes before TOD."

"Thought you'd like that," Cox called from across the room.

"Thanks," Leslie managed to say between bites. She was even hungrier than she had thought.

"Just doin' my job. Boots said you might be takin' some time off. That true?"

"True, she said I should. Not true I will."

"Great!"

Now it was Leslie's turn to study Cox. "And just what makes my vacation time important to you?"

"Because Boots assigned me to work with you on the Fuller case now that Fish is outta action. They've pretty much kept me away from homicides. Don't really know why. Hey, don't look so glum. You're the lead. I may have seniority over you, but Boots made my role clear. I've read the file and have some ideas."

Stifling the first thought she had, Leslie calmly informed her new partner, "I've been ordered to take the weekend and Monday off. Can't work on it until Tuesday."

"That'll give me time to study the file, get up to speed. Run down loose ends type of thing. I hear your car is off-limits for now. Part of the unreleased crime scene. How about I give you a ride home? You can brief me on the way."

"Not necessary," Allen injected, not comfortable with where this was going. "Her ride home's covered."

"Okay, then, partner," Cox quickly agreed. "See you Tuesday. Need anything, anything at all, give a shout. I'm here for you. Got your back all the way."

When Cox was out of hearing, Allen said, "Must be nice to have a new BFF. Anything, anything at all, give a shout. I'm here for you."

"Allen don't go getting yourself worked up over him. Word around the office, he's harmless."

"Far's I'm concerned, school's out on him," Allen replied, his nose wrinkled. "Harmless until he's not. School's out."

When Leslie didn't respond, Allen said, "When I learned they were giving you time off, I took the liberty of booking us up at Lakeridge Winery for two nights. I'm thinking I'll spend the night at your place tonight and we'll leave in the morning. Be good to get a change of scene."

"How did you…"

"Stetson told me she was giving you Monday off. Is that okay? It's what we…"

"It's fine," Leslie said, less enthusiastically than Allen had expected. "A long hot shower and a good night's sleep and I should be as good as new." Even as she spoke, she had her doubts. Her former husband had been shot and killed in much the same manner as Fischer had been, both being in the wrong place at the wrong time. But for a lucky break, she herself would now be in a refrigerator at the morgue, a name tag tied to her toe, waiting for the medical examiner to cut her open and prowl through her body looking for God knows what.

The thirty-minute drive from the hospital to Leslie's house was mostly silent. Allen asked several questions, each answered with a few words. When Allen glanced over, her affect was flat, her eyes revealing nothing.

"Would it upset you," Leslie asked when they turned into her driveway, "if we didn't go to the winery tomorrow. I need alone time. Time to regroup."

Having anticipated the question, Allen replied, "I'll cancel. Should I rebook, say a month from now?"

"Let's talk about that down the line."

Allen took her hand and gently pulled, forcing her to turn sideways in the seat and face him. "What you're not saying, Leslie, is as important as what you are saying."

"Just what am I not saying," she snapped, pulling her hand free.

"I think you're asking me not to spend the night. Right?"

"I suppose I'm saying that as well. Please don't be upset. I need alone time."

"Did I do something to...to upset you?"

"Nothing you did. It's me I'm concerned about. Darn near died today. Need to come to grips with that."

"All the more reason for me to be with you. Someone to talk to."

"Nothing to talk about. My partner's in the hospital with a bullet through his arm. I'm lucky to be alive. I could have saved all of us from all of this if only I had drawn faster."

"My God, Leslie! You'd most likely be dead if you had drawn faster! I worked the streets for years in uniform. One thing I learned; you can't outgun a shooter who already has his weapon out. The laws of physics are against you."

"I just need to work through it — alone. Thanks for the ride — and the Sox shirt and jacket — and for being my friend. I just need time to myself. Please understand."

"I'm fine, if you are," Allen said, putting his hands back on the steering wheel. "Call if you need anything. Tomorrow we can go pick up your car if you want. Lunch?"

"Let's let that wait till morning," she said, slowly walking to her front door, fumbling for her keys.

Allen waited until she was safely in the house, hoping she'd turn and blow him a kiss.

Disappointed, when she didn't, he slammed the car into reverse and shot backwards out of the driveway.

# THIRTEEN

LESLIE'S HOT SHOWER RAN COLD by the time she stepped out. Terrig's blood was long gone, but the trauma it represented was still very much with her. The bruise where her shoulder had slammed into Fischer's car was shades of blue and red. The doctor had accurately predicted it would be sore and instructed her to take ibuprofen as required. Despite the medication, her body ached.

She slipped into bed and closed her eyes, hoping sleep would quickly overtake her. No such luck. Fischer's voice in her head begging her to keep the shooter alive overpowered the quiet of her bedroom. She now realized his plea to save the shooter's life was made to protect him from a homicide charge should his firearm discharge be ruled excessive force. Desk duty was automatic any time a weapon was fired, and Leslie asked herself if that was why she had fumbled drawing her weapon. Helping people in distress is what she lived for. Watching the protests across the country made it difficult, but she knew this was her calling and couldn't imagine doing anything else.

Between the mental anguish of reliving the sight of the victim's head exploding, the image of the shooter's gun pointing directly at her, and her being slow to draw her weapon, sleep was impossible. She paced the floor several minutes, gave up and went downstairs to work a jigsaw puzzle hoping to focus her mind away from the shooting. This puzzle had carved thin wooden pieces forming a picture of a turbulent ocean beneath an angry, dark sky. It was a present from Allen and was rated difficult. Many of the pieces had flat or almost flat edges, even though they were not part of the border. The shade differences across the sky were subtle and not much different in color and texture from the water.

An hour passed. Then another. Progress on the puzzle was slow. Into the third hour she decided that if she was up anyway, she would be better served by working on the Fuller file.

She constructed timelines beginning when the security service, Gables International Protective Services, picked up the Chladni euphon at Fuller's home. One timeline for Fuller; one for his lady friend, Selma Fritz; one for the euphon's owner, Ernst Chlad; one for Chlad's wife, Carol. She also began timelines for the three potential buyers known to her: Stratis, Colton and the Kumars.

Finishing as much as she could with the timelines, she turned to the case file. As always when she read files, Leslie made follow-up checklists. She was starting on her second page of notes when her eyes drooped, and she felt herself nodding off. Finally, she thought, I can get to sleep.

It was not to be. The next entry in the file log brought her wide awake.

INTERVIEWEE: COLTON, ALEXANDRE
INTERVIEWER: COX, SIMEON
INTERVIEW DATE: 01/15/2021
INTERVIEW TIME: 18:20
LOCATION: OFFICE OF ATTY S. MOREHOUSE

Leslie had checked out of the hospital at 5:47. Cox had left a few minutes earlier and apparently had gone directly to Morehouse's office to meet with Colton. He had to have known about the interview when they had spoken yet failed to mention it. Yes, Cox was senior to her in the department. But it was her case, not his. He had agreed to allow her the lead. To make matters worse, Cox was alone without backup ears. Not an ideal situation. To his credit, the entire interview had been recorded with Morehouse's agreement.

Leslie listened to the recording:

MOREHOUSE: For the record, this interview has been granted for background purpose only in the investigation of the death of Dr. Sigmund Fuller on January 13th of this year. My client has been informed that he is not believed to have participated in Dr. Fuller's death. Is that a correct statement?

COX: It is.

MOREHOUSE: You may proceed.

COX: Thank you. Also, for the record, Attorney Morehouse, you have agreed to this interview being recorded.

MOREHOUSE: That is correct.

COX: Mr. Colton, what is your relationship to Dr. Fuller?

COLTON: I collect artifacts, many of which have significant value. Often, the value of such artifacts stems from their geographical and/or historical importance. Dr. Fuller is, was I suppose I should now say, one of the world's leading experts on European culture.

COX: Did you have occasion to consult Dr. Fuller, say within the past year, on any matter?

COLTON: I became aware that the original Chladni euphon had been found in Poland. Chladni died in 1827, in Breslau. The Potsdam Agreements gave that part of Germany to Poland, so today that area is called Wrocław. As I understand it, Dr. Fuller was hired by the Chladni owner, a Mr. Ernst Chlad, to find the euphon.

COX: Which he did?

COLTON: Which he most certainly did.

COX: If you know, how did Dr. Fuller determine that the instrument he found was, in fact, Chladni's original euphon and not some copy?

COLTON: Fuller prepared an extensive report for the Polish Government. I won't go into all the details, but it was convincing. Convinced the authorities.

COX: Do you have a copy of that report?

COLTON: I've seen a copy. It was thorough. I can say that much.

COX: What makes this…this what do you call it? A you-phone? What makes this you-phone so valuable?

COLTON: The euphon is a first of its kind musical instrument using vibrating glass rods of different lengths. You would have to understand the Seminal Society collectors to understand its true value.

COX: Please enlighten me.

COLTON: The Seminal Society begins with Oswald Wolkenstein, a song composer back in the fourteenth century. After his death, the Society believes his creative soul passed to Leonardo da Vinci, himself an artist and inventor. Da Vinci's soul then passed to Galileo Galilei, who, as you must know, was served well by it. The soul then went to the greatest of all, Sir Isaac Newton. Then on to Ernst Chladni. And finally, to Thomas Edison.

COX: Frankly, I've never heard of this guy Chladni. Can you help me here?

COLTON: Seminal Society collectors regard Chladni as an important person in the chain of genius evolution. He discovered acoustics and how to measure sound. These men were true geniuses, including Chladni, and they all produced novel devices and discoveries. These inventions are called Firsts and are extremely valuable. Chladni's euphon was lost when he died. I had hoped to purchase it.

COX:  Is that why you're here in Florida?

COLTON:   I'm here because of another. The Blue...

MOREHOUSE: Don't go there.

COLTON:  Let's just say, I came to your lovely state for several reasons. For one, the Chladni that I was hoping to purchase. The one Dr. Fuller certified as being authentic. I wanted to hear directly from Fuller how the Carnegie finding could possibly be true."

COX : Did you talk with Dr. Fuller?

COLTON:  I called him late Tuesday night when the Carnegie announced it was closing the exhibit.

COX:  Tuesday the twelfth?

COLTON:  Yes.

COX:  Time?

COLTON:  Around midnight I'd say.

COX:  Did you speak with him?

COLTON: Not then. He didn't answer. I called him again in the morning.

COX:  At what time?

COLTON: Around 7:30, give or take.

COX:  Did you talk to him at that time?

COLTON: He said there had been a mix-up at the Carnegie. That he could explain everything. He said to come by his home between 11:30 and noon and he would prove to me the euphon was authentic.

COX: And did you go to his house?

COLTON: Of course. I really wanted that First! If Fuller could convince me that the Science Center was wrong, then I was still in.

COX: When did you arrive at Dr. Fuller's? Please be as accurate as you can.

COLTON:  About 11:30. Maybe a bit earlier. Could have been closer to 11:15.

COX: Why so early? I thought he said between 11:30 and 12.

COLTON: Misjudged the driving time, I guess. Like I said, I wanted to own that First. Didn't want to be late.

COX: Was there anyone else there when you arrived?

COLTON: Didn't see anyone.

COX: Did Fuller satisfy you the original you phone was in Pittsburgh?

COLTON: He went over his report and showed me pictures. He assured me he had made no mistake. Said the original Chladni was transported by secure messenger to Pittsburgh. He said he'd put his reputation on that statement.

COX: Did you believe him?

COLTON: I have no reason to believe he's lying. Let's put it that way. On the other hand, I have no reason to think the Carnegie report is wrong.

COX: Do you know why Carnegie is skeptical?

COLTON: Something to do with the size of the rods. One of them is wrong, or out of order, or something along those lines. Didn't match up, was what I understand.

COX: Help me here. the Pittsburgh Science Center was not the first exhibition as I understand it. So why was the you phone here in Florida?

COLTON: In fact, Pittsburgh was the last exhibition in the States. After every exhibition the euphon was returned to Fuller for recertification.

COX: Why?

COLTON: That's the way the Polish authorities wanted it. Fuller had to certify it before and after each exhibition.

COX: Is that usual?

COLTON: Highly unusual. From my experience anyway.

COX: And you don't know why?

COLTON: I'd be guessing.

COX: Was Dr. Fuller alive when you left him?

COLTON: Very much so. Agitated, if anything.

COX: And what time was that? When you left him?

COLTON: About fifteen minutes after I arrived. I suppose there's a video record of me leaving through the main gate. Don't those places keep such stuff?

COX: I'll certainly check. And again, you said Dr. Fuller was alive when you left his home. Is that correct?

COLTON: Like I said, he definitely was.

COX: You said the size of a rod was off in Pittsburgh. Wouldn't Dr. Fuller have known the proper sizes before it left Florida?

COLTON: One would suppose. He's the one that certified it. He told me it was correct when it left his house.

COX: Did you ask Dr. Fuller about the sound error?

COLTON: He said there was nothing wrong when the instrument left his house.

MOREHOUSE: Detective, I believe we are finished answering questions. Mr. Colton, I instruct you to answer nothing further.

Time: 19:40

# FOURTEEN

LESLIE'S BEDSIDE CLOCK GLOWED 3:58
AM. when she last saw it before finally falling
asleep. The clock displayed 10:17 when she next
came awake. Sitting up, she massaged her sore
shoulder a moment before going into the bathroom. A few minutes later she was again in the
shower, the comforting water flowing over her
body still doing nothing to wash away the vision
of Amelia Bishop's head exploding in front of her.
One thing was for certain, losing herself in work
was what any doctor knowing her would order.
Captain Stetson had all but ruled work out with
her order to stand down until at least Tuesday.

Leslie considered going to the office despite
the order, reasoning that for her the more she tried
to not think about the shooting, the harder her
mind would work at it. Coming downstairs, she
entered her code into her computer in preparation
for reviewing the Colton interview, only to discover
that she was now blocked. Going into the office
could, she thought, trigger even further action,
such as forced leave.

"Damn them!" she shouted, suddenly feeling
alone — and vulnerable. She wasn't at all sure who
"them" was in this situation, but it felt as if the
universe was lining up against her. She turned
to the half-finished puzzle as a consolation. The
first piece she picked up had the physical shape of
a ladies high-heel shoe and fell into place almost
immediately. She then spotted an opening that
would accept a small arrow-shaped piece. She was

116

searching for it when her doorbell rang. Expecting it to be Allen, she took her time answering the door, ambivalent about his presence and concentrating instead on locating the arrow among the pieces spread around the table.

One great thing about Allen; he brought an enjoyable lightness to her. They could discuss life, work, politics, all without judgment. She had looked forward to spending the weekend with him at the winery and now felt guilty — and angry with herself — at having canceled the mini vacation. Thinking of Allen, her mood brightened. She hurried across the living room, flinging the door open, fully prepared for a much-needed hug and kiss.

Leslie froze when she realized it was Simeon Cox, and not Allen Smith, standing in her doorway. Cox held a box of Dunkin Donuts in one hand, a cardboard tray with two cups of coffee in the other. The anger she had felt while reading his Colton interview welled up.

"Hey, don't just stand there," an upbeat Cox called. "Coffee's already cold. Invite me in."

"What the hell you doin' here?" Leslie demanded, taking a step back in preparation for slamming the door in his face.

"Invite me in, I'll tell you. Don't know 'bout you, I'm starved."

Against her better judgment, she removed her hand from the door and took another step back, undecided as to how to play this.

"Where's the microwave?" Cox asked, kicking the door closed behind him. "Need to heat these up."

"What the hell you doing here? I'm supposed to be..."

"Working. I'll explain. Let me..."

"Where the hell else would a Microwave be? Back there in the kitchen!"

Leslie followed Cox into the kitchen and stood, hands on hips, waiting for him to explain himself.

Cox closed the microwave door and hit the start button. "You're blocked," he said, turning to face her, "from the computer system. I'm here to do what a good partner does. Keep you in the loop."

"You that hungry, you coulda eaten a doughnut, or a dozen if you wish, on the way over here. What gives?"

"And miss breakfast with my new partner. I guess at this hour I should call it brunch."

"How did you know..."

"You were awake and home? Home I guessed. Awake's another matter. Waited for you to try and log in."

"How the hell did you know I'd try? And how did you know when I did?"

"Every attempt at logging in is recorded. Pays to have friends in IT."

"Still don't know how you knew I'd..."

"Homicides don't take vacations. Neither do dedicated homicide detectives. Before you go giving me credit for that, it came from Boots. Warned me to do my homework. Said you don't suffer fools — or lazy cops. She tipped me you'd find a way into the files."

"What about going behind my back? Did she also warn you I'd go crazy if you went off on a lark of your own?"

"You talkin' 'bout my Colton interview last night. Let me..."

"Bingo! Who the hell do you think you...?"

Cox held up a silencing hand. "Need to hear the whole story before you go off on me. Thing is, Attorney Morehouse was being her normal asshole self. Refused to allow Colton to say anything. That Pittsburgh detective friend of yours came through big time. Tipped me to the Blue Footed

Golden Booby being a fake. Having that piece of information meant the possession of international listed artifacts, or whatever the hell that Interpol list is called, couldn't stick. The interview was in exchange for dropping all charges on the possession matter. Allen okayed it."

"That explains the why," Leslie acknowledged, bristling when she realized Allen had also known about the interview and hadn't told her. "But does nothing for the timing," Leslie added, regaining her mental balance.

"You think Colton, with a private jet a few miles away, planned to hang around waiting to be questioned? It was then or never. Just say, thank you, Detective Cox. Glad you were there to jump in, Detective Cox. You did a great job, Detective Cox." He broke a donut in half, dunked it in his coffee and took a bite. A moment later, still waiting for Leslie to say something, he did the same with the other half. Finally realizing that his new partner was still pissed, he continued, "Placed Colton at the homicide within a window of probable times. In case you're wondering, the timing Colton gave me checks out with the surveillance footage from the main gate."

"I didn't see anything about the surveillance check in the file," Leslie scolded, reminding herself Cox was certainly a wild card. She had worked with a few like him in Tampa with mixed results. One, a woman, seemed to be as scatter-brained as they came. Never doing what you'd expected her to do. In the few instances when lives were on the line, she came through with flying colors. She had an instinct for being in the right place at the right time doing the right thing. Leslie had also worked with many by-the-book types. Often, a bookie, as she called them, would be missing in action when it counted most.

"Gotta learn to trust, partner," Cox said, starting on his second donut. "Got the time checks after you closed the file. Check there now if you like."

Calling his bluff, she said, "Show me in the file where you logged the time check."

"Sure thing, partner." Cox opened his laptop and pulled up the file. Turning the screen to her, he said, "See for yourself."

Leslie checked the file stamp for the time entry. Sure enough, Cox had entered the confirmation earlier this morning. "Just why are you here?" she asked, looking up. "You know I'm off duty at Captain's order."

Ignoring her question, Cox said, "So, you're a jigsaw puzzle person. Happens, so am I. By chance you know where an arrow-looking piece is?"

"Over there," Leslie said, this time spotting it immediately.

"It goes..." Cox picked up the dark blue arrow piece and triumphantly placed it in the upper right quadrant. "...right here."

"Hate to burst your bubble, but I already had spotted that location. I was looking for the piece when you rang the bell."

"Great minds think alike. Sometimes it just takes two to tango."

"Cox, why the hell, exactly, are you here?"

"Truthfully, I didn't think you'd take well to being out of the loop with an open homicide on your plate. I know you can't come to the office, so I brought the office to you, so to speak." Smiling broadly, he added, "Tell me I'm wrong, I'll get out of your hair. Otherwise, let's get to work."

Leslie knew herself well enough to understand that the only thing keeping her from dwelling on Fischer's injuries and how close she herself had come to being shot was to deep dive into the Fuller homicide. Even concentrating on the jigsaw hadn't worked as well as she had hoped. Nonetheless, it felt wrong to be hiding out in her den with a person she barely knew — detective co-worker or not — in violation of Stetson's direct order.

Reading her eyes, Cox stood. "Didn't mean to make this such a problem for you. I'll just finish my coffee and we can pick it up Tuesday, or whenever you're in next."

"Sorry." Leslie replied, motioning Cox to be seated. "This just feels, well, strange is all." Taking him at his word, she asked, "You have something specific in mind?"

Sitting, Cox said, "Thought we could begin by understanding where and how Fuller found this you-phone thing and why in the hell anyone in their right mind would pay over a hundred million for an old musical instrument no one has ever heard of. Colton says it's because some Seminal Society collectors want it because it is a First. That make sense to you?"

Not yet willing to impart information to Cox, Leslie simply said, "I've had discussions about these so-called Seminal Society collectors. Billionaires, I suppose, don't need justification for how they spend their money. They want it. They buy it. Period."

"I suppose so. I haven't found much online," Cox added. "Except I did find a picture of a small xylophone-looking device standing about two, two and half feet tall." When Leslie remained silent, he continued, "Heard you had an insurance contact that helped you with the Edison investigation. Suppose he, or perhaps she, would know about the Chladni?"

"Good thought," Leslie acknowledged. "That is his business after all." Reaching for her phone, Leslie realized she had turned it off late last night so she wouldn't be disturbed. "I left my phone upstairs. Be back in a moment."

When her phone came back on, Leslie saw several text messages from Allen. She was about to listen to a voice message from him when the doorbell rang. She hurried down the steps in time to see the front door open and Allen, carrying a large plastic bag labeled Ginger Bistro, standing in the doorway, a puzzled look on his face.

"Cox!" Allen exclaimed, planting his feet and not coming into the house. "Seems I'm interrupting some..."

"Nonsense!" Leslie called from across the room, stopping herself from hurrying over to hug him. "We were just...brainstorming the Fuller case. Come on in and join us."

Allen looked over at Cox who hadn't moved from the corner of the sofa where he was comfortably ensconced. "I thought Stetson had you off duty through Tuesday," he said, closing the door behind him. "Must have heard wrong."

"Cox's been working the file. Had some info he wanted to run by me."

Allen looked first at Cox and then back to Leslie. "When you didn't answer my calls, I assumed you slept in. Came over to be sure you were okay. Brought your favorite lunch." Glancing in the direction of the Dunkin' Donuts box, he added, "It appears I'm late to the party."

"Lunch'll roll around soon enough," Cox replied, "as we work through this file. Les, I didn't know you were a Bistro fan. Best Chinese anywhere. You and I'll have lunch over there sometime soon, partner."

Leslie didn't reply to Cox. Instead, she hugged Allen before taking the bag from him. "Thoughtful of you. I'll put it in the fridge. We can heat it up for later."

"Should I hang around or leave you two alone?" Allen asked, still confused over the situation and not understanding his role in this three-way dance. "I wouldn't want to hold up progress."

"I don't suspect this'll be more than an hour, two at most," Leslie called from the kitchen. "You can join us or go out back and relax."

"I have a brief I'm working on," he quickly replied. "I'll get my computer and set up in the kitchen. Be right back."

"Two hours isn't near enough time," Cox commented when the door closed behind Allen. "We'll just be getting started."

Leslie studied her new partner a moment before responding. "Don't push it. I'm officially off duty and, to tell the truth, not one hundred percent with it. Two hours and we'll pick this back up on Tuesday."

"Have it your way, partner."

Leslie considered throwing Cox out. Instead, she dialed Jack Silver, CEO of Great Southern Insurance Company, a man who took pride in insuring the world's most precious artifacts. It was highly likely one or more of the bidders for the Chladni euphon would have contacted him preliminarily to research insurance coverage. As best as Leslie could determine, Jack and his wife Precious, lived aboard their converted Boeing 727 and could be anywhere in the world at any time.

As expected, her call was intercepted by a messaging system, instructing Leslie to state what she wanted, promising a call back as soon as possible. "This could take hours, days, or not at all," she told Cox when the call ended. "There's really no reason for him to call back."

"Except a man is dead. The very man who vouched for the authenticity of the you-phon. It's his business to know what's going on. My money, for what it's worth, is on a return call."

Changing the subject, Leslie said, "The way I see it, we have two possible persons of interest. The owner of the euphon, Ernie Chlad, who might have been deceived by Fuller and who admits being invited to Fuller's house at the critical time. And second, your buddy, Colton, a Seminal Society collector who has his mind set on the artifact. According to your interview, Colton also visited Fuller within the critical time window. For completeness, I suppose we can't rule out the woman friend, Selma Fritz who found him. That makes three."

Cox thought a moment, then said, "I'd add Carol Chlad, Ernie's wife. She had a stake in selling the you-phone as well. If her husband was deceived, so was she. For all we know, her…her shall I say battiness, could be an act. And I'd not be so fast to eliminate any of the other Society collectors. Their names are in the file. Dexter Stratis. And the couple, Sanjay and Riya Kumar."

Leslie paced the room, her head down, her shoulders slumped forward. "I suppose you're right," she agreed. "We shouldn't rule out anyone with an interest in the Chladni."

Leslie's phone chirped. Silver GSI popped up on the screen. "Detective Hodges here," she immediately answered.

"Leslie, how are you?" Silver replied, his voice gracious and as smooth as she recalled.

"Fine, and you?"

"No complaints on my end."

"Where are you?"

"Not important."

"Mind if I put you on speaker so my partner can hear?"

"Please don't. And no recording. Agreed?"

"Agreed," she reluctantly replied, removing her finger from the recording button.

"Your message mentioned the Chladni euphon and Sig Fuller's authentication," Silver paused before continuing. "Such a shame about Sig. We've relied upon his expertise for decades. He was a great friend and will be missed. Do you know what happened?"

"Can't comment on the investigation. But we'll get to the bottom of it."

"I understand," Silver replied. "Well, all I can add in response to your inquiry is that Great Southern did offer to insure the Chladni for up to three hundred million."

"For whom?"

"Not important."

"Are you satisfied with Dr. Fuller's assessment? I mean that the euphon he certified is the actual original Chladni instrument."

"Our insurance offer is based on his analysis and report. And, might I add, the acceptance of his findings by the Polish authorities."

"Are you still willing to insure the artifact? Given the Carnegie finding?"

"We are. Providing confirmation of three things."

"Which are...?"

"The veneer on the euphon matches Sig's report.

"The veneer? What..."

"According to Sig, the veneer used in the construction of the euphon matches a rare veneer used by a German piano maker in a few of his pianos. Sig found documentation showing Chladni had engaged that exact piano maker to build the euphon's frame. A piano with that same veneer, made by the same piano maker, is in a decorative arts museum in Prague. We need certification that the euphon in question is constructed with the same veneer that is on the piano in the museum."

"And the second thing?"

"The original euphon had particular interlocking joints that made it relatively easy to assemble and take apart for traveling."

"Also used in that same piano I assume."

"Exactly," Silver confirmed. "So, if a buyer can convince us that the euphon currently in Pittsburgh matches up with the piano in the Prague museum in those respects, then Great Southern will insure it."

"You had a third condition?"

"Has to do with the suspect glass rod. Certainly, the euphon must have the proper rods. That goes without saying. But because Sig had certified the euphon as being genuine before it went up to Pittsburgh, my hunch is that someone purposely substituted the rods. We're of the opinion the euphon at the Science Center is genuine — with switched glass rods."

"Why would anybody do that?"

"You'd have to ask the mastermind behind the substitution."

"You know who that person is?"

"I have my suspicions."

Leslie paused to digest what she had just been told. Realizing Silver wasn't about to impart a name, she asked, "You called back, so I assume there's something you have for me."

"Don't know how important it is, but I learned from Sig that one of the Society collectors, a husband and wife team, had a meeting set up with him the morning poor Sig was killed."

"Did he say what the meeting was for?"

"Apparently they had gone down to Florida to negotiate with the owner of the euphon. They reached out to Sig when they heard that the euphon had a wrong rod."

"Did they have that meeting?"

"They tried and somehow got spooked and went up to Tampa. Judging from something they said, they plan to fly to Europe later today or in the morning."

"Any chance of you having a contact number for them. I'd like to talk..."

"Let me see what I can do. Hold a few moments if you can."

"I'll wait," Leslie said, anticipating several minutes of silence followed by an apology for not making a connection. She glanced over at Cox who had his head down studying the puzzle, his hands moving every few minutes to insert a piece in its proper place. The man was good with puzzles. That much she conceded

"Sorry to keep you," Silver said, after an eight-minute hold, "but you'll like the news. The Kumars agreed to remain in Tampa through tomorrow. They'll meet you for lunch at the Columbia Restaurant in Ybor City noon tomorrow. They know as much as anyone does about the euphon. Sanjay and Riya Kumar. They're longtime friends of Sig's and want to do what they can to bring the culprit to justice."

"I'll be there. Thank you." Before Leslie hung up, she said, "Question if you don't mind. What makes you believe Fuller's hanging wasn't suicide?"

"Sig loved life. Lived for his work. I pride myself on knowing people and I can tell you straight out, Sig didn't take his own life."

"The Science Center threw a major cloud over Dr. Fuller. If it's true he was wrong in his authentication, he'd have trouble reestablishing his credentials. Isn't that true?"

Silver took a moment before answering, "As I said, I've known Sig a very long time. He's been my go-to resource for authentication of European artifacts for more years than I care to discuss. In all that time, he's never been wrong. Polish government bought off on his report. He's not wrong this time. Subject's closed."

"I assume my partner is welcome at the Kumar meeting tomorrow?"

"I can't speak for them, but if they have a problem he can always eat alone. Columbia Restaurant never disappoints."

The line clicked dead.

"What the hell was that about?" Cox asked when Leslie dropped her phone onto the table. "Get anything worth repeating?"

"Tell you on the way up to Tampa. Pick me up at nine in the morning. You're driving. Now get your ass out of here. I have a lunch date."

# FIFTEEN

COX TURNED INTO THE COLUMBIA Restaurant parking lot at exactly eleven. It had been an uneventful ride north on Interstate 75 with Leslie explaining that her insurance contact was Jack Silver, CEO of Great Southern Insurance Company, and that GSIC specialized in insuring high value art. She didn't communicate that she knew the tail number of Silver's 707 and had looked up his most recent flight plans. She also kept to herself the fact that his plane was scheduled to touch down at the Alejandro Velasco Astete International Airport in Cusco, Peru within an hour of when they spoke yesterday. That put him in Inca territory close to Machu Picchu. Colton and his Blue Footed Golden Booby came to mind. She made certain to instruct Cox that her arrangement with Silver was that everything, including his name and company, was off the record.

"That goes for you as well," she had said. "Don't cross me on this."

"Of course," Cox confirmed, "but why the owner of an insurance company would give you as much information as he does, let alone set up this meeting with the Kumars, is puzzling."

"Good question. I have no easy answer, except to say he makes his money insuring valuable — and sometimes questionable — artifacts. The more information sources he has the more information he can gather. In his world, information is money. Big money as we now well know. But, Fuller was his friend — and one of his go-to experts. Maybe he just wants the case solved."

"And just maybe," Cox retorted, smiling broadly, "he's just blowing smoke up your ass."

"Remains to be seen," Leslie said, falling silent.

Cox then asked what she knew about Morris Dexter Stratis. Her response was short and to the point. "Stratis is a Seminal Society collector," she said, "and presumably the purchaser of Edison's original phonograph. As you know from reading the file, the Edison phonograph went missing the night its owner, Scotty McDermitt, was murdered."

Cox's smile disappeared. "How'd you know I read the McDermitt file?"

"Same way you knew I'd be itching to get back into the Fuller file."

The car parked, Cox studied his partner and could not avoid noticing her usually vibrant green eyes were now dull and flat. "I say or do something?" he probed. "You look as though you're fix'n to..." Cox was about to say 'cry'. But instead, said, "bite my head off."

"Sorry, Sim. It's not you. It's only..." Leslie couldn't bring herself to say it was Junior, her Tampa detective husband who had been killed in the line of duty not far from where they now sat. He had been her life for seven wonderful years, one of which she had spent on patrol right here in Ybor City. "Nostalgia, I suppose. I once patrolled these streets. On a bike no less."

"You have a favorite haunt to visit? We have an hour to kill."

"If we weren't having lunch, I'd suggest a Cuban sandwich. Best in Tampa down Seventh half a block." She pointed over his shoulder to an empty space between two sets of townhouses. "On that lot over there stood the last of the cigar factories. Cuban tobacco came in on ships that docked just south of here. The bales were loaded on the backs of donkeys and hauled to the factories. The men — and women — worked ten-hour days drying, cutting, selecting, and rolling the tobacco into the best cigars in the word. Or so I'm told."

"Speaking of cigars, I could go for one right about now."

"Be my guest. It's your car."

"Have to buy it first. Know the best place?"

"Gone now. Sorry. The place we're going for lunch has a store. You can pick one up there."

"Join me in an after lunch cigar? I'm buying. We can go over by the water and kick back."

"I think I'll pass, you don't mind."

They fell silent for several minutes before Cox said, "I'm sure you know, this place has a long history of mob activity. You get involved in any of that?"

"I've heard the stories. Some are true, most embellished. I walked — rode — a beat. Mobs were above my paygrade." Leslie's answer was accurate as far as it went. For six months, she had been the eyes and ears for a joint task force with the FBI and the Alcohol and Tobacco Tax and Trade Bureau. She was pulled out a week before six men were arrested, four for tax evasion, one for bribery and one for capital homicide. Within a week, three men, one a police officer, believed by the mob to have been snitches, were shot and killed. One officer died not twenty feet from where they were now parked.

"Judging from your silence, I take it you'd rather not talk about your time in Tampa. So be it. I also assume you'd rather go inside and be early."

"Good plan," Leslie said. "It's a big place with several rooms. Give us time to pick the location we want."

The two Lee County Sheriff detectives approached the hostess, a late-twenties, dark-skinned Latino woman with black hair flowing over her shoulders. "Reservations for..." Cox began.

"Kumar party?" the hostess, whose name badge read, 'Julian', replied, a touch of Cuban flavor in her voice.

"Right," Cox said, startled she knew who they were.

"They're already at the table. Follow me, please." Julian proceeded through an archway leading to the dining area. They strode through the main dining room, noting the COVID-required table spacings, and continued into a side room where again the tables were safely spaced. Julian continued on to a door and pushed it open, ushering the detectives into the room beyond.

Sitting at a table for four, with three place settings, were perhaps the two most elegant people Leslie had ever seen. The Indian man, wearing a custom-made silk suit, stood in greeting. He was tall and narrow shouldered, with a smooth face and expressive brown eyes. "You must be Detective Leslie Hodges," he said in clipped British English, extending his closed hand in greeting. "Pleased to meet you. My name is Sanjay Kumar. Our good friend, Jack Silver, spoke highly of you." Sanjay turned his attention to Cox. "Sorry for only three settings. We were not expecting a fourth."

"This is Detective Simeon Cox," Leslie quickly said. "He's my partner. I took the liberty of asking him to join us. I trust you don't have an objection."

Kumar studied Cox a long moment. In response to a small nod from his wife, he said, "Please allow me to introduce my wife, Riya. I will request another place be set."

Riya pushed her chair back and stood facing Leslie, allowing her bottle green sari to flow freely to the floor. She wore a wide, gold-braided belt around her waist. "I was told I'd recognize you by your lovely green eyes," Riya said. "They are every bit as beautiful as I imagined. This sari was selected in your honor."

"I'm flattered," Leslie managed, momentarily flustered by the grace and beauty of the woman. "It's nice to meet you." Leslie was always uncomfortable discussing attributes a person is born with. This was no exception.

Riya turned her attention to Cox, who was having trouble looking away. "Sorry for the inconvenience. It should only be a moment before the table is made ready for you."

Sanjay raised his hand and almost immediately a young man appeared, received the order to add a setting and quickly disappeared. "The ladies should be seated while you and I wait for a chair to be brought," Sanjay said to Cox.

"Mr. Kumar, please be seated," Cox replied. "I'm certain it will only be a moment."

"I'll stand, thank you. And please call me Sanjay, Detective." Turning to Leslie, he said, "I've learned you were a police officer right here in Ybor City. I assume you are familiar with the menu. What do you recommend?"

"Everything is excellent," Leslie finessed. "I was thinking of having the grilled grouper if it's still on the menu. I recommend it if you're in the mood for fish."

"Grouper sounds delightful," Riya commented. "Sanjay and I are fish eaters. And the grouper is indeed on the menu."

The door to the private room opened and in came a man in a light blue suit who Leslie recognized as one of the owners. He carried a chair and positioned it opposite to her at the table. A man dressed in black slacks, white shirt and a black vest followed the owner into the room. He set the fourth place in front of the newly positioned chair. The owner looked at Leslie, his eyes blinking twice in recognition. "Welcome back, Señora," he said, slightly dipping his head. "Nice to have you dine with us again. Please enjoy your meal." He took a step backward, turned and walked from the room, pulling the door closed behind him.

Any question Leslie had as to her being recognized was now settled. She had been the first responder to a late-night break-in at the Columbia and had arrested the burglar in the back parking lot, recovering a gym bag stuffed with over fifty thousand dollars. The owner had told her to bring her husband in for 'the best dinner you've ever had.' Junior had died before she took him up on the offer.

"Three grilled groupers," Sanjay told the waiter a moment later, looking over to Cox for his order.

"I'm going with the Cuban sandwich," Cox responded. "I enjoy fish, but Leslie mentioned Cubans and that sounded good."

"I was talking about the place down the block," Leslie said, feeling the need to clarify. "But they're good here as well."

When the waiter was gone, Sanjay said to Leslie, "We understand you are interested in the Chladni euphon. First let me be very clear, Riya and I are no longer in the running for that particular artifact."

"Pardon me for being confused," Leslie responded. "But, if the euphon is a fake, why would anyone continue to pursue it?"

It was Riya who answered. "It is not at all certain that the euphon on display at the Carnegie

Science Center is a fake. In fact, everything points to it being the original, just as Sig said."

"Do you then disagree with the museum's forensic report?"

"Not necessarily," Sanjay replied. "To my knowledge, they didn't actually claim it was not the original euphon as located by Sig. Rather, based on one rod being of the wrong size, they couldn't confirm that it was the original."

"Please explain the difference if you will."

"We trust Dr. Fuller had it right. He is — was — much too good at his job to have it incorrect. Or to lie about it. Sig was the definition of integrity. The world will miss him dearly."

Leslie thought a moment about what she had just heard, then said, "My mother always said money does strange things to people. This seems to be one of those situations."

Riya leaned forward. "Sig was above all that. He was in the art and objects world most of his life and I think you will find he is a wealthy man in his own right. In the end, he valued his reputation above all else."

What Riya was saying matched exactly what Jack Silver had told Leslie.

"So, let's assume for the moment you're correct in your assessment. I have no reason to believe otherwise. How then do you account for the discrepancy?"

"Confidentially speaking," Sanjay said, "not to be attributed to us. Is that possible?"

"I can't absolutely promise, but I'll do my best to keep whatever you tell us confidential."

Sanjay turned to face Cox. "And you, Detective Cox?"

"I'll follow Hodge's lead."

"As I said, we dropped out of the bidding primarily because it was getting over our limit.

Money's no object for Stratis. And that newcomer, Alexandre Colton, that man has bad money behind him. We'll pass this time around. Not because the euphon's not genuine. Oh, no. It's genuine all right. At least that is what Riya and I believe. Our theory is that someone wanted that exhibition closed. That same someone arranged for a rod to be exchanged after the euphon left the hands of dear Sig."

"I'm confused as to why?" Leslie said.

"To make the Pittsburgh euphon appear to be fake. That's all I'm prepared to say."

"No, please continue," Leslie prodded. "We drove up here to gather information that could possibly help us learn how Dr. Fuller died. There's a high likelihood Fuller's death is linked to the substituted rod. The more you tell us, the closer we get to the perpetrator."

Sanjay remained silent.

Leslie turned to Riya, who followed her husband's lead and said nothing.

Breaking the silence, Leslie changed course. "Please tell us about Dr. Fuller. How did he locate the euphon?"

Riya again leaned forward. "He was a dear friend — and a lot more. We relied on his judgment and expertise implicitly. He was the best in the world at what he did. Honest to a fault. People trusted him. They would tell him things they wouldn't tell anyone else. He and his friend, Selma Fritz, must have interviewed several hundred people looking for the euphon. I won't bore you with all the rumors of its location that have floated around over the years. Somewhere along the line, he, or Selma, had the idea of tracking down every possible relative of Chladni. That required forming a genealogy tree and going back ten generations. Fuller interviewed all those living that he could locate. Then, painstakingly, he went through the estate records, what there are of them, of each person."

"How long did this all take?"

"I think he began the project before his wife died. So, what was that? Eight years now?"

"About that?" Leslie acknowledged. Recalling it was closer to six. "Is it a coincidence that Chladni's actual heir, the person who has undisputed ownership of the euphon, lives in the same community as Dr. Fuller?"

"Not in the least," Sanjay replied. "Fuller lived in Coral Gables when his wife died. Sig wanted to move away. As he said, the house had too many memories. For a few years he spent so much time in Europe it was a non-issue where his home was. When he determined Ernst Chlad had the only clear right to the euphon — this even before Sig had located it — he went looking for Chlad. Found him living in Fort Myers in an area called Miromar Lakes. Sig visited Chlad, and when it became clear they would be working together Sig decided to buy a home in that area 'to be close to my client,' he said. Selma moved over from Miami a year or so later."

"Do you know how Dr. Fuller located the euphon? You said he interviewed people and examined records. I don't suppose the location was written down anywhere?"

"That's just it! There was no record of it anywhere. That fact bothered Sig immensely. He and I had dinner often while he was in Poland and Germany, 'on the hunt', as Sanjay likes to call Sig's missions. He told me over and over the lack of any record troubled him."

"I suppose that's important, but I don't see how," Leslie confessed.

"Sig figured that no record could mean it was not part of Chladni's estate when he died," Sanjay filled in. "Sig made a wild guess that Chladni had the euphon with him when he died in Breslau, Prussia. As it happens, at that time in Prussia, as with so much of Europe, the proprietor of boarding houses and hotels had to maintain records of everyone spending the night. The police collected those records and like most governments, once they get information in their hands, they never give it up. Sig, knowing the place and date of death, tracked down 200-year-old police records and eventually found Chladni's name at a boarding house, miraculously still standing. That was his first big breakthrough."

"What was his second?" Leslie asked, recalling Chlad's story of the euphon being found inside a fake wall.

"His theory was that if the euphon hadn't been found when Chladni died it couldn't have been listed in his estate, which it hadn't been. If that was so, Sig believed the proprietor spirited it away before the police even arrived."

"But it's never surfaced," Leslie probed. "Wouldn't the proprietor have sold it?"

"That's the key! Sig decided the proprietor hid it in one of the secret spaces aristocratic houses of that era had. And died before it was safe enough to sell it."

"Secret spaces?" Leslie asked. "What's that mean?".

"House structures at that time were basic stone blocks. Rich families covered the stone with fancy wood. They had the builder construct hidden spaces so they could hide their valuables from thieves — and the king's tax collectors. Sig believed the proprietor hid the euphon in such a hidden space and sealed it up. He couldn't just sell it right then and there. Eventually the proprietor died without anyone knowing what he had done."

"So, how did Fuller locate it?"

"Money. Sig was so certain that he paid the owner five thousand dollars to allow him access to all the rooms. He promised an additional fifty thousand dollars to remove anything he found hidden in any secret place. He used a scanner. Essentially, he imaged the walls to locate it."

"How did the Polish government get involved?"

"The owner of the house was standing right there when Sig found the euphon. He told someone who then told the Polish authorities. The government declared the euphon a national treasure and took charge."

"It's one thing to declare something a national treasure," Leslie said, trying to line up the pieces. "It's quite another to have the world's cultural heritage community accept that something."

"That is exactly why it was so important to the Polish Minister of Culture to have the euphon authenticated by the acknowledged expert, Dr. Fuller. From what Sig told us, the U.S. tour was part of his agreement to provide the report. That, and he wanted to do the work at home."

"So that's why the euphon is on tour in the U. S.?"

"That, and the publicity involved. I would not be surprised if money changed hands as well."

"Sanjay is right," Riya concurred, "and I would add something else. Sig's authentication is of great interest to historical object collectors, such as ourselves. You know, in our world, the value of an artifact is in the absolute knowledge of its uniqueness. We all wanted to know the Chladni didn't come with shadows."

"By, our world," Leslie said, "I assume you mean the Seminal Society."

"Yes. And not all antiquities are as important. I'm speaking of Firsts. The phonograph of Edison.

The euphon of Chladni. Perhaps, a hand-written version of Newton's original Principia. We can well imagine the ultimate price of the Chladni being over five hundred million dollars. As I said, Sanjay and I are out for the Chladni."

"But some members are obviously in. For example, Alexandre Colton," Leslie said. "Can you tell us about him? Who he is? How'd he make his money?"

Riya's eyes narrowed. "We're not here to talk about Seminal Society collectors, but we'll make an exception for Mr. Colton. He's new to the bidding and not a long-term Society collector. Frankly, his background is a mystery."

"Well, yes and no," Sanjay interjected. "Let's face it, there are indications he is with the Russian Foreign Intelligence Service, the new KGB. Laundering money appears to be his stock in trade."

"How does that work?" Leslie asked. "I mean, he pays half a billion dollars for an artifact. And then what?"

"I won't go into how money laundering works. Let's just say that if Colton is, in fact, working for the SVR, the euphon could be central to any number of possible money launderings, usually resulting in terrorists obtaining weapons."

"SVR?" Leslie queried.

"Oh, sorry. 'Foreign Intelligence Service' in Russian is Sluzhba Vneshney Razvedki, SVR. The Russians love their letters as much as anyone."

"Can you please be more specific how it would all work — the money laundering I mean?"

"Our meal has arrived," Riya cut in. "Let us continue this discussion over coffee." She checked her watch. "We have plenty of time."

During lunch their conversation was of travel, with Riya telling about her favorite restaurants in several cities, from South America to the

Netherlands. For a woman as slender as she was, Leslie found her food fixation interesting.

Near the end of the meal, Leslie said, "I would be remiss if I didn't ask you where you were around noon this past Wednesday?"

"The day poor Sig died?" Riya asked, her eyes again going dark.

"Yes."

"I prefer if we didn't answer," Sanjay interrupted.

"Your choice. But I must tell you, we'll trace your movements and eventually we'll know exactly who was at the Fuller home that morning. Please believe me when I tell you we will piece together a comprehensive timeline. You can give us your version or wait for us to come to you with ours."

"I suppose it can't hurt," Sanjay conceded. "We went to Sig's house around that time at his request so he could convince us the euphon was genuine. He didn't answer the bell and we left."

"How long were you there?"

"A few minutes. No more than five."

"Were there any other cars parked on the street or in the driveway?"

"Nothing in the driveway. As to the street, I can't say that I noticed one way or another."

"Was the garage door open?"

"No."

"What door did you knock at?"

"Front door. I did not knock. I rang the bell."

"Anyone answer?"

"I said no."

"And you saw no one in the house?"

"No."

"Did you see anyone at all near the house? Next door? Down the block?"

"A woman in the driveway next door," Riya said. "I was sitting in our car, a rental, when she drove up in a red car and parked in the driveway.

She carried a shopping bag up to the front door and left it there. I noticed her because of her lovely white hair."

"See anyone else?"

"Didn't see it, but the woman had a dog in her car. Heard him bark. Oh yes. There were also two women walking. They stopped to chat with the first woman as she was about to get back into the red car."

"Any description of the two women would be helpful. Age? Hair color? Build?"

"Age in their fifties. Both blond and...buxom."

"That would describe half the women living in that neighborhood," Cox declared, causing Sanjay to glare at him.

"Mind if I ask a few questions?" Cox asked, looking from husband to wife, oblivious to Sanjay's glare.

"Go ahead, Detective," Sanjay said, his face revealing nothing. "What is on your mind?"

"You said you went to Dr. Fuller's home the morning of the thirteenth."

"We did."

"Why? I mean what was your reason for going there?"

Sanjay looked to his wife for help. Seeing none, he said, "I told you. We wanted to learn how he could have missed the rod."

"Why not just ask him on the phone? You could have accomplished what you required by phone and saved a trip, could you not?"

"For something this important, in person is preferable," Sanjay snapped. "You should know there is no substitute to looking someone directly in the eye."

"We arrived in Fort Myers Tuesday, early evening," Riya added. "We went to dinner and when we returned to the room, I discovered my cell had been off. When I turned it back on, I found a message asking us to come to Sig's home at 11:45 the next morning if we were still interested in the euphon."

"Who left the message?"

"Sig."

"What exactly did the message say?"

"I didn't memorize it, but he said something to the effect that we should come to his house at eleven-forty-five in the morning if we were still interested in the Chladni. He said we'd hear proof that the instrument he sent off to Pittsburgh was the genuine euphon from Poland that he had validated."

"Did you save the message?"

"I am sorry. I did not."

Leslie interrupted. "What do you think the significance is of you hearing proof? For one thing, you said you weren't still interested in buying it."

"I did not know it then," Riya began, "but we now know the problem at the Carnegie stems from a wrong sized glass rod. Sig would never have made such a substitution. What possible reason would he have had to do that? Up until that point, we were anxious to own the Chladni. Learning of a possible substitution cooled our enthusiasm."

The table was cleared, and coffee was poured for all four of them. Desserts were waved off. Riya, cup in her hand, said, "Earlier, you asked about Colton and money laundering. I didn't give you the entire story as I see it. Money laundering works in many formats. Assume that Colton, or his Russian handlers, wanted to transfer a large amount of money to, say, Iran so that the Iranians can buy weapons from, say, China. Instead of cash, the Russians give the Iranians the original euphon. The Iranians turn around and inform the Seminal Society collectors that they have the euphon. Before you know it, the Iranians have a half-billion in cash and the Society collector has the prized First. What is more important to the Russians, it cannot be traced."

Leslie thought for a moment. "But in your scenario," she began "the Chladni is gone, and the Polish Government is cut out. How does that work?"

Riya glanced at her husband. Leslie caught a slight nod before she said, "It is our belief a duplicate euphon has been constructed. One so perfect that it will pass even the most exhaustive examination. The duplicate will be delivered to the Polish National Museum where it will be accepted as being the original."

What Riya had just said lined up perfectly with how Leslie had pieced together the facts. "How much of what you just said is speculation?" she asked, trying to calibrate her own analysis.

"Let me just say, hundreds of millions of dollars do not exchange hands on mere speculation."

"That all means that the euphon is still in play?"

"Very much in play."

"And speaking of hundreds of millions," Leslie said, "where would Colton get that kind of money? From the Russians?"

"That's certainly a real possibility. But as I see it," Riya said, her eyes twinkling. "Alexandre Colton, or whatever his real name is, has no intention of paying for the Chladni. His plan all along has been to steal it and let the chips fall where they may."

# SIXTEEN

ALLEN WAS DRIVING, LESLIE DOZING next to him. The discussion with the Kumars had pulled Leslie out of her funk. He knew how much she had dreaded coming back to Tampa, but the bounce in her step told him all he needed to know.

"You should have seen Cox's face when I told him you were picking me up" she had said, leaning over the console to kiss him. "If I didn't know better, I'd think he had made overnight plans for the two of us."

"Why doubt your instinct?"

"Against the rules, for one. For two, not my type."

"Think he cares about either of those points?"

"Man's bright enough. But...but something's off. Hey, mind if I catch a few Z's on the way? Didn't sleep well for two nights and this interview with the Kumars exhausted me."

"You have about an hour. Sweet dreams."

———◆———

"How long was I out?" Leslie asked, her eyes flicking open.

"Little under an hour. Winery's ten miles ahead."

"I needed that. I'm thinking it's more mental than physical."

"You're not surprised, are you? That bullet missed you by millimeters. Witnessing a woman's head blown off. Your partner going down. Who the hell wouldn't be exhausted — or worse?"

"I've trained for that. This should..."

"Look, I was a cop. So, go easy on the macho talk, okay. Underneath, we're all human. Seeing what you saw and realizing but for the grace of God go I impacts us. You're no exception, tough as you are."

Leslie acknowledged the truth of what Allen had just said by remaining silent.

"Here's the deal," Allen said, breaking the silence. "We're here to enjoy ourselves. Put this behind us. So please, no more shop talk."

"That's a plan. You know, when I lived in Tampa, we drove around this area. This is a pretty part of Florida, if you're an orchard lover. To my eye, I could use a few rolling hills."

"Don't bad mouth the area. I was born not far from here. Maybe tomorrow we'll run on over and I'll show you around my old stomping grounds. I didn't actually do much stomping, left when I was five. But I still consider it home."

"Show me the house you were raised in?"

"Gone years ago. It wasn't much then and went downhill from there."

They fell silent until Allen pulled off the road and stopped under the brick overhang that served as the Lakeridge Winery check-in area. Two men wearing large straw hats leaned against a wooden fence, one strumming a banjo and the other blowing into a harmonica.

"Orange Blossom Special."

"What's that about a special?" Leslie asked, stepping from the car. "What're you talking about?"

"They're playing the Special. A bit slow if I were to judge, but that's it. Hear the harmonica simulating the pulse of a train moving along the track. You can just picture smoke billowing around the curve as the train approaches the station. People say it's the best fiddling tune of the century."

"Didn't know you were into fiddling."

146

"Oh, I don't play. Just listen."

"You never told me."

"Didn't think it important. My pap was a fiddler. Pretty good at it too. He often played with Will McLean. He even got me a job at the annual Florida Folk Festival not far from here in Brooksville. Festival was moved up to White Springs in 2007, but I worked it for several years. Got to meet all the top players."

"Who's your favorite?"

"Beside McLean, I'd have to say Gamble Rogers. Guy told stories like no one I ever heard before — or after. Speaking of McLean, that's Osceola's Last Words they're now playing. One of over three thousand songs and stories he wrote. Guy was the best ever."

They waited for the duo to finish the tune before heading inside. Check-in went smoothly with the clerk saying, "Your timing's perfect. A group's forming just over there." He pointed in the direction of people milling around in a corner of the lobby. "They're getting ready for our most popular winery tour. I'll have your bags taken to your room. You don't want to miss this one. It ends with a wonderful wine tasting and happy hour. The Southern Red is magnificent."

An hour later, with the tour group gathered around a table spread with several cheeses and crackers, Allen held up a half-glass of the Southern Red and in an official sounding voice said, "This wine derives its full-bodied unique fruity flavor from a Noble variety of Muscadine grape." When everyone laughed, he continued, "Note the true balance of aromas with a refreshing aftertaste." He emptied the glass in a single swallow.

The group saluted him by holding their own glass high and draining the contents.

Leslie leaned close. "What's that about? I didn't know you were a wine authority. Learning something new about you every hour."

Smiling broadly, he replied, "Don't know jack squat about wine. Just memorized the website blurb. I'm not even certain I matched the slogan with the right wine. Just having fun. Trying to impress you is all."

"You're impressive enough already. Come on, let's walk the grounds before dinner. Work up an appetite."

"I'll walk with you. But I remind you, I'm not the one who had lunch at the Columbia. I'm already hungry enough to polish off that cheese."

"You still bristling over Cox?" Leslie said, squeezing his arm as they moved back outside. "Told you, he's not my type."

Refusing to engage on the subject, Allen instead replied, "Believe it or not, I've never been to the Columbia Restaurant. Is that a place you and Junior went?"

Leslie's eyes clouded and she looked off into the distance as she spoke. "We always meant to, but for one reason or another, never managed." She again paused, sucked in her breath, took Allen's hand in hers, before continuing. "But I've eaten there several times myself when I worked Ybor City. Love their menu. They claim they're the largest Spanish restaurant in the world. No reason to doubt them. The Kumars travel the world and claim this is one of their favorites."

"Got me sold. Kumars still bidding on the euphon?"

"They're out — or so they want us to believe. Meeting was to give us background on the euphon and on the players."

"Sorry," Allen said, "I promised no shop talk. But you might want to hear about my case with

Colton. It's got nothing to do with your investigation. Just a fun set of facts."

Leslie pulled Allen close and kissed him. "What a nice place. Thanks for suggesting we come here. Tell me your fun facts as we walk."

"You know about the tip you received suggesting that Colton had in his possession an artifact on Interpol's list called the Blue Footed Golden Booby. Right?"

"I do."

"The Blue Footed Golden Booby, as it turns out, weighs about seventy-five pounds, stands ten inches tall, is roughly four inches by four inches, and was carved from solid gold — pure solid gold. The gold is worth about two and a half million, making the Booby's artistic value far greater than its intrinsic mineral value."

"What's so special about a gold bird?"

"The real Booby, the one worth perhaps a half billion, was crafted by a tribe from a South Pacific island that did not have any gold. Where — and how — the tribe came into possession of such a large pure gold block is the mystery that drives up the value."

"So where did the gold come from?"

"Shipwrecks! The island is surrounded by ragged reefs. The islanders rowed out at night and moved the channel markers. Ships, mostly from New Zealand, sailed onto the reef. Easy prey."

"And I always thought living on a Pacific island would be ideal. What island was that?"

"It was crafted on the island of Aurora, now called Maewo, the republic of Vanuatu. From what I gather, the Vanuatu people were adventuresome and sailed east, eventually landing and exploring coastal Peru. Apparently, the explorers found fish by following the boobies. Once back home, they crafted the Blue Footed Golden Booby in tribute to their good fortune. How the Golden Booby got back to Peru is another mystery. Most likely it was stolen from them by pirates operating in the South Pacific."

"Half a billion? For a statue of a bird?"

"Here's the thing. Anyone who has claimed ownership of the Booby over the years has met with disaster. And always, the Booby goes missing. My favorite story is the one where Al Capone comes down to a little island off the south shore of Texas, an island called South Padre, to retrieve what he believes to be the real Golden Booby. But it's a trap. Most of Capone's men are shot and killed on the beach. Capone himself escapes, only to be arrested in Chicago a few months later for tax evasion."

"Al Capone," Leslie responded, "that happened almost a hundred years ago. What's that got to do..."

"Nothing," Allen answered, smiling broadly. "The truth — if you can ever really know any truth with these stories — is that the real Blue Footed Golden Booby was never even in Texas."

"So, where was it?"

"As best anyone knows, it never left Peru. An illusion. Just like the piece Colton had in his possession. A fake. Oh, the gold's real enough, or the weight would be off. But the carving isn't."

"Shouldn't Colton have known that when he first got it?"

"I believe he did."

"I'm slow today. So why..."

"A diversion tactic. He wanted law enforcement eyes on him."

"Why would that be?"

"Gives him a perfect alibi for what he saw coming."

"Alibi failed. He was out of custody at the time of Fuller's death."

"He'll have to sue his lawyer. She sprung him way too fast."

# SEVENTEEN

"THAT MEAL WAS EXCELLENT!" ALLEN said, stretching his back as he stood. "I don't know which was better, the lobster or that fabulous wine."

"I vote for the wine. Not knocking the lobster, but the wine was perfect."

Leaving the dining area, they passed two couples they had met on their earlier vineyard tour. Sasha and Hendrik, celebrating their three-year wedding anniversary; and Scot and Mark, also celebrating their wedding anniversary, only it was their eighth.

"Leslie," Mark asked, "just what are you and this gorgeous hunk of a man celebrating?"

"Friendship," Allen answered. "Four-month friendship."

Scot lifted his glass, prompting the others to do the same. "Here's to five months of...friendship." Eying his partner, he added, "and to many, many more months. Hopefully, even years." He took a long drink.

"To all of us," Sasha added, draining her wine. "May we all have many more years together of happy times."

"You want to dance?" Allen asked, when Sasha dragged her husband toward the dance floor.

"Not my thing, I'm afraid. At least not this fast music. Mind if we go to our room. I'm exhausted."

"Not at all," Allen said, turning to the two men. "Please excuse us. Been a long day."

"Something we said?" Mark asked, frowning.

"No, it's just..."

"Let them go, Markie," Scot winked, "I can see why she's exhausted."

"Nice meeting you both," Leslie said, taking Allen's outstretched hand. "Enjoy the remainder of your night. And please make our apologies to Hendrik and Sasha for us. Maybe we'll catch you at breakfast."

"Not unless you call eating at one p.m. breakfast," Mark answered.

"I call that lunch and we'll be long gone by then." Leslie responded, planning to leave early enough to allow for a stop at the hospital to visit Fischer.

Despite her intentions, they didn't walk onto the patio where breakfast was being served until just before ten. On the way down, Leslie pulled Allen close, kissed him, and said, "That was a nice surprise. I mean the silk night gown and all. How'd you know my size?"

"Been sleeping with you for months. Not a tough problem to solve."

She kissed him again, this time pulling his body tight against hers.

Coming up for air, Allen said, "You thinking of skipping breakfast and..."

"Love to, but..."

"Head back to the room?" Allen offered. "Or quick bite first? Either works for me. Then we can drive around Lake Apopka to the town where my birth house was."

"How 'bout a leisurely brunch to top off a perfect night — and morning — skip the old home visit and head for the hospital? I'd like seeing firsthand how Fish's doing."

Hiding his disappointment, Allen responded, "We can do my hometown another time. Give us a good reason to come back up here. Anything particular you want to talk with Fish about?"

"Just checkin' in. Showing the flag as it were. Thanks for being so understanding."

"Wonder how that shooter, Terrig I believe that's his name, is doing?"

"As of twenty minutes ago, he's still in critical, but stable, condition," Leslie answered.

Allen shook his head. "Thought you were locked out of the system."

"Called the hospital while you were in the shower."

"You worried?"

"About?"

"Him dying and his shooting escalating for the two of you?"

"Did nothing wrong. Neither did Fish. Man had a gun pointed at us. A gun he had just fired. Justified no matter how you slice it."

"It's not me who slices it. I'm thinking of the media."

"No story here. White cop shoots white man. No agenda in that. God, I hate that aspect of our job." Changing the subject, Leslie said, "I don't know what to make of Cox. He's certainly bright enough. But...but I don't...exactly trust that guy."

"In what way?"

"Nothing specific. Lack of impulse control I suppose. He reminds me of a partner I once had whose instinct was to fire first and sort out the facts later."

"Anything on his record suggest that?"

"Nothing I found. No citizen complaints, nothing of that sort. It's just, as I said, a feeling."

"Ask for a reassignment."

"I'll let this run a while before I play that card. Hey, this trip was just what I needed. Thank you."

———————

They drove in silence until they were south of Tampa. "We're making good time," Allen said. "Traffic's light." Not receiving a reply, he looked over expecting to see Leslie asleep, instead he found her deep in thought. "Dollar for your thoughts."

"Oh, sorry," she replied. "Whatever happened to a penny? Inflation I suppose."

"I'm thinking you're into some mighty heavy thoughts. Worth a lot more than a penny."

"You're wasting your money. I was thinking of Fuller hanging from his belt in his garage. Makes no sense. Even if he lied about the authenticity of the Chladni, why kill him? Who's been harmed? Suicide makes the most sense and even that's on shaky ground."

"Certainly, the euphon's owner, that guy Chlad. Maybe he was conned into putting up the money in hopes of a big payday."

"Can't tell you why, but I'm not like'n Chlad. But I do need to interview him again. See if we missed anything."

"I suppose you've reread your initial interview of him."

"I'm blocked from the file until I'm cleared for work tomorrow — or whenever."

"Could it be longer?"

"If the shooter, Terrig, dies, this could drag on."

"But it's a murder investigation. Isn't time of the essence?"

"Cox'll run with it. He's senior to me in the department. For all I know, I've already been replaced."

"Just yesterday you two were in Tampa getting background information. Why would Boots — or whomever — cut you out?"

"If my situation impedes the investigation I'll be replaced, that much is for certain. Cox was pissed big time when you picked me up. No telling what he's capable of."

Changing the subject, Allen told Leslie stories of his time on the fiddle circuit, as he called it, with his father. "I'd walk from table to table holding my hat upside down while he played."

"People step up?"

"Some did. Some waved me away. Got a lot of coins, not so many dollars. What really pissed me off, you want to know, was the pennies. Still makes me angry."

"Last night," Leslie responded, replaying their conversation, "you said, 'Osceola's Words.' What does that mean?"

"Osceola. A Seminole chief. Lived in the early 1800's here in Florida. There was a truce in place, but the Seminoles were still being driven from Florida. His brother begged him to fight, but he implored his brother to lead them to the grassy waters where no white man can invade and leave them dead and cold."

"That's heavy."

"One of the best songs ever written."

———◆———

Pulling up in front of the hospital, Allen said, "Sure you don't want me to wait and drive you home? Not a problem if you do."

"I'll be fine. Thanks for a wonderful getaway. And for the nice present!" Leslie leaned across the seat, squeezed his arm and kissed him before getting out of the car. "Love you," she called. "Talk tomorrow."

Fischer was sitting up in bed, the silent TV tuned to CNN. "Hey, partner!" she called. "You're looking a lot better than the last time I saw you. Any thoughts of when you can get out of here?"

"You're a sight for sore eyes, Leslie," Fischer responded, pulling himself up straighter. "Hey, you're looking rested. That's good."

"And you're ducking my question. How're you doing?"

"Maybe tomorrow. I'll need rehab."

"I'll miss you," Leslie said, surprising herself.

"You got Cox. What more can anyone want?"

"Need I answer that?"

"Taking the fifth is reserved for criminals."

"I'm still not answering."

"Hope you don't mind my saying," Fischer said, "but other than you not being there, Cox's interview of Colton was textbook."

"How the hell did..."

"Friday magic."

"Bullshit, Fish. How did you..."

"I said Friday magic. As in Sergeant Joe Friday."

"Pain meds must be getting to you. What're you on?"

"Nothing at the moment as a matter of fact," Fischer's eyes held a twinkle. "Time you learn." He flipped his computer open, brought up the main database log-in screen and turned the keyboard to face his partner. "Use this login," he instructed. "SGTJOEFRIDAY. All caps, under username. Then for password use 6, 5, 4, 3, 2, 1. This is a universal login, access to everything. Guard it with your life. Use it wisely."

Leslie accessed the Fuller file and immediately exclaimed, "What the hell's going on? Who authorized that interview?"

"Cox did it on his own, far's I can tell. Take a moment and read it. You can sit over there if you like," Fischer said, pointing to the chair where Leslie had last seen Fischer's wife.

"I can't believe that asshole interviewed Chlad without me!"

"Could have been worse."

Sunday January 17, 2021

Interview Began: 10:53

Leslie skipped over the formal requirements and the introductory remarks.

COX: You understand that when I refer to the Chladni I am referring to the Ernst Chladni original euphon built by him in 1791. The one that disappeared at Breslau, Lower Silesia upon his death.

CHLAD: I do. Yes.

COX: Do you claim ownership of the Chladni?

CHLAD: I do.

COX: What makes you believe you are the true owner?

CHLAD: I trace my heritage back ten generations to Ernst Florens Friedrich Chladni.

COX: Direct descendant? Grandparent?"

CHLAD: More like a great uncle.

COX: Polish?

CHLAD: German, actually.

COX: Did you locate the instrument?

CHLAD: Heavens no. Dr. Fuller did. He's also the one who produced the family tree showing I was the rightful heir.

COX: Are there other heirs claiming rights?

CHLAD: Not to my knowledge.

COX: No one other than yourself has come forward claiming ownership?

CHLAD: I know of no one.

COX: I'm trying to figure out how you're so positive you own it.

CHLAD: Dr. Fuller put together the paperwork. Convinced me and the Polish Government.

COX: Let's talk about the day Dr. Fuller died. What time did you wake up that morning?

CHLAD: About 7:15. Got a call from a potential euphon buyer.

COX: Then?

CHLAD: Then I puttered around the house. Sig called shortly after nine asking me to come to his house at noon. Said he'd explain it all. Told me not to answer any questions from the press.

COX: Did he tell you what happened?

CHLAD: Only that Carnegie believes the instrument they had to be suspect. The problem had to do with a glass rod having the wrong dimension. He said Carnegie was in error.

COX: Did you believe him about the Carnegie having it wrong?

CHLAD: He's the expert. Why would I not believe him?

COX: What did you do after you hung up?

CHLAD: This and that. I was agitated.

COX: Your wife home then?

CHLAD: Carol had a women's luncheon, Hearts of Miromar I believe it was. She left a little after eleven.

COX: Did you go to Fuller's house?

CHLAD: Yes.

COX: And?

CHLAD: He wasn't home.

COX: Did you go inside?

CHLAD: I just told you, he wasn't home. Didn't answer the door.

COX: You walk from your house or drive?

CHLAD: Walk.

A moment later the interview ended.

"This really pisses me off!" Leslie exclaimed, handing the computer back to Fischer. "I needed to be there."

"You have to admit, he's thorough."

"I would have probed more around how Sig knew Carnegie had it wrong. And exactly what he wanted to achieve by going over to Fuller's place. Also, I wish he'd have pinned down the times with precision. If Chlad's our guy, we need to place him at the scene before Fuller died not after."

"There's always tomorrow," Fischer said. "There's always tomorrow."

# EIGHTEEN

TUESDAY MORNING LESLIE WALKED INTO Sergeant Oakmore's office not knowing what to expect. Oakmore had the reputation as a no-nonsense manager, but you couldn't prove that by Leslie. As she had said to Allen on several occasions, "He's giving me all the rope I need to hang myself." She had yet to determine whether or not he had her back.

"Just keep that rope away from your neck," Allen had quipped, a sparkle in his eye.

"I sense that's where it's already wrapped," she responded, not picking up on his reference to the Fuller hanging.

"So, you did come in today after all," Oakmore said when Leslie walked through his mostly always open door. "I lost to Boots. She said you'd be here first thing in the morning. I had my money on tomorrow."

"And let Cox continue to piss on my case. Not on your life."

"I didn't see anything he did that was so bad. He's senior to you, you know."

"He's senior, I grant you that. But I can't help thinking if you wanted him leading this case you would have assigned it to him to begin with."

"If I'm ever asked, I'll deny it," he said, flashing a rare smile. "You're right. You feeling okay? Stetson said the shooting got to you."

"If it wasn't for Fish, you'd be attending my wake."

"Who said I'd attend?"

"There's that, I suppose."

"You do know you saved the shooter's life. Blood loss was massive as it was. I hear he's expected to pull through."

"Doing my job's all."

"I know you gave a statement to IA. You've had time to think, clear your mind. Anything you need to, or want to, add? Anything you might have overlooked? This can be just between you and me if you wish."

Thinking something was amiss, she asked, "Is there something wrong? Fish's not in trouble is he. He's the..."

"Nothing I know of. Maxwell and Cakecroft are two of the best. Straight shooters all the way. No agenda that I know of."

"At least something's going right. All I need now is to be cleared for..."

"Already done," Oakmore said, smiling again. Checking his watch, he continued, "Better hurry, Cox set up an interview at ten with Chlad's wife. You saw what he did with Chlad. Didn't wait for you."

"How'd you know I saw that file?"

"Joe Friday reviewed the Fuller file twice yesterday. I suppose the first was Fish nosing around. Can't keep him down. The second, I'm guessing, was you. Here's the thing," Oakmore said, reducing his voice to barely a whisper, "You and Fish are quarantined from each other, so don't tell me how or when you learned of the Friday code. Just don't let Cox screw this up."

Cox answered on the first ring. "Leslie, I was hoping it was you. Been cleared?"

"Move the Carol Chlad interview to ten-fifteen and don't go in without me," she barked, not bothering to answer his question.

"Hey, just remember who's senior..."

Leslie heard nothing of his reply. She had already hung up. As a practical matter, her GPS had indicated she would be at the Chlad house at 9:55. The delay instruction was designed to smoke out Cox's willingness to work with her.

"I thought you couldn't make it for another twenty minutes," Cox scolded when Leslie walked up to his car window just before ten. "Mrs. Chlad's not expecting us 'til then."

"That'll give us time to talk," Leslie said. "Coordinate ourselves." She held up two coffees as a peace offering. "My car or yours?"

"Get in," Cox said, reaching for the cup she held out. "Damn right we gotta talk."

Before the door closed behind Leslie, Cox started in on her. "It's clear you don't trust me. And, for the record, coffee won't work as a peace offering. I suppose you've read my interview with Chlad. I also suppose you're pissed. Sometimes after a shooting like you were involved in it takes weeks to be cleared for active duty. I have reason to believe Chlad is about to leave town. That's why I set this one up for this morning with his wife. Didn't want to chance missing them. I hope that answers your concerns."

"If they're really planning on leaving town, it does," Leslie replied, about to add, 'for now', but thought better of it.

"Then how about trusting me."

"It's not a matter of trust. It's..."

"Of course it is! We go up to Tampa, two hours in the car, you barely speak. You don't bother telling me you have plans with your boyfriend. That your definition of trust? God only knows what the hell else you're withholding."

Leslie turned to face him. "I'll say this once, and once only. Trust is earned. You don't do a damn thing more on this file without my approval! Make that my prior approval. You hear me?"

Cox knew four important facts. One, he was senior and didn't have to take orders from her. Two, rookie detectives are never designated as lead on homicides, but she had been. Three, Fischer was far senior to either of them, and even he had deferred to her on the two cases he had worked on with her. Four, and perhaps the most important of all, he had reached out to a friend on the Tampa force and the sheet on Leslie was that she was fair-minded, but tough. She certainly wasn't someone you wanted as an enemy. This knowledge, coupled with her hard-set cold eyes, prevailed over his ego. "I hear you alright," he conceded. "But that doesn't make it right."

"I know my being junior to you grates on you. I may be a rookie here in Lee County, but I've been a cop for over eleven years. And I'm running this case until the brass tells me to back down. You don't like it, tell it to Boots."

When Cox didn't respond, she asked, "You going to work under my rules or not?"

"That's my plan. But..."

"No buts! You will or you won't! Which is it?"

"Just exactly what do you want from me? I'm nobody's errand boy! I've got a mind of my own!"

"Just run your ideas past me before you act."

"What else?

"I take the lead in questioning. You fill in the blanks."

"That's what I did in Tampa with the Kumars."

Leslie played back the scene at the Columbia and realized Cox had essentially said nothing, allowing her to carry the interview. "You did. That's all I ask." Even as Leslie said it, doubts lingered.

Cox remained quiet a moment before asking, "Mind if I set up an interview with the Fritz woman. Like to go over some stuff with her."

"Good idea," Leslie replied, visualizing the slightly built woman and replaying their conversation immediately after the woman had found her fiancé hanging in his garage. The horror of it again sent a shiver down Leslie's spine.

While Cox was calling Selma Fritz, Leslie thought about the upcoming talk with Carol Chlad and how when she had spoken with her previously the woman seemed disoriented. Her age, Leslie had determined by cross-checking birth and driver's license records, was fifty-nine. Normally, not old enough for dementia, but one never knew.

"Okay," Cox announced after a brief phone discussion, "got it set for one-thirty with Fritz. That work for you?"

"Works for me. Let's go talk with Carol."

Unlike the previous visit where Carol Chlad had worn an ankle-length skirt with an untucked blouse and wide scarf tied at her waist, this time she looked more like a prisoner in a one-piece light beige jumpsuit, a hair band across the top of her head keeping the strands from her eyes. She wore a color coordinated mask covering her lower face. "I remember you," she said to Leslie, surprise in her voice. "I wasn't told you'd be coming. A man called..."

"Detective Cox," Leslie said. "We're working together. As you may recall, my name's Detective Hodges. May we come in?"

"Oh, certainly. Where's my manners? Follow me." Chlad took several steps, then added, "I thought we'd sit out in the lanai. It's such a nice day today. Don't you just love January days? It's my favorite month for being outside." She led the way through the magnificently furnished home to the outdoor lanai area containing furniture every bit as upscale as inside. "Here we are. Please excuse me, I have coffee made and I baked bread. You know, in one of those bread machines. This one is whole grain."

While she was gone Cox asked, "Was she this... this ditzy in your last interview? You didn't note it."

"Giving her the benefit of the doubt," Leslie replied, "She seems marginally better this time. We'll see what develops."

It took over five minutes before Carol returned, followed by the maid, Bekka carrying a large tray. Carol removed saucers and cups from the tray, placing them carefully beside the detectives. She then poured coffee into each cup, her hand shaking slightly as she did so.

"Bekka please bring us cream and sugar. I prefer mine natural. You must try the bread. This is a first time for this...this...I forgot what we used."

"Whole grain, Miss Carol," the maid said, her voice carrying a pleasant Jamaican lilt.

"Oh, yes. Now I recall. I so hope it came out nice."

Judging from the bread's hard-looking, lumpy surface, Leslie thought eating it was going to prove a challenge.

Bekka placed a slice in front of each person, then backed away and disappeared inside the house.

"Let's start with last Wednesday morning," Leslie began. "I know we briefly discussed this already, but let's do it again now that my partner's here."

"He's a different man," Carol said, surprising Leslie with her memory.

"Yes, this is Detective Cox. Detective Fischer is...is busy."

"I liked Detective Fischer. He's a nice man."

"So is Detective Cox. Please tell us what you did last Wednesday from the time you woke up until you arrived at the clubhouse."

"One day is the same as the next. Remind me why you are asking."

"Wednesday, I believe you said you had a luncheon. Hearts of Miromar? Does that help?"

"Oh, yes. Now I recall. I had breakfast and went for a swim. The pool is heated you know."

"After your swim? What time would you say your swim finished?"

Before Carol could answer, Bekka returned with the cream and sugar.

"I'm okay," Leslie said, silently kicking herself for not speaking up before the maid had gone back to the kitchen.

"I'll take a little cream," Cox volunteered.

When Bekka turned to leave, Carol said, "I'm sorry. I forgot the question."

"I asked what time would you say your swim finished?"

"Oh, yeah. Ten-thirty exactly. I know that because I cut it short. It takes me an hour to get ready for the bridge luncheon. I showered, did my hair and makeup. Not like today when I didn't have time to properly get ready."

"What time did you leave for the luncheon?"

"Before eleven-thirty. Maybe a bit sooner. Maybe Bekka can remember better."

"I'll talk to her later. Did you drive straight there?"

"It's just around the corner down there at the clubhouse. Where else would I drive to?"

"Just being certain we understand. So, you drove directly from this house to the clubhouse?"

"That's what I did. That's what I always do on Wednesdays. Go to the club for lunch with the girls. We always have lunch on Wednesdays at the club."

Leslie glanced over at Cox, signaling that he was free to ask questions. Sitting back, she picked up the bread and took a cautious bite. It was a good thing she bit into it softly, otherwise she might have cracked a tooth. How Carol, or Bekka, had sliced it, was a mystery. The crust was nearly impenetrable.

Leaning forward, Cox asked, "Tell me, Carol, how long a drive it is from here to the club?"

"Five minutes. Maybe seven at most."

"If the security camera shows you walking into the clubhouse at five minutes after noon last Wednesday, what would you tell me about what time you left this house?"

While Cox was asking his question, Leslie quickly removed the bread from her mouth and buried it under a cocktail napkin.

"I'd tell you the security camera was wrong. I left here when I said I did."

"And you drove straight over to the clubhouse?"

"That's what I said. Yes. Where else would I go?"

"That's what we're here to determine, Mrs. Chlad. Where else you might have gone."

"I know what I did and did not do young man! And I don't appreciate your questions."

"Carol," Leslie interrupted, trying to save the interview, "last time we spoke you said your father sold a business..."

"To Federal Express."

"And you also said you bought this lovely home and this furniture and artwork with the money your father left you."

"We traveled around the world buying the art."

"If I recall right," Leslie prompted, "you said you still have the same amount of money in the bank."

"Not in a bank. In investments. With a broker. Ernie handles all that. It's way beyond me. Did you enjoy the bread, my dear? It's rye, you know."

"You said it was...," Cox began before Leslie cut him off, saying, "I did. But I'm not very hungry this morning."

"That's a shame. Made it especially for you. Maybe next time."

"I also believe you said you paid Dr. Fuller over a million dollars to secure the Chladni euphon?"

"My husband is in charge of our money. You must ask him."

"It's your money, I take it."

"Our, money," Carol corrected. "Our money."

"A million dollars is a lot of money. Aren't you concerned..."

"Not in the least. We have plenty of money!" Carol abruptly stood. "Bekka will show you out. I have to finish packing."

"Packing for what?"

"Vacation."

"Where are you going?"

"Europe," she replied, excitement in her eyes.

"Where in Europe?"

Carol's eyes quickly dimmed. "I...I don't remember where exactly."

"It's January," Leslie said, recalling that Chlad had indicated his wife didn't like traveling in the cold.

"Of course, it's January. It's my favorite month. Need to go now. Bye." Carol abruptly turned and walked into the house, disappearing into a bedroom.

A moment later Bekka appeared. "May I show you to the door?"

"We're quite capable of finding our own way out of here," Cox said, taking out his frustration over Carol's sudden departure on the hapless maid.

# NINETEEN

SELMA FRITZ LIVED ON THE top floor of a five-floor condominium called White Sands located just off the Tamiami Trail four miles west of the deceased's house at Miromar Lakes. "What a nice view," Leslie exclaimed, when Fritz opened the door to reveal a glass-lined wall on the far side of the living area that overlooked an expansive tree-lined lake with what appeared to be marsh land beyond the lake. Several small sailboats were darting about, taking advantage of the light breeze. "I'm new to the area and haven't been here before. Is this a new development?"

"Only if you call twenty-two years new. They keep it up well. Unlike some I know. And who, pray tell, is this?" Selma asked, eyeing Cox.

"Excuse me. This is my partner, Detective Simeon Cox. Detective Cox, let me introduce Selma Fritz."

"What happened to that other detective who…"

"Detective Fischer. He's on leave."

"Oh, yes. Now I remember. It was on the news. Is he okay?"

"He'll be fine. I'll tell him you asked about him."

"Please do that. Come along, I'll show you two around."

Following Fritz across the apartment, Leslie said, "That's a lovely scarf you're wearing. I like the vibrant colors."

"Pashmina. This time of year, I'm hardly ever without one. Started wearing them years ago to stave off the cold in Europe and just got in the habit. I have several."

"This space is larger than I thought," Cox commented. "How many bedrooms do you have?"

"Two and a den."

"Love your art!" Leslie said, admiring the many paintings and sculptures. "Is this all from America? Or is it from other countries?" she asked. "I've only seen art like this in…in exhibits."

"You have a good eye, Detective. Museum quality. I held the Zelnick Chair of European Art at Miami University. Got to travel the world."

"I suppose we should call you Doctor then."

"Selma works just fine."

Leslie, seeing no pictures of a husband or children, or even parents, said, "May I ask, were you ever married?"

A cloud fell over a face that was already grieving. It took Fritz several seconds before she said, "Married to Milton for twenty-eight years. He was a sales rep for RCA and traveled more days than he was at home. I travelled as well. Only we were seldom in the same time zone. He started with RCA in the mid-seventies and did well until they put him in charge of CED Videodisc sales. It was downhill from there."

"Pardon me. I've never heard of…"

"CEDs. That's the problem. No one has. RCA pioneered video recording so people could play movies on their TVs. Only they tried to do it in the analog mode. Today, as you know, it's all digital, or optical. RCA was into capacitance as the recording medium and lost their shirts. GE, who had owned them originally, reacquired them. Milton was working for GE when he dropped dead of a heart attack the day after his fifty-fifth birthday. I was in Italy when it happened." She looked away before forcing a smile. "I still get a small pension from them. Sit, I'll pour us coffee and we can talk some more if you like."

When Selma returned to her seat, she seemed smaller, and far more vulnerable than Leslie remembered. Everyone processes family losses in their own way, and Leslie knew from her own counseling sessions there is no right or wrong way. Time, she had been instructed, would dull the pain. From her own experience, time wasn't working all that well.

"Here's what I recall from our last conversation," Leslie began. "You have a PhD in medieval history and are a collector of European furniture." Looking around the room to a pair of tall magnificent wooden chairs with worked leather padded seats flanking an ornate carved oak sideboard, Leslie added, "I see what attracts you to this style. I don't recall ever seeing anything quite like it. At first, I thought those curved bands on the sideboard were some sort of rose metal. I'm now thinking they're glass. Glass curved in a shape I've never seen."

Fritz's eyes lit up; her face came alive. "Compound curve. Indeed, it is glass. You most certainly do have a good eye. This is a one of a kind. Took me half a lifetime to assemble this collection. Museum curators are dying to get their hands on it."

"I can see why. I recall you saying you met Dr. Fuller, Sig, in Bamberg. Upper Franconia."

"My, you have a wonderful memory. Wish mine was as good as yours."

"Comes in handy," Leslie said. "But I couldn't begin to make heads or tails out of all this. You have a unique talent."

'It's just something I love doing and researching. Like your job, it takes a lot of digging and chasing clues to find old pieces, often in strange locations."

"Please tell us about the euphon. As I understand, Sig located it in Poland. Hidden in an old building. We also understand Chladni traveled with it around the country. Wasn't it awful heavy?"

"That's one of the beauties of it! The wood the piano maker used is light and was designed with interlocking pieces easily disassembled. Fits into two large bags, similar to golf bags. One person, obviously someone stronger than me, can carry it."

"What made Sig think to search in that building?" Leslie knew the answer but wanted to hear it from Fritz directly.

"He was an expert in European artifacts and had an exceptional ability to follow even the slightest of leads. The dear man was focused beyond belief. Just a hint of a clue drove him to exhaustion as he worked every possible scenario. Hypos he called them. Short for hypothesis. He'd find a clue, possibly in a piece of literature, once even in a folklore song, and then he'd make up hypos as to possible locations of an object. He'd continually change the hypo until every possible mutation was eliminated. He thought of it as a massive three-dimensional human puzzle with continuously changing borders."

"What clue — hypo — was he working from to find the euphon?" Leslie probed.

Fritz studied the ceiling a moment, then focused on the lake, seemingly lost. Cox leaned forward, about to ask a question.

Leslie signaled her partner to wait.

Almost a minute passed in silence before Fritz, her eyes now slightly red, returned to the present. "Pardon me," she began, "but I couldn't help seeing Sig, recalling how happy he was with this 'great adventure', as he called it."

"Chladni is not exactly a household name. Certainly, not many people have ever heard of a euphon. What triggered Dr. Fuller's interest in such a...such an obscure artifact?"

"The Seminal Society? Do you know about them?"

"We do." Leslie affirmed. "Group of wealthy people who collect art."

"Not just any art. Primarily, their passions run to possessing Firsts."

"We've heard that as well."

"The euphon is a true First. For many reasons. It was the first instrument to have ever made musical notes using vibrating glass rods. But the fascination goes beyond that alone. Think about the souls honored by the Society. Edison, Chladni, Newton, Galileo."

"There are more than that," Leslie injected. "Goes back even earlier."

"For our purposes that's far enough back. You know, of course, Edison was fascinated by sound and invented the phonograph to record it. What you might not know is that Galileo himself was experimenting with sound vibrations in metal. The Society believes Galileo's soul passed to Edison through Newton and Chladni. It was Chladni who perfected the technique of representing sound vibrations as a function of frequency in various materials."

Fritz's passion captured Leslie's attention. "You mean the euphon is a provable — tangible even — bridge from Galileo to Edison?"

"That's why at one of the Society's gatherings, several years back the euphon was discussed in detail. After that discussion, a man by the name of Morris Stratis spoke to Sig to see what Sig knew about the euphon. The more dear Sig dug, the more excited he became. Put yourself in the shoes of a Seminal Society collector. Money being no object, would you pass up the opportunity to own the original — and perhaps the only — tangible proof of the soul linkage from Galileo to Edison?"

"You're not saying Dr. Fuller was a Seminal Society..."

"Oh, heavens no! He just drew energy from their passion!"

"Is it fair for me to believe a Seminal Society collector would stop at nothing to own the Chladni euphon?"

"You must admit the original euphon is extremely valuable." Fritz began crying again and this time it took a few minutes for her to compose herself. "I'd say that was a fair statement."

Cox, having received a nod from Leslie, said, "Did you help Sig? I mean interview people. Track down records? That sort of thing?"

"We spent the better part of a year in Masovian. I worked with him some."

'When was that?"

"2018."

"This is 2022. It took four years to find it after that point. Did I miss something here?"

"I don't like what you're insinuating, Detective."

"Sorry, I'm not insinuating anything. Just trying to understand the timeline."

"These things take time," Fritz snapped. "Finding a long-lost high-valued object is only the beginning. You need to establish title, and... and you have to negotiate to get it."

"Negotiate with whom?" Cox probed.

"As I said, I didn't directly participate in that aspect. I do know Sig paid several people what he called consultant fees, to secure possession of the euphon. Getting it out of Poland legally was the big hurdle. National treasures, I'm sure you know, are difficult to remove from a country."

"Did Sig pay consultant fees to secure exit permission?"

"I repeat, Detective Cox, I wasn't involved. I dare say I'd not be surprised to learn that fees were paid. That was a tense period."

"Let's focus on ownership, shall we?" Cox said, changing gears. "Exactly how did you establish ownership?"

"I didn't. Sig did that. My expertise is in furniture. His is in authenticity — and ownership." Fritz gathered herself and stood. "I'm sorry, I can't help you any further. You must excuse me. I didn't think this would take this long and I have another engagement." She stood, walked to the door and held it open.

"Here's my card," Leslie said, passing the frail looking woman on her way out. "Please call if you remember anything further that might be of help."

# TWENTY

BACK AT HEADQUARTERS, COX HOVERED behind Leslie as she reviewed the file. She turned to face him. "What's troubling you?" she asked. "You're pacing like an expectant father."

"I screwed up!" he blurted. "Interview was going so well. You and Fritz were on the same wavelength. I ask a question and whamo, she throws us out."

"If I'm not upset, you needn't be either."

"Would I even know if you're upset?"

"Haven't you learned by now? I have something to say, I say it. Period."

"But I..."

"You hit a sensitive spot. The heart of the matter you ask me."

"How so?"

"Far as we know, everything was going along fine. Fuller finds a lost artifact. Fuller traces ownership to Ernie Chlad. Chlad pays Fuller for expenses. Chlad comes into possession of something of great value, something worth possibly a half-billion to the right buyer. The artifact goes on exhibit around the country and ends up at the Carnegie Science Center in Pittsburgh. Everything's on track for a huge payday for Chlad — and for Fuller. Then the wheels fall off! Carnegie determines that the newly arrived Chladni euphon doesn't match the specification — a specification presumably provided by Fuller himself. Within a day, Sigmond Fuller, the man who pronounced the euphon genuine, is murdered."

"I understand all that. I still don't see how that ties in with Fritz throwing us out."

"Your line of questioning pertained to ownership. The euphon originally belonged to Chladni that's a given."

"Only if it's genuine," Cox stipulated, "as Fuller claimed it was."

"There is that to consider. Yes. Presumably Fuller was correct in his assessment. Then..."

"I suppose you're right, Les. Polish government thought Fuller was correct. They declared it a national treasure and granted permission for it to leave the country for a limited time."

"Good point," Leslie conceded. "The euphon, hidden as it was, could not have been sold, so it passed down ten generations in the Chladni family. Then the question becomes; how in the hell is everyone so positive Ernst Chlad, of Lee County, Florida, has undisputed ownership? Fritz appears to be sensitive on that subject. Your questions smoked that out."

"You think she knows more than she's saying?"

"Bet my badge something's bothering her. By the way, there's nothing in the file about Carol Chlad arriving late for her luncheon. Where did your security camera question come from?"

"From video I got from a friend who works security over there. Trouble was, when I saw the video, I didn't know what she looked like so I could be confused. Now that I've seen her in person, I'll review the footage. The person I saw came in closer to twelve-fifteen than eleven fifty-five as she'd like us to believe. I didn't put it in the file because I wasn't certain I had the right woman."

Leslie, noting that her new partner had friends everywhere, asked, "What do you believe accounts for her tardiness?"

"Could be just doddering. Or could be she ran an errand on the way over. Or...or it just could be she visited Fuller. After all, he may have cheated her out of a big pay day."

"A pay day to the tune of over a hundred million depending how you view it," Leslie added. "You like her for the hanging?"

"In your initial interview she refused to go with her husband to Poland to work on getting the Chladni because she doesn't like cold weather. Now she's leaving for Poland. Guess what? It's January — and cold in Poland."

"If human inconsistency is enough for a person to become a homicide suspect, then we're all in big trouble."

"Just sayin', don't rule her out."

"I'm more interested in the husband. He admits being at the Fuller house at the right time. He says he didn't get to see Fuller. That remains to be seen. His alibi, such as it is, consists of him then going to the beach alone. Had lunch at a vendor stand we can't confirm."

"Plan?" Cox asked, content to follow Leslie's lead.

"Plain and simple. We need more on Chlad. As well as on all the folks who had the most to gain with Fuller dead."

"I suppose we should add to your list people who had big dreams riding on the good doctor being correct in his claim of authenticity."

"Good point," Leslie conceded. "I suppose you have the Seminal Society collectors in mind."

"I'd start with the ones bidding for the Chladni. Colton's one. The Kumars are another, except for the fact they seem to have dropped out."

"Or so they want us to believe," Leslie added. "Riya seems to be the driving force in that marriage. At least as a collector."

"Why does that surprise you?"

"Stereotype of Indian marriages, I suppose. Have to add Stratis to that list as well."

"Who the hell's Stratis?" Cox demanded. "Fritz mentioned that name as well. Can't find his name in the file."

Leslie had just screwed up. Her conversations with Stratis during the McDermitt investigation had been off the record. She had communicated her Stratis interview in person to Fischer and to her direct boss, Sergeant Hudson Oakmore. Sharing the information with Cox could prove counter-productive. On the other hand, now that Cox had a thread, he would pull on it until everything unraveled. Not sure how this would turn out, she took a chance. "I'm about to tell you something that must remain off the record and between you, me, Fish, and the brass. Will you honor that?"

"So long as it doesn't involve breaking the law."

"I assure you Hud and Boots both know about it. So far, it's not much of anything. It's future possibilities we're playing for. A heads-up here and there type of thing."

"I'm in."

Leslie sucked in her breath. "His name is Morris Dexter Stratis. Family business is window technology based in Pittsburgh. Worth in the multi-billions. He's an art enthusiast and supports galleries and museums around the world. Nothing happens in the art world without his knowledge. He's a member of the Seminal Society and I'm positive he has his sights on possessing the Chladni."

"Assuming it's not a fake."

"No one, especially not Stratis, is paying that much money for a fake. We're missing something here."

"Then you believe the original is still in play."

"I don't know what to believe. But, for the Fuller investigation, I think we should assume the Pittsburgh euphon is the original and play our cards accordingly. That is, until we learn otherwise."

"You think there's a second euphon running around somewhere?"

"That would make sense. Unless I miss my guess, the second one, the real fake, will find its way over to Poland and be accepted as the genuine original."

Cox thought a moment, then added, "With the expert, Fuller, dead, it certainly makes it easier to pass off a duplicate as the original."

"My thought exactly.

"From the little I remember of high school physics," Cox added, "I think the length — and possibly the diameter — of a glass rod determines the frequency of its vibration — and hence its musical sound. We did an experiment with crystal glasses. Tapped them and they vibrated, making whistling sounds."

Leslie, impressed with Cox's scientific approach, added "We did the same. Only I remember something about lead in the glass. And, let's not forget the wood with the special joints and the veneer. There are, I can imagine, several factors to consider for authentication. We can confirm all that later. In truth, our concern is Fuller's homicide, not missing artifacts. I only care about the Chladni in so far as it leads us to the killer. Need to let Poland — or the insurance company — straighten out authenticity. Not our concern."

"It strikes me," Cox replied, "the Polish government believes the original Chladni was on display in the U.S. Can't believe they'll do nothing about the loss — if there is one."

"Good point. That would involve the State Department and who knows how many federal agencies. Let's keep our heads down and dot the i's and cross the t's. How about you going over the financial records of Fuller and Fritz, say for the past five years. All deposits, expenditures. You know the drill. I suggest lining up a Criminal Investigative Assistant to help. Try to get Lizbeth Hillard assigned. Woman has a double masters from Florida Gulf Coast University in Math and Criminal Justice."

"Know her well. Good woman. Anything specific you're looking for?"

"Anything that stands out," Leslie answered, silently berating herself for not realizing Cox would know an attractive single woman. "I was thinking along the lines of foreign transactions, accounts, partnerships, trips to money laundering countries. Don't forget Fuller's cell phone. If you need search warrants, they should be easy to obtain."

"And you? What will…"

"I'm thinking of putting together an argument for a search warrant for the Chlads' financial records. As I see it, our friends, Ernie and Carol, are sitting in the eye of the storm."

———

"Allen," Leslie said into her phone when Cox retreated to his own desk, "dinner at your place or mine?"

"What ever happened to, hello, how are you? Having a good day?"

"Thought I'd cut to the chase. Judging from the sound of your voice when you answered my call, I knew you were having a good day. Am I right?"

"As rain. Trial's going as well as a trial can go. You're forgiven. How about mine, seven-thirty. Have back-to back hearings in the morning, but for once I'm ahead of them."

"That brings me to another subject. Need a search warrant. Financial and phone records for a possible suspect in the Fuller homicide."

"So, dinner talk was a ploy to soften me up for legal help."

"Maybe the warrant question is an afterthought?"

"Nothing in your life Leslie is an afterthought. I don't kid myself. Nothing! So, who's the target?"

"Ernst and Carol Chlad."

"The owner of the Chladni? Didn't you say it was a fake?"

"I don't know about it being a fake, only that a glass rod dimension was wrong when the euphon arrived in Pittsburgh."

"I thought Fuller certified it before he sent it up to Pittsburgh. Something change?"

"That's what's so troubling here. Could be Fuller was part of some sort of a fraud being perpetrated on the Chlads. They paid Fuller a lot of money to find the euphon and certify it genuine. Now the authenticity is called into question. That's a strong motive for homicide — for both of them. And they both had opportunity. Because Fuller was a hanging, they both also had means. Do I need anything more than that for a warrant?"

"Get me the Chlad's full names, address and whatever other info you have on them. I'll put something together for their bank accounts."

"I suppose their house is off limits?"

"Now you're pushing it. Be lucky to get the financials."

"Please get me what you can. As soon as you can. Appreciate it. Love you. See you later."

While she was talking to Allen a text arrived from JAK.

PICK ME UP TODAY — 7:18 RSW — ALONE.

Unfortunately, dinner with Allen would have to wait.

# TWENTY-ONE

LESLIE CAME TO A STOP at 7:15 PM directly in front of the door serving American Airlines arrivals. American, she had determined, was the only airline with a plane scheduled to land at 7:18. While waiting, she replayed her previous work in Pittsburgh with Pete Jakowski, the fifty-some-thing detective. She had pleasant memories of the well-maintained large man with the shoulders of a former Steeler defensive lineman, which he had been. His hard-set jaw and firm grasp were offset by jovial eyes. She recalled him being a great listener and an astute detective who loved leisurely dining.

"Thanks for picking me up, Leslie," he said, interrupting her thoughts. Throwing his jacket and small bag in the back seat, he slid gracefully into the passenger seat. "Nice seeing you again. What great weather you have down here. How've you been?"

"Can't complain," Leslie answered. "And you? COVID treating you and your family okay?"

"Knock on wood, everyone's fine. Heard about your partner getting shot. Understand you're both lucky to be alive."

"How the hell..."

"No great mystery. I called Boots to brief her. Apparently, she doesn't...let's just say, have a lot of faith in that guy Cox working with you now."

"Then why the hell did she assign him to me?"

"Can't answer you. Never been able to explain what bosses do. Put on earth to harass you. That's

185

my take. One of those mysteries of the universe I suppose. Hey, I'm starving."

"What're you in the mood for?"

"Haven't had a Cuban in years. Know any good places? I'm buying."

"Matter of fact, not far from here. Artisan Eatery over on Daniels. Less than ten minutes. Curious. What's a Pittsburgh guy like you know from Cuban food?"

"Probably more than a Mississippi girl like you."

"First of all, my girlhood is far behind. Secondly, I lived in Tampa for over seven years. They have the best Cubans."

"You'll have to take me up there sometime. Back when I played ball a bunch of us looked forward to playing the Tampa Bay Bucs. Often, we'd arrive in town Friday late afternoon and head straight for Ybor City and a great little place. Carmines. Been there since the late forties. Nobody does deviled crab like they do."

"You're a restaurant connoisseur, I see. Loved Carmines. I remember the place you took me to in Pittsburgh. Great little place. Quiet. Good food."

"What else is life about? My wife loves to cook, but to me there's something special about restaurants." Jakowski studied his phone a moment. "How long to where we're going?

"About five-seven minutes. Why?"

"Need you to instruct Cox to get over to Page Field as soon as he can. Cargo plane's landing with the Chladni from Pittsburgh. Exhibit was canceled. I want him to note in the file the time of unloading, the description of the freight, the location they take the cargo to, time of delivery at that location. Under no circumstances is he to be seen or to interfere in any way. Once the location is determined he's to get the hell out of there."

186

"Timing?"

"It's 7:25 now. Plane's scheduled for 8:45, give or take. Tail marking, Specialty Forwarders. Gives him an hour and change to get over there."

"How the hell's he supposed to witness what cargo comes off a plane. That'll happen in a hanger somewhere."

"He's a cop, isn't he? He's got a shield. It's a small field relatively speaking. He'll manage."

A few minutes later Leslie pulled into the Artisan Eatery parking lot. "We're here. I'll text Cox. But why him?" she asked. "We're not that far away. We can handle it ourselves."

"You and I'll be busy with your friend Stratis. His plane lands a little later. At nine-fifteen."

"Won't we be tripping over Cox? Thought you didn't want him knowing you're here."

"Stratis lands in Naples."

"Gives us about an hour, a little less, for dinner," Leslie said, doing the math.

"Come, we'll go in and over our sandwiches you can tell me how you're progressing with Allen."

Bristling, Leslie took her time before responding. "If you don't mind," she finally admonished, "let's concentrate on the investigation. I prefer not to mix work with pleasure."

"So, Allen's pleasure," Jakowski said, holding the door for her. "That's good. Order and I'll fill you in." The restaurant was practicing social distancing, allowing plenty of space between tables.

While they waited for their order to arrive, Jakowski said, "From what you said, I assume you're uncomfortable with Cox as a partner."

Leslie, caught off guard by the question, took a moment to answer, debating how truthful she wanted to be with a detective who worked a thousand miles away, but who seemed to know everything about her job and relationships. "Truthfully," she began, "he's conducted two interviews that I wish I had been there for. If I'm being honest, I'd say he did a good job. And for each of them he had a reason to go it alone — because of timing."

The waiter arrived, his mask now hanging below his nose, and placed their order on the table. Cuban sandwiches for each of them and a side of sweet potato fries for Jakowski. Water for both of them.

"A beer would sure go well with this sandwich," Jakowski commented, "but we're both on duty. Order one if you want. I won't tell."

"As you said, we're on duty."

"Leslie, you're being entirely too nice. It's your case, Cox's assigned to assist. From what I gather he's overstepping."

"You've been around this business about as long as I've been alive. You can demand what you want. I'm barely out of diapers down here. I've cut one tooth — with your help I might add — so I can't be throwing my weight around. It'll take a while, but I'll get Cox in line, even though he's senior to me."

"He's only senior in Lee County. You have years on him in uniform. Just know you have Boots' blessing to do what you must."

"You and Boots," Leslie said, realizing he knew far more than what a police captain with Stetson's reputation would normally confide in anyone, let alone a man from another police department, "speaking of relationships, what'm I missing here?"

Now it was Jakowski's turn to fall quiet. For the first time since she'd known the big guy, he turned his head away when he spoke. "Karen and I...well, we had a relationship back when we both first started. We were teamed together in an FBI training group at Quantico. One thing led to another. We've managed to remain friends ever since."

"Am I the last to know?"

"Matter of fact, you're the first—and only. Please keep it that way."

"If it doesn't need to go into the file, then it doesn't pass my lips. Easy rule to follow."

"Okay, I promised to brief you. Here goes. I'd like to start at the beginning, but I'm not certain there is one. The Chladni was last documented as having been seen at Chladni's death. After that there are all kinds of rumors and stories, some dealing with Russian generals, others with the Germans. As it turns out, none of them are true. The euphon was stolen at Chladni's death and hidden in a false wall. That's where Sig—the deceased Dr. Fuller—found it."

"I've heard the stories," Leslie commented. "Truthfully, I don't know what to make of the euphon, or of the discrepancy uncovered by the Carnegie Science Center, as it all pertains to Fuller's murder."

"Frankly, I don't either. But that's your matter. I'm here at the request of the Feds."

"Feds? What's that about?"

"I'm a Stratis expert. Thought I had him several times, but the guy's a frickin' genius. A clever genius at that. We know full well he commissions forgeries of very substantial art pieces."

"If everyone knows he's a forger," Leslie commented, confused, "why continue to support him?"

"Because so many of his pieces are in museums around the world, they don't want their world crashing down. Museums are content with the status quo. IRS has been investigating him for tax fraud for years. It's now believed they have an internal leak and that's why he slips through their traps. I've been tasked to assist."

"Lucky you."

"Change of scene. Good every now and again."

At 8:40 Leslie read a text from Cox saying the cargo plane had landed a few minutes early and was taxiing to Hanger 16.

"Let me know when the cargo we're interested in is loaded on the truck," Jakowski instructed.

Leslie dutifully sent instructions to Cox and then turned to the big detective. "If we're to be at the Naples airport at nine-fifteen, better get going."

"I've changed my thoughts as to how we should handle Stratis. We'll allow him to come to us. All we really need is to know where the euphon is being delivered. Cox will provide that information. Everything else will work from there."

"Not been unloaded yet according to Cox."

"Then we sit tight."

At 9:05 a message from Cox confirmed a crate had been unloaded onto a Specialty Forwarders van. Jakowski called for the check, left money on the table and the two of them went out to the car.

"We'll sit here a while, see where that van goes."

At 9:15 a message from Cox told them the truck was heading south on Route 41.

"All's going according to plan — so far," Jakowski said.

"Mind letting me in on this plan?"

"The euphon, unless I miss my guess, is going to the home of Ernst Chlad."

"Ernst Chlad, the owner?"

"One and the same. Once that's confirmed, that's where we're heading."

"And?"

"And wait for your friend Stratis to show up."

"And?"

"And if Stratis leaves Chlad's house with a euphon we'll know for certain it's the genuine article."

"And just how will we know that? More to the point, how will Stratis know the genuine one from a fake one?"

"He'll use a frequency meter. They'll test each and every glass rod. If all the frequencies line up, its genuine. Trust me, Leslie, Stratis has been in this game far too long to pay for fakes."

"Best guess. How much will the Chlads be paid?"

"I'd say around a hundred million, possibly as much as one and a half, in one form or another. It'll be deposited in some obscure bank account in the Cayman Islands or wherever."

"Your part in all this?" Leslie asked, not sure where Jakowski fit in and how much she should believe.

"Just guessing. I'm here to be certain the right euphon is returned to Poland. I'm to document what I see and hear. Let the IRS do the rest."

At 9:15 Jakowski studied his phone, then said, "Stratis just landed. Game on!"

Several minutes later Leslie's cell buzzed with a message from Cox saying the van was unloading the crate at Chlad's house.

"Okay," Jakowski said after being told where the crate was going. "Let's roll. To Chlad's place."

They drove in silence a few minutes before Jakowski asked, "Who you have for Fuller?"

"I personally like Chlad. Had plenty of motive if he thought Fuller had defrauded him. Can't account for his time in any meaningful way. His wife's timeline's not much better. The woman seems to have memory issues. Then there's Fuller's fiancée, Selma Fritz. She had access, but no apparent motive. We can toss that Seminal Society collector, Colton, right in the middle of the heap. Speaking of Seminal Society, I'd add Stratis as well. While we're at it, the Kumars belong on the list as well."

"Stratis? He wasn't even down here."

"You know that for a fact?"

"His plane just now landed."

"Could'a been here and gone. Coming back to the scene as it were."

Jakowski changed the subject. "Let's return to the Chladni euphon and Poland. Fuller convinces Chlad that he's a distant relative of Chladni. That much is accurate as far as we know. Fuller then persuades Chlad to accompany him to Poland, initially on Fuller's dime. Fuller continues working on finding the euphon and eventually convinces Chlad to pony up expenses. Apparently, Chlad's wife had inherited a large sum from her father. When Fuller finds the euphon, all hell breaks loose in Poland. Lots of publicity, the whole nine yards. The problem suddenly switches from finding the treasure to getting it out of the country legally."

"Hold up a moment," Leslie said. "I'm not buying ten generations. Chlad, if he has ownership at all, would have to share it with perhaps a hundred, or even more, others. How could he...?"

"Here's the thing, Leslie. Poland declared it a national treasure. That being so, they don't need a true owner. They just claim it as theirs, and it really is theirs."

"I can buy that. Then why bother dealing with Chlad at all?"

"Problem with that approach is it would result in costly and protracted litigation. Better for them to certify one person as the true owner. That person is our Ernst Chlad. Poland then can take title back from the true owner. Effectively makes it easy — and quick — for the Polish courts to decide ownership. Nice and neat. And that's exactly what they did."

Leslie's eyes narrowed in cynicism. "You're saying the Polish government signed with Ernst Chlad to expedite the process."

"Between you and me, it's naïve to believe money didn't exchange hands."

"That a fact — or speculation?" Leslie asked, as she turned onto Chlad's street and slowed.

Instead of answering her question, Jakowski instructed, "No, don't park in front of his house!" A light was on in a back bedroom. Other than that, it was dark. "Go down the block and park out of sight of the house. We'll walk back and find an observation spot. I want to see, and be close enough to hear, exactly what happens when Stratis arrives."

"You know," Leslie said when they were half-way back to Chlad's, "we could have followed the Chladni ourselves from the airport and accomplished the same thing. Didn't need to get Cox involved at all."

"And give up a great Cuban?" The big guy laughed, his face and eyes animated. "No, seriously, you've been complaining of him leaving you out of the loop. How would you explain this if you hadn't included him?"

"He's being excluded right now. What will I tell him?"

"You're clever. You'll figure something out. Now, we need to be absolutely certain it's Stratis who visits Chlad. If not, my whole plan is wrong."

"And if your plan is right, then what?"

"Then you and I are on the morning flight."

"To where?"

"Warsaw."

# TWENTY-TWO

WHILE JAKOWSKI FOCUSED ON THE on-going operation, Leslie struggled to process what she had just heard. Nothing the big cop said made sense, especially the part about going to Poland.

"The euphon from Pittsburgh is now in Chlad's possession," he whispered as they approached the house. "If it all works out, he's off to Poland in the morning on the early flight. Goes through Paris. You and I leave a bit later and fly into Frankfurt."

"Isn't his wife going with him?" Leslie managed, forcing herself to focus. Carol Chlad had said she was traveling, so that part added up.

"Originally, yes. Plans changed. He's going alone."

"I assume you've cleared all this with the brass. I can't be..."

"Goes higher than that," Jakowski interrupted. "If we get that far, I'll brief you on the plane."

"I need to let Allen know I'll be..."

"All you're authorized to tell him is that you'll be undercover for a while and not to expect communication."

"He's to be told nothing!"

"Boots'll brief him."

"You kidding me? Boots'll brief Allen? That makes no sense at all!"

"Do I look like I'm kidding? And that goes for Cox, as well."

"This is bonkers! I'm a local detective. A freshly minted one at that. Now you have me traveling the world, getting involved in God knows what! My

194

job's right here working on the Fuller homicide, not trying to solve a global art fraud — or money laundering — or tax fraud — or whatever the hell's going on."

"They go hand in hand. Solve the fraud, you'll solve the homicide."

"'I'm not buying that!" Jakowski wasn't making sense, causing Leslie to wonder what she was missing. Frustrated, she asked, "Why, if Stratis saw the euphon at the exhibit in Pittsburgh does he need to also see it here in Florida? You've lost me."

"The man's about to spring for a hundred or so million. He needs to see, touch, and listen to the prize up close and personal. That's what he lives for."

"But it's a fake!" Leslie corrected herself. "Carnegie found that the Chladni euphon had an improper glass rod. That makes it suspect at best."

"Never mind what the Carnegie report said. Someone may have substituted a wrong glass rod for the proper one to have the euphon declared suspicious. Fuller was too good to get that wrong. If Fuller certified the euphon as being genuine, then trust me, it was genuine when it left his possession."

"Carnegie thought it was suspicious enough to pull the exhibit. They didn't do that lightly!"

"Carnegie pulled it because exhibition funding was revoked by Stratis after the rod was found to be wrong. That doesn't make the euphon fake. Not by a long shot."

"Are you suggesting Stratis orchestrated the substitution?"

"The possibility crossed my mind," Jakowski replied, his eyes again on his cell.

"You still haven't told me why we're going to Poland?"

"For reasons I will elaborate on the plane, the Polish Government has reason to trust me. They must sign off on the return of the original. I'll vouch for the fact that Stratis is satisfied and that will go a long way to satisfying them."

"I see no need for me in all this. I add nothing to the Polish side of this."

"It's a task force joint operation. You were assigned to the task force. I believe Boots even briefed you."

"Feels wrong, is all."

"You want to explain that to your management?"

"Why must the Poles sign off?" Leslie asked, not responding to the big guy's challenge. "I mean it's theirs, isn't it?"

"If somehow the original goes missing, or a fake is introduced, then this all becomes a cultural art theft and Interpol becomes involved. The FBI is called in and the shit hits the fan. Our job is to avoid an international incident."

"Let me understand you. You're saying that if the Polish Government is satisfied with the returned euphon being genuine then law enforcement stands down."

"Exactly what I'm saying."

"Then just why is Stratis still interested? It doesn't add..."

"What if a second euphon has been constructed. One so perfect that even the Poles can't detect it. The original would then be available to the highest bidder."

"Jak, if I'm hearing correctly, you and I may be delivering a copy of the original euphon to the Polish government. You seem prepared to put your name on the dotted line. I want no part..."

"Speculation, Leslie. Speculation. For all we know, the euphon from Pittsburgh, but with all the correct rods, will be on that plane with Chlad.

Now get yourself hidden. Stratis is no more than five minutes out."

Leslie, being as slender as she was, had no trouble slipping in behind an oak without a shadow showing. It was a different story for the former footballer who had to settle for sitting on the ground behind an over-grown hedge near the front door. She had to give him credit. Once he was settled, she couldn't see him even though she knew exactly where to look. The lawn was still damp from what Leslie guessed was an earlier watering and the thought crossed her mind that football players just didn't care about things such as wet and grass-stained slacks.

Eight minutes later a black Lincoln Town Car turned the corner and rolled to a stop in front of the Chlad house. The doors remained closed for several minutes and the dark windows yielded no clue as to the occupants. Leslie half-expected the Chlad front door to open and Ernst to walk out to the car.

Slowly the back car door opened allowing Leslie to see a man who she tentatively identified as Morris Dexter Stratis, sitting with a small leather bag in his lap. A moment later the man climbed out, pausing to study the surroundings, before proceeding to the house. The car then continued down the street, coming to a stop not more than twenty feet behind her parked car.

Leslie confirmed her initial identification.

The light over the front door turned on and the door opened as Stratis approached. Leslie heard Ernst Chlad say, "It is nice to see you again, Mr. ..."

"Please," Stratis interrupted. " I prefer we talk in the house."

"I'm so sorry," Chlad apologized. "Come on in." The door closed behind Stratis, but the light remained on.

The silence was broken by muffled voices coming from inside the garage. Leslie motioned to Jakowski, who signaled he heard nothing.

Soon, musical sounds penetrated the closed garage door. Leslie recognized them as coming from vibrating glass rods, most likely those of the euphon. One note at a time in progression from lowest to highest in frequency.

The sounds ceased, allowing an unsettling silence to fall over the yard. Leslie pressed tighter against the tree expecting Stratis to emerge from the house. But the front door remained closed.

Then the notes repeated, identical to the first time, but spaced closer together. "Ghostly," Leslie told herself. "Positively, Ghostly."

Again, silence settled in, with no further sound from the garage.

Ten minutes passed and nothing changed until the detectives heard the Town Car approaching, its engine a low hum.

The front door opened. "Have a safe trip and good luck in Warsaw," she heard Stratis say before the door closed. He then walked briskly to the waiting car carrying an elongated crate. His driver met him halfway, took the crate and fitted it into the large trunk. A moment later they drove off.

"Now what?" Leslie inquired of the slowly rising big man.

"Didn't do my pants much of a favor," he whispered, brushing mulch, dirt and grass-clippings from his trousers. Jakowski didn't speak again until they were seated in Leslie's car. "All in a day's work, I suppose. So, what did you hear?"

"Euphon — or at least I think it was the euphon. Only it sounded like individual tones and not music. Twice. Someone played the notes twice."

"Not unexpected. As I said, Stratis had a meter with him and took frequency measurements."

"Should I then assume he was satisfied and took the euphon with him? Is that what was in the crate?"

"You took a picture if I saw right."

"He had his back to me. Looked safe enough." She brought the picture up on her phone and sent him a copy.

"Text it to Cox as well. See if he recognizes it."

Within a minute they had their answer. That's the crate delivered to Chlad at 9:26 PM.

An instant later, a time-stamped picture appeared on her phone from Cox showing the exact same crate, including a greasy smudge on the top left corner.

"In answer to your question about what we do next. Drop me at the Hilton Inn. Plan to pick me up in the morning at six."

"Six? I thought we're on a later flight."

"Chlad's flight's at nine. We need to see him check his bags and make certain he boards. We also need to verify the security folks are in place."

"You don't need me for that. Airport's a mile away from your hotel. Take the shuttle. Or call an Uber."

"I have no jurisdiction without you."

That comment made no sense — unless he was planning to arrest someone. Which also made no sense. Instead of debating the issue, she drove the two miles to the hotel in silence anxious to be rid of the big guy.

Missing her dinner with Allen bothered her more than she had thought it would. The instant Jakowski closed the car door behind him, his last words, "Don't forget your passport," still ringing in her ears, she hit the speed-dial code for Allen.

A groggy voice answered. "Gave up on you an hour ago," he mumbled through sleep-laden lips. "What's going on?"

"Sorry to wake you. I wanted to apologize for skipping dinner tonight. I'm sorry. Stuff came up at the last minute."

"What kinda stuff?"

Leslie visualized Allen now sitting up in bed, his mind engaging. "Just know I love you."

"You say that as though something bad is about to happen — or happened."

"I wish I could tell you, but I can't. Just know I'm safe and everything's okay."

"Sounds to me as though it's not. What's up? Are you in...in some kind of trouble?"

"I'm going under-cover for a while. Will be out of contact."

"For how long?"

"That's just it. I don't know."

"You weren't trained for..."

"Actually, I was. Allen honey, please let's not debate this. I can't..."

"Are you coming over here tonight or..."

"Can't. Gotta go to my place. I'm sorry."

"I'm sorry too. This have something to do with Cox?"

"Now why would you be asking that?"

"I've checked around. He has a reputation for..."

"Allen! Enough! It's been a long day! I'm exhausted. Need to get up early and..." She caught herself before saying, "pack," and substituted, "...meet the team."

"It's just that..."

"Need to go now. Love you. Talk when I can."

"Okay. Love you as well. Please stay safe."

She wanted to reply, "As safe as a cop ever can be." But that wouldn't be at all helpful. Instead, she said, "Good night, my love," and clicked off before he could respond.

Before going to bed, Leslie tossed a week's worth of blouses, slacks and undies in her bag, added an extra pair of shoes and a travel toiletry bag, took a shower and set her alarm for 5 AM. Sitting on her bed, she pulled up the file and entered all that had happened since meeting Jakowski, who she identified only as Informant.

# TWENTY-THREE

LESLIE PARKED IN FRONT OF the Hilton Inn a few minutes early and watched as two men and a woman boarded the shuttle bus. She focused on the upcoming trip and bitter-sweet memories flooded in. Leslie and Junior had planned a Paris trip for their fifth anniversary. They had to cancel at the last minute when Junior's father was hit by a car and nearly died. He was in a coma for six days and Junior wouldn't leave his bedside. By the time his father had recovered, vacation days were gone. They postponed Paris until their tenth. Junior died one month shy of their ninth.

The tap on her window startled her. "You're in your own world," Jakowski said when she rolled down her window. "Pop the trunk and we're outta here."

"Sleep well?" he inquired, pulling the passenger door closed behind him.

"As well as can be expected," Leslie replied. "Did you?"

"You sound down. Thought you'd be excited. This being your first time out of the country."

"My travel history's not your concern," she snapped, angry with herself for being so transparent.

"What's with that bee in your bonnet? We've got a long day ahead of us, so let's get to the bottom of what's troubling you."

"Your antics got Cox rousted by your secret friends! What the hell's that about?"

"Let's just say he got himself rousted by staking out Chlad's house against instructions."

Leslie looked at him, her eyes narrowed in controlled anger. "Busted by a Homeland Security agent? Since when does DHS waltz in and take over local cases? I call bullshit, you wanna know!"

"Hold on a moment," Jakowski replied. "I'm working with Treasury, not Homeland Security. I've no idea what..."

"File says Boots removed him per DHS."

"I thought you wanted him gone."

"So, you're admitting it was you and not DHS?"

"You have to admit, he didn't follow your directions."

"Then it's up to me to take action! I don't need you — or anyone — swooping to my rescue! You obviously have connections, seeing as how you know my travel history."

"A little research goes a long way. And, for the record, I didn't swoop to your rescue. I briefed Boots and she did the rest on her own." Leslie remained silent and Jakowski continued, "The plan right now is to go to Chlad's house and — from a distance — escort him to the airport."

"Explain again what that's about." Leslie knew the plan, but it hadn't made sense last night — and still didn't.

"There's no percentage us traveling all the way to Poland only to learn Chlad didn't bring the euphon. Can't leave anything to chance."

Skepticism written across her face, Leslie commented, "Sounds squirrelly to me. You're not making sense."

"Humor me on this. IRS expects me to stay close to him. They want a record of everything he does. That includes loading his car, making certain the euphon is on that plane and that it's delivered to the Polish government. When they bust him for tax fraud, they want solid proof."

Remaining unconvinced, Leslie nonetheless turned right onto Ben Hill Griffin Parkway and headed south toward Miromar Lakes. "I hope you know what the hell you're doing."

Jakowski didn't answer, remaining silent for the six-minute drive. Turning into the gated community, Leslie said, "You ask me, this entire operation is...well, it doesn't pass the smell test."

"Depends on who's doing the smelling. Part of the reason I'm going is that I'm a known entity to the IRS as well as to the Polish officials who will be certifying the authenticity of the euphon."

"Dubious, I'd say, at best."

"What's dubious?"

"Authenticity. We both believe Stratis has the original. The Chladni at Chlad's house, if, in fact, there is a Chladni at Chlad's house, is a duplicate. You'll be certifying a phony!"

"I'm not certifying anything. Just providing security. My role is to vouch that the euphon traveled from Pittsburgh to Chlad's house in Florida. And from Chlad's house to Warsaw."

"And my job?" Leslie asked, remaining confused.

"A Florida police officer witnessing that the euphon traveled from Chlad's house in Florida to Warsaw."

"I don't even know what's in those bags."

"That's someone else's problem. We just need to certify we saw the bags leave Chlad's."

Leslie slowed the car in front of the Chlad home prompting Jakowski to say, "Go up the block, turn around and park where we did last night. We can observe the house from there."

"You wanted to see him load his trunk. How the hell you gonna..."

"He'll open his garage door before he loads the baggage. Everybody does. If not, we're screwed."

Twenty-five minutes later, the Chlad garage door, as Jakowski had predicted, started up. "Okay now," Jakowski instructed, "drive slowly down the street. I'll video as we go. Stop just before their house. He'll pay no attention."

"What if he makes me?"

"Wave. Stop. Get out and tell him you knew he was leaving today and you had one more question."

"What question?"

"Make something up. Hey, we're in luck. I see the leather bags. Slow, so I can zoom in. Okay, now keep moving. We'll wait down there a few houses for him to pass. Plan's working."

"Glad to hear it," Leslie replied. "Now your Florida cop can report she witnessed a man in Florida place his bags in the trunk of his car."

"That'll mean a lot to the Polish authorities," Jakowski replied, his attention remaining focused on Chlad, apparently unaware of Leslie's sarcasm. Less than five minutes later Chlad's light green Mercedes drove past them. "We know where they're heading," Jakowski said. "So keep a good distance back."

"Aye, aye," Leslie answered, suppressing the urge to throw a salute.

"Now what the hell's bothering you?" the detective asked. "You always this moody?"

"Screw you!" Leslie barked. "I'm tired of your damn games!"

"To what do I owe this outburst?"

"Those bags you threw in the trunk. That's what!"

"What about those bags? What the hell's eating you?"

"For starters! When I picked you up at the airport last night you had a small bag. Now you have two bags. You're playing me! That's what!"

The big detective looked at her a moment before responding. "Bags missed the flight. All I had was my carry on. Those two were delivered to the hotel while we were staking out Chlad's, if you need to know."

Leslie immediately felt foolish. Two partners, first Cox and now Jakowski, brought out the worst in her. Was it them — or her? "I apologize for the outburst," she said. "My bad."

A few minutes later the green Mercedes pulled to a stop in front of the international drop off gate. Leslie parked several car lengths behind Chlad. A porter approached his car, the trunk went up, and one large suitcase was removed and curbside checked. Chlad then drove off.

Jakowski nodded and Leslie followed from a distance. Halfway around the large airport oval Chlad turned left under the sign reading: Long-Term Parking.

Leslie followed.

"Hang back a bit," Jakowski said. "Don't want him making us. Stop out of the way, but where we can see him unload the two leather bags. He'll carry them on board. Too valuable to check."

Leslie followed instructions while the big detective captured video of Chlad parking his car and then proceeding to the shuttle carrying a small handbag along with the leather bags.

"Good news," Jakowski quipped a moment later, "got a good video record for our Polish friends. Go park. We'll catch the next shuttle to the terminal. We'll pick him up at the ticket counter."

The parking lot shuttle bus took longer than expected to pick them up and when the two detectives finally arrived at the terminal, Chlad was nowhere to be seen. "Let's try security," Leslie suggested, having noticed a long line.

"Good call, Hodges," Jakowski commented five minutes later when they spotted Chlad about to display his boarding pass to TSA.

"Come on," Jakowski said to Leslie after having watched Chlad and two security guards, a man and a woman, pass through screening, "let's check-in, get our boarding passes and do the TSA bit. Then we can keep an eye on him as well as catch breakfast. Coffee will go good about now."

"Best thing you've said all morning," Leslie replied, following Jakowski in the direction of the ticket counter. "That coffee's calling."

Leslie was surprised to learn they were going First Class and would be served several meals en route. "You'll be pampered," the ticket agent assured her. "That's our specialty. We want you to arrive in Warsaw ready to go. Is this business or pleasure?"

"Little of each," Jakowski answered. "Isn't that the way to do it?"

"I suppose," the agent said. "Never had the chance myself."

The next three hours went by in slow motion. Chlad's flight left five minutes late, with him, the leather bags, and the security detail, safely aboard.

Breakfast seemed to take forever. Since there was nothing for them to do but wait for their flight, it made no difference. After eating, Leslie browsed the bookstore, buying several magazines and two books, one titled, *Owning The Grill — Never Burn Another Steak*. She planned to read it on the plane as a surprise to Allen who chided her every time she grilled something, and it came out charred. The other book was a mystery/thriller titled *The Padre Puppets* by David Harry, an author she had never heard of. The puppets on the colorful cover had caught her attention.

At 10:30 the gate area speaker system announced that First Class for their flight would be boarding momentarily. She checked the Fuller file one last time and was surprised to see a note addressed to her from Sergeant Friday requesting a call back. No number was listed. She dialed Fischer and the call went directly to voicemail. She then read a private note to her posted by Cox at 10:25 simply saying, "I was set up." There was no indication what he was referring to.

She redialed Fischer. Same result. She then dialed Cox and received a busy signal.

"First Class passengers," a male voice on the overhead speaker system announced, "you may proceed to check-in. Welcome aboard."

The First Class line began moving forward.

Jakowski said, "We're off. This should be a fun trip. A little business. And as I said to the agent back there, a little pleasure."

"What does Cox mean by I was set up?" Leslie asked.

"Leslie, what are you talking about?" Jakowski responded. "A little context for your question will help."

"Cox sent me a message saying., I was set up. Is he talking about last night?"

"Who the hell cares what that character's jabbering about? He disobeyed your direct order to not linger in front of Chlad's house. In fact, he set up surveillance, had his camera focused on the house. Got his ass busted. Not your problem."

Jakowski held out his boarding pass to the agent and the scanner dinged approvingly. "Welcome aboard, Mr. Jakowski," the agent greeted. "Enjoy your flight."

When the agent reached for her boarding pass, Leslie pulled it back and asked, "Do I have time to visit the Ladies' Room?"

"You can use the facilities aboard the plane if you wish."

"I prefer out here. Do I have time?"

"You have twenty minutes. The nearest rest room is directly across the concourse," she said, pointing to a blue toilet sign. "Hurry back."

"I'll go with you," Jakowski called.

"Sir," the agent said, stepping between them. "I'm afraid you cannot leave once you're checked on-board. If you do, you'll not be permitted to reboard."

"Be back in a moment," Leslie called over her shoulder, hurrying across the hallway to the rest room. She entered the first open stall, closing and locking the door behind her. Sitting on the toilet, she again called Fischer. Still no answer. Cox didn't answer either. She checked the file and saw that nothing new had been added.

She waited five minutes and tried both numbers again. Same result.

Checking her watch, she realized she only had ten minutes until boarding was closed. She waited another five, tried both numbers again without result.

She stood, unlocked the stall door, washed her hands out of habit, and marched out into the common terminal area fully expecting the massive former Steeler to be waiting for her.

Jakowski wasn't anywhere to be seen. In fact, the entire boarding area was now empty, except for the gate agents and a woman emptying the trash baskets.

"Paging passenger Leslie Hodges," a speaker above her head blared. "Please report to Gate D1. Your flight is in the final stages ready for departure.

This is the final call for passenger Leslie Hodges. Please report to Gate D1."

Leslie took two quick steps toward the gate area. But instead of continuing across the concourse and boarding her flight, she turned and walked briskly toward the front of the terminal.

# TWENTY-FOUR

IF LESLIE WAS LESS AGITATED, she would have realized she was being followed from the gate area, onto the parking lot shuttle, and off the bus when it stopped at her car. "Go ahead, get in," a solidly built woman said in a tone radiating authority. The woman was slightly taller than Leslie, standing five-nine, and outweighing her by perhaps seventy pounds. Leslie didn't recognize the woman, but she certainly recognized the stance. Feet slightly apart, knees flexed, ready for anything that came her way.

Leslie replayed the last five minutes and now realized that she had first seen the woman inside the terminal standing near the women's restrooms. When the woman had climbed on the shuttle a slight bulge showed in the middle of her back under her jacket.

A gun inside security. Not likely. Replay the scene.

Same result. Only now Leslie was positive. This was the same woman she had seen milling around the news shop.

"Leslie Hodges! I said, get in the car! Do it!" The woman's eyes were now as menacing as her voice.

The interior of the car was where her weapon was stored. Except it was locked in the gun safe. There was no chance Leslie could overpower this woman, not starting from the relative positions of the two women.

"I'm reaching for my key," Leslie said, trying to keep the woman calm.

"I know you are not armed," the woman said, her eyes softening ever so slightly, "you just came from the secure zone and didn't report your weapon."

Leslie pushed the unlock button on the key fob twice and both doors unlocked.

Once inside the car, the woman held up her ID long enough for Leslie to grasp who she was. "As you can see, I'm Agent Maxine Ghana, Department of Homeland Security. Please be advised everything you say is being recorded and can and will be used against you."

"I bet you're the hard ass who busted my partner last night! What the hell's going on? Why the hell are you reading me my rights?"

"All in due course. Now tell me in your own words, why didn't you board that plane?"

"Am I under arrest?"

"Not yet, you're not."

"What the hell's that mean? Not yet?"

"Means what it sounds like it means," Ghana shot back, her eyes boring into Leslie. "Just answer my questions."

"Why the hell should I tell you anything? Get the hell out of my car!"

"Remember who has the weapon."

"You remember what the hell country this is! I don't have to tell you shit! Now get out!"

Ghana's right hand reached behind her.

Leslie's tipping point had been reached. "You pull your weapon on me, that'll be the last time you ever do that! I'm a sworn peace officer in my own jurisdiction! That gun comes out you better shoot me dead or I'll arrest you for pointing a gun at a police officer. See how that plays in Washington. One thing I'll tell you for certain, it won't play well before a local Florida judge! I've done nothing improper, and you haven't said otherwise. So, tell me what the hell this is about!"

Ghana paused, saw the determination in Leslie's eyes and heard the resolve in her voice, and slowly withdrew her hand from behind her back. "Okay," Ghana said, "Suppose we start over. Perhaps we have a few things confused. Answer me this: Whose idea was it to go to Warsaw? Jakowski or you?"

"Why the hell would I ever even suggest going to Poland? My investigation is here in Florida. I have nothing to do with Poland!"

"Answer. You or Jakowski"

"Jakowski."

"Tell me why you missed the flight."

Leslie thought a moment before answering. Naively deciding the truth never hurt, she quietly responded, "It just felt wrong. Everything about leaving Florida felt wrong. My partner was removed from the investigation we were working for no good reason. It's all wrong. I don't belong in Poland. I belong here." She stopped talking, took a deep breath, then continued, her voice again in command. "Now it's time for you to explain yourself. What the hell's DHS got to do with a murder in Lee County, Florida? And you better make it good."

"Okay. Fair enough. We owe you that much, Hodges. I'll give you what I can. But a few more questions first if I may?"

Leslie reluctantly nodded consent, then added, "I'm not here for twenty questions. So, don't go fishing."

"First. Did you invite Jakowski to Florida?"

"No."

"Did you book any of the flights?"

"No."

"Did you book the hotel reservation?"

"Goodness, no! What makes you think I did?"

"Not important what I think. So, your answer is, no?"

"My answer is no."

"Let me show you an image." Ghana tapped several keys on her cell, made sliding motions across the screen with her finger, then turned the cell so Leslie could read what looked to be a receipt from At Your Service, an on-line travel booking service Leslie had never heard of.

HOTEL: RAFFLES EUROPEJSKI WARSAW
NIGHTS: 4
NUMBER IN PARTY: 2
NAME: MR. & MRS. LESLIE HODGES
RATE: $415 US/NIGHT

"What the hell!" Leslie exclaimed.

"Precisely what our team said when this popped up. Seems your cop friend has more than work on his mind. Did you know of the sleeping arrangements?"

"Of course not!" Leslie replied, reeling from what she had just read. "I don't know what to say about all this. How about you telling me..."

"Give me a moment. Need to clear it with the team. I'll step outside. You can retrieve your weapon while you're waiting."

Leslie opened the gun safe using the combination known only to her, being careful to shield the numbers. In less than five minutes Ghana was back in the car.

"Good news," the DHS agent announced. "The team has now confirmed the room was indeed booked by Jakowski, using an alias he's known to have used previously. Two other things you should know. One is that you and I are no longer being monitored by my team. And two, you're cleared for partial read-in."

"Partial?"

"This is far larger than even I'm cleared for. You're cleared for the Florida piece. Your boss, Stetson's provisionally cleared as well. Neither Cox nor Fischer have clearance."

"What about Sergeant Oakmore? I report directly to him."

"For now, he's not. If there's a need later perhaps that can be arranged."

"Stetson you say is provisional. What's that..."

"Means she's the one approved Jakowski coming to Florida. She approved you going to Warsaw with him. She's the one approved Cox for file removal. Need to vet her."

Leslie knew Jakowski had confessed to an affair with Boots causing Leslie to wonder if her boss was actively working with him on the euphon, or just plain being blackmailed. Looking directly at Ghana, she said, "How about beginning with Jakowski. What's his connection to all this?"

Ghana sat back in deep thought, apparently working through what she could reveal. Making up her mind, she looked Leslie directly in the eyes and said, "I'll fill you in on all I can, but I still need a few questions answered."

Leslie again nodded.

"Mind telling me when you first met Jakowski. And how that came about?"

"I was working a homicide. One of the suspects lived in Pittsburgh. Actually, in a suburb. I was authorized to fly up and someone, I think it was Boots..." Seeing the confusion in the agent's eyes, Leslie added, "...Captain Stetson...who arranged it with Jakowski. He met me at the airport and insisted we have dinner and do the interview the next morning."

"I take it you had no romantic involvement with Jakowski on that trip?"

"I've never had a romantic involvement with him — or anyone!" In response to Ghana's frown, Leslie added, "Other than Allen."

"Your prosecutor friend?"

"Is there anything you folks don't know about me?"

"Wouldn't be doing our jobs if there was. Now, would we?"

"I have no idea what your job is. Why don't you tell me?"

"What I can, I will. You know about the euphon. It was discovered in Poland a while back by Dr. Sigmund Fuller. You're assigned to his homicide. One of the people who facilitated the euphon leaving Poland is referred to as Esquire. He runs interference for a man we call the puppet-master. Man by the name of Morris Dexter Stratis."

"I suppose you know the real name of this guy you call Esquire?"

"More about him in a moment," Ghana promised. "As I just said, Esquire works for — or at least was hired by — Stratis for the purpose of getting the euphon legally out of Poland. I'm certain you know it's a Chladni First. Fuller authenticated the instrument and we have no reason to doubt his report. Truth is, even if it's a fake, we don't care."

"What do you care about then? What has DHS so agitated you have my partner removed from a homicide investigation?"

"I told you, that wasn't us who had him removed. Yes, I asked him to leave Chlad's house last night. That's all I did. It's Colton we're locked on to. We have reason to believe Alexandre Colton is a Russian agent. Real name: Dmitri Volkov. Reports directly to Ivan Lenkov, head of the SVR. Should Lenkov be lucky enough to live a few more years I wouldn't be surprised if he takes over from

Putin." Ghana paused. "Hey, your eyes are glazing over. You following this, or should I repeat?"

"I'm following alright. I'm working the connection of this to the death of Dr. Fuller and coming up blank."

"The murder's your jurisdiction, not ours. Frankly, his death, I hate to admit, is a footnote to our investigation."

Shocking as that sounded, Leslie knew it to be true. "If the euphon is a fake," Leslie asked, "why does Stratis remain interested? And Colton for that matter?"

"What makes you think Stratis gives a honk about the euphon?"

"Saw him last night go to Chlad's house to check out the euphon, the one delivered from the Carnegie. I believe he took it with him after having it played for him note by note."

"That's where you come in, Hodges. Jakowski, primarily because of his relationship with Stratis, has earned the Polish Cultural Minister's trust. Jakowski's flying over to Poland to vouch for the authenticity of the instrument Chlad will be delivering."

"Where do I fit in then? They don't need me to verify the euphon."

"Local police officer. Vouch for the authenticity. Window dressing mostly, want the truth."

Leslie's head filled with questions. The first being: "How could it be authentic? The exhibition was canceled because the one in Pittsburgh had a wrong glass rod."

"I assure you Chlad replaced the wrong rod with the correct one when the euphon arrived back from Pittsburgh. It won't be the rod that causes a problem. That is, if there is a problem."

"Possibly. Then why drag me to Poland? There are any number of ways Jakowski could vouch for the euphon not involving me. All that veneer and joint stuff. They could see for themselves. Why the hell go to the trouble of folding me into his scheme?"

"Allow me a bit of speculation. First, you are indeed a credible witness, being a Florida detective and all. Polish government officials are fascinated with U.S. police. Go figure." Ghana's lips formed into a thin smile. "And second, extracurricular activities with his wife, the lovely Leslie Hodges."

"Never! He and I? You got to..."

"You have to admit, sex sells. Distracts focus."

"I can promise you nothing would have..."

"Go with me on this, will you? Assume nothing of the...the romantic nature happened. That won't stop the underground gossip. The authorities will believe it because they want to believe it."

"You kidding me? I can't believe..."

"And that's just the beginning. Jakowski'll have photos, hotel records, recorded sound bites, you name it. He'll have you in his control, perhaps as he has Stetson, for a long time to come."

"Why don't you roll him up? Obviously, you have enough on Jakowski to..."

"The devil you know is better than the one you don't. So long as Stratis believes in Jakowski, it works to our benefit. Like I said, my mission is Colton. Euphon's going to Poland, you can lay money on Colton being in Poland. Colton, and his Russian bosses, want that euphon. He'll stop at nothing to get it. Be glad you're not in his sights."

Thinking about what Ghana said, Leslie asked, "Who's the potential buyer? I suppose you think it's Colton. I have my money on Stratis."

"Enjoy your lunch at the Columbia?" Ghana asked sidestepping the question.

Surprised at the response, Leslie responded, "You don't believe it's the Kumars do you? They

218

said they're out of the running. You telling me something different?"

"Those two can charm the pants off the devil. Who knows if they're still in the hunt or not? All I know is that DHS, with help from the IRS, has them in their sights."

"I'm convinced the Kumars dropped out."

"Don't allow that charm to fool you. Those two are masters at what they do. Especially the wife. She's as deadly as they make them. Trust me on that."

"From what you said before, it's not the Kumars you're concerned with. It's Colton."

"We believe Colton is planning to buy—or steal—the euphon in Poland. Stratis is setting him up."

"Colton? Why would Stratis promote a First with the idea of having a rival buy it? Please explain."

"Would this make more sense to you if you knew there's more than one euphon making the rounds?"

"Is there?"

"Everyone believes the euphon in Pittsburgh is—was—the genuine original, even though someone changed the glass rod to make it appear fake."

"Why? I mean, why change the rods?"

"To prevent Colton from stealing it out from under Stratis."

"Now you see it, now you don't," Leslie said. "Real bait and switch. So Stratis has the original and Chlad is taking a duplicate to Poland. And you think Colton will try to steal it over there?"

"I'm a grunt. Not a thinker. Below my pay grade," Ghana answered. "But I ask you, if there's one copy, why not two?"

Leslie hadn't considered that possibility. "I suppose..." She took a moment to think through the possibilities, before saying, "The second copy is being used for..."

"A private sting operation."

"Stratis? Stratis is stinging Colton? To what end?"

"To ruin Colton with his handlers. He'll buy the fake for his masters, the Russians. They'll give it to some terrorist state. When its ultimately sold, which it must be if the terrorists are to raise money, then it will be proven to be fake. That's when the shit — in the form of Colton — hits the fan. End game: No more Colton."

"Where does that leave the Polish Museum? Or wherever the original euphon is supposed to be displayed."

"Oh, they'll certify the one that arrives with Chlad. That much has been wired. A done deal, so to speak." Ghana flashed a knowing smile. "All signed and sealed. You were mere window dressing — a distraction. A name for the official records."

"What's the going rate for bribery over there?" Leslie asked, hiding her anger as she came to grips with what Ghana had been hinting at.

"I'll deny I said it. I believe in this case it's twenty-five million. Give or take."

"Paid by?"

"My guess — Stratis."

"What's he get for all this effort — and money?"

"That's where the rubber meets the road. A twofer. Stratis wins and we win. He secures his beloved First — which we believe he did last night — and we eliminate a Russian agent. Which we hope to accomplish very soon."

"In your scenario, where Stratis delivers Colton, does he get an added bonus?"

"What are you thinking?"

"IRS looks the other way."

"Can't speak for the IRS. But you might be on to something."

"Reminds me of the three-card Monte flim-flam you see in New Orleans," Leslie said, finally getting her mind around all the double dealings. "Hand is faster than the eye. The card is never in the position you think it is."

"Got taken in once long ago in New York City," Ghana confessed. "Thought I could follow the ace. In fact, I did. Won a few dollars. Guy next to me started betting hundreds and won big. Got me all excited. I put down a twenty and won. At one point I had two hundred of their dollars in my hand. Needless to say, I lost their two hundred, plus sixty more of mine, plus…plus my watch. Got taken big time. Learned my lesson. Professionals play for keeps — as do Colton and Stratis."

"Sorry for your loss," Leslie said, remembering how close she had been to laying down a twenty-dollar bill in New Orleans, the only twenty she had, certain she knew which one of the three face down cards was the ace. "I take it you believe the original euphon is in Florida."

"Not my concern where the devil that original is. My focus is on catching Colton interchanging money with the Russian Lenkov. You're right you know. Following the euphon is like following the ace. Now you see it, now you don't."

"If Colton's your target, why are you here with me? Colton, I believe is long gone."

"Mopping up loose ends. Your boss Stetson's a loose end as far as Jakowski's concerned."

"What's that mean?"

"If she was duped by Jakowski into sending you to Poland that's one thing. If she's a willing participant, we need to know that as well. In that same vein, we need to know if Jakowski's working for his own account or officially."

"Why not ask his bosses in Pittsburgh."

"Not Pittsburgh. Verona. Reason to believe someone up there's been compromised. Every time IRS gets close to nailing Stratis, the operation goes...well...off track is the nicest way to say it."

Leslie let that play a moment before responding. "If you're asking me to gather information on Boots, the answer is no!"

"Just a little..."

"I'm a rookie for God's sake! Already in far over my head! I go up against the brass, I'll be lucky to stand guard over the canned corn at Publix."

"You're a detective, aren't you? Just ask her a few questions. We'll listen in."

"That's for Internal Affairs. I can't! And I won't!"

"Leslie. It's just you and I in this car. Two women trying to get ahead in a male world. You help me, I'll see you're protected on the way up. You fight me, well, who knows what'll be."

Leslie didn't believe in the male dominated world scenario and said so.

"Okay, then, let me be blunt," Agent Ghana said, her eyes narrowing to slits. "Either do as I ask, or the file showing you boarding the flight to Poland with Jakowski finds its way to the sheriff with a note as to how much money changed hands and explaining how we pulled you off that plane at the last moment."

Both women knew that such action would effectively end Leslie's career. Once when Leslie had questioned the wisdom of Junior going along with a not so well thought out FBI operation, he had responded by saying, "I've learned the hard way to never fight the Feds on my own. Bound to lose every time. Just don't have the resources to set the record straight." Junior's advice coincided with what her evidence instructor, a lawyer, had told the class. "Military plane crashes in a potato field in Iowa. You'll be lucky to prove the existence of the field. Never mind the fact that an airplane, military or otherwise, was even in the vicinity."

Conceding this round to Agent Ghana, she said, "Let's hear what you want me to do before I decide." Remembering a lost thread from earlier, Leslie said, "First, let's talk about that character you called Esquire. The one who, according to you, negotiated the arrangements with the Polish authorities. Who have you penciled in?"

"Indelible ink is more in keeping. Your good buddy, Pete Jakowski."

# TWENTY-FIVE

LESLIE'S CONVERSATION WITH AGENT GHANA looped in her head as she drove from the airport to headquarters. She was upset to learn that Pete Jakowski was the man working behind the scenes in the euphon's discovery. She had unquestionably trusted him, even going so far as to substitute his judgment for hers in an ongoing homicide investigation. He had unforgivably duped her into betraying her partner by not revealing she was working with him. Her behavior was inexcusable, even though she believed she had Captain Stetson's tacit approval.

Junior's comment on con artists came to mind. "Remember, Leslie," he had replied to her question as to why so many people fell for transparent schemes to separate them from their money, "the hallmark of the con game is believability of the artist. It's natural for people to be sucked in by the promise of getting something for nothing. Even smart people suspend their learned knowledge in favor of their basic inborn tendencies of trust."

"Aren't you the one," Leslie had replied, "who always preaches, 'when something feels wrong, it usually is'?"

"Good motto to work by," Junior had said, "But with a top con artist, it doesn't feel wrong. That's what makes the con work."

Although she couldn't articulate it at the time, perhaps that's why she intentionally missed the flight. It just felt wrong. "Thank you, Junior," she said aloud. "You saved my sorry butt yet again."

Leslie paced the hallway outside Stetson's office waiting for — dreading is more to the point — the door to open. She had committed to Ghana to ask the questions DHS wanted answered but had drawn the line with real-time surveillance. One wrong word and her career, she knew, would be in shambles.

The door opened, revealing her immediate superior officer, Sergeant Hudson Oakmore, sitting across the desk from the captain, the look on Oakmore's face barely concealing his anger. The situation had suddenly gone from horrible to catastrophic. "Come in, Leslie," Stetson called. "I understand you asked to see me."

Protocol required Leslie to process all up-line communication through the chain of command. Oakmore took pride in knowing everything that was going on with his people and that could explain his apparent foul mood. "I did," Leslie acknowledged, confessing the obvious. "It's about..."

"Presumably," Stetson interrupted, "it's about the shooting you witnessed and our little conversation at the hospital. Let's hold that a bit, shall we? Hud's here about the problem with your partner, Cox. Seems you asked him to follow a package from Page Field to its destination. The file shows he followed your instructions but didn't leave the scene immediately as you had instructed him to do. According to his report, a DHS agent, acting without prior notification to us, escorted him from the scene in a rather forceful manner."

"I can..." Leslie began, intending to defend Cox, as well as herself.

"Why Cox didn't follow your instructions is beyond me," Stetson continued. "Hud's suggested assigning him to direct traffic over at Fenway

South Park. I think that's overkill. I'm suggesting a reprimand. He needs to know that when the lead detective gives an order, that order is to be followed. What's your take on that?"

Where to begin? Lying to your boss is a bad idea under any situation. When you work for top detectives, it's not even an option. Leslie remained standing as she told them about Jakowski having her pick him up at the airport and the bizarre events that followed. While Leslie spoke, she watched the captain's eyes for a sign that she had coordinated any of this with Jakowski. Her eyes revealed nothing of significance.

"Are you suggesting," Stetson asked, when Leslie fell silent, "this is all a misunderstanding?

"That's how I see it. I'm not happy with what Cox did, but truthfully, he was trying to gather evidence concerning a person of interest in a homicide investigation. DHS didn't register with us, so he had no way to know he was interfering with them. I passed on Jak's instructions and perhaps I wasn't as clear as I should have been."

"Since when does an out of jurisdiction officer give orders to a Lee County Sheriff Deputy? Have I misjudged you?"

"I thought..." Leslie selected her words carefully, not being free to say what she wanted while Hud was present. Asking Oakmore to leave was career suicide, assuming she had much of a career left. "...you had granted Jak permission to..."

"Me? Why in the world would you think that?"

"He told me he had your blessing."

"And you believed him?"

"Sorry, but I did."

Turning to Oakmore, she said, "Seems Cox is not the only one screwing up last night. He shouldn't have remained on site, but I can't fault that. The order made no sense in the context of our investigation. I assume Leslie here has no objection if we assign him back to the Fuller matter."

"No objection, Captain," Leslie replied, relieved at the outcome, but still on edge knowing the tough discussion with her captain was yet to come.

"Hud, I think that's all we have for now. Leslie and I have administrative matters to discuss concerning the shooting. This is best handled in private. That's why she didn't tell you about this meeting. My instructions."

Oakmore stood to leave, started to say something to Leslie and changed his mind. He took a few steps toward the door and turned back to face her. "Detective, when you're done here come by my office." The door closed behind him.

Leslie was now confused about how to proceed with her captain, the only person standing between her and unemployment. She had carefully worked out her exact words which had been predicated on Stetson acknowledging she had invited Jakowski into Lee County to work with Leslie. Either Stetson had lied when she denied working with Jakowski, or...

"Leslie," Stetson began, her eyes hardened, "I saw a file note about you being at the airport this morning. What's that about?"

Leslie's first thought was to answer by simply saying she was there to drop off Jakowski. Thinking better of it, she confessed, "I was booked on a flight through Newark to Warsaw with Jak."

"Warsaw? Who the hell signed off on that? Hud knew nothing about you traveling. I certainly didn't."

Captain Stetson was either in this deeper than Leslie had allowed herself to imagine, or...or Leslie had been completely played by Jakowski — and perhaps even by Agent Ghana. "Captain," she said, making a quick decision, "I think it best I begin at the beginning. I believe I've been played. Worse, I believe you have been as well."

"Sit," Stetson ordered. Checking her watch, she hit the intercom button on her phone. "Cancel my appointments for the next hour. And intercept all calls." She then looked across her desk directly at Leslie, her eyes narrow and still determined, "Let's hear what you have to say, Detective."

Leslie began with the text she had received from Jakowski asking her to pick him up at the airport and to not inform Cox. She relayed Jakowski's instructions about what Cox was tasked to do, and how Jakowski and she were going to watch Chlad's house in the hope Stratis would show up. Leslie then added, "Captain, you specifically told me it was okay to work with Jak on this matter. A tip you had received from DHS or something along those lines. This collaboration was to be handled off the books with me direct reporting."

"I'm well aware of my instructions. I'm also aware that Stratis is a billionaire living in Pittsburgh. Member of some group believes spirits pass from person to person or some such thing."

"Seminal Society. I met with him when I investigated the missing Edison First Phonograph."

"I remember. Go on."

"I asked Jak who had approved his working on the file. He said you did, and that you had approved of our working together. I suppose I should've confirmed that."

"I would have noted the file."

Sucking in her breath, Leslie replied, "That would have been impossible if Jak being here was being kept from Cox." Even as Leslie said this, she knew how wrong she had been. Jakowski had played her from the beginning. That was exactly why Cox was to be left out. It prevented her from annotating the file.

"And why on God's earth would I approve such a bizarre situation — and not tell you directly?"

"Lapse of judgment on my part, brought on by..." Leslie felt her face flush and as professional as she could muster, continued, "Jak convincing me you and he had...had been an item at one point." Rushing on, Leslie said, "According to him you were together at Quantico early in your careers. One thing leading to another type of thing."

Stetson's face stiffened, her eyes now on fire. "That's a damned lie! Yes, we were together for two weeks. Yes, we had dinner privately twice. But, no, we were not, as you say, 'an item'. Not then. Not ever!"

"It's not my..."

"Damn right it's not your business. So why..."

"I need to tell you about Homeland Security Agent, Maxine Ghana."

"I've met Max once or twice," Stetson said, a puzzled expression forming. "Hard driving. Ambitious. What's Agent Ghana got to do with any of this?"

"She, or the Team, as she refers to the agents working with her," Leslie began, violating her promise to Ghana and deciding to play her hand as honestly as possible, "believe Jak is working for Stratis. According to DHS, he's the person who negotiated with Polish officials for the transportation of the euphon in the first place."

Stetson's silence forced Leslie to continue.

"They believe you're working with Jak."

"They? Meaning..."

"Agent Ghana. DHS, I suppose."

"To what end?"

"Do you mean, to what end would you be working with Jak? Or to what end would you want me in Warsaw?"

"Actually both. Start with me."

"You working with Jak insures we never find Fuller's killer. I suppose that's the same answer for why I was tagged for a trip to Poland. DHS believes something's going on here. Stratis, Colton, or someone, wants both of us out of the way. Hate to sound like a conspiracy theory nut, but..."

"But even a conspiracy fanatic's right every now and again. I assume they asked you to report our conversation — this conversation — to them?"

"In fact, they wanted me to wear a wire."

Stetson was on her feet, fists clenched, face bright red, jaw clenched. "Tell me you didn't!"

"No way, Captain. But I did agree to report to them your response about you working with Jak."

"And just what do you plan to say?"

"I have no doubt you are not in any manner involved."

"It's a damn good thing you didn't record this — or wear their frickin' wire! If you had, this would be your last minute in law enforcement — ever! As it is, I need to think about what to do with you. Why the hell would you ever agree to question me in the first place?"

"Ghana convinced me if I didn't, she was prepared to take it to IA directly. Then it'd be on your record permanently. Affair and all. I tried to protect..."

"There was no affair!"

"But if IA considered an affair a given because it came from DHS, they might not have bothered to ask about it."

"You've said enough! Get out! For now, you're still on the Fuller case. You and Cox. Nothing of this conversation gets to Cox. Understand?"

"Understood," Leslie said, walking out of Stetson's office as quickly as she could before her boss had a change of mind.

# TWENTY-SIX

FOLLOWING UP ON HER COMMITMENT to touch base with her immediate boss, Leslie crossed the floor to his office. "Hud's out," his assistant, Marge Harvey, informed her. Harvey had worked for Lee County through several Sheriffs and had her ear to the ground. Nothing happened in Lee County she didn't know about. "Hud said for you to carry on. He'll catch up with you later."

"Thanks, Marge," Leslie replied. "Could you please buzz me when he comes in."

"I'll tell him you came by." She lowered her voice and in a conspiratorial tone, added, "Between you and me, he trusts you more than I've known him to trust anyone. Don't screw that up. Know what I mean?"

Leslie didn't know but guessed that Oakmore had been tipped off as to the essence of what Leslie had been asked to find out about Stetson. Briefing him as to their conversation was not possible. "Thanks for the heads up. Appreciate it. By any chance is Cox around?"

"At his desk ten minutes ago. Maybe in the break room." Lowering her voice again, she added, "Better watch that one, if I was in your shoes."

———————●———————

"Heard you were looking for me," Cox said fifteen minutes later when he appeared at Leslie's desk. His face was neutral, but his stance defiant.

"We need to talk," Leslie said, "I owe you an explanation. Pull up a seat, this may take a while."

"How about the interview room? Only private place we have."

When they were seated, Leslie proceeded through everything that had happened beginning with Jakowski's text to meet him at the airport. She omitted only the discussion of the affair with Stetson.

Cox, to Leslie's surprise, turned out to be a good listener. When she finished, he simply said, "Thanks for going to bat for me with the boss. Means a lot. Now it's time to get back to Fuller. According to you, one of our suspects is now out of the country. That's not good. On the other hand, one of your theories seems to be that they wanted you out of here because something big is about to go down."

"Just a thought. The more I think of it, the more convinced I am whatever's about to happen concerns the euphon and not the homicide. The way I see it, the euphon's not Lee County's problem. Not yet anyway."

"Theft of a valuable object is most definitely our jurisdiction," Cox responded.

"It would be, if, and only if, the euphon owner filed a stolen property report. Chlad never did that. Even when the euphon, the one on display at the Carnegie, was determined to be suspicious, he didn't file a complaint."

"So, what's your plan?"

"Frankly, I'm fresh out. Tell you what, let's pick this up in the morning. How about you locate Colton. I doubt he's still in town. But on the off chance he is, I'd like to meet him. Stratis' plane landed at Naples about the same time as the cargo plane from Pittsburgh you were watching. Try and find out where he is. I'll see if I can locate insurance on the euphon and see if a claim's been made."

"For having no plan, you did right well, ma'am," Cox said, chuckling at something he must have thought funny. "Have a great rest of the day." Without further comment, he left the interrogation room and walked back toward his desk on the far side of the Pit.

Leslie watched him go, thinking about the divide between them she had created. She knew full well their lives could depend upon mutual trust, which unfortunately right now, was at a low point. Time would have to repair the rift. She realized, however, time was not on their side.

———————

Leslie called Allen, the connection going directly to voice mail as it often did late in the afternoon on court days. "How about dinner tonight?" she asked the recorder. "My place?"

"I assume," Allen said twenty minutes later when he returned her call, "from your invitation that you've again become available. Quick assignment?"

"Tell you about it later." Was it her imagination, or was Allen sending her a message? "Steaks okay? I bought a book on how to..."

"Only if I grill them. See you at..."

"Make it seven. That work for you?"

"Seven it is. Love you. Bye."

Last night wasn't the first time she had stood him up for dinner. Police work was anything but a nine-to-five business. Missing meals was commonplace. Getting called out of bed in the middle of the night was routine. It was important for her to know, sooner rather than later, if her lifestyle annoyed Allen.

Her call to Jack Silver at Great Southern Insurance Company also went to voice mail. "Hi, Mr. Silver. It's Detective Hodges. I have a quick question. Can you please call me?" She provided her phone number, not being comfortable leaving her question about Chladni insurance coverage on voicemail.

———◆———

Once home, Leslie flopped on the sofa and opened her computer. Within minutes, mental, as well as physical, exhaustion set in. Leslie found herself reading the same screen over and over, struggling to assimilate the information. She flipped the computer closed and shut her eyes. Instead of the intended quick cat nap, her mind focused on Allen and his distracted demeanor.

Allen arrived precisely at seven and answered her hug with enthusiasm quelling her earlier doubts. "Come," she said, "the grill's on and ready for you. Dinner tonight is basic. Steaks by Allen, baked potatoes, which are almost ready to come out of the oven, a nice salad I picked up at Publix, and a surprise dessert."

"Sounds nice. I see you have the cab poured and ready to go. Give me a hint of dessert?

"You'll like it," she said winking at him. "That's all I'm going to say. Now go and cook the steaks. I skipped lunch today and I swear I could eat the whole cow."

"The way you eat, there'll still be half a steak left when you're done. Never seen anyone eat as little as you."

"You suggesting I'm too thin?"

"My, you're sensitive. Just stating a fact is all. A jealous fact if you must know."

Indeed, Leslie was sensitive about her slim figure. Her mother always said she was all bones. Seen skeletons with more meat on them than you, girl, she had told her on more than one occasion. Food had never been a priority for Leslie although she had learned her way around a kitchen for no other reason than to please her mother. Now she was putting those skills to good use, even though tonight's dinner was mostly store-bought.

"Two medium steaks," Allen called, coming in from the outside. "Perfectly cooked if I do say so myself." He placed the plates on the table and held his refilled wine glass high, proclaiming, "Bon appétit!"

"I'll drink to that," Leslie replied, dropping a potato onto each plate. "How about we eat the salad last?"

"Works for me. You must be hungry alright." A few bites into his steak, Allen said, "So what's the mystery about? Last night you said you were going under cover, and I wouldn't hear from you for a while. You couldn't tell me how long. Less than twenty-four hours later we're grilling steaks as if nothing happened."

"Nothing did happen. Operation was called off."

"Why? What changed?"

"Change of direction's all. What's the big deal?"

Allen finished his steak in silence and sat back as Leslie picked at her dinner, moving food around on her plate aimlessly. When she put her knife down, he asked, "When were you planning to tell me about you and that Pittsburgh cop traveling to Warsaw?"

"How in the hell..."

"The important question, Leslie, is not how I know, but why you're hiding it?"

"I'm not hiding anything!" Leslie snapped, dropping her fork onto her plate. "It's part of an ongoing investigation."

"Last I checked, you're a Lee County Deputy Detective with no jurisdiction outside Florida. And especially not in Poland."

"Last I checked, I'm sitting across the table from you eating a steak you cooked to perfection. I'm not on an airplane anywhere! And I'm certainly not in Poland!"

"What changed your mind? You were definitely on your way to Warsaw."

"If you must know, I was duped. Almost got my ass fired over it! Matter of fact, I'm not yet out of the woods. Had I boarded that plane, I'd have been arrested."

"Arrested! What's that..." Leslie's face tensed, causing Allen to switch away from his question to a statement of concern. "I'm sorry the job's not going the way you planned. You're an excellent detective — a natural. If there's one thing I've learned, it's that being a detective is messy at best. Wish I could help."

"Thanks. But I somehow got myself into this shit, and somehow I'll get myself out."

"Spoken like a true tough ass. If anybody can do it, you can." Allen fell silent, draining the last of his Cabernet.

"Okay. Allen. Out with it. Something's eating at you. What is it?"

"I promised myself I wouldn't ask. After what you're going through this is a horrible time."

"Can't imagine any better time — at least not in the near future. Out with it."

Taking a deep breath, and focusing on Leslie's eyes, he asked, "Have you slept with him?"

"Allen!"

"Have you?"

"The answer is no. Hell, no! The fact you have to ask tells me more than I want to know!"

"Did you plan to?"

"Of course not And I don't..."

Allen produced a folded sheet of paper and threw it on the table. "Explain this?"

Before Leslie had it fully open, she knew it was a copy of the printout of the booking reservation from the Hotel Raffles Europejski. The words 'Mr. & Mrs. Leslie Hodges' leaped from the page. Leslie leaned forward, her face angry, the voice of her former husband reminding her that if her defense wasn't holding it was time to switch to offense, "Screw all this cat and mouse shit! Why the hell did you even bother to come here? Allen, either you trust me, or you don't! Obviously, you don't! As I said, I was duped into that flight and had the good sense not to board. Homeland Security's involved and that's all I can tell you!"

"The reason I am here is that I do trust you. If I didn't, I wouldn't have returned your call. I just had to hear you say it."

"You satisfied?" Leslie demanded, pushing her chair back from the table. Her eye caught her plate and she realized Allen had been right. Her steak was only half-eaten. This man knew her better than she knew herself.

"Relieved," Allen responded. "Relieved is the right word."

"Thanks for being honest."

"I went to law school because I didn't want to live a cop's life, never knowing what's about to happen. Trusting nothing. Suspecting the worst in everyone. Frankly, it tires me out. I'm struggling watching you."

"I'm sorry to be the source of pain for you Allen. You want to end it? Is that what you're telling me?"

"Hell, no! I'm in love with you, Detective Hodges. For better or worse. I just wanted you to know how I feel."

What Leslie wanted to say was, You make me feel like Junior made me feel. But that seemed wrong. Instead, she said, "You make me feel loved.

And I do love you, Allen." Then, to lighten the mood, she said, "You're right, you know. I do eat like a bird. Save room for dessert?"

"You bet. You have me intrigued."

"Your choice," Leslie said, smiling broadly. "German chocolate cake here in the dining room? Or...or...me in the bedroom?"

"Bedrooms," Allen answered, squeezing Leslie's hand playfully, "always take priority over dining rooms.

# TWENTY-SEVEN

COX HAD SET THE MEETING with Selma Fritz for 9:30. Leslie arrived in the parking area of the White Sands complex shortly after nine and immediately brought up the Fuller file. Criminal Investigative Assistant Lizbeth Hillard and the Digital Forensic Unit had done their jobs well. She began by reviewing Fritz's cell phone records. Nothing of interest caught her attention.

Leslie then went over Fritz's income, noting the regular monthly entries of $1430.08 from GE, $1750.23 from SSA Treas, $1021.86 from BambArt, and $3245.43 from Fidelity. In round numbers that comes to $89,400 per year.

Leslie questioned whether that was enough to support the lifestyle Selma Fritz appeared to lead. Her question was answered when she saw that for the past five years Fritz had been receiving a quarterly payment of $25,000 from an entity identified as FreeForm Holdings, Ltd. The last of those payments was deposited on June 2, 2020. There was no record of the September 2020 or December 2020 payments being deposited. Reading further she found that FreeForm Holdings, Ltd. had declared bankruptcy in November 2020.

"Have you seen the report on Fritz's finances?" Leslie asked Cox when he sauntered over to her car at 9:25.

"Seems her income stream's been impacted by some fund going dry. But, hey, she still has over eighty-nine K a year. Not so shabby."

Leslie thought of her own income and nodded in agreement as she joined Cox, the two of them walking into the lobby together. The concierge's desk was empty with a 'Be Right Back' sign in the center. The detectives took the elevator up to the fifth floor just as they had the last time. The door to Fritz's apartment opened even before they knocked.

"Saw you coming on the video." She pointed to a small white circular plate with a button in the center mounted on the wall beside her door. "Sees and hears all. Come on in. I know cops love donuts, so I apologize for only having blueberry muffins. But I did make them myself."

"That was nice of you," Cox said, covering for Leslie who he hoped would force herself to eat the pastry out of politeness — or at least out of converting this session from a homicide investigation to a coffee klatch.

The detectives were again seated on opposite ends of a slightly curved sofa while Fritz fussed with the coffee service. Leslie allowed a muffin to be placed on her plate. When their hostess finally settled in a chair facing them, Leslie said, "I must learn to make these. Do you share recipes? Many people don't."

"I usually don't, actually. But in your case, I'll be happy to make an exception."

Leslie sat back, her mask still in place. "I know we went over this before," she began, "but how about once more? Please start from the time you woke up on the morning of..."

"January 13th. I know all too painfully what day you're referring to, Detective. My reason for living ended that day."

"I'm so sorry to be the source of your pain, but if we don't get the times exactly right, we'll have even more difficulty determining what really happened to Dr. Fuller."

"All the same, this is very..."

"Please, Selma, just walk us through your day up until you found Dr. Fuller — Sig."

"Is this really necessary?"

"Afraid so," Leslie said, taking a bite of muffin. "This muffin is good. Please do send the recipe."

Selma remained silent several seconds before responding, "I just don't know exactly what time I did what. You know, the days blend together."

Cox broke his silence. "How about guessing as to the time you woke up and walk us through what you did from that point onward until you arrived at Sig's house. We'll try and match it up with a timeline, see how close we come."

"Wake up time I know. Seven-ten. Clock is set for that time. Stayed in bed maybe five, ten minutes at most. Then went to...must I go into all the details?"

"Do your best," Leslie coaxed, taking back the lead. "You got out of bed and..."

"Went to the bathroom. From there into the shower."

"How long were you in the shower?"

"I don't know, exactly. Long. I washed my hair. Maybe a half-hour?"

Half-hour, Leslie knew was far longer than likely. But that could be revisited later. "After you got out?"

Leslie led Selma through her morning routine step by step, learning that after her shower Fritz had put on her robe, gone to the kitchen and boiled two eggs. "I like them soft with toast," she added. "Rye when I can get it."

"After breakfast. What did you do?" Leslie gently prodded. "I'm thinking the time was then eight-forty-five, maybe nine?"

"I finished reading the newspaper. I have the NY Times delivered every day. I think it was closer to nine-thirty, maybe even later, when I finished reading an article I got involved in."

"Do you always spend that much time with the paper?" Cox asked.

"There was an article on European artifacts triggered by the opening of the Chladni exhibit. Well done article, I must say."

"And then?" Leslie gently pressed.

"I picked out what I was going to wear. As I told you, Sig told me we were going out to celebrate. I then blew out my hair. Did my makeup. You know, at my age, makeup is a woman's best friend."

Leslie, whose experience with makeup was limited to an occasional application of lipstick, didn't know. But she nodded in agreement, nonetheless.

"Took me longer than usual and anyway Sig called and moved lunch back an hour. He was upset and told me about what he called, 'the mix up at the Carnegie'. He said he was meeting with Ernst Chlad around noon and I could come then if I liked."

"You and Mr. Chlad know each other I assume."

"We spent time together getting the euphon all worked out. Getting back to the timeline; it usually takes me twenty minutes to drive from here to Sig's. Like I said, I wanted to get a card, so I left here around eleven-fifteen or so. Went to Target, got the card and then drove to Sig's."

"How long were you in Target?" Cox asked.

"Don't know."

"Please guess."

"Fifteen, twenty-minutes. More or less."

"You then drove to Dr. Fuller's."

"Yes."

"Directly?" Cox pressed.

"Yes."

"What time did you arrive at Dr. Fuller's?"

"I believe it was just after noon," Fritz answered, frowning.

"It was twelve oh three to be exact," Cox volunteered. "Okay, now, if you don't mind, we'd like to go over your finances. We can begin with your sources of income?"

Fritz sat upright, her chin quivering slightly. "My income is a private matter. I believe you are overstepping your bounds."

Cox started to respond, but Leslie cut him off. "Like I said before, Selma, this is a homicide investigation. I know it feels intrusive, but for us to do our jobs we need to understand everyone with access to the murder scene. We need to know where people were at the time of death as well as their lifestyles."

"Am I a suspect?"

"We're just gathering facts at this point."

"Do I need a lawyer?"

"Only you can decide that. We are asking factual questions. The facts shouldn't change with a lawyer. But if you want one, we can meet you at his or her office if you wish."

"What was the question?"

"Your sources of income."

"I don't see what this has to do with anything. I get my husband's pension from GE. I get Social Security. My own pension from Miami. And an annuity."

"Tell us about the annuity."

"I discovered an artifact in Kosovo from the Bulgarian Period. I made the discovery at the time the Serbian and Yugoslav governments were negotiating with the UN over the future of the territory. My discovery of the artifact strengthened Yugoslav's position and the Serbians arranged for an investor to buy the artifact for his private collection. I was paid a handsome sum and the artifact disappeared from public view all without the Yugoslavs ever knowing. I was advised to buy an annuity with the money, which I did."

"What artifact would that be?" Leslie asked.

"Sorry, Detective, I am bound by a legal document to never discuss it with anyone. I must honor that agreement."

"When was that?"

"Sorry, I can't talk about any aspects of what or where exactly, or even when. But I will say, I spent time in Croatia just after the turn of the century."

From the information Fritz had given, and from what they already had from her financial records, Leslie was positive the digital forensics experts would be able to piece it all together if need be. "Okay, let's talk about the euphon itself. How about describing it to us and walking us through the steps of finding it."

"As I said, Sig did most of that."

"But you were with him were you not?"

"I was."

"Tell us what you saw and heard and did."

"The description is easy. It's made of wood, looks somewhat like a small piano, keyboard kind of instrument with glass rods instead of keys. The rods are different lengths and supported by bamboo. The rods are positioned beside each other across the face of the instrument. The player runs moistened fingers lengthwise along each glass rod causing the rod to vibrate. Once a rod begins to vibrate it continues for a few seconds allowing an accomplished player to produce blended sounds."

"Do you have recordings of the euphon you discovered?"

Without comment, Selma produced her cell phone, poked around a bit. Soon, musical tones filled the room.

"Sounds like music from outer space," Cox commented. "If you ask me."

"A modern instrument, called the Cristal Baschet, produces very similar sounds. And indeed, the Baschet is often used for space movies.

"It certainly is different. Unique," Leslie agreed. "And you say the sound is generated by stroking glass rods with wet fingers to make the rods vibrate?"

"That's how it works. The artist can, and does, truncate the vibrations by touching the rods at certain locations. Chladni traveled around Germany performing euphon concerts. His music was very popular."

"I appreciate we went over this the last time we spoke, but it's important we get it right. Please again walk us through how you — Dr. Sig — found the original euphon."

"As I told you, he and I made several trips to Poland and Germany over many years, travelled all over. Mostly, I went along as company. Did my own thing. Sig spent the days in the field, as he called his work, interviewing people."

"Where was your — his — base of operations? In what city?"

"Mostly in Breslau, Poland. That's the city where Chladni died. In his day it was the Kingdom of Prussia. From there, Sig traveled around from town to town, village to village, sometimes he was gone days at a time."

"Mostly interviewing people?"

"Putting together an ancestor log. Talking to distant relatives. Trying to find the euphon and at the same time determining ownership."

"Did you or Sig have help locating the euphon?"

Fritz looked away, lost in thought. Leslie and Cox sat quietly, waiting. It took a few minutes, before she said, "I don't really know. Sig spoke to anybody and everybody. People were always giving him information. Somewhere Sig came up with the idea that the euphon had been stolen by the proprietor of the boarding house where Chladni stayed his last time in Breslau. He thought it was most likely hidden inside the building."

"Did anyone other than you and the Chlads know about Dr. Fuller's investigation?"

"Near the end, people began asking questions. Some directly, some through other people."

"Any names you recall?"

"Man by the name of Colton. Another man, also. Introduced to us only as Esquire. There was an Indian couple as well. Maybe others, I don't recall."

"This Mr. Esquire," Leslie said, searching her phone for an image of Jakowski. "Could this possibly be the same man?"

Fritz's eyes answered the question, even before she managed to say, "That's him! How did you know?"

"I've heard of him."

Cox, who has sat mostly quiet, asked, "You mentioned the name Colton. Have you spoken to him since?"

Selma looked away before saying, "He's very interested in buying the euphon. Called me several times. Mostly he wanted assurance it was genuine."

"What did you tell him?"

"That he had to speak with Sig."

"Did he?"

"I don't know."

"I read somewhere," Cox said, "that often it's the rumors that drive up the price of a lost artifact. So, my question is, if there were no rumors, what makes the euphon so valuable?"

"The Seminal Society collectors want it. Colton, I understand, is a collector. And what they want, they get — and pay for." Tears ran down her cheeks.

She dabbed at her eyes with a napkin. "Sorry. I was thinking of Sig. He often said, 'When elephants fight, the earth shudders — and people die.' Poor Sig. Unfortunately for him, he was so right about that." She again brushed the moisture from her face. "I hope we're almost finished here. I have..."

"Almost," Leslie sympathized. "Just a few more, mostly background questions. Do you know what material the euphon is made from?"

"Chladni had a piano maker, a man named Johann August Tischner, make it. His workroom was in Saxony, Germany."

"What materials were used to make it?"

"The wood frame is spruce, and the sounding board is maple because of its excellent tonal qualities. Woods of today just don't carry sound as well as they did in the 1800s. The glass rods are, of course, glass with a high lead content. Bamboo is used for supporting the rods."

"One final question," Cox said, brushing crumbs from his tray into a napkin. "How did Sig authenticate the euphon? I mean, what makes him — and you — so positive it's genuine even when now it's thought to be a...a possible fake?"

"It boils down to two main factors. Now don't get me wrong, there are countless little facts that need to be right. Such as the glue and the joint style. The two most significant factors are the veneer used by Tischner and the glass rod dimensions. Tischner used a rare mahogany that he imported from India for the veneer. Sig was able to confirm that pianos built by Tischner, pianos that now reside in several museums, use that very same veneer. There is no question Tischner's veneer was on the euphon Sig located."

"And what about the rod dimensions?" Leslie asked.

"Sig found, among Tischner's business documents passed down over the years, his work ledger for 1791 showing the specification for Friedrich Chladni. The lengths, diameters, and exact spacing of each rod was neatly listed. There is no question that the instrument Sig located in the wall was the Chladni euphon. It's a genuine First. There is no question at all."

# TWENTY-EIGHT

BACK IN HER CAR, LESLIE checked her messages and found one from Jack Silver. If your question is, did great southern insure the chladni? the answer is yes, as certified by Fuller. will await your return call if I have answered the wrong question.

Leslie motioned for Cox to join her as she dialed Silver's number.

Surprisingly, the call was answered on the first ring. "I was expecting your call," Silver announced. "Did I not answer your question?"

"You very much did. Thank you for that. I just need a clarification. In interest of full disclosure, I have my partner, Detective Cox, with me. With your permission I'd like to put this on speaker."

"I learned years ago that conversations with police officials are rarely off the record, so do what you need to do."

"Appreciate that. My question is: What does, as certified by Fuller, mean?"

"Without getting into the technical weeds, the policy Great Southern Insurance Company has on the Chladni is limited in scope. It requires GSIC to return the artifact to its owner, Ernst Chlad, at his Florida home in the same condition as it was in when it left Dr. Fuller's home on its way to Pittsburgh. If it can't be returned for any reason, GSIC will pay a stipulated amount. There is no evidence the artifact was tampered with in transit to the Carnegie Science Center, nor while it was in their possession. In fact, the insured artifact was under constant surveillance from the time it left Dr. Fuller's possession until it was returned to the Chlad home. At that point, Great Southern's obligation ended."

"You are, of course, familiar with Carnegie's inspection report are you not," Leslie asked.

"I am. Certainly."

"Does that mean no claim has been made?"

"I'm not at liberty to discuss specific claims. I will, however, emphasize that the insured euphon has been delivered to Ernst Chlad in the exact same condition it was in when it left Dr. Fuller's home. That is what our policy required."

Leslie digested what she had just heard, then pressed, "Are you at all concerned that a claim will be made?"

"We live with the risk of claims every day. Let me put it this way. As risks go, at this point the euphon is not high on my radar."

"Why is that? I mean, in light of the reported improper rod?"

"It would be difficult at best, for the insured to file a claim with GSIC when the Polish authorities have accepted the euphon from Chlad as the original."

"I assume the Polish acceptance has occurred."

"I'm told that will occur very shortly."

"The amount of insurance?"

"I won't talk in specifics. You can assume it is — was — in excess of a hundred million."

"Where is it now?"

Silver remained silent for an uncomfortably long time. When he next spoke, his voice held a slight edge. "Just opened the file. Looks like the euphon's at the Hotel Raffles in Warsaw in a connecting room to Ernst Chlad. Security detail is in the connecting room. Room is registered to..."

"I know. Mr. and Mrs. Leslie Hodges. I can exp..."

"Man by the name of Esquire is in the connecting room, along with three armed guards. Polish officials are due within minutes. Chlad can't very well claim an insurance loss while at the same time certify the return to Poland of the exact same euphon that was allowed out. No, I have very little concern."

"Thank you for the information."

When the line went dead, Cox said, "Silver may not have asked for an explanation, but I'm sure as hell curious. What's this about, Mr. and Mrs. Leslie Hodges?"

"Frankly, none of your business."

"You said it on a call with an informer. I heard it. Makes it my business."

"This Mr. Esquire. That's Jak, covering his tracks by using my name. Nothing more."

"So you say."

"I don't appreciate the innuendo! And if you know what's good for you, you'll stop it right now! That clear?"

"Clear as can be."

She glared at him before saying, "That informant was Jack Silver, CEO of Great Southern Insurance Company. Met him when I was investigating the missing Edison. GSIC insures valuable artifacts for museums and collectors. If there's a high dollar item anywhere in the world, he knows about it. He and his wife live aboard their private jet and who knows where he was just now. Across the street, or across the world. Husband and wife team fly the plane for them. What's your takeaway?"

"From the conversation with Silver? Or Fritz?"

"Either. But I was talking about Silver."

"Nothing major. The only confusing part was about the hotel room being in your name?"

"I told you, Jakowski set that up! Part of his scam."

"You and him?"

"I told you to stop!"

"Touchy."

"Get out!"

"Or?"

Leslie drove off, saying nothing. They were a mile north on Route 41 when she slowed for a light. She purposefully remained in the center lane to make it difficult for Cox to escape.

"Where are you taking me?" he demanded.

"I'm not taking you anywhere. You're the one refusing to leave my car."

"Stop and I'll get out!"

"Not safe on the highway." She accelerated when the light turned green.

"Pull over and let me out!"

"When you apologize."

"For what?"

"For being an asshole! And that's for starters!"

"Okay, I apologize."

"For what?"

"For what you said."

Leslie sped up.

"Okay. Okay. For being an asshole."

Leslie rolled her hand signaling she wanted to hear more.

"For teasing you about your personal life."

"And it won't happen again."

"And it won't happen again."

At the next intersection she pulled into a Shell station and stopped.

"How do I get my car?"

"Should have thought about that before you harassed me. Now go!"

Cox didn't move.

Leslie stepped on the gas.

"You frickin' win! Stop the damn car!"

Leslie jammed the brakes. The car stopped dead, sending Cox forward against the locked seat belt.

"You play hard," he complained. "Could have broken my shoulder."

"You continue screwing with me, you haven't seen the beginning!"

"That what they taught you up in Tampa?"

"There and Gulfport. Learned from the best rednecks the world's ever seen. Now go! Got a meeting with Hud in fifteen. Don't want to be late. I'll tell him you got delayed."

"Shit! I better go with you. Get my car later."

"Do that and you better hope you don't catch a call. Shit'll hit the fan then. In or out?"

Without a word, he opened the door and climbed out.

Leslie had lied about the meeting. It was forty-five minutes out and Cox would have known the time if he had been paying attention. For his sake she hoped he would check his messages while waiting for a ride back to his car. Not for the first time, she tried, but again failed, to work out just why Cox got under her skin so easily.

———◆———

"Just checking in," she said a few minutes later when Allen answered her call. "How's your day going?"

"About as well as can be expected. You caught me on break. Judge had to go potty. Or call his stockbroker, or something. Defendant's counsel has objected to every other question I've asked. Judge's with me. Overruled almost every objection. Day's going well. How's yours?"

"Great, if I ignore Cox."

"What's he done now?"

Leslie relayed what had happened and con-fessed her confusion as to why he grates on her.

"From what you say, he's bright enough as a detective. Has all the right instincts. Must be personality."

"It's something alright. Hey, I'm at the office. Gotta go. Talk later."

"Your place or mine?" Allen asked.

"Gotta catch up on laundry and cleaning. Mind if we take the night off."

"Okay," he responded, disappointment in his voice. "Talk to you later."

———————

Oakmore's door was closed when Leslie arrived. His assistant said he was finishing up a call and would be available in a few minutes. Eight min-utes passed before Leslie was instructed to go on in. Just then, Cox turned the corner and slipped inside the small office a few seconds behind her.

Oakmore motioned for them to be seated before saying, "Just got off the phone with DHS Agent Ghana. First, I should tell you, Boots had a long talk with that woman's supervisor and they banged out the ground rules you and they'll be playing by. Their interest is only in Colton and his activities with respect to the euphon. If Colton is a suspect in a crime originating in Lee County then that's our jurisdiction regardless of where it takes us. Same for Morris Dexter Stratis. DHS has agreed to not interfere in any way. In exchange, you're to cooperate with them. Any information pertaining to the Chladni euphon you'll immediately pass on."

"Essentially," Leslie said, when her boss fell silent, "we've been given the green light to work with DHS, but to continue to pursue the Fuller homicide."

"You got it. Now for the factual update. The euphon that came from Pittsburgh to the home of Ernst Chlad, and which he took to Warsaw, has been returned to, and accepted by, the Polish Government. As I understand it, Chlad's on a flight back here. Further, I know not."

"Is that all?" Cox asked.

"What the hell more where you expecting? You're sure as hell not going to find Fuller's killer sitting here! That's your priority!"

"I seem to be tripping over everybody today," Cox commented when they were back at Leslie's desk in the Pit. "Hey, look, I'm sorry for offending you earlier." Holding his hand straight up, he said, "Peace?" and added, "If I had a peace pipe, I'd pass it to you."

"Offer accepted," Leslie replied. "But, let the record show I would never touch any pipe you smoked. Okay, time to track down Agent Ghana. See what she's willing to tell us."

A moment later she announced, "Meeting Ghana for late lunch over at Jason's. You can get yourself one of those muffulettas you were talking about on our way up to Tampa."

"Thought you weren't paying attention to anything I said."

"It's called multi-tasking. I'm blessed, or maybe cursed, with high recall on what I hear."

"Rumor has it once you read something you never forget it. That true?"

"I wouldn't say I never forget what I read or hear. But recall is high I must admit. Speaking of that, something's troubling me. I reviewed Fritz's financial information this morning and if I remember correctly there was a monthly entry labeled

White Sands-Maint. I assume that's the condo monthly maintenance fee."

"I saw that. Those condos with the community pools and exercise facilities and God knows what else, are expensive."

"But $2200 a month? For a two-bedroom unit! Granted, she has a great view and plenty of room, but..."

"You want me to look into it?" Cox asked.

"Please."

———————

Twenty minutes later Leslie, Cox and Agent Ghana were seated at an outdoor table, waiting for their lunch to arrive. They had been talking about sports teams and boating, killing time until Ghana had assured herself that they were not being overheard, either by someone close by, or electronically from a distance.

"We've been given the green light," Ghana said after consulting her watch. "No electronic devices."

"Just how does that work?" Leslie asked. "I can understand picking up a receiver planted close by. That's one thing. But a receiver off in the distance? How in the world would you even know it was there?"

"Join Homeland Security and you'll learn." Ghana smiled. "We have more technology than you can imagine. More than even I know about. Speaking of technology, let me play some sound for you. To set the stage, this was taken at the Chlad house a few nights ago when your friend Stratis paid a visit shortly after the euphon was delivered by messenger."

"That's when you ran me off," Cox interjected. "Wasn't right to do that."

"Sorry 'bout that. But time was critical. You were directly in the line of sight for the video recorder."

"I take it you had a warrant for that recording?" Cox responded, barely concealing his anger despite the apology.

"Foreign Intelligence Surveillance Act warrant," Ghana replied.

"That works for foreigners, "Cox pressed, not backing off. "Chlad's a U.S. citizen. And so, I believe, is Stratis."

Holding her ground, Ghana responded, "Colton, however, is a Russian National. You were briefed, weren't you, that everything we discuss is confidential?"

"We were," Cox replied.

"Good. Take it seriously. Colton is the focus of our investigation. The euphon is the center of his activities right now, so the court has granted us approval to follow the euphon. We expected Colton to come for the euphon, so we placed a transmitter inside. Rules require us to not identify U.S. citizens, so we won't tell you the names of the participants. You should be able to work that out yourselves."

Ghana proceeded to play the recording.

"Nice to see you again, Mr. Str..."

"Please. Let us speak in the house."

"I'm so sorry. Come in." Sounds of a closing door.

"Mr. INAUDIBLE. This is my wife, INAUDIBLE. INAUDIBLE, this is Mr. INAUDIBLE."

"I trust you had a pleasant trip south. The Chladni was delivered about an hour ago and I took the liberty of assembling it. I trust that is okay with you?"

"I would have preferred seeing it come out of the bags, but that's only a minor problem.

Please assure me this is the original as it came from Pittsburgh."

"This euphon is most definitely the original one Sig, Dr. Fuller, located in Poland. The same one he certified before it went to Pittsburgh."

"Then I trust you won't mind playing each rod one note at a time. I have brought with me a meter, the same kind employed by Dr. Fuller I believe, to measure the frequencies. I will measure each reading against a chart taken from his report. Now give me a moment to turn the meter on and we're ready to go." Sounds of fabric rustling were followed a moment later by the same note by note vibrations Leslie had heard as she had listened from outside the house the night this recording had been made.

"The frequencies all match perfectly. We have a deal then. I will take this with me. The funds will be in your account the moment I receive confirmation from Esquire that the Polish government is happy with the package you deliver to them."

Footsteps. Door opening. "Have a safe trip and good luck in Warsaw."

The tape stopped. "That's all I can share at this point," Ghana said. "As I said, I trust you know the players."

"So, what's your take?" Leslie asked Ghana. "You've had time to think about this."

"Truth is, this isn't Colton speaking so it's not high on our priority list. I would say there are definitely two euphons. How they fooled the Poles I don't know. But fool them they must have. Chlad will soon be home from Poland."

"Exactly why are we being briefed?" Leslie asked, remembering all the times Junior told her of DHS coming in and clamping everything down. They wouldn't give him the time of day.

"Colton's still here. He's focused on the euphon. Man seems obsessed with having it."

Cox asked, "You have a basis for saying that? Or is that a guess?"

"Got some timing info for you. Our target arrived at Fuller's house at 11:10 the morning Fuller died. Target was inside for thirty-five minutes until 11:45. We have some sound, but it's essentially unintelligible. Technicians believe it was scrambled professionally. From what little we can reconstruct, there may have been three men, maybe an argument, we can't be certain. We believe Colton was in the garage at some point. One of the sounds has been tagged as possibly someone falling or stomping the ground. But remember, that's speculation based on an unreliable recording."

"How about copies?" Leslie asked, knowing that would be near impossible.

"You know the answer to that, Detective. Not a chance in hell! With all the politics around FISA warrants, sound bites from us will kill your case. I can, however, tell you that Chlad arrived at eleven-twenty-five. Team saw no car, the assumption being he walked from his home. About a ten-minute brisk walk, I'd imagine."

"Chlad? Assume you mean Ernst?" Leslie recalled Chlad saying he'd stopped by, got no answer, and went off to the beach — alone.

"He rang the bell," Ghana said. "A moment later he went around back. Don't know if he got in the house. As I said, Colton left at 11:45. Chlad left five minutes later."

"Is it possible Chlad's voice was the third one you heard?" Leslie asked.

"With the recording as messed as it is, anything's possible. But...timing's wrong. The three voices, assuming there were three voices, were detected before Chlad arrived."

"Let me get this clear," Cox said, "if the three-voice analysis is correct, someone, a male, was already at the Fuller home when Colton arrived. Is that accurate?"

"As accurate as we can be with this recording. Yes, Detective."

"That all you have at the Fuller residence?" Leslie asked, still not comfortable as to why DHS was yielding this information.

"We're tasked with surveilling Colton. Where he goes, we go. Another fifteen minutes or so at the Fuller residence and we would have giftwrapped the killer for you."

"What fun would that be?" Cox quipped. Seeing the agent's response, he said, "Agent Ghana, you're shaking your head. I hate to say it, but I wouldn't be at all surprised if DHS had video of the hanging and refused to share it."

"Cox!" Leslie exclaimed. "There's no need..."

Ghana raised her hand. "Detective Cox, you and I got off on the wrong foot. I should have explained why I wanted you to move out of our line of sight. I wasn't authorized to read you into the operation. I just couldn't think of a plausible reason fast enough."

"Try the truth!" Cox shot back. "Whatever that is in this case!"

"Simeon!" Leslie snapped, quickly stepping between the two. "Enough!"

"Need to clear the air if we're to work together! Here we have DHS practically witnessing a murder and the first we learn of it is a week later! Who knows what the hell they recorded? Trust them if you like, Leslie. I find it difficult!"

"Peace," Ghana calmly said, "In fact, we do have video of Colton. It's not going to help you much, but in the spirit of working together I'll release what we have. It's all been recorded outdoors, so

260

not subject to privacy concerns. The team will run a check to be certain we're in compliance with all our warrants. You'll have what we have within the hour."

"That's a start," Cox said, taking a step back. "We'll see what you have."

"And what about Jakowski?" Leslie asked.

"What about him?"

"I thought you had him in your sights as well."

"Don't know why you'd think that," Ghana winked. "He's done nothing wrong far's we know."

Leslie breathed a sigh of relief, surprising herself by her reaction. "To sum up," she said, diverting attention away from herself, "you believe there are two euphons and Stratis has the original."

"Pretty much."

"Then why rig it so Carnegie would cry foul?"

"Stratis is known for diversion. I think he created the fake by arranging for the wrong rod, knowing the Carnegie security examination would uncover the deception."

"Why would he sabotage an exhibition he paid for?"

"I learned long ago it's impossible to guess how a billionaire will spend his dollars. They don't view money the way we mere mortals do. For them, their wealth is used for diversion and fun. In this case, Stratis believed, and rightly so, that Colton had planned to steal the euphon from the Carnegie. Had the theft worked, the euphon would have been lost to Stratis forever. Either Colton would have it, or we would. Either way, Stratis wouldn't. You know about the Seminal Society Firsts. The euphon is a First and Chladni is the bridge from Newton to Edison. We believe Stratis has the Edison First Phonograph. Stratis won't give up easily on the euphon — and neither will Colton. You can put money on that."

# TWENTY-NINE

LESLIE SPENT THE REMAINDER OF the day going over the financial report put together on the Chlads by the Digital Forensics Unit. Nothing unusual popped out. Her Criminal Investigative Assistant, Wanda Hill, hadn't spotted anything either. Leslie then did the same with Fritz, noting only that the annuity she claimed she received every month had stopped several months back. That, and the fact that Fritz's condo maintenance fee was higher than Leslie expected, were the only items remaining for follow-up.

Shortly after five, Cox came by to say good-night. "Did you get a chance to go over the video from Ghana? Came in an hour ago."

"Didn't. Been busy with the financials. Anything jump out?"

"Mostly Colton driving from place to place. Starbucks for coffee type of thing. Captured him entering Fuller's place and then leaving. Time stamps match the times Ghana gave us. One thing, however."

"And what's that?" Leslie asked, now upset with herself for not having already watched the video.

"It appears Colton threw something into the center-divider hedges on the main Miromar Lakes roadway. You can see, at time stamp11:49:08 into the video, his arm coming out of the car window in a throwing motion. I can't actually see anything leaving his hand, but the motion's there."

While Cox was talking, Leslie pulled up the video and fast forwarded to 11:49. A blue BMW was thirty yards ahead when its brake light came on. The car slowed and an arm suddenly appeared out of the driver's window eight seconds later at 11:49:08 just as Cox had said. Leslie made a mental note of the scene and said, "Need to search there, see what turns up."

"I'll do it on the way home."

"I'll go with you?" Leslie volunteered.

"No need. Have a good one," he replied. "Tell Allen hello from me."

"Asshole," she thought. It wasn't so much what he said, but the tone. No wonder she disliked the man. "See you at nine," she said as upbeat as she could make it. "Be prepared to lay out all the theories you can dream up based on the facts we know. Right now, three people had access to Dr. Sig within the margin of error time frame. Let's put together likely scenarios and timelines assuming each is the killer."

"Got it. See you in the AM."

———■———

Sleep for Leslie, when it finally overtook her, was fitful. She didn't usually remember her dreams, but when she did, they were vivid and real. For the most part the images she usually recalled had no real meaning in her life, serving only to instill a sense of foreboding. But every once in a while, a dream turned out to be a premonition of something that came true. Such as the time her mother was diagnosed with possible breast cancer. Days before the biopsy Leslie saw the doctor sitting across her desk saying, "I have good news, Mrs. Barnwell. The tumor's benign." That's exactly how it turned out, with Leslie sitting next to her mother and her mother saying to the doctor, "That's exactly what my wonderful daughter here told me last week."

Leslie woke up from a dream where she was walking on a beach hand in hand with Allen. A wave rolled up and soaked his shoes. "See what happens when you don't listen," she said. "I told you to leave them in the car."

Allen quickly dropped her hand and turned to face her, his face blazing with rage, his eyes on fire. "Just stop telling me what to do!" he barked, "One mother's enough!" He raised his hands high over her head and a long sword appeared. Leslie struggled to run, but her feet were mired in the sand.

The sword slowly lowered, coming even with her neck. Then it turned toward her. Now not only were her legs frozen, but her arms as well. The sword was inches from her throat when a booming voice yelled, "Police! Put that sword down and step back!"

The sword dropped to the sand and Allen moved backward until he disappeared into the surf. The dream ended, but not before Leslie recognized the voice as belonging to the solidly built Pittsburgh detective, Pete Jakowski.

She sat upright in bed, shaken. The time was 4:18 and she held little hope of getting back to sleep.

Jakowski! What did that mean? And why was Allen involved? Around and around her thoughts went, settling on nothing. At six she was out of the shower and dressed for work. She started for her car, stopped, fished out her cell, found Jakowski's official department phone number, and called.

"Please connect me with Detective Jakowski. Pete Jakowski," she instructed the officer who answered.

"It's six in the morning! Is this an emergency or what?"

"How about a message to call me. I'm Detective Leslie Hodges of the Lee County Sheriff's Office in Florida."

"Funny you're calling from Florida. That's where I understand Jak went."

"He's on assignment?"

"He took a month leave of absence. Starting about ten days ago."

Puzzled, Leslie managed, "Okay. Thanks."

When Cox sauntered into the office at nine, he found Leslie bent over her computer. "On that list of yours," he began, "I understand Chlad, Colton and Fritz. But who the hell's BG?"

"Lower your voice, I don't want BG's name out yet."

"I'm good," Cox said, sitting on the corner of her desk. "What gives?"

"BG is Jak." In answer to Cox's frown, she added, "the Pittsburgh guy who..."

"Oh, shit! You think he's..."

"Frankly, I don't know what to think. We have reason to believe that when Colton visited Fuller there was a third man there. If Jak was in town..."

"Your notes say you picked him up at the airport a few days ago. That's a week or so after the murder."

"Here's the thing — a flight from Pittsburgh landed at that time, that much I know. I also know he walked out of the front door of the terminal shortly after that flight landed. Until I know he was actually on that plane, he's a suspect. Trouble is, he may have a contact in the department, so it's BG for now."

"You working the flight list?"

"Digital Forensics is on it. But he's good enough to cover that base. Bring up the ME file. Check these timelines with me. TOD, 11:30 to 12:15, with low likelihood of it being any earlier."

Cox flipped open his computer, logged in and brought up the file. He studied it a moment before saying, "I concur."

"Hey," Leslie said, "before we dig into the file, I see you found a needle and syringe in the Miromar Lakes median. Could belong to anyone. Tell me about it."

"Lab's working it now. There seems to be a smudge on the needle. I'm thinking it's blood. Went back and studied the video. The needle was in a bush where the video showed something landed. Looks as if Colton was wearing gloves."

"Him throwing the needle out should be enough to tie him to it. Let's see where that goes."

"Next?" Cox asked, not wanting to get ahead of his partner.

"Now that we agree on the range for TOD, we'll compare possible scenarios. Want to begin?"

"The euphon appears to be the common denominator," Cox immediately said. "Found in Poland, classified as a national treasure. The Polish government allowed it to go on tour. Question: Who arranged for that? Tour was going well when Carnegie detected an improper rod. They labeled the euphon as suspect. Remainder of the tour was canceled and the euphon returned to Florida. Returned to Ernie Chald's house to be precise. We believe the improper rod has been replaced by the proper rod. We also know..."

"Hate to break it to you, partner," Leslie interrupted, "but that's not exactly a scenario. It's a compilation of events — a timeline if you will. Here, let's do it this way." Leslie brought up a fresh screen and began typing, Cox looking over her shoulder. Soon, the screen displayed:

Two euphons-one original, one copy. Maybe a third?

Fuller certified the Pittsburgh bound euphon as the original

Certified euphon transported to Pittsburgh under bonded guard

Was the rod switched?

if so, by who?

Where was the switch made?

In Florida?

In Pittsburgh?

the Pittsburgh euphon was returned to Chlad untouched (containing wrong rod)

Proper rod was in place for Stratis to hear

Where did chlad (or whomever) get the proper rod?

From Jak?

Someone else?  Who?

A second ??? euphon went to Poland

Polish authorities accepted the second ??? euphon as genuine

is there a third euphon?

Where did second (or third) euphon come from?

Was it made in Europe or US?

 Assuming a second (or third) euphon, then where did the wood (and veneer) come from?

Where did the glass for new rods come from?

"Let's focus on item 4," Cox said. "If neither the transportation security company nor Carnegie security was breached, then the substitution was made before the euphon left Fuller's house."

"I concur," Leslie replied, putting a mental check mark beside item 4bI. "Anything else?"

"I think you have the scenarios lined up. How the hell this helps with putting a name to the killer eludes me."

"Now we look for motives and opportunities."

"When hundreds of millions are in play, there are plenty of motives," Cox said, pacing the area behind Leslie, his eyes closed as if in deep thought.

"That leaves opportunities. We have four possibilities based on who was at Fuller's within the boundaries of our agreed TOD. Chlad, Colton, Fritz, and possibly Jak."

Cox, lost in thought, didn't answer immediately. "I like Chlad," he eventually said. "He was to be paid a million a year when the euphon returned to Poland. Fuller, in Chlad's mind at least, did something, either on purpose or by error, to cheat Chlad out of his money. That fits well with the financial forensics. Chlad's behind on HOA maintenance fees, as well as late on his mortgage. Two of his credit cards are maxed out. He was at the crime scene at the right time. I say he's our man."

"Never hold in court," Leslie commented, tamping down her partner's enthusiasm. "I think you may be right, but we're not there yet. We need to tie him with physical evidence to Fuller, or at the very least, eliminate all the others. Why did you eliminate Colton? Especially now that you have a possible needle linked to him?"

"Guy might be a user. For all we know, he was injecting himself. Besides, what's his motive? The money's coming from him. That eliminates money as the motive. For him, the goal is him getting his hands on the original euphon. Killing Fuller doesn't move him one step closer to that goal."

Leslie thought about what Cox said. "But, and here's the trouble with your analysis. Colton remained in Florida after Fuller's death. If Colton killed Fuller, with his Russian training, he'd be long gone. Perhaps he went to Fuller's house to find out where the original was. I can imagine him wringing the truth out of Fuller, but not by hoisting Fuller up by his neck. Not a good way to torture someone into talking because the victim can't speak with his neck in a noose."

"I see your point. Assume for a moment Colton hung Fuller to make him reveal the location of the authentic euphon. Assume then that Fuller somehow signaled that he was willing to give Colton what he wanted. Colton then would have lowered Fuller so he could speak."

"I'm good with that," Leslie said, visualizing the gruesome scene in the garage. "Where you going with this? And why hoist Fuller up again?"

Cox quickly responded, "To keep Fuller from identifying Colton for attempted murder."

"Good point. So, you like both Colton and Chlad? Make up your mind."

"I suppose you're right," Cox conceded. "The pieces don't yet fit properly. Assume Fuller refused to give Colton anything of value? Then what would be gained by killing him? He would have let him down."

Leslie thought a moment before beginning a new chart.

TIMELINE

| | |
|---|---|
| 11:10 am | Colton arrives at Fuller's |
| 11:25 am | Chlad arrives at Fuller's |
| 11:30 am | Fritz left her condo |
| 11:45 am | Colton left Fuller's |
| 11:50 am | Chlad left Fuller's |
| 12:03 pm | Fritz arrived at Fuller's |
| 12:07 pm | First Lee County Sheriff Deputy to arrive |

Cox studied the timeline, before saying, "You left out your Pittsburgh cop friend, Jakowski."

"If Ghana is right, he would have arrived at the Fuller house before 11:10 and left before 12:07."

"So, who was actually there at TOD?"

Leslie clenched her lips together in frustration. "Unfortunately, this is one of those situations where actual TOD is of marginal help. The time we need to determine is what time the body was lifted off the ground. Not the actual TOD. According to the ME, strangulation could have begun as early as 11:15."

"That points right back to Colton. Assuming the timeline is correct." Cox pulled up the medical report. "ME says the most probable time strangulation began was between 11:45 and 11:55."

"Fritz claims she didn't touch the body when she arrived, so we don't know for certain if Fuller was actually dead at that point. Deputy found no pulse. Body temperature wasn't taken until the ME team arrived, so TOD is, at best, an estimate." Leslie remained silent for several minutes before saying, "The hanging, while not likely, could have occurred before Colton arrived. Based on what we have, I'm back and forth. One minute I like Chlad, the next, Colton. We need to build a case against both and see where that takes us."

Leslie's computer beeped, signaling an answer to a request she had made to Investigator Lizabeth Hillard about Jakowski's travel schedule.

After studying the response, Leslie said, "According to Hillard, Jak arrived in town on January 12th. That put him here the day before Fuller died."

"Puts him squarely in the running," Cox commented.

The next entry caused Leslie to suck in her breath. Jakowski landing Fort Myers in four hours. Looking at Cox, she said, trying to keep her voice neutral, "Let's move Jakowski to the top of that list. Use BG as an alias. I now believe he was in town at the critical time and didn't bother to tell me, either before Fuller died — or afterward."

# THIRTY

LESLIE WANTED COMPANY FOR LUNCH, someone she could talk with, discuss the thoughts banging around in her brain. Allen, of course, was her first choice, but he was tied up in a trial. Her next call was to her partner, Daryl Fischer, who she was surprised to learn was still in the hospital. He sounded excited about her bringing sandwiches.

"Anything special?" she asked.

"Surprise me," Fischer responded. "Anything's better than the lunches in this place. I guess that's not fair. Food's not so bad, only it reminds me of my high school cafeteria. The menu names change every day, but the food tastes the same."

Leslie put Fischer's comments down to boredom. Lee Memorial was known for its excellent food service.

Logistically it worked out that her route took her past the Artisan Eatery where she picked up two Cubans, bringing to mind Pete Jakowski and the almost disaster of her traveling with the big guy to Poland. She chided herself for even considering going along with him, but everything had seemed so logical. According to Agent Ghana, Jakowski worked for Stratis as…as what? If the Verona Police Department's rules were anything like Lee County's, then all off-duty work would have had to be pre-approved. While waiting for her sandwiches, she sent a message to Investigator Hillard asking for details of all off-duty police-related activities of Pete Jakowski.

"This is really a nice surprise, Leslie," an up-beat Daryl Fischer proclaimed when she walked into his hospital room carrying two Artisan Eatery bags. "You're a sight for sore eyes."

"Thought you'd be long gone from here. Doin' okay?"

"I'm told I'll be outta here tomorrow. Believe it when it happens."

"Back to work?"

"Rehab for a month. Then ride the desk until this Wallace Terrig fiasco weaves its merry way up through the ranks to Tallahassee." He tossed off the sheet and threw his legs over the side of the bed, struggling to keep the flimsy hospital gown closed.

"Hey, what're you doing?"

"Doc said to walk. Doesn't want me lazing around all day."

"Lazing? That a technical term?"

"Suppose so. Besides, it's my shoulder. Nothing wrong with my legs. How about we eat in the visitor's room? Change of scene."

When they were seated and the sandwiches arranged, Leslie said, "Fish, I need you back on the job. Cox is...well let's just say he's a piece of work. I can't believe this whole thing with the review boards and all. It should be cut and dried. You shot in self-defense."

"Sorry to say, it's anything but. Terrig's lawyer claims his client was shot with his hands up."

"That's not true! I told..."

"Seems it makes no difference what you told them. There's no video. Allows the defense to say what they want."

"For a man who can't work, you're taking this rather upbeat."

"Is there another way? They want to give me full pay for answering the 9-1-1 line, so be it."

Leslie knew that not to be true. Not working was eating at her partner. Unable to do anything about it, she changed the subject. "I see your fine footprint all over the Fuller file. Have any theories you care to share?"

"Thought you'd never ask. You almost got your ass snookered by that fast-talking northerner."

"I don't need a reminder, thank you," Leslie replied, feigning annoyance. "But here's something you may not know. That room, the one in the name of Mr. and Mrs. Leslie Hodges, that was a room adjoining Chlad's. Used to house armed guards protecting the euphon. It wasn't a sleeping room."

"You got that info from...?"

"A source I can't talk about. Sorry."

"Ghana?"

"How'd you..."

"Little Birdies," Fischer answered, his eyes smiling. "You mentioned Cox. How's he working out?"

Leslie bristled. "I shouldn't say this, but that man gets under my skin. Don't know why."

"You're not alone in that feeling. Guy's smart, though."

"Smart's not the problem. He just..."

"I can get him removed."

"The devil you know is better than..."

"I know the saying. The man gets under everyone's skin. His brain's not always focused, but he's brilliant — like you. Who put together that fact chart? You or him?"

"Did it together."

"Good piece of work. One suggestion. Need to nail down a few things. If there's a second euphon, who made it? Figure out who that someone was. If there's only one euphon, it's an entirely different ballgame. A third's stretching it."

"Why's that such a game changer? I mean for the homicide investigation if there's only one?"

"If there's no duplicate, then I'd suggest the killer is somebody desperate to own the original at all costs. Stratis, Colton, or even the Kumars. Frankly, any of the Seminal Society collectors would be in that category."

"If there's a second euphon?" Leslie asked, anxious to learn from her former partner.

"I'd take all the Society collectors out of contention, including your friend Jakowski. Fuller was more value alive to any would be owner because he could validate the original. Chlad would be high on my list, but don't forget Fuller's lady friend."

"What would Fritz gain by Fuller's death? Doesn't add up. If we take Jak and Colton out, that leaves us with Chlad."

"Won't argue with you. If Chlad's on your radar, his wife should be as well."

"Carol? She's..."

"Losing it, I agree. Do your due diligence. See what her neurologist is willing to tell you. Never know what you'll find."

"You think she's faking?"

"Do your due diligence's all I'm saying."

"Cox likes Chlad for the perp."

"And you? What's your take?"

"On and off."

"Whatever's bothering you, be sure to run it to ground," Fischer instructed.

"I'm going in circles."

"Speaking of going in circles, you know," Fischer said, lowering his voice, "you're not teamed with Cox by coincidence. Hud doesn't like the guy. Sarge's done everything in his power to kick Cox to the curb. Boots sees something in him. I think it's his out of the box thinking. Pairing you with him tells you what the captain thinks of you."

"I'm a frickin' rookie! How the hell am I supposed to cultivate a guy like that?"

"You, dear partner, may be the only one in the department smart enough — and dare I add, strong-willed enough — to rein him in. You're most likely his only chance."

# THIRTY-ONE

"THANK YOU FOR AGREEING TO see us on such short notice," Leslie said to Carol Chlad when she opened the door shortly after four pm. "You remember my partner, Detective Cox?"

"Hello, there. Oh, I thought that other nice man was coming."

"Detective Fischer is taking some time off. Detective Cox is filling in for him." They had gone over this on their last visit. Either Carol was an award-winning actress, or...or what?

"I hope he's not sick or anything. So many people are sick these days. Ernie keeps telling me to wear a mask, but I forget. Tell me again why you are here."

"May we come in? I'll explain it to you."

"I'm so sorry. I seem to forget things these days. Please do come in. I don't have anything to serve you. My husband is away."

"You didn't go with him?"

"He's on a business trip. Somewhere. I don't remember where he said he was going. Maybe New York. I didn't feel up to it."

"Will he be gone long?"

"Sometimes a week. Sometimes a month. I don't know which."

"Did he take the euphon with him?"

"What?"

"Did he take the euphon, the musical instrument, with him?"

"I don't know what you are asking. He went on business."

276

"The musical instrument. The euphon."

"He doesn't play a musical instrument. You must be mistaken. Oh, I just remembered, I have cookies. I can get you cookies."

Before Leslie could stop her, Carol was out of her chair and on her way to the kitchen. Turning to Cox, she said, "Either this woman deserves an Academy Award, or she's far too gone for us to continue this interview."

"I agree. Anything we get could be tainted. I'd love for her to show us around, see what we can see. A good lawyer will eat our lunch about informed consent. Better play by the book."

A few minutes later Carol was back, a box of chocolate chip cookies in one hand and a pile of paper napkins in the other. "Here are some nice cookies." Placing the box and the napkins on the side table, she sat down where she had been. "Now, what were we talking about?"

"I was asking about a musical instrument. The euphon. It's wood with glass rods. Did your husband..."

"Oh, yes, now I remember. It came out of two golf bags. Strange, I didn't know he played golf."

"Did he play the euphon?"

"The euphon? Afraid I don't..."

"Have you ever heard the euphon played?" Cox asked.

"Sig's friend. Don't recall her name, she..."

"Selma. Selma Fritz."

"Oh, now I remember. Selma. Yes, Selma played something. I do not recall its name."

"What sound did it make?"

Carol's eyes went dead. Her fingers opened and closed rapidly as if she was trying to grasp something and missing. "Oh, now I remember!" Her eyes coming alive as she said, "Outer space music. It was outer space music."

"Did your husband take the euphon with him to Poland?"

"Poland? Did he go to Poland? I thought he went to New York. I like Poland."

"Did you ever go to Poland?" Leslie asked. "Just you and your husband?"

"With Dr. Fuller and his friend."

"Selma?"

"Yes, Selma. She was looking at furniture.

"Did you buy anything?" Cox asked, looking around. "Antiques?"

"Oh, no! I wouldn't know anything about buying antiques. Selma and Sig did that. I just watched."

"What did you watch?" Leslie asked, her curiosity aroused.

"Selma was so fussy about the wood — and the glass. It had to be just so."

"Are you saying Selma was more concerned about what type of wood the furniture was made from than about the furniture itself?"

"Not the furniture. The glass. I remember her asking questions about the glass and…and…oh, lead. Especially about the lead. I didn't know glass had lead in it."

While Carol spoke, Cox looked up lead glass in his phone's browser. "Here's something," he said, reading from his cell. "Lead is used to replace calcium in potash glass. That's how crystal glass is made. It also says you can determine if glass has lead in it because it rings when tapped. The higher the lead, the more ringing it does. I think we may have just found where the Chladni rod glass came from."

Leslie recalled Fritz's condo and the European furniture with its fancy colored glass. The piece that came directly to mind was positioned at the end of a hallway. Floor to ceiling display case having colored glass shelves. An unusual piece in an unusual place.

Carol's phone rang. She said into the phone, "I'm really glad you called. Those detectives are back asking questions."

She listened a moment before saying, "Okay, I will." She then held her phone out to Leslie. "My husband wants to speak with you."

Leslie took the phone. "Detective Leslie Hodges speaking. Is this Ernst Chlad?"

"Who the hell else would be calling my wife?" a very distressed voice said. "Please leave our house right now! Carol is not in any condition to be speaking to police!"

"We're just trying to piece together what we can on the euphon."

"Forget the damn euphon! It's been returned to the Polish National Museum! Everything is in order."

"I assume you delivered it yourself."

"I did. Not that it's your business what I do with my property!"

"And they accepted the one you delivered as the original?" Leslie pressed.

"What're you implying, Detective?"

"Just being certain we have our facts straight?"

"The euphon is not your business! I own it! I can sell it to whomever I like! And I don't have to account to you — or anybody!"

"What is our business, Mr. Chlad," Leslie replied, her voice sharp and to the point, "is the timeline on the day your friend, Dr. Fuller, died. During our previous conversation you stated you left your home at approximately eleven in the morning and you went to Dr. Fuller's home. Is that correct?"

"I also said he didn't answer the door, so I left."

"Is that entirely accurate?"

"Yes."

"And you then went to the beach and spent the day walking the sand. Do I have that correct as well?"

"After leaving Sig's house, I drove straight to the beach. What the hell's…"

"Let me ask the question another way. Did you see Dr. Fuller the morning of January thirteenth?"

"No."

"Did you at any time have in your possession a second, or duplicate, euphon?"

"I certainly did not. And I resent…"

"What would you say if I told you we have evidence suggesting you were in possession of a second euphon?"

"I'd say, talk to my lawyer! I'm not answering another bloody question without counsel! And neither is my wife! Leave my house this instant! You understand me?"

"Perfectly well, Mr. Chlad. The next time we talk it will be with your lawyer." Leslie paused, was about to ask another question and thought better of it. "And just who might that be?"

"Jack Huntington," came the quick reply, as if he had already hired the well-known Fort Myers criminal defense lawyer.

"As you wish," Leslie replied. "And when do you plan on returning to Florida?"

"I have an early morning flight. Gets me to Fort Myers around noon tomorrow."

"Have a nice flight Mr. Chlad. I'll hand the phone back to your wife." Holding the phone out, Leslie said, "Your husband wants to talk to you. We'll be leaving now."

"Is there something wrong? You're leaving without eating even one cookie."

"Everything is just fine, Mrs. Chlad," Leslie gently replied. "It's too close to dinner. Thank you anyway."

"What do you make of all that?" Cox asked when they were outside. "Think she's hiding something, or...."

"I'd say she's lost. Eyes were too flat. My question: What's bugging the husband that he needs a thousand dollar an hour criminal defense lawyer?"

"For starters, he lied to us about the second euphon. And we have him at the scene within the possible kill time. We're closing in."

"My take, he hasn't actually hired Huntington yet. It's just the first name that popped to mind."

"Based on...?" Cox asked.

"Huntington's too good. The first thing he would have insisted is that Chlad tell us nothing. We just got information from the man. Either he wasn't listening to advice of counsel, or he had no counsel—not yet anyway." A thought struck Leslie. "We need to consider the possibility that Dr. Sig might have been the one to substitute the wrong sized rod for the proper one, all to Ernst Chlad's economic detriment."

"Why would Fuller do that?" Cox asked, puzzled.

"I don't know. Maybe someone paid him a lot of money to do it."

Before Cox could respond, Leslie's phone buzzed with a text.

DINNER 7:30 -JASON'S DELI, JAK

# THIRTY-TWO

ALLEN'S WORDS RANG IN HER head as Leslie pulled to a stop in front of Jason's Deli. He had asked her point blank, "Why the hell you having dinner with a guy who damn near smoked your career? Sometimes, my love, I swear you need your head examined."

"And I love you too," she had snapped before hanging up.

The truth was that Allen's question was exactly her own question. Why the hell was she here? If this meeting was necessary for the criminal investigation, then why had she cut Cox out? Most likely Allen had tumbled to this inconsistency before she had, accounting for the tinge of jealousy she had detected.

Stepping through the restaurant door, she refused to acknowledge that a large part of why she was here was deeply personal.

Jakowski sat with his broad shoulders to the door, his eyes focused on his cell, thick fingers racing across the keyboard. Leslie slid into the seat across from him, positioning herself in front of a tall root beer he had ordered for her.

"Missed you on the plane," Jakowski said, not taking his eyes from his cell. "Give me a moment here."

She sipped her drink, biding her time until he finished.

"Sorry, Leslie. Had to send that. Thank you for joining me. You missed a nice time in Warsaw."

"Got sick in the Ladies' Room," she said, not wanting to explain all that had transpired. "Plane was gone before I was feeling well enough to come out. Hope I didn't screw up your operation."

"Anything serious?" he asked, genuine concern in his voice.

"Fine now. Thanks for asking."

"It wasn't my operation I was worried about. It's yours. I have video for you of Chlad certifying to the Polish minister that the euphon he was returning to Poland was the same one that had left Poland originally."

"And just why is that important to my homicide investigation? I assume it's the homicide you're referring to."

"Removes motive from Chlad. He made a deal with the Poles to allow the euphon to go on tour. Now the euphon is back home in Poland safe and sound. Chlad's getting his yearly fee from Poland. Happy camper."

Jakowski had a point about Chlad not having motive. But she reminded herself the critical time for the motive wasn't yesterday in Poland; it was at the time of the murder last week in Fuller's garage. And at that point, Chlad knew only that the Carnegie euphon was suspicious. "You here to bust my chops, or help?"

"Help, of course. But I sense anger. You're the one stood me up. Not the other way 'round. Let's order, then we can straighten this out."

They studied the menu in silence, ordered, then drained their glasses. "Another, while we're waiting?" Jakowski asked. "Or would you prefer the real thing?"

"Enough for me." She refrained from adding, "I'm on the clock." Instead, she said, "Exactly when did you first arrive in Florida?"

"About seven years ago."

"You know what I mean."

"Why don't you tell me what you mean? I thought we were friends, colleagues, working a case. It seems I'm mistaken."

"If by being colleagues you mean trusting each other, how about starting when you asked me to pick you up at the airport! I believe you were already here in Florida before that. I'm right about that, aren't I?"

"As a matter of fact, you are."

Leslie couldn't determine if the big guy was surprised at her knowing he had been in Florida early. If he was, he hid it well. "Want to tell me about your time down here? When you got here? What you've been doing? That sort of thing? Things colleagues tell each other — when they're being colleagues."

"Can't."

"And just why not?"

"Working an assignment."

"For the City of Verona? Or private?"

"Former."

"I was told you were on leave of absence."

"That's for cover. Working a Stratis angle."

"How do I verify that?"

"You don't. Here's where trust comes in. Either you're with me or you're against me. Time to declare."

"You're the one needs to declare! You could have told me you were working a matter. No! Instead, you had me pick you up at the airport as if you had just arrived. Perfect alibi to cover a murder the way I see it."

Their muffulettas arrived and again they fell quiet, Leslie struggling with her thoughts. Eventually, she said, "What can you tell me? My focus is on the homicide, anything you can give is welcome. Start by telling me how you got around before I picked you up?"

"Blue Ford rental with a racing stripe down the hood. Last car on the lot type of thing. Promised myself I'd switch it out. But, hey, I grew to like it. Guess I'm just a teenager at heart."

Leslie closed her eyes and used her near photographic memory to bring up an image of the hotel parking lot the night she had dropped him off after their surveillance of Stratis visiting Chlad. Sure enough, the image of a Ford sports car formed, racing stripe and all, parked four cars down from the main entrance. "Okay, so you came to Florida. For what purpose?"

"The goal is to catch Stratis performing an illegal act in the procurement of the euphon. The bidding has gone wild, that we knew. We also know Stratis will stop at nothing to secure that euphon. One of these days he's bound to get careless."

"But Stratis wasn't here at the time. Why were you here?"

"No one ever knows where that man will show up at any given moment. You know how the President uses two planes, one as a decoy?"

"I do."

"Stratis does the same. Sends planes to different places. He's not always on the plane."

"I thought he sponsored the Chladni at the Carnegie. Wouldn't he naturally have been in Pittsburgh?"

"Nothing Stratis does follows any conventional notion of natural."

"You came down here on opening day. Suggests to me you knew something was going to happen to delay or postpone the opening. Did you know the euphon was going to be declared suspicious?"

"Colton decamped from Pittsburgh and I followed Colton," Jakowski answered. "Theory being he was headed to where the original Chladni was."

Leslie took a moment to process what she had just learned. The detective had evaded a direct answer to what he knew but had provided helpful information. A thought struck her. "Around that time, we received a heads-up from DHS about Colton and the Blue Footed Golden Booby. Any chance that info came from you?"

"Not at liberty to confirm or deny."

"I'll take that as a confirmation."

"If it floats your boat. Be my guest."

"You say'n I'm wrong?"

"Not saying either way."

"You came down to tail Colton."

"Among other things."

"What does that mean?"

"The Stratis operation is confidential. No notes. No reports."

"I'll do my best."

"I trust you, Leslie, but I fear that's a one-way street. Colton planned to steal the Chladni from the Science Center in an elaborate scheme he had cooked up. He bribed several security guards. One of them went to the Feds. From what I understand, it was a brilliant operation, and except for the faithful guard, would have worked. Stratis sniffed out the plan and to prevent the heist he concocted a scheme to have the Chladni declared a fake."

"By substituting out one of the glass rods. Then Fuller was in on it!"

"You know about the glass rods? Good. "

"What I don't know is where in the world a duplicate glass rod came from. You can't buy it from Amazon. Had to be custom made."

"The same place the rods for the second euphon came from."

Jakowski now had Leslie's full attention. "Second euphon? You believe then there's more than one? How the hell many are there?"

"Great question, Leslie. You just put your finger on a major problem. Ask yourself this: What happens to the value of the euphon when more than one shows up?"

"Disaster for the Seminal Society, that's for certain," Leslie answered, recalling the conversation with Riya Kumar at the Columbia Restaurant when she had said, "You know, in our world, the value of an artifact is in the absolute knowledge of its uniqueness. We all wanted to know the Chladni didn't come with shadows."

Jakowski was quick to say, "Imagine parting with five hundred million dollars and finding out several other Seminal Society collectors have original Chladnis in their collection."

"Enough for..."

"Murder!" Jakowski interjected. "But here's the thing. These folks are too good to be involved in major crimes. Brings way too much official scrutiny."

"Didn't you just finish telling me about Colton planning the heist of the century? You're going in circles."

"Colton's a rather new member of the Society and connected with the Russian mob. That's not good for anybody. I suppose that's why DHS is on his case so heavy."

Leslie fell silent, sorting through what she had just learned, meshing it with what she already knew. A fuzzy picture was forming, akin to being halfway finished with one of her jigsaw puzzles. She could almost see the completed image, but a few key pieces were still eluding her — maybe even more than a few. Sensing Jakowski had told her about all he was prepared to tell her, she ventured one further question. "Your turn to be honest with me, Jak. Were you at the Fuller house at the time of the murder?"

# THIRTY-THREE

THE "SERGEANT HUDSON OAKMORE" SIGN outside Hud's office was upside down in its holder when Leslie approached, most likely the result of a chewing out received by one of his many direct reports. Oakmore wasn't known for mincing words when a deputy crossed the line. This meeting hadn't been her idea, she had been summoned to appear in his office at 8:30 a.m. After her discussion last night with Jakowski, she welcomed the meeting. Guidance was required.

"I don't suppose you know why you're here, Hodges," Oakmore began the instant she stepped through the doorway. "Close the door and take a seat."

Sitting, she knew from office chatter, meant there was something important he wanted to discuss. Standing in front of his desk was reserved for verbal beatings.

When she was seated, Oakmore began, "Please tell me everything that happened this past Friday...." Consulting a note pad, he added, "January 15th. Begin from the instant you stepped out of that pawn shop."

"What's this..."

"Never mind why! Just tell me exactly, and I mean exactly, what you saw! If you're guessing at something, be sure I know you're guessing. I'm recording what you say. Now focus! Go!"

Leslie closed her eyes a moment, recalling the images that had been burned into her brain. Then, keeping her voice calm, as if narrating a scene from a favorite old movie, she related exactly what had happened movement by movement, adding her thought process when appropriate. The pain she now felt was as real as it had been in real time.

Oakmore stopped her when she got to the part where she vomited on Officer Brownwell's patrol car. "You're absolutely certain the perp, one Wallace Terrig, shot that woman?"

"I didn't know his name at that time. But yes, the man Fischer shot is the same man I saw shoot a woman in front of the hair salon."

"At the time Fischer discharged his weapon were you pointing your weapon at Terrig?"

Again, Leslie closed her eyes for an instant. "I'm embarrassed to say I wasn't."

"Embarrassed? Why so?"

"For the ten years I was in uniform I wore my weapon on my right side. Now that I'm not in uniform I wear it on the left under my arm. When I heard the shots, I inadvertently reached to the right. I did finally get my weapon out, but it was not yet fully aimed when Terrig fired. I'd be dead if Fischer hadn't shot him. That much I know for certain."

Oakmore flipped the recorder off. "Sorry to put you through this, but..."

"What's going on?"

"Don't you read the papers? Watch TV?"

"Sorry. Been busy these last few days."

"That lawyer, Huntington, held a press conference last night. Claims Terrig shot Fischer in self-defense. Says the two of you were in plain clothes and he had no idea you were cops. Says you pulled your gun and were about to shoot him when he fired at you. He claims he missed you and hit Fischer."

"That's bullshit!" Leslie exploded. "He's lying! What's he say about shooting his girlfriend"

"Claims it wasn't him. Says he dropped her off at the salon and a guy in a car on the other side of his truck shot her. He was taking aim at the other guy when you pulled your gun on him."

"That's ..."

"Crap! I know. I wanted to be sure your story's solid before you go see Lieutenant Maxwell over in IA. That's today at two. Any problem with that?"

"I suppose not. I've already given her my version. Can't imagine what else they want."

Hud studied her a moment. "Something's bothering you, Detective? What're you not saying?"

"Nothing to do with IA. It's the Fuller case."

"If Cox is the problem, then..."

"Mind if we postpone a discussion on Cox? It's working about as well as can be expected. He and I've come to an understanding."

"Good luck with that! If it's not Cox, then what?"

"Boots asked me to set up an eyes-only file. Have you..."

"She briefed me. What about it?"

Leslie told Oakmore about her dinner with Jakowski and her assessment that the Pittsburgh cop was pretty much telling the truth.

"I assume you asked him directly whether or not he was at the Fuller house the morning of the homicide."

"That's why I'm here. He acknowledged he was in or near the house from before Colton arrived until just before noon when Chlad left. Claims he walked in from the main road and left the same way. He says Colton came to the door, Fuller and Colton argued and Colton dragged Fuller out to the garage. At some point Chlad arrived, rang the bell, walked around back and came in through the open lanai door. Jak hid and Chlad never saw him. Chlad, hearing noise from the garage, went out there. Jak says Chlad and Colton began arguing — or yelling — and then Colton left, followed about ten minutes later by Chlad."

"What were they arguing about?"

"Jak says he doesn't know. I don't believe him."

"Why don't you trust him?"

"That's where I need help. He claims he's on an official investigation into Stratis sanctioned by his department. DHS, while they didn't say this exactly, has me believing Jak's freelancing and is working directly for Stratis. Running interference for him the way I understand it."

"And you want me to press Pittsburgh?"

"Verona, not Pittsburgh. But yes. I'm far too low for that."

"Who then? Me? Boots? Who do you have in mind?"

Leslie had anticipated the conversation would find itself at this juncture. Problem was she didn't think Captain Stetson was the right person either because of Jakowski claiming her as a former lover. A misstep here and Leslie's career would be at an end. She straightened her back, took a deep breath and said, "Can I talk to you off the record? I know I should let this drop, but...but I need help."

"Off the record to the extent you don't give me information about criminal activity." Oakmore was playing this by the book as she had hoped he would.

"Fair enough," Leslie agreed, welcome for the opportunity to receive input from a person she trusted. Lurking in her mind was the possibility her captain hadn't been entirely truthful with her even though Stetson had denied in the strongest possible terms having had an affair with Jakowski.

"Interesting," Oakmore said after Leslie laid out what Jakowski had said about their affair and what Stetson's response had been. "One thing we know for certain, one of them is lying. I'll put my money on Jak playing you. But the truth is we never know."

The silence in the room was overpowering. Leslie had always heard that when this happens the first to speak loses. Loses what? That was the question she had asked herself the first time she had heard that old negotiating rule. It appeared to Leslie that she had been dismissed and Oakmore was now waiting for her to politely leave his office. She resolved to hold her ground, forcing him to issue a verbal order to leave.

After what seemed an eternity, Oakmore cleared his throat. "Here's my advice, for what it's worth. I know you're aware that how you resolve this will ultimately affect your performance ratings and your career. So, I need not tell you to proceed with caution. Since I agreed to keep it off the record, I'll honor your request." Oakmore paused before continuing, appearing to carefully select his words. "If I go to Boots on your behalf, she'll know you told me about her possible affair and didn't trust her. Personally, I'd be pissed off you did that to me."

Processing what her boss had just said, Leslie responded. "I assume you're suggesting..."

"I'm suggesting you go directly to Boots, tell her what you want done and be upfront with her that because of Jak's allegation of an affair, while you personally believe her, which it sounds to me you do, it would be best for all concerned if the Sheriff himself makes the inquiry."

Leslie had not thought of involving the Sheriff. That would indeed clear the air. "Thank you, Sarge. Good advice. Appreciate you taking the time to hear me out."

Leslie wasn't back to the Pit a minute before Cox appeared. "What did Hud want?" he asked without preamble.

"No, hello? No, how are you this fine morning?"

"Thought you didn't like small talk. Shit, Leslie, you confuse me. What the hell'd Hud want? About me?"

"Personnel matter."

"Me?"

"No. Not you. Me. Wanted to know what I saw at the pawn shop."

"Thought that was in the bag."

"I think the justified shooting part is. This has to do with the criminal trial. They're claiming perp shot Fish in self-defense."

"That's crap! Ballistics supports your version."

"One can only trust. Any luck with the Fritz woman?" Leslie inquired, refocusing the discussion. "Her condo maintenance fee thing. What about those BamArt payments? Where'd they come from? What're they for?"

"That's why I'm here. Investigator Hillard just posted her report. BamArt appears to be short for Bamberg Artysta, Ltd., a company registered in the Channel Islands."

"Who the hell is Bamberg Artysta?" Leslie asked, her eyes rolling in puzzlement. "And where the hell are the Channel Islands?"

"Wait for it. Drumroll. Bamberg Artysta is none other than Selma Fritz! She's managing director. Channel Islands are in the English Channel off the coast of Normandy. Had to look it up myself. Understand it's a tax haven."

"What's this Bamberg company do?"

"Can't get their financial info. But did manage to find their charter. Buying and selling European classic furniture and antiquities."

"Fits with her background. What do you mean, you can't get financials?"

"Channel Islands is a low transparency jurisdiction. Set up that way for tax havens, you name it."

Leslie grabbed her phone.

"Whoa," Cox exclaimed, "Who the hell you calling?"

"Agent Ghana. Let's see just how much clout DHS actually has around the world." When Ghana didn't answer, Leslie left a message outlining what she wanted.

"And just what is that piece of valuable information you just promised Ghana?"

"I'm now positive there's a second euphon. Perhaps they're both fakes. Perhaps the second was copied from the first. That's my take."

"In either case," Cox replied, immediately picking up on the thread, "the forger would require wood and glass from the late 1700's. Where the hell would that come from?"

Leslie looked Cox straight in the eyes saying nothing.

"What? What's that look for?"

Leslie continued staring, as if to say, come on now, it's all right there in front of you.

"Oh, shit!" Cox finally exclaimed. "Bamberg Artysta! Buying and selling furniture. The euphon is a piece of furniture when you think of it."

"Assume Fritz bought the furniture for its wood and glass values," Leslie prompted. "Someone would have had to make the actual euphon. That someone would be highly skilled at woodworking and possibly glass blowing."

"Now who're you calling?" Cox asked.

"Same person." Again, Leslie's call went directly to voice mail. Again, she left a message, this time saying, "Agent Ghana, how about a list of employees of Bamberg Artysta Ltd.? Surely, your Interpol contacts can get that for you without breaking a sweat. Thanks."

"Hey! Look at this!" Cox said excitedly, his eyes focused on his computer screen. "I think I found what we're looking for."

Leslie looked over his shoulder at a Bamberg Artysta webpage showing a pin located in Bamberg, Germany, near something called the Linker Regnitzarm. "This appears to be a store!"

"Says here the proprietor, Heinrick Nowak, is a master cabinet maker specializing in reconstructed furniture, from modern to antiquities."

"You're making progress," Leslie said. "What can we find about this Nowak guy?"

Cox went silent for several minutes as he browsed through the Internet. "Oh, shit!" he exclaimed. "Store closed two months back."

"Alert Investigator Hillard to the store and to Nowak. See what she turns up." Leslie turned her attention to her ringing phone, the name Ghana being displayed. "Leslie here," she answered. "So glad you called back."

Ghana, her tone defiant, asked, "Now just what do you have for me that would make me waste a valuable Interpol IOU on getting that information you requested?"

"I believe there are two euphons," Leslie said to the DHS agent. "Both may be fakes. But I think not. I believe a fake copy went back to Poland."

"Tell me more."

"Will you obtain the financial info for us?"

"Perhaps."

"Bamberg Artysta runs a shop in Bamberg specializing in copying antiques. Guy by the name of Heinrick Nowak is the main person. Selma Fritz is the managing partner. I believe Fritz collected old furniture and was able to find the exact wood, veneer, and glass as used in the original euphon. Nowak copied the euphon."

Leslie was greeted with a moment of silence, followed by, "You did well, Detective Hodges! Took us months to arrive at the same conclusion. Colton, just two hours ago, we believe, came to the same conclusion. The euphon Chlad returned to the Polish Government was the fake. The real one, Colton believes, remains in Florida."

"If he's right about the real euphon being here, then Stratis already has it and it's long gone."

"If a hundred million dollars appears in an account owned in any way by the Chlads, then you're right," Agent Ghana replied, her tone softening.

"I thought the price was five hundred million," Leslie said, thinking the DHS agent had misspoken.

"Beggars can't be choosers," Ghana said. "Stratis had Chlad over a financial barrel. Guy's tapped out. But you're still missing one piece of the puzzle."

"And what's that?"

"Who made the glass rods? They had to have been copied as well. And tuned to absolute perfection. The frequencies had to match perfectly for every rod. My sources tell me that's not an easy task. For one thing, the original rods and the copy would have to be in the same place for a period of time in order to perfect the tuning."

"I'm assuming they made the duplicate euphon at the Bamberg shop."

"Could be. But the shop's now closed," Ghana replied. "Your guy Heinrick Nowak was last seen at immigration in Buenos Aries in transit to parts unknown. Also, you should know there's no glass making equipment on the premises. And judging from the pictures I'm looking at, there never has been."

"Don't really require glass making. Those rods can come from other sources. Just need to be tuned. What about sound testing. They would have to get the sound right."

"If you are asking about a sound-shielded area, there definitely could have been that. All the equipment has been removed, but I see holes where speakers could have been."

# THIRTY-FOUR

STANDING OUTSIDE HER CAPTAIN'S OF-
FICE, Leslie was surprisingly calm waiting for
her turn in the barrel. She had taken Oakmore's
comments to heart and was prepared to lay everything out, the chips falling where they may.
Nothing else made her comfortable. Head up, face
forward, go at it! her mother liked to say. Always
following with, Just be ready for the consequences my dear.

"You can go in now, Detective," Stetson's
assistant said. "But be fast, she has a luncheon
engagement."

"Must be a command performance," Leslie
commented, surprised because it was a source of
pride with Captain Stetson that she never took
lunch unless required to for official duties.

"Old friend," the assistant winked. "Going for
Cubans. Promised to bring one back for me."

Alarm bells sounded in Leslie's brain. Lunch
most likely was with Jakowski, causing her to
rethink her plan.

Stetson's voice boomed, "Whatever it is you
want, Hodges. Make it quick, I gotta run in a
moment."

Too late to back down, Leslie forced her head
up. "Captain," she began, willing her arms to hang
naturally at her side, "I need to update you on a
conversation I had with Pete Jakowski last night."

"I read your report. It's all there, I presume."

"It's complete, as far as it goes. But I…"

"You're concerned about whether he's free-lancing for that guy Stratis or working undercover for the Verona Police Department. That's why you're here, right?"

Stetson's astute directness caught Leslie off guard. "I'd like..."

"I'm concerned as well," Stetson said, not waiting to hear Leslie's response. "That's why I've asked Sheriff Radclif to personally call Jakowski's chief and find out, top guy to top guy, what the hell's going on. Protocol would have required such a communication before he ever arrived down here, I'll grant you that. But sometimes folks don't dot all the i's, especially where the Feds are concerned. Those folks are notorious for not even telling each other what's going down. Thought it best if the Sheriff makes the call himself. Because of what Jak told you about me and him I think it best if I stay out of the loop. Want nothing tainting your thought process."

"Appreciate that, Cap," Leslie managed, trying hard to keep her face quiet, not giving away her relief. "How long do you expect that to take?"

"By end of shift. Tomorrow at the latest." Stetson studied the rookie a long minute. "Why? You getting close to something?"

"Hard to tell. We're pretty certain we know all the players who were at the Fuller house at the critical time. Now we need actual evidence linking one or more of them to the hanging."

Standing, Stetson said, "Detective, I'd love to hear your theories, but your friend Jak's waiting. He suggested a place over at Cape Coral. Casa Rojas Cuban Bakery. Man seems to be a Cuban sandwich fan."

"He is that," Leslie agreed, starting for the door.

"Oh," Stetson said, following Leslie into the hallway, "I see Ernst Chlad hired Jack Huntington.

That lawyer's got more skins than a python. You're going to face him in the Bishop homicide trial, so be careful what you say to him now. I'd suggest allowing Cox to do most of the questioning."

"Thanks for the heads-up, Cap," Leslie called to Stetson as her boss disappeared into the parking lot. "Enjoy your lunch."

Leslie headed down the drab hallway to the Pit area, Cox's voice interrupting her thoughts before she made it to her desk. "Les, you know that question you had about the maintenance fee on the Fritz apartment seeming high?"

"You have something?" Leslie half-heartedly asked, her mind continuing to dwell on her conversation with Stetson.

"Got an answer. Well, a partial answer anyway. The fee's high because there's additional space. She combined her apartment with the one next door. Have a request in to the county for remodel plans. If there's anything, we'll get them late today or first thing in the morning. My take: Remember that hallway ending with a bedroom on the right? I think we'll find that hall leads into the apartment next door."

Forcing herself to focus, Leslie replied, "There's a gorgeous piece of furniture at the end of that hall. Floor to ceiling, curved, or wavy, colored glass. There's a wall behind it. No door that I recall."

"Oh, and before I forget," Cox said, "Chlad lands at eleven-forty today."

"Can't intercept him at the airport, if that's what you're thinking. Call his lawyer, set something up for as soon as you can, preferably tomorrow afternoon. You take the lead on this with Chlad."

"Any reason?"

"You like Chlad for the homicide. Go for it."

"I thought you liked Chlad as well."

"Thing is, Huntington's the lawyer on the Amelia Bishop homicide. I'm in Huntington's cross-hairs. Perp claims self-defense. Says I was aiming at him. Best for me to lay low."

"Got you covered. Next steps?"

"We have Jakowski, Colton, Fritz and Chlad at the scene in the critical time frame. Let's start eliminating them. We'll see who's still standing when we're done."

"I thought we eliminated Colton."

"In theory we did. I think the fact DHS believes he's a Russian asset plays into it. Anything on that needle you found? Nothing's in the file yet."

"Nothing yet," Cox confirmed.

"I'm working on Jakowski. You have Chlad to prepare for. I'll take the easy one. Lady friend Selma Fritz."

"What makes her so easy?" Cox quizzed, a puzzled look in his eyes.

"Good question. Timing's wrong. So are the mechanics. Got to the party too late. And I don't see how she could have positioned Fuller under the rope, wrapped the belt around his neck and hoisted him up. It doesn't add up." Leslie paused, again visualizing the garage as it had been when she first saw Fuller, the bike leaning against the workbench, the body hanging several feet above the floor. "If it was Fritz, she wasn't alone."

Cox agreed, adding, "Fuller had no ligature marks on his arms, so he hadn't been tied. Unless he was drugged, you're right, it's not likely Fritz could have done it alone."

A thought struck Leslie. "Pull up the final ME report. Let's be certain nothing's changed."

"Unless I'm reading this report wrong," Cox called out a moment later, "there were drugs, sco-polamine hydrobromide to be exact, in Fuller's system. That's new. Cause of death is listed as bradycardia from compression of the carotid sinus. Sounds like he was choked, not hung. What's your take?"

"Let's not guess," Leslie answered. "Van Deere's the ME. Worked with her on the McDermitt file. Woman of few words, but on her game. I'll call."

Van Deere answered on the first ring. "Detective Hodges, nice talking to you again. I anticipated your call. The Fuller matter I presume?"

"That's the one. Mind if I put this on speaker?" Leslie asked. "My partner, Detective Cox, would like to hear what you have to say."

"No problem. Tell me when you're ready."

"Hello, Dr. Van Deere," Cox said. "Thanks for taking our call. Ready when you are."

"I assume you've both read the report, so I won't repeat what's in it. Hangings are tricky. Death can occur from suffocation, as when the windpipe is blocked. Also, from blood being cut off to the brain. In some instances death can occur from broken or crushed vertebrae. Complicating matters further, time to die, as measured from the start of the trauma, can be anywhere from one minute to perhaps fifteen, even twenty in extreme cases."

"In this case, can you narrow it down?" Leslie asked.

"I'd say Dr. Fuller was brain dead within two minutes of when the belt tightened around his neck."

"Why so fast?" Cox asked. "If the range is ..."

"He had traces of scopolamine hydrobromide, which you might know as truth serum. In the twenties and thirties it was used by police forces to discover the truth — or so they thought. No real evidence that it worked. Scopolamine is used to reduce nausea, so alone that's not significant. But coupled with the sodium thiopental it appears someone injected chemicals to induce Dr Fuller to reveal something he otherwise would have been reluctant to disclose. I've been waiting for a call back from a friend who specializes in Russian trade craft. They've been known to use a drug called SP-117 to induce prisoners to give up accomplices. I don't know the exact chemical composition of SP-117, but my speculation is a combination thiopental and scopolamine."

Leslie followed up with, "From your report it appears the injection wasn't the cause of death. So, why's that important?"

"It helps explain the short time from when the belt was tightened to when his brain ceased functioning. As I said, the actual cause of death was bradycardia induced by compression of the left carotid sinus, aided by an arteriovenous occlusion. Usually, in hangings, a rope is tied around the neck. In this case, as you know, a belt was used. The buckle slid tight and pinched off his blood supply."

The image of Fuller hanging in the garage again flooded back to Leslie. Now that her attention was focused, she saw that his bloated face was leaning over to the left obscuring the buckle.

"You know," ME Van Deere went on, "my thought when I first saw the crime scene photos was autoerotic asphyxiation. The belt and all. The fact the wall plate where the rope was tied was possibly within range of his arm lent credence to the hypothesis."

"What directed you away from that line of thought?" Leslie inquired, not yet entirely following the ME.

"Initially, I was skeptical because of his age. There's no real statistics on this, but I believe auto-erotic behavior is for thrill seeking individuals. Fuller, I believed, was beyond that stage in his life. Then two factors came to bear that out. One, the pulley above his head broke just after his feet left the ground. The broken pulley caused the rope to jam. The system wasn't designed for his weight, ruling out repeated usage. Two, timing's wrong. From your report I note he was waiting for his woman friend — fiancée, if your notes are correct. She was expected before noon. So, as I say, the timing's wrong."

"He was drugged, then hanged," Cox said. "Same person? Different person?"

"There is no evidence I can point to that argues either way. One could reasonably conclude that whoever injected him with SP-117, or whatever cocktail they were using, was facile with chemicals. If that person wanted Fuller dead, why not just inject him with a deadly dosage. Hell of a lot less work than hanging. The forensics bears that out, as well."

"In what way?" Leslie inquired, scanning the report as she spoke.

"Remember, my area is medical. Lang is assigned to this case from a physical evidence point of view. You should talk to him about that aspect of the file."

Lang, Leslie knew, was Langston Williams, the man she had had lunch with. "I assume the two of you consulted. Mind giving us your take. We'll touch base with Williams as well."

"Start with the guest bedroom. Note the blanket had traces of Fuller's blood, as well as traces of sodium thiopental. I believe that's where Fuller was injected. The inside door handle leading to the garage from the house revealed traces of the guest blanket, as well as prints matching Selma Fritz."

Leslie interrupted. "Since this was Fuller's house, I would assume his prints would have been there as well."

"Good assumption. Not, however, in this case. May have been wiped down. Don't know. Fritz's prints were on the garage side door handle as well. That's consistent with Fuller never leaving the garage. But, as I say, Lang's the expert on that. And Fuller's DNA was found on the needle you recently sent over. Traces of SP-117 were also found in the needle."

"What about prints on the pulley rope?" Cox asked. "Whoever hung him had to have pulled down on the rope."

"Nothing in the report showing prints on the rope, or on the cleat. But there were fibers. As if someone had wrapped the rope in a rag, or a cloth."

"Gloves, perhaps?" Cox suggested.

"Again, I defer to Lang. The fibers are in the 4-to-8-centimeter range. Suggesting to me animal hair, possibly cashmere. But that's pure speculation."

"Thank you, Doctor. As before, you've been a great help," Leslie said. "Anything else we should know?"

"A bit of conjecture here, if I may," Van Deere responded. "There may have been a rod of some sort in a table drawer in that little soundproof area."

"I didn't see any rods listed in the inventory," Leslie said, puzzled.

"Correct. We didn't locate a rod. But there was an indentation in the felt drawer liner. Again, my conjecture, but I'd say a rod had been lying in that drawer. Judging from the extent of the bent fibers, I'd say the rod had recently been removed."

"What was the size of the indentation?" Leslie inquired.

"Seventeen centimeters long with a seventeen-millimeter diameter."

Leslie, trying to visualize the scene, asked, "Can you determine the shape of the rod? I mean is the circumference round? Or does it have points like…like a hex tool of some sort?"

"I don't see anything suggesting points. I'd call it round. Lab techs made a mold to preserve the shape."

"Again, I'll ask," Leslie responded. "Is there anything more you'd like to tell us, Doctor?"

"Nothing I can think of," came ME Van Deere's answer.

# THIRTY-FIVE

DHS AGENT MAXINE GHANA KEPT her word. Shortly after the detectives hung up with the ME, several pages of financial information appeared in Leslie's electronic inbox. Judging from the volume of transactions, the business Selma Fritz had owned had been doing nicely, buying, restoring, and duplicating furniture. It was difficult to tie a specific purchase of material to a particular sale, but in the few instances where Leslie could match them up, the profit margin was in the five-hundred percent range. The banking records were not sufficiently detailed to allow for full profitability calculations. However, the labor costs were essentially three people, with Heinrick Nowak, the master craftsman, receiving eighty percent of the salary entries. Leslie noted that the business closing did not appear to have been precipitated by a financial crisis.

"Fritz did rather well from Bamberg Artysta," Cox noted. "We're in the wrong business."

"How are you with woodworking?" Leslie responded. "And glass blowing?"

"Does hanging shelves count?"

"Better keep your day job. Any luck getting those plans for Fritz's condo?"

"Not 'til morning, I'm told."

"Okay, I'm knocking off."

"Got dinner plans?" Cox asked, smiling his crooked smile.

"I told you to knock that shit off!"

"So, you're having dinner with Allen."

"I said, none of your business!"

"Why so sensitive? Allen's a nice enough guy — for a lawyer."

"I'm outta here," Leslie said, flipping her computer closed, locking her desk, and standing, all in one sweeping motion.

Cox took a precautionary step backward, not exactly certain what his unpredictable partner might do next.

Not further rising to the bait, she marched past him, down the hall and out to her car, sitting several minutes clearing her mind.

A text from Allen popped up. JURY CAME BACK SOONER THAN EXPECTED. GUILTY AS CHARGED! YOU UP FOR CELEBRATING?

Allen's text was a welcome break to the gloom that had descended on her. Death and dying was now a steady part of her life and would be until she hung it up. But that wasn't a new revelation. Her deceased husband, Junior, had worked the same job, yet it hadn't seemed to affect him. Why, she asked herself, should it be any different for me?

Responding to Allen's text, she said, LOOKING FORWARD TO IT. TIME? PLACE? AFTERWARD? YOURS OR MINE?

His reply was immediate. 7:30 DaRuMa BELL TOWER, MINE

The timing of dinner allowed Leslie enough time to go home, shower, change out of her work clothes and pack her overnight bag before driving to the Japanese restaurant.

Her phone rang several times while she was in the shower. Stepping out she glanced at the screen, noting three missed calls from Jak. So be it, she thought. Remembering that Stetson had lunch with him earlier in the day, Leslie didn't know what to make of the fact that she had not received any feedback. Also, she had heard nothing about the

Sheriff's talk with Jak's chief. Not good omens. Jakowski could wait until morning.

On her way out to her car, JAK appeared on her now vibrating cell screen. Against her better judgment, she accepted the call. "Make it fast," she snapped, "I'm running late."

A stern voice said, "Hadn't expected you to brief Karen on what I had told you. That wasn't a good move."

"You have some nerve lecturing me on bad moves!" Leslie shot back, her patience gone. "You think you can wind me up and I'll do your bidding? Think again!" Except that's exactly what she had been doing—his bidding. "Frankly, I've had enough of your interference!"

"Leslie," Jakowski said, his voice heavy with contrition, "please allow me to apologize. I overstepped my bounds and I called to say I'm sorry. I used my relationship with Karen because I wasn't authorized to discuss Stratis and what I was doing for him—all with the blessing of both the FBI and my chief. You'll be fully briefed in the morning as to everything."

"So, you were working for Stratis?"

"As far as he believed, I was. All kosher I can assure you."

"Why didn't DHS know that?"

"FBI and DHS have their own feud going. Treasury department is mixed in there somewhere. When billions of dollars are floating around, lots of coffers fill up. Hey, for all I know, Agent Ghana's on someone's payroll."

"Why should I believe you over her?' Leslie replied, skeptical of what she was being told. "Or over anyone else for that matter?"

"Believe who you want—or even better, believe nobody. As a peace offering, I'll give you two pieces of information. Do with them what you wish. First, you know I went to Fuller's at the time he was hanged. I went there to retrieve the original seventeen-seventeen from Fuller's garage."

"The what?"

"Fuller referred to each glass rod by its length and diameter. Seventeen-seventeen means seventeen centimeters long with a seventeen-millimeter diameter. For reference, a dime is approximately seventeen millimeters in diameter."

"Is that the one, this seventeen-seventeen rod, that was in the original euphon?" Leslie asked, thinking back to her conversation with Medical Examiner Van Deere and the indentation the forensics team had found in the sound booth drawer in Fuller's garage.

"In Pittsburgh, Carnegie measured it as being seventeen-fourteen," Jakowski replied. "The proper rod would have measured seventeen-seventeen."

"Same length, smaller diameter?" Leslie said, making certain she understood what Jakowski was telling her.

"You nailed it. I was leaving Fuller's when Colton arrived, forcing me to hide in the bath."

Puzzled, Leslie asked, "Did Fuller just hand the rod to you? Or what?"

"I went in through the back door. Fuller was on the phone, never saw me. Got it from the sound room."

"How'd you know where the rod, the seventeen-seventeen as you call it, was?"

"Selma Fritz. She had put it in a drawer in the garage sound room."

"How did she…"

"More on that in person."

Not at all happy with Jakowski's evasion, Leslie debated pursuing this line of questioning, but decided to get what else he was willing to give and circle back for the rest later. "I assume you were in the house when Colton arrived. Tell me about him."

"From what I could hear, Colton demanded that Fuller hand over the original euphon. From the way Colton was talking, he had a weapon of some sort. A gun, or possibly a knife. He had no intention of paying for the instrument. Fuller refused, claiming the original was in Pittsburgh. The two of them got in a screaming match. Then suddenly all went quiet. I heard a door slam. In hindsight, I believe it was the door into the garage from the house. I came out of the bath, about to slip away, when Chlad showed up. He couldn't get in the front door and came around to the back. I intercepted him and told him Colton was inside and he, Chlad, had better get away from there because Colton was armed and had no intention of paying for anything."

"Did Chlad leave, as you suggested or..."

"Chlad confessed that he had come for the seventeen-seventeen as I had and wasn't about to leave without it."

"How'd you know that?"

"Told me so. Said he wasn't afraid of Colton getting his hands on the original euphon because he knew for a fact it was at the Carnegie. He then said the original seventeen-seventeen was in the garage."

"How'd he know that?"

"Same way I knew. Stratis had arranged it."

"Chlad started shouting and I clamped my hand over his mouth. The last thing I wanted was for Colton to know we were outside. I handed the seventeen-seventeen to him and told him to get away from the house as fast as he could."

"Did he?" Leslie asked, mentally comparing what she was hearing to the timeline she and Cox had constructed. So far, his story was lining up.

"We both did."

———■———

Allen was in a good mood and doing his best to dispel the cloud hanging over her. He was succeeding, relating how the jury deliberated only a few hours, beating the office prediction by a full day. It had been Allen's first shooting case, a home invasion, the one Allen had told her about. The charge was second degree attempted murder. The kicker being that it was the homeowner on trial and not the burglar.

"The homeowner?" Leslie questioned, when Allen had first said it. "How the hell'd that happen? Homeowners are presumed to have reasonable fear of imminent peril of death, or at least great bodily harm, when someone breaks into their house. From what I learned at the academy, that essentially gives the homeowner a license to shoot an intruder."

"Your understanding is spot on — as far as it goes. But, as you well know, facts, and timing, are important. In this case, the home invasion occurred at 12:59 AM. Homeowner, a guy in his mid-fifties, lives alone, was out drinking. This dude claims he drove into his garage, parked his car, and entered his house through the laundry room. He saw the perp in his living room, pulled his gun and shot him."

"Where's the timing come in? Homeowner walks in, sees an intruder, and shoots. Seems cut and dried. What am I missing?"

"The burglar was caught on the dude's surveillance camera coming in the back door. He has..."

"Homeowner have a name?"

"Ralph Watson. White, as I said. Mid-fifties. Forty or so pounds over-weight."

"Go on."

"Watson's got himself one of those fancy Arlo camera systems. As Watson's rolling on home, feeling no pain I might add, his cell phone beeps. He sees the perp carry out his flat screen TV. A moment later the perp is back for more of his stuff."

"How do you know what Watson saw?"

"It's all right there on his phone. In a storage file. And what's more, a traffic cam shows Ralph two blocks from his house at 1:04 AM. That made his story of being surprised by the intruder an outright lie. It didn't help his cause that he didn't call 9-1-1. Ol' Ralph shot the perp in the back of the leg. He was found two blocks away getting into his car."

"Sounds like you could have charged the homeowner with first degree attempted homicide as well."

"I wanted to. Was overruled. Proof of premeditation is sketchy. I argued that the video we had of Ralph coming into the house with his weapon out and cocked was more than enough to show premeditation. Defense would argue the gun was out because he knew about the burglary. Ralph was protecting himself as he had a right to do. I don't buy it, but the boss wanted a win. We got a win! I'm celebrating."

Leslie lifted her wine glass. "To a win for the State of Florida." She then added, "And for Allen Smith, my love."

# THIRTY-SIX

FRITZ APARTMENT HAS ADDITIONAL SPACE, was the text message greeting Leslie when she checked her phone the next morning. "Space is located at the end of the hallway where that glass display case is positioned," an upbeat Cox reported when she called him in response to the message, "just where you thought it would be. The drawing shows a door behind that cabinet at the end of the hall. The door opens into a walk-in closet serving a bed and bath area just beyond the closet. A small kitchen is off to the side. You can also enter that separate apartment from a door in the common hallway leading directly into the kitchen."

"Why would a single woman, with no children, need so much space? And why partition it off in any event?"

"That's the exact question I asked the White Sands management office. Apparently, she rents the unit out to a man who travels a lot. She pays her maintenance fees on time and has no complaints from neighbors. The manager is pissed at Fritz for trying to get her fired."

"Why? I mean why did Fritz try to get the manager fired?"

"Manager allowed the maintenance crew into the apartment to repair something. According to the manager, Fritz has a hair-trigger bad temper when she's crossed."

"There's no record of rental income."

"You're right," Cox confirmed. "Must be off the books."

"Maybe there's a business account we overlooked," Leslie suggested, falling silent a moment to mentally review the file, visualizing the timeline. "Remember that woman who saw Selma drive into Fuller's driveway?" Not waiting for Cox to respond, she continued, "One of the reasons we ruled Fritz out as the perp is because she arrived at her boyfriend's house several minutes too late. We constructed that timeline from her cell phone records of when she called 9-1-1."

"And of the cell phone records of a woman dropping off something next door," Cox reminded Leslie. "Where are you going with this?"

"Tell me about that woman. What all do we know?"

"Something to do with dropping off a Hearts of Miromar package next door. One of the deputies interviewed her. Lives in Miromar Lakes, but in a different neighborhood. I don't understand, Les, timeline's still wrong for Fritz. If you tell me Jakowski's out of the running, then..."

"I'm not yet writing Jak off. He says he just went in and took the rod. Only Chlad saw him. Left no prints, no trace, nothing. A real ghost."

"He's an experienced detective, Leslie. Wouldn't expect someone like him to slip up and leave trace evidence," Cox argued.

"Everyone slips up," Leslie said, following her deceased husband's belief.

"Noted," Cox acknowledged. "That leaves Chlad. We're set up for two today. At Lawyer Huntington's."

"And Colton?" Leslie asked.

"What about Colton?"

"Don't count him out. ME's probably right he would've used a lethal injection, but a chemical death using Russian drugs might be a bit too obvious. In fact, right now, I'd say he's our highest priority. You up for getting an arrest warrant?"

"Based on?"

"Video showing him coming and going from Fuller's house within the critical period. Also showing him throwing a needle and syringe out of his car shortly thereafter. Fuller's DNA and traces of SP-117 on the needle. SP-117 in Fuller's blood. Ties him directly to Fuller. That's enough for a warrant."

"But Les," Cox protested, "Fuller didn't die from SP-117. He died from hanging."

"If you're uncomfortable with homicide, make the warrant for aggravated assault. We certainly have enough for that. It'll give us enough to search his plane — and anything else he owns. Never know what might turn up."

"Don't know what Ghana and her folks will say about this."

"Don't tell them. What they don't know won't…"

"There's nothing they don't know."

"That's what they want you to believe. Are you going to prepare the warrant? Or should I?"

"I'll do it," a reluctant Cox said as the call went dead.

"What was all that about?" Allen called from the kitchen. "I made breakfast. I was hoping you'd have time. I should know better by now."

"Coffee's all I need. Thanks. Something you said last night's playing in my head."

"I love you?"

"That as well. But I was thinking earlier. That surveillance camera, the one that tripped up your homeowner."

"Which one? There were two. The traffic light camera and the homeowner's own security camera."

"Both. Fritz has a doorbell security camera outside her door in the common hallway. Do I need a search warrant for stored images?"

"If they're stored on her personal computer or phone you do. The fact that the images were captured in a public space lowers the bar for the judge. You can file that yourself online."

Leslie explained to Allen about the added apartment space, asking, "Can I get a warrant to search that area?"

"Search for what?"

"Whatever's in there I suppose."

"You just answered your own question. Court won't allow fishing. Need probable cause for a different apartment."

"Spoil sport! What about good old break down the door?"

"Didn't hear that. You gotta stop watching old detective movies. That's Philip Marlowe, Sam Spade stuff. Finesse is today's MO."

"Don't knock my heroes." She bent to kiss him. "Knock 'em dead. See you tonight. My place."

"Can't wait," he called to her retreating back.

———————

Leslie stood in a corner of Attorney Huntington's spacious lobby waiting for her teleconference with Judge Sonya Gonzales to begin. The conference had been set for 1:45 and it was now 1:55 with only silence on the line. Gonzales, she had been told, was usually punctual. The good news, Huntington, according to the receptionist, was running fifteen minutes late.

"Detective Hodges," the judge's brisk voice interrupted Leslie's thoughts, "I've reviewed your paperwork and I'm prepared to grant the warrant. I must remind you this warrant covers only the video from the hall camera and nothing further. Do I have your assurance?"

"I understand, your Honor."

"I don't want this to be a fishing expedition. If you find anything on that video that warrants an expansion of the warrant, you are to reapply. Do you understand me?"

"I do, Your Honor."

"Don't overstep or I'll throw it all out."

"I appreciate that. Thank you, Your Honor."

"Okay. It's signed. Clerk will log it and it'll be available in the file in a few minutes. Give it ten minutes and you're good to go. Good luck, Detective."

"Thank you, Your Honor," Leslie said, quickly hanging up the phone. The electronic version of getting out of Dodge.

"Detectives," a pleasant voice called from across the lobby, a voice not belonging to anyone Leslie had seen before, "if you'll follow me. Attorney Huntington will see you now. I'm Ann, Mr. Huntington's assistant," the early-forties blonde said when the two detectives fell in behind her. She wore a tight-fitting blouse, and an even tighter fitting skirt, leaving nothing to the imagination. They followed Ann down a wide hallway with small, but pleasant looking offices on both sides. Leslie noted the lawyers at their desks, evenly divided male and female, their heads buried in computers, stacks of paper around them. Cox's eyes remained focused on Ann.

Turning a corner, Ann announced, "Mr. Chlad is with Mr. Huntington. They'll both join you in a few moments." She pulled open a conference room door. "Can I get either of you anything?"

Leslie declined. Cox remained silent.

"What about you, Detective Cox. Is there anything you require?"

Sometimes you don't have to speak to be heard. And Leslie heard Cox's silence loud and clear. It wasn't coffee he wanted from the shapely blonde. The woman heard it as clearly as Leslie had.

"Nothing now, Ann," Cox finally answered. "At least not at this moment. But thank you just the same."

"I'll leave you two now. Use that phone over there and dial three. I'm just around the corner."

"Your lucky day," Leslie teased when the door closed, giving back to Cox what he had been giving her over Allen. "Your new BFF?"

"Am I that transparent?"

"Could have tripped over your tongue. Now get your mind back on business."

"It never left business."

"That, partner, is not an accurate statement. In fact, it's a flat out lie."

The conference room door opened and in walked a short, overweight, bald man followed by Ernst Chlad. "Hello, Detective Cox," the lawyer said, reaching his hand out to shake hands with Cox. Remembering COVID etiquette, he quickly withdrew his arm. "And this must be Detective Leslie Hodges. Been reading a lot about you my dear," he said. "Pleased to finally meet you in person. Taller than I imagined."

"Pleased to meet you as well," Leslie replied, biting her tongue at his condescending manner, and remembering to say as little as possible.

"The reason we're here today," Cox began, "is to ask Mr. Chlad here a few..."

"Pardon me, Detective. Which of you is the lead detective on the Fuller matter? That is why we are here today, is it not?"

"It is," Cox replied. "What difference does..."

"I asked a question. I expect an answer! Which of you is the lead detective?"

"I am," Leslie answered, guessing he already knew that fact. "Detective Cox is taking the lead today."

"Like hell he is! You're lead on this matter; you conduct the interview. Period."

Recognizing this was his way of intimidating her, Leslie refrained from engaging, telling herself to focus on the mission. "If you insist, then…"

"I insist."

"Okay, let's begin with a series of timeline questions pertaining to the morning Dr. Fuller was found dead in his own garage. You recall that day, do you not Mr. Chlad?"

Chlad glanced at his lawyer before confirming that he did.

"We discussed this at length the last time we spoke, but please repeat for us exactly where you went that day when you left your home. Please include the times involved. You can begin at ten A.M. to, say, one P.M. the day Dr. Fuller died."

Again, the glance at Huntington. Again, a barely perceptible nod. "As I told you, I called Sig, Dr. Fuller, about nine, went over to his house around eleven-thirty, give or take. When he didn't answer his door, I went to the beach for the day."

"When you were at Dr. Fuller's home, did you speak to anyone?"

"Hold up, Detective," Huntington said, his arm in the air as if to cover his client's mouth. "I've instructed my client to say nothing about any possible visit he may or may not have had with the deceased on the day of the murder."

"You're assuming Fuller's death is a homicide," Leslie said, "ME's report's not been released yet."

"If it's not a homicide, why are you wasting our time?"

"Trying to determine the facts is all."

"You'll have to determine the facts without my client testifying against himself. You are familiar, aren't you, with the constitution? The fifth amendment to be exact."

"Is your client invoking the fifth amendment?" Leslie retorted.

"As to any conversation that may or may not have occurred between my client, Mr. Chlad, and the deceased on the morning of his...his demise, yes."

"Then," Leslie said, pushing her chair back, "there is nothing more to be discussed here today is there?"

"Not so fast. As I understand the facts, and please correct me if I'm wrong," the lawyer began, "but am I to understand you have reason to believe Mr. Chlad spoke to someone at the residence at the time in question?"

Leslie looked the lawyer straight in the eye and replied, "I see no advantage in providing information to you if you won't cooperate with us."

"Sit down, Detective. How about we do this on a theoretical basis."

"How's that work?" Leslie asked, playing dumb to see how far she could push.

"Ask theoretical questions. We'll answer as best we can."

"I'll play your game. First bullshit answer and we're out of here. You cooperate, you'll get what we have. You screw us over; you won't get shit until the Grand Jury indictment is handed down. We clear about that?"

"Ask your questions. Theoretical questions."

"If you had met or spoken with anyone at the Fuller home that morning," Leslie began tentatively, "who would that have been with?" Looking toward the lawyer, she asked, "Theoretical enough?"

"Answer the question," Huntington instructed Chlad.

"A man I had met in Poland who...who negotiated an arrangement with them to allow the euphon to go on tour."

"Does this theoretical man have a name?"

"Don't answer that," the lawyer advised.

"And what would this theoretical man have said to you?"

"Not to go inside the house because a man named Alexandre Colton was there trying to force Sig to give him the euphon."

"Did you go inside?"

"No."

"Did you leave?"

"Yes."

"Before you left did this theoretical man give you anything?"

"Don't answer," the lawyer again advised. "Not theoretical."

"I'll ask the question this way," Leslie said. "If this theoretical man had offered you something, would you have taken it?"

"Depends."

"On what?"

"On what was offered?"

"If he had offered you a glass rod. Say one with a 17-centimeter length and a 17-millimeter diameter."

"Theoretically speaking, yes."

"To what end would you accept such a rod? Again, in our hypothetical."

Chlad looked at Huntington who again nodded.

"The euphon, as it was in Pittsburgh, was highly devalued. With the seventeen-seventeen, the instrument had great value to a collector, such as Mr. Stratis."

"In theory, why would Dr. Fuller have been in possession of the seventeen-seventeen rod?"

"It was at his house."

Leslie closed her eyes a moment to visualize the transaction. the Pittsburgh euphon, she knew, was eventually delivered from the Science Center in Pittsburgh back to Chlad in Florida by messenger the night she and Jakowski had dinner. That euphon, in theory, then went to Poland the next morning as the original. Yet Chlad essentially had just said he sold, or was about to sell, the original to Stratis. "Continuing in theory Mr. Chlad. You do agree with me it would not be possible to deliver the original euphon to both the Polish government and to Mr. Stratis, do you not?"

"That's a fair hypothetical statement. Yes."

"Then in my mind one of those entities, Poland or Stratis, received a duplicate. Again, in my hypothetical."

"Hypothetically speaking, one of them would have received a duplicate, yes."

"Would I be wrong in assuming Stratis received the original? Assuming, of course, he paid the hundred million."

"Hypothetically, one does not pay a hundred million for a duplicate."

"Would I be right in concluding a bribe...call it a finder's fee...was paid to the Polish authority who accepted the fake euphon and certified it as genuine?" Seeing the lawyer's head come up, Leslie added, "Hypothetically speaking, that is."

"Authorities, plural," Chlad responded, smiling broadly.

"Would I be wrong in thinking, again in my hypothetical, a second, recently fabricated euphon had been substituted for the original euphon?"

"Hypothetically speaking, there would be no other way." Chlad was obviously having fun, telling his part of the con game.

"It also strikes me, Mr. Chlad, hypothetically speaking of course, that the fewer people who knew about the con the better."

"I'd say so. Yes."

"Dr. Fuller, of course, would know. Who else?"

At the mention of Fuller's name, the smile disappeared from Chlad's face, and his eyes went dark.

"That's enough!" Huntington snapped, his arm again in the air. "Time for these folks to give us what they have."

"Fair enough," Leslie said, knowing she had received all the information she was likely to receive from Chlad. "For starters," she began, "we know your client arrived at the Fuller house at the critical time. He's told us that much. We also have testimony that he was given the seventeen-seventeen glass rod when he arrived. We can also prove he gave Mr. Morris Stratis the original euphon the night before he flew to Poland with a duplicate in his possession — a counterfeit if you will."

Chlad threw himself back in his chair. "How is that possible? I never..."

"Say nothing further!" Huntington sternly instructed. Standing, he said, "Interview's over!"

"And when the money from Stratis," Leslie continued even as she stood, "shows up in your account we'll have you for fraud on the Polish government, if nothing else."

Chlad's eyes involuntarily opened wide. Leslie saw it clearly. So did Huntington. "I said, meeting's over!" He took his client by the arm and marched him to the door. Turning back to the detectives, Huntington said, "Ann will show you out." To his client, he instructed, "Not another word, you understand? Nothing further!"

# THIRTY-SEVEN

"WHAT THE HELL WAS THAT about?" Cox asked when they were in the parking lot. "All that hypothetical crap got us nowhere. We're chasing our proverbial tails, you ask me. Biggest takeaway for me was that Polish authorities were definitely bribed. No surprise there."

"Not a total waste of time," Leslie countered. "That's what happens when a client doesn't fully brief his lawyer. Huntington knew nothing of the duplicate euphon, or we would never have been able to get this interview. We've now confirmed there are at least two euphons. And the knock-off is in Poland."

"Hypothetically we know that," Cox said, irritation slipping into his voice. His cell vibrated. "About time," he announced. "Arrest warrant for Colton just issued. Judge went along with the search of his plane as well as his hotel room and any vehicle he may have rented."

"Order $^{24}/_7$ surveillance on him," Leslie instructed. "ME Van Deere had a good point. Once Colton injected Fuller, why not finish him off with the drugs? Traces would be found anyway. Before we make the arrest, we need to review every detail of the file. The answer's sure as hell in there. We're just not seeing it."

"We have the Fritz warrant for the doorbell video? It would be nice to see what it shows before we..."

"Good thought," Leslie said, checking the time. "Four-ten. Let's head over and serve that warrant."

326

"Protocol requires a uniform," Cox reminded her.

"Have someone meet us there. How about four-forty-five? Should be out by five or so."

Serving warrants was always stressful for Leslie. She was aware that even the mildest mannered person can become aggressive when the police show up to search their home. For some, the agitation level can go through the roof. It was no different this time when the two sheriff deputies, with the uniform in front, knocked on Selma Fritz's door. Leslie was on edge not knowing exactly what to expect.

Selma answered on the second knock, a smile on her face, a glass of wine in her hand, a magnificent rose colored paisley pashmina draped over her shoulders. The smile quickly turned to fury when Cox, smiling his best smile to ease the tension, announced, "Mrs. Fritz, I'm here with Detective Hodges to serve a warrant for..."

"Get the hell out of my house!" Fritz bellowed, her eyes blazing with anger, the veins on her neck bulging. "This is harassment! I won't allow you in!"

"Selma," Leslie calmly said, "this will take us just a few minutes and we'll be gone. We have a court order."

"I said, no! You're not coming in!" She pulled the shawl tighter, covering what remained visible of her cleavage. "And I mean it! Go away!"

"Selma, please," Leslie said. "We have a warrant, so we are coming in! You can make this easy. Or hard. Your choice."

"A warrant for God sakes! What's that about? What are you looking for?"

Leslie glanced at the doorbell camera. "Images from this camera. We have a court order allowing us to take a copy of the images from this camera. That's all we're here for. Just the images. Are they stored on your phone? Perhaps on your computer?"

"On my phone!" Fritz snapped, her feet remaining solidly planted but her agitation seemingly lowering. "Allows me to see who's at the door before I open it. What exactly are you looking for?"

"Primarily, the time you left your house on the day Dr. Fuller was…"

"I told you! It was around eleven-fifteen."

"Here's a copy of the order," Cox said, handing Fritz a printout he had made on the car printer. "We can look at your phone out here in the hallway if you wish."

"I don't see why you…"

"Selma, please," Leslie said, focusing on the dining room table behind her clearly set for two, an open wine bottle in the center, "this will only take a moment and we'll be out of your hair."

Fritz again said, "Tell me again what you're looking for?"

"Timeline. We need to determine exactly what time you left your home on the thirteenth. You said eleven-fifteen. If the time of your doorbell camera matches that time, then I can eliminate you from the possibilities list."

"Oh my God! How could you even think I could….Oh, my God, is that what you think? How could you even think that?"

"In truth, we have all but eliminated you. This is really the final piece." Leslie answered as truthfully as she could. "I'm certain you want us to get to the bottom of Sig's death. We can't do that unless we eliminate all possibilities."

"Who are the possibilities?"

"Sorry, we're not at liberty to discuss that."

"My poor Sig's dead," Fritz sniffed, "and you won't even tell me who you think did it! And now you even blame me. I can't..." A tear appeared under her right eye. Fritz made no attempt to dry her face.

Leslie waited in silence for Fritz to gather herself. "What part did you play in finding the euphon?" Leslie finally asked, remembering their conversation with Fritz where she professed to have little to do with locating it."

"I helped Sig. I...oh, never mind. Take what you're after and go away!"

"You said the information we need is on your cell phone," Leslie reminded her. "The Arlo app to be accurate. We need..."

"Here," Fritz said, thrusting the phone at Leslie, "take what you came for and let me alone!"

"Tell you what," Cox suggested, "how about we just transfer the camera file from your phone to mine and we'll view it later."

"Do what you need to do and make it quick." Fritz handed Cox her phone and again pulled the shawl close around her. She appeared to be on the verge of crying, but her face remained dry.

The transfer operation went smoothly and a few minutes later they were in the parking lot where Cox asked, "You thinking something's wrong with that woman?"

"Thought crossed my mind. Something's off. Don't know what."

———•———

Halfway back to the office, Leslie's cell rang. "Sheriff Radclif," Leslie said in surprise, sitting up straighter when the big boss announced himself. "What can I do for you?"

"Boots asked me to call you directly. Seems you poked a hornet's nest, young lady. Spoke to Chief Roberts up in Verona. Mixed bag on Jakowski. He's assigned to Morris Stratis as part of an FBI ongoing investigation. The part about Jakowski being in Lee County on official business is accurate. That's the good news. The bad news is he was supposed to check-in and coordinate with Boots. He didn't manage that part of the equation as you already know. He certainly isn't authorized to carry water for Stratis in any capacity. Appears he's off the reservation on that. Chief Roberts shared speculation that Jakowski's the reason Stratis has never been caught with stolen artwork. FBI's working that aspect, so be warned. Going forward, take your marching orders directly from Boots. Need I warn you, don't get caught up in that nasty operation?"

"I have no intention of doing anything improper, sir. Thank you for the update."

Sheriff Radclif remained quiet a long moment, then added, "Nobody begins with intention to do wrong. The slippery slope is alive and well. One little step leads to another, and soon...well, you know the drill. Just be careful out there." Changing the subject, he said, "I hear you're making progress on the Fuller investigation."

Leslie had no idea the sheriff himself paid attention to ongoing investigations. "Ups and downs," she replied, trying to be as accurate as she could without being overly optimistic. "One minute I think we're close. The next is uncertain."

"That's not all that uncommon. Are you receiving all the help you require? Got your DHS wires uncrossed?"

"I believe so. Yes. And Investigator Hillard's been excellent."

"Good to hear that. Let me know if I can help in any way. It'll feel good to get this off our plate. The sooner the better. Have a good day, Detective."

Leslie wasn't sure if she had just been praised or scolded. Most likely the latter. No time to dwell on it. Before the call she had been replaying their conversation with the Medical Examiner and something was nagging at her. It wasn't what she had heard, but rather what she had visualized. She called lab tech Langston Williams to follow up.

"Lang," Leslie said when he came on the line, "I have a quick question on the Fuller file. Now a good time?"

"Good as any. Shoot."

"Your report shows fibers on the rope. I assume those fibers were in the area where hands would have tightened to pull the body up."

"They were."

"Van Deere speculated on the fibers being cashmere. Is your..."

"About to post the report now, matter of fact. As always, ME's spot on. Cashmere from the neck of the Changthangi goat."

"You know it's from the neck," Leslie joked, thinking he was pulling her leg. "That's impressive, I must say."

"A pashmina. Sometimes, size does matter. Human hair can be anywhere from 40 to 100 microns thick. These fibers are under 15 microns. Makes tracking them that much easier. There were more than enough fibers to track down the manufacturer and the dye lots for several of the colors. In fact, the final report will have a note to the effect that there is a high probability the material was deformed, possibly torn. My thought is the damage to the cloth occurred when the pulley jammed and the rope stopped moving, allowing the pashmina to slide down the rope."

"How long will it be before we get the analysis?"

"Best guess, a week. Ten days at most and we'll have a list of buyer's names. Can't be all that many with Florida addresses."

"Please include the entire list in your report," Leslie instructed.

"Of course. Standard practice. You think it was someone from outside the state?"

"Just covering the bases," Leslie replied, thinking of the beautiful Sari Riya Kumar had worn to their Columbia restaurant meeting and visualizing her, on a different day, wrapped in a colorful paisley pashmina.

———■———

"You wanted to see me," Leslie said to Captain Stetson. "Saw your note."

"I understand the boss spoke with you. Tell me about the call."

Caught off-guard, Leslie answered with the first thought that came to mind. "Sheriff seemed miffed. I had the feeling he's not happy with the progress on Fuller."

"Man's always miffed. Good boss, but over the top, you ask me. He's okay with the pace of the Fuller investigation. It's DHS that has him spooked. Anyway, I want to clear the air with you about Jak. First off, I need to apologize for not being entirely honest. Jak and I did have an affair years back."

Leslie started to respond, but her boss held up her hand, palm wide open. "No, don't say anything. Just listen. At the core, he's a good man. Has your back all the way. But he has a son, let's just say, special needs. Costs him tons of money for private nursing twenty-four-seven. That's no excuse, just a fact. He gets money for his son's medical bills by running interference — high level errands if you will — for Stratis. Nothing illegal, mind you."

When Stetson fell silent, Leslie asked, "Errands? What kind of errands would that be?"

"Like delivering objects from one place to another so Stratis can be assured it's done right. Jak's trusted to get it right. Negotiating for security, things like that."

"We ran a financial check on Jak and found nothing unusual," Leslie said, frowning.

"Stratis pays the son's bills directly. To my knowledge, Chief Roberts up there in Verona is aware of everything Jak does."

"Could Jak have murdered Fuller?" Leslie blurted, throwing caution aside. "He was there at the right time?"

"I find it impossible to believe he could do such a thing. But then again, I am compromised."

"If he saw it happen, or knows who did it, would he tell me?"

"I believe so, yes. He's a cop first and foremost. And a damn good cop at that. Enough true confession! Out of here."

———◆———

Back at her desk, Leslie tried to determine whether Jakowski had been declared a good cop by Stetson's brain — or her heart. Sorting it through, she mentally moved Jakowski from the bottom of the list of potential killers to just below Chlad. She wavered on Colton. One minute agreeing with the ME that Colton would most likely have used a lethal injection, and the next moment liking him as an accomplice. Riya Kumar, all but eliminated from contention before cashmere had been identified on the rope, was now floating around as well. Stratis didn't feel right. Neither did Jakowski.

Leslie brought up the video from the doorbell camera and in less than thirty seconds it was clear Selma had indeed left her apartment precisely when she said she had on the morning of Fuller's murder. Remembering the judge's lecture about not overstepping the bounds of the warrant, she turned the video off at noon that day.

She then pulled up the Miromar Lakes neighborhood canvas report pertaining to the 13th. She was most interested in the interview with the woman driving a white Lexus who had pulled into the driveway next to Fuller's at 11:59. The woman driver was in her late sixties, white hair and glasses. The interview was keyed to a separate file containing the woman's name, address, phone number, driver's license, Social Security number. The woman had told the deputy that while she was delivering a package to the neighbor, a white Prius had pulled into the Fuller driveway. She had started to walk over to take a closer look because the car was identical to a Prius she had just sold. She was curious to see if it was the same car. The woman had received a cell phone call at precisely 12:02 and stopped to take it, turning her back on the Fuller house. The time of the incoming call corresponded to the time Fritz claims she opened the Fuller garage door and called 9-1-1.

Finished reading, Leslie again said to the empty room, "I'm missing something here. What the hell is it?" She reached for her cell to call Cox, intent on arresting Colton, if for no other reason, out of frustration.

Cox materialized at her desk before she hit the send button. "You won't believe this, but we may have just got lucky. There's a traffic camera at the entrance to Miromar Lakes. My brain's numb from looking at video, but here it is. A white 2016 Prius V turned into the complex at eleven forty-six the morning of the thirteenth." Cox pulled up the Fuller file and played the video clip for her. "It sure as hell doesn't take seventeen minutes to drive from the front gate to Fuller's home. Five at most. And that's generous."

"We don't know whose car that is," Leslie said. "There's more than one white 2016 Prius running around. Got a license number?"

"Can't make it out. Sorry."

"Not helpful," Leslie replied, frustration level continuing to rise.

"Les, I see you uploaded the doorbell video from Fritz. I haven't had time to go through it. Anything there?"

Leslie shrugged, "Nothing."

"Mind if I look?"

"Knock yourself out."

"I see what you mean by nothing," Cox admitted a moment later. "Selma left her apartment exactly as she said she did."

"Okay," Cox said, "let's see what else's on this puppy."

"Stop!" Leslie cried, "You can't go beyond the time of the murder. The warrant won't allow..."

'Shit! Look at this!" Cox exclaimed, ignoring Leslie's stop command.

"What date?"

"Fifteenth. Two days after the murder."

"That's outside the warrant! You'll get our whole case tossed!"

"She's pushing a cart out of her apartment carrying a wooden travel crate exactly like the one you videoed Stratis carrying when he came out of Chlad's house! Except the top's off. Inside the crate there's two leather bags."

"Cox! I said, stop! It's not admissible! Anything we find now can be thrown out! Shit, you've messed this up something awful!"

"Les, cool your damn jets! Get out the frick'n warrant," he snapped back at her. "There's no end date to the timeline! This is the common hallway. I'm not going beyond the video from the door camera."

Leslie pulled the warrant up on her screen, studied it a long moment, then sheepishly said, "You're correct. I told the judge I wanted the video for the morning of the murder to check an alibi.

But the warrant just says, all video captured by the hallway surveillance camera positioned to view the common hallway outside apartment 603 in the White Sands Condominium Complex.

"Say you're sorry," Cox teased, "for doubting me."

"I apologize," Leslie sheepishly replied. "You're right."

"I suggest," Cox said, "you use your magic to get us a warrant to search the premises. We now have probable cause to believe evidence of a crime is, or has been, stashed at her residence."

"I don't...This'll take some time to put together. I need to add the ME report and other data."

"We also have the traffic cam stuff I just told you about," Cox reminded her. "Same type of car. Piece by piece it's coming together — maybe."

"As I said, can't tie that car to her — not yet anyway. I was just reading a witness statement from the canvas at the scene. Woman mentioned the white Prius. Maybe she can elaborate."

"I'll follow up with that witness, see what she can tell me."

———————

Leslie's progress on putting the search warrant information together was almost non-existent. One step forward and two back type of thing as she struggled to make her case iron clad.

Allen called about dinner and she told him she'd be lucky to be available before midnight, if then. He said he understood and agreed he'd talk to her in the morning. Wished her a nice night.

Around eight, Cox went out for Chinese. The two of them ate while they worked on the expanded search warrant request. Leslie continuing to insist that it be perfect. Bullet proof, she repeated every time Cox was ready to submit it.

Exasperated, Cox finally exclaimed, "What exactly are you worried about? This looks frigg'n bullet proof to me. What the hell's bothering you?"

"The foundation for this warrant is your viewing the surveillance tape beyond the date of the murder. That won't be lost on the judge."

"But the warrant allowed it," Cox reminded her.

"If we assume the judge made a mistake in not limiting the time frame, she could easily decide to remedy her mistake by killing the new warrant."

"Not likely. This is a camera in a public space. We didn't invade anything! Hell, we didn't even go inside the apartment to get the information. Fritz handed it to us. I say, file the bloody thing already. You're overthinking this."

Her patience about shot, Leslie held her ground. "I'm not convinced we have enough."

"Have it your way! Sleep on it. Give it fresh eyes in the morning."

"Maybe that's a good..."

Cox's phone interrupted Leslie. "This is that witness getting back to me. The one parked in the neighbor's driveway." Into the phone, he said, "This is Detective Simeon Cox. Thanks for returning my call. I have a couple of quick questions. Do you have a moment to answer them?"

"A few minutes, yes," came the pleasant reply.

"Mind if I put you on speaker? My partner, Leslie Hodges, would like to listen."

"I see no reason why not."

"And do I have your permission to record this conversation?"

"Of course."

"Do you recall the morning, noontime it was, when you saw the white Prius pull into the Fuller driveway?"

"How could I ever forget? That poor man was murdered right there in his garage."

"I believe you were dropping something off next door at the time?"

"I was. I social distance to an extreme. Had a birthday present for my friend, Louise."

"I believe you told the deputy you had driven in through the front gate and parked in the driveway of your friend's house. Correct?"

"Correct."

"You then walked up the driveway, rang the bell, laid the package — the present — down and were heading back to your car when you saw the white Prius pull into Dr. Fuller's driveway. That's what the report says."

"One thing wrong with what you just said," the witness volunteered.

"And what was that?"

"I laid the package down before I rang the bell. Not after."

"Okay. I'll correct the report. Now please listen to my next question carefully and think before you answer."

"I always think before I answer."

"Okay, then. As you faced the street, which direction was the front of your car faced? To the left or to the right?"

"Neither. I parked in the driveway. The front of my car was facing me."

Cox replied, "My mistake. You did say you drove into the driveway. Okay, just so we get our bearings straight here, as you looked out from the front door where you dropped off the gift, what direction is the exit from the subdivision? Left or right?"

"To the left? Is this a trick question?"

"Not intended to be. No. So when you drove away, what direction would you turn from the end of the driveway to leave the complex? Left or right?"

"I said left."

"When you were standing in the driveway facing the street, which direction was the Fuller house? To your left or right?"

"Left."

"When you first saw the white Prius, where were you standing?"

"Halfway down the driveway, next to my car."

"On the driver's side?"

"Yeah."

"From where you were standing your car would have been between you and the white Prius. How were you able to see it?"

"It came down the street from behind me."

"You mean, from your right?"

"If I had been facing the street, yeah."

Cox struggled to hide his surprise. He had fully expected the witness to confirm the Prius had entered from her left—the direction of the front gate. "You are positive the white Prius that we have been talking about, the one that parked in Dr. Fuller's driveway, came from your right?

"I'm sure."

"And turned left into the Fuller driveway?"

"Yes."

"To your knowledge, is there any way to enter the community from the right?"

"It's a dead-end street. There is only one way in. And that's the way I came in, from the left."

"Thank you for taking time to speak with us. Do you have anything you would care to add or change?"

"No. I've told you what I know."

"Thank you for that. If you think of anything, anything at all, please call and ask for Detective Cox or Detective Hodges."

"I will."

"Have a good evening."

"We now have Fritz in a lie!" Leslie exclaimed, when Cox hung up. "Good work! I'm going to attach this recording as an exhibit."

"I wouldn't do that if I were you," Cox warned.

"Just why not?" Leslie asked, puzzled.

"Witness is wrong. She admitted there was only one way in from the left. She said the Prius came from the right. Those two facts are inconsistent."

"Not if what the witness saw was Fritz returning to Fuller's house after perhaps circling the block, or parking down the street, for several minutes. I'm going with it."

"I suggest sleeping on it. Morning light is always brighter."

"While you were talking to the witness, I had a thought. Why would Fritz kill her boyfriend? They were about to be engaged; everything was going right for them."

"Any conclusions?"

"Nothing concrete, just a vague uncomfortable feeling as though we're overlooking something. And exactly who was she entertaining in her apartment? Drinks for two?"

"Could be anybody."

"And why in the world would Fuller switch out the rods knowing the euphon would immediately be classified a fake and ruin his reputation? And where in the hell would he even get a wrong rod? For that matter, where in the hell would anybody get rods for a fake euphon?"

"I don't know. Maybe Stratis got to Fuller. With a hundred million in the bank, who in the hell needs a good reputation?"

"Assume someone got to Fuller. Did he do it without Fritz's knowledge? Why? He was planning on marrying the woman. Why cut her out at the last moment?"

"You seem to be going somewhere with this thread," Cox said. "I'm stumped."

"What I was thinking while you were on the phone, was what if we have it backward? What if Fritz was cutting Sig out?"

"How could she have done that? The euphon was delivered to the security messenger by Fuller directly. To change the rod, the messenger would need to know how. And he'd have to have a replacement rod. Not exactly something you can buy at Lowes."

"That road, dear partner," Leslie said, suddenly realizing how to resolve her confusion, "leads us directly to Fritz."

"What the hell're you searching for now?" Cox asked as Leslie frantically scrolled through her early notes. "Something's got you worked up."

"I can't find it!"

"What? What are you searching for?"

"A conversation I had early on with... Shit, I don't recall who that conversation was with!"

"That's unlike you not to recall anything. About what?"

"About how the euphon was moved from Florida to Pittsburgh by messenger." Leslie closed her eyes, concentrating on forming a picture — a picture in this case that simply wouldn't form. "I'm sorry, I can't..."

"Sometimes when you try too hard it blocks. Try..."

Suddenly, the image formed, the image Leslie had willed to the surface. "Got it!" she cried, realizing it was a sound sequence and not a visual image that she was struggling to recall. "Gonzalez Whitacre! Head of security for Gables International Protective Services. The man who supervised the delivery from Fuller to the Science Center. We need to know exactly what he did and saw when he picked up the euphon. Get background on him and his company. He may hold the key to what really happened."

"Are you thinking the security company could have changed the rods? That would throw a whole different spin on this."

"See what you can find," Leslie instructed, still troubled by a thought triggered by something else she had heard. A thought now gone from her mind. Focusing back on Cox, she added, "Be sure you walk Whitacre step by step through what he did and saw. I want any inconsistency resolved."

"Shouldn't be that hard to find him. You think he can — or will — help?"

"Worth the chance."

"You polish the warrant. I'll round up Whitacre." Cox trotted back to his own desk, leaving Leslie to her thoughts.

An hour later a jubilant Cox was back. "Listen to this. Caught Whitacre just as his flight was called. He was flying from Miami to Tel Aviv to escort a load of diamonds back to New York. He remembers the euphon being picked up from Fuller's house. Only, it wasn't Fuller who gave him the crate. It was a woman."

"Fritz?"

"He positively identified her."

"What do we know about this Whitacre? And about this Gables International Protective Services company?"

"Company's rated one of the best in the world. Called a friend down in Miami. He knows the company well. Says, he's never heard of a problem. FBI contact says the same."

"Cox, is there anyone you don't know?"

"Pays to have friends. That's all I can say."

"And Whitacre?" Leslie asked, ignoring the thinly veiled suggestion that she didn't have a support system.

"Whitacre's always assigned to supervise Stratis deliveries anywhere in the world. He's trusted. No reason to believe he'd lie. Could lose his license if we filed a complaint."

"So, what did he tell you about picking up the crate from Fuller?" Cox's obvious excitement boosting her spirits.

"The woman, Fritz, who answered the door said Fuller had taken ill. She told Whitacre the crate was in the garage and had him wait while she opened the garage door. Not seeing Fuller troubled him, but since it was Fuller's house and the crate matched exactly what he had been sent to escort, he examined and sealed it."

"You said he positively identified Fritz."

"He identified her from a line-up of pictures I sent him. According to Whitacre, before he sealed the crate, she handed him a leather bag saying, and I quote, here are the glass rods, each in its own labeled pouch. "

"Where does that lead you?" Leslie asked, her excitement now matching Cox's.

"If I wasn't before, I am now certain it was Fritz who changed out the glass rod. How about you?"

"I suppose," Leslie responded, tamping down her elation. "Fuller himself could have made the substitution."

"Les, you always so low key? What's got you now?"

"Truth is, I'm liking Jakowski more and more. I'm willing to concede the rod was changed at Stratis's direction. Then I think of motive. If Stratis is paying Jakowski's medical bills, why screw that up with a senseless, and frankly, rather clumsy, murder?"

"If Fritz knew about the substitution, why isn't she at the top of our list?"

"Motive. What's in it for her? My late husband always said, in murder cases, follow the money — or the passion. For Fritz, we have neither."

# THIRTY-EIGHT

THE WARRANT TO SEARCH SELMA Fritz's apartment was issued by the on-call judge at 3:17 in the morning after a fifteen-minute give and take with Leslie. Tough, but fair, Leslie concluded. Allen would have been proud of her. The judge, a man Leslie had no knowledge of, had suggested that because of Fritz's age, the small likelihood of violence, the many families in the building, some perhaps with small children, she postpone serving the warrant until after nine in the morning.

Cox, who had been napping on the conference room table, nodded his agreement to wait until morning, rolled over and went back to sleep.

Leslie wrote a note telling Cox she would meet him at nine at White Sands. I'll arrange for a uniform, she added. Placing the folded paper on top of his cold coffee cup, she went home to catch a few hours' sleep.

———■———

Allen's car was in her driveway, forcing her to park on the street. "Where you been all night?" he mumbled when she slipped in beside him. "You with Cox all this time?"

"He was sleeping when I left," was the first thing that came to mind. Realizing Allen would not appreciate her humor, Leslie simply said, "Talk in the morning." She turned on her side, her back to him.

She didn't hear him answer, "It is morning."

At 7:30 her alarm came alive. The smell of coffee wafted past her nose. Sitting bolt upright, it took her a moment to orient herself. "So, it hadn't been a dream," she exclaimed, forcing a tentative smile when he appeared in the doorway, a coffee cup in each hand. "What a nice surprise."

"You look like shit!" he responded. "I've arrested more presentable drunks."

"And I love you too! Hand me that coffee and step aside. I need to shower, comb my hair and do things girls do."

"Why start now," he teased, stepping back out of slugging range.

"You're the last thing I expected to see in my bed. Care to explain?"

"You said you'd be home late. Didn't anticipate an all-nighter. Planned to surprise you with a late dinner. Fell asleep waiting."

"Good thing I didn't bring Cox home," Leslie teased.

"You want Cox, just say the word and I'll pack my toothbrush."

"I almost did, you know. He was too tired to drive. Thought about bringing him here so at least he'd get a few hours sleep. He was out cold on the conference room table when I left. I thought of calling a ten-fifty-four on him. Truthfully, I didn't have the energy."

"Ten-fifty-four? Possible dead body? That wouldn't have gone over well with him — or the brass."

"Sounded funny at the time. Chalk it up to sleep deprivation. Bet he's still out."

"What's going down?"

Leslie briefed Allen while she showered and dressed for the day.

"Let me understand," Allen said when Leslie fell silent. "The only thing tying the girlfriend to the correct timing for the hanging is some neighbor lady who may not know her right from her left. That's not going to hold up."

"Judge bought it."

"No disrespect intended, but sometimes judges get bored like the rest of us. Especially at three in the morning. The way I see it, you have one shot at that Fritz woman. You blow it now, find nothing with that warrant, there'll be no going back. My money's on the Russian."

"You been watching too much TV, you ask me."

"That's a low blow. Why in the hell would Fritz inject sodium thiopental, or whatever, into her boyfriend? That's most definitely a Russian thing. They love their drugs."

"On the way home last night I worked out a theory. It's half-baked, but better than nothing. Colton, that's the Russian, figured out the game Stratis, or whoever, was playing. He believed the euphon at the Science Center was the genuine euphon and that its glass rod was changed to make the genuine euphon appear to be a knock-off. All Colton needed to restore the Pittsburgh euphon was the seventeen-seventeen rod."

"Seventeen-seventeen? What's that?"

"The proper size glass rod. Seventeen centimeters length, seventeen millimeters diameter. If Colton had the seventeen-seventeen rod, his plan to steal the euphon would work. He went to Fuller's house and demanded the seventeen-seventeen. Fuller denied knowing anything about the missing rod. That's when Colton drugged Fuller to make him talk. When that didn't work, Colton hauled Fuller out to the garage, I'm thinking to torture him. Seeing the bike lift, Colton decided to scare Fuller into talking, hoping the truth serum would work. Colton hoisted Fuller up and immediately lowered him so he could talk."

Allen processed what he had heard, before saying, "So, Fuller didn't give Colton what he wanted because poor Sig didn't know where the missing rod was."

"That's my latest theory," Leslie confirmed.

"So, what did Colton do then? Leave Fuller dangling from the ceiling?"

"That's as far as I got. Perhaps he was interrupted. I don't know."

"So then why didn't Fuller free himself?"

"Perhaps the drugs would account for that," Leslie answered, not entirely convinced. "Fritz could have shown up, and..."

"And, under your theory, she what? Pulls the rope and hangs her boyfriend? Now who's watching too many old detective stories?"

"I know. I know," Leslie replied, mentally recreating the scene where Fritz, dressed for a celebration lunch, comes upon her soon-to-be fiancé? "It doesn't hold together. But it's the best I got."

At nine, a disheveled looking Cox stumbled from his car in front of Selma Fritz's condo building, his hair uncombed, his shirt mostly unbuttoned, his eyes bloodshot.

"What the hell happened to you?" Leslie asked, not certain she wanted to know the answer.

"You don't want to know."

"Try me."

"Assholes faked a dead body call, as though they didn't know I was sleeping. The tech team played it up, been busting my butt since five. You didn't have a hand in that did you?"

"If I did, I wouldn't confess."

"I'll find out you know. Payback is hell."

"Speaking of hell, you better pull it together. We have work to do. Button your shirt. Do something with your hair."

"You sound chipper. How do you do it?"

"Good living habits. Avoid sleeping on tables, stuff like that."

Leslie's cell buzzed. A woman named Jada, the deputy assigned to them for executing the warrant, announced she'd be twenty minutes late. Leslie told her to take her time, they weren't going anywhere without her.

Deputy Jada slammed her cruiser to a stop almost exactly at the twenty-minute mark. Cox was nowhere in sight. "Are you expecting trouble?" Jada asked, her hand resting on her service revolver. "I thought there were two detectives. I'll call for backup. Might be a while 'til they get here."

"Partner went for coffee. I shouldn't think we'll need force. We served a warrant on her yesterday, no real problem. But you never know. Need to be on our game."

"If that's your partner coming across the lot, you better tell that to him," the deputy replied. "Appears his game is long gone. In the old days I'd arrest him for vagrancy."

"He'll pull it together," Leslie said, noting Cox now looked worse than when he left. "You ready to serve the warrant, or what?" Leslie asked when he approached her car. "This is Deputy Jada."

"As ready as I'll ever be," he mumbled. "March on, as if to war." His arm was up in mock tribute to some unseen audience. "Jada can lead the way."

"You been drinking?" Jada asked, looking as though she was prepared to call it in.

"Good question," Leslie responded. "Cox, have you been drinking?"

"Not in the least. I'm playing with you two. Let's get this over with so I can go get some shuteye."

"At least button your shirt and pretend to have it together," Leslie chided him. "Want to look good for the security cams."

"Sure we don't need backup?" Jada again asked, this time with her thumb on her transmit button.

"Positive," Leslie nervously replied. "Let's go."

Jada, looking from Leslie to Cox and back again, said, "Against my better judgment I'll go along. At the first sign of a problem, I'm calling it in."

———◆———

Fritz didn't answer on the first knock. Nor on the second. Not even on the third.

"Hate to break down such a nice door," Leslie said. "You two stay here and I'll go see if management has a key."

One flash of the search warrant in the concierge's face did the trick. He was a tall slender man sporting a broad smile and the name Jenkins on his name tag. He immediately entered numbers into a touch pad on the face of a small key safe. The door swung open, he extracted a key, handed it to Leslie, saying, "Don't really know why you need the key. Ms. Fritz hasn't gone out yet today."

"Would you know if she did?" Leslie asked, curious why Fritz hadn't responded if she was home.

"It's my job to know."

"What makes you so certain?"

"It's not unusual for her to sleep in on days she's traveling."

"Traveling? Where's she going?"

"Night man left a note saying she's being picked up at noon. Instructions are to send the driver up for her bags."

"She travel a lot?"

"Ms. Fritz's always going somewhere. Mostly to Europe."

"That where she's going this time?"

"Note said, Montenegro. That's all I know."

Leslie took the key and hurried back up to Fritz's apartment. Pulling Cox aside, she said, "Fritz is being picked up around noon. Going off to Montenegro. Ever heard of that place?"

"Think it's in Europe but can't place it." Cox reached for his cell and entered Montenegro. A moment later he said, "On the Adriatic, near Kosovo. Oh, in case you're wondering, there's no extradition to the U.S."

"Shit!" Leslie exclaimed, remembering Allen's comment about having one chance to nail Fritz. "Unless we find something solid linking her to the Fuller homicide, she'll be gone — for good."

"You two gonna stand in the corner over there and mumble," Deputy Jada called, no humor in her voice. "Or are we doin' what we came to be doin'?"

"Your body cam and mic on?" Leslie responded.

"Been on ever since we came out of the elevator," the deputy replied. "Ready to go."

Another unanswered knock and Cox called, "Police!" loud enough for the neighbors to hear him.

The deputy drew her weapon.

Leslie inserted and turned the key. The door opened inward. Cox again called, "Police!"

The deputy followed up by calling, "Police. We have a warrant."

Silence greeted them.

The deputy went in first and quickly checked behind the door. She motioned for Leslie to follow. Cox entered the apartment last. Leslie crossed the living room, passed through the office alcove and signaled to the deputy to push open the master bedroom door.

Weapon still drawn, the deputy did as instructed. The bed was made, the bathroom in perfect order. No Selma Fritz.

The small den was likewise empty. "Nothing back here," the deputy called, retracing her steps to where Cox and Leslie were positioned.

"This side of the apartment appears empty," Leslie said, more for the record than to advise her colleagues. "There's another bedroom in the hallway over there," Leslie pointed to the hallway off to the side. "Cox, push that door open and step back."

Cox slowly twisted the handle, pushing on the door with his foot.

Deputy Jada stood at the ready, her weapon pointed toward the doorway.

Still nothing.

"Do the same with the guest bathroom over there," Leslie instructed. "Ready. Go!"

The bathroom was also empty, causing the deputy to exclaim, "So, where the hell is this Fritz woman hiding? Seen this movie before and it doesn't end well."

Cox, studying a glass shelving unit at the end of the hall, said, "Isn't this where the entrance to that added space should be?"

"What added space?" the deputy asked, suddenly alert for trouble.

"A year or so back," Leslie explained, "the owner of this apartment bought the unit next door. The plans show a door right here," Leslie said, pointing to the shelving. "And a walk-in closet on the other side of this wall. And beyond the closet is a bedroom and small kitchen."

"I don't see no door!" Jada exclaimed, her face crinkling into a deep frown. "You folks know what you're doing?"

"I'm telling you what the plans show," Cox explained. "That's all we know."

"Does that apartment have a door to the hall?" the deputy asked. "We could go use that door. Better than busting through this here wall."

"Search warrant is only for this apartment," Leslie patiently explained, acknowledging to herself the stupidity of what she had just said.

The deputy's frown deepened. "I don't follow. If we can go in through this here wall, why not through the front door? Get to the same place."

"I don't make the laws," Leslie answered. "I try to follow them. We enter through this apartment or...or we go get a new warrant. I don't want the case blown by screwing up."

"If Fritz's leaving in two hours, doesn't give us much time for a new warrant," Cox argued. "I'm with Jada here. Let's go use the door down the hall."

"And do what? Screw up the case?"

"Won't screw up anything if she opens that door for us."

"We have no warrant for that apartment," Leslie argued, trying to convince herself she was right.

"If we don't and she's in there then a murderer might skip town."

Leslie thought a moment, considered following Cox's lead, but then said, "We have no evidence she's anything other than who she says she is. A woman whose fiancé has just been murdered."

"Going to Montenegro," Cox answered. "Isn't that enough to hold her?"

"Another guy watching too many old movies. Fritz is a European art expert. Didn't she find an artifact or something over there near Kosovo? Not unreasonable for her to be going there. Not at all."

"Speaking of movies," the deputy volunteered, "as a girl I watched movies on TV. In situations like this, they just pushed on one side of the bookshelf — and it turned." Jada holstered her weapon, took a step forward and gave the side of the shelve unit a playful push.

"Holly shit!" Cox exclaimed, drawing his weapon. "It's turning!"

# THIRTY-NINE

PROTOCOL DEMANDED THE UNIFORM GO through the opening first. "Police!" Deputy Jada announced, stepping through the wall, her eyes wide in anticipation. Leslie and Cox slipped through behind her.

"It's not a closet!" the deputy announced, shining her flashlight around the area. "It's a workshop of some sort."

It soon became clear that this was no ordinary workroom. The walls and ceiling were soundproofed. Several work benches were spread around the room interspersed with professional-looking woodworking tools.

"Shine your light over there," Leslie said, pointing to a wall off to the right. "There! Hold it." Following the light, Leslie walked over and inspected a box that appeared to contain several glass rods of varying sizes. "Spare rods for the euphon, I guess," she announced. "Move the light more to your left," she instructed. The outline of a booth identical to the soundproof one in Fuller's garage appeared. Beyond the booth there was a wall of meters and various pieces of equipment Leslie couldn't identify.

Cox, studying the equipment, said, "I'm certainly no expert, but that looks like a professional grade sound booth. Those meters likely measure sound."

"That would allow Fritz to tune the glass rods to the proper frequencies," Leslie added. "Bet we find glass cutting tools somewhere around here."

Cox motioned the deputy to continue moving the light around the room. "You think she melts the glass herself, say to get the right shape?"

"I don't see a furnace," Leslie answered, "or anything like that. But she might use a local glass-blowing place — or school. Oh, shit! That could explain the burn on her arm!"

"Is there a light switch for this room," Cox asked. "I didn't see one when we came in."

Deputy Jada played her light up and down as she slowly turned in a circle. "There it is," she announced, when the beam landed on a switch plate. "Should I turn it on?" she asked.

"I see no reason why not," Leslie responded.

The sudden light was blinding. But Cox had caught a glimpse of something in the corner just before the overhead lights had come on. "Look over here!" he exclaimed, careful not to stumble on anything while his eyes adjusted. "Looks like someone threw away one of those…"

"Pashminas!" Leslie exclaimed, hurrying over to the trash where Cox was standing. Bending down for a closer look, she said, "Take a look, Jada. What would you say happened to this cloth?"

"Looks…looks…ripped. Maybe burned, you ask me."

"Cox," Leslie said, "call Lang and have him out here to process this room. Deputy, don't allow anyone other than the ME Team in or out of this area. Call for back-ups if necessary. This is now a crime scene."

"Isn't that a bit premature?" Cox said. "Shouldn't we find Fritz first?"

"Most likely, long gone," Leslie replied. "She's the murderer. That much I now know."

"Leap of faith, if I must say so," Cox said, not understanding his partner's sudden resolve. "What's triggered you?"

Leslie wanted to say, I had a vision. Instead, she said, "You weren't there when I first met Fritz at Fuller's house immediately after she had called in his death."

"No, but I've seen the photos and read the file."

"So, what was Fritz wearing?" Leslie challenged.

"Don't recall exactly. Well dressed. In preparation for celebrating her engagement."

"What was missing?" Leslie pressed.

"I'm sure you're about to tell me."

"According to her, she always wears a pashmina to keep her warm in January. Her shawls are color coordinated with her outfit. The one over there contains shades of blue. The blouse she was wearing that day was blue. I'm willing to bet that pashmina over there is hers — the one she wore that day."

"Not to burst your bubble, Leslie, but you still don't have motive. After all, she and Fuller were to be married. That counts for something."

"It's her. I know it," Leslie insisted. "It's her alright. Now to prove it!"

"It's a long way from what we have to beyond a reasonable doubt," Cox reminded his partner. "A real long way."

"I know it's not my business," Jada injected, "but where the hell did she get to? Didn't you say she was still here?"

"That what the concierge told me. He's covering for her the way I'm seeing it," Leslie responded.

"Need to finish our search of the premises," Cox reminded them. "According to the plans, there's a bedroom over there." He pointed in the direction of the sound booth. "But I don't see a door."

"Maybe she's in the next-door apartment," Jada suggested, taking a step toward the opening in the wall back to the main apartment. "I'll go around and see."

"Not without a new warrant, you won't," Leslie instructed. "Instead, check inside the sound booth."

Jada opened the booth door and looked inside. "Spooky in there," she said, pulling her head back out. "Can't see shit!"

"Doors got to be here someplace," Cox said, grabbing Jada's flashlight and disappearing inside the booth.

Leslie heard a faint mumble from inside the booth and moved over to listen for it again. She heard nothing.

"Shit!" Cox exclaimed a moment later as he emerged from the booth, a smile appearing at the corner of his lips, his eyes now showing a semblance of life. "What the hell you two waiting for? Found the door."

"I'll go first," Jada instructed, motioning Cox to step aside.

The two detectives followed Jada into the small booth and through a now open door. Something directly ahead of them moved. Jada's light beam swung forward catching a naked Selma Fritz sitting upright in bed, a bewildered expression on her face. It took Fritz an instant to realize people were in the room and a still further instant to pull a sheet up to cover herself.

"And who do we have here?" Leslie asked, the flashlight beam falling on the still prone figure lying face down beside Fritz, his face partially covered by a sheet.

Receiving no answer, Leslie walked to the bed and pulled the sheet away. "Oh, my God!" she exclaimed, "this is too much! Everything now makes perfect sense!" Leslie stepped aside so Cox could see for himself. "Partner, if this isn't beyond a reasonable doubt, then I don't know what is!"

Then, almost as an afterthought, she said, "You both are under arrest for the murder of Dr.

Sigmund Fuller. You have the right to remain silent. Everything you say, can, and will, be used against you in a court of law. Cox, cuff this one. I'll do award-winning actress Selma Fritz."

A confused Deputy Jada, her gun trained on Fritz, said, "I take it you know these people."

"Deputy. Let me introduce you to Selma Fritz and her accomplice — and apparent lover — Ernst Chlad."

"Didn't you say earlier," the deputy replied, struggling to put it all together, "Fritz here and the deceased were...engaged to be married? Then why is she here with...?"

"This woman's a loner," Leslie responded. "In her first marriage she and her then husband were almost never in the same city. Her relationship with Dr. Fuller may have begun real enough, two kindred souls pursuing their passion for art in Europe. But her ambition took hold of her. Apparently, she had no qualms about scoring a huge payday and disappearing into the sunset. That's where Ernst Chlad came in. A hundred million from Stratis for the original euphon. Fritz, likely working with an art collector named Morris Stratis, produces a duplicate euphon authentic enough to satisfy a bribed Polish government. Everyone wins. That is, except for Fuller, a man of integrity, who would never have participated in duplicity. Fuller and Fritz, two mismatched souls if ever there were any."

"A deadly combination," Cox added, unaware of his pun. "I suppose Detective Jakowski was the facilitator between Stratis and Fritz."

"That's the way I see it," Leslie answered, deeply troubled by the duplicity of the big Pittsburgh detective.

Cox, pulling Chlad to his feet, said, "So why not just take the money and disappear into the Montenegro sunset? Why kill Fuller?"

"I didn't have anything to do with that! Nothing! Selma found him in the garage where Colton had left him. Sig had been drugged and..."

"Shut your mouth!" Fritz screamed. "Say nothing!"

"Hell with that! You didn't have to kill him! You could have..."

"Shut up!"

Chlad continued, "Colton had drugged Sig, trying to find out where the seventeen-seventeen was. No doubt Sig would have reported the attempt on his life, which would have screwed up all the plans. Selma flew into a rage and activated the bike hoist."

Cox turned to Fritz, now lying face down on the bed rapped in a sheet, her hands cuffed behind her. "I'm curious as to what your long-term intentions are — were — with Chlad here. Assuming, of course, we hadn't caught you? You planning on living together? Getting married? What?"

Fritz remained silent.

Leslie looking directly into Chlad's downcast eyes, said, "My advice to you for what it's worth, stay out from under bicycle hoists."

E n d

# Thank You

EDITORS ARE CRITICAL AND I am blessed with several great ones. My wonderful daughter-in-law, Brenda Goldberg Tannenbaum, spends countless hours carefully tracking down errors I continually try to introduce. Along with Brenda, my stepson, Charles Kappauf, Jr., Debi Bass, and Lori Cameron, have done an exceptional job with their thoughtful comments and suggestions. A big thank you also to Charles Ryan for his insightful comments. Their careful attention to detail is invaluable.

I very much appreciate the hard work and encouragement of my publisher, Red Engine Press and particularly of Joyce Faulkner, (an accomplished author in her own right). The Seminal Society is in good hands with Red Engine Press at the helm.

As has been my good fortune for more years than I care to acknowledge, my longtime friend, Ronald Slusky patiently calls to my attention words, phrases, sentences, paragraphs and chapters that are incorrect, misplaced, redundant or worse. We don't always agree, but more times than not he's right. Sometimes I learn that by hindsight. Errors and omissions that remain after all the hard work of so many people are mine and mine alone; my sword to bear for not listening to their advice.

Thank you as always to Mary Tannenbaum, my wonderful wife, for continuing to make my writing life possible. I don't know what I would do without your continuing encouragement and green florescent marker ink on draft after draft.

# About The Author

David Harry Tannenbaum and his wife, Mary, have a home in Miromar Lakes, Florida. When David isn't writing, he enjoys swimming, model train building, and walking Franco.

# Communications

David can be reached at author@seminalsociety.com and followed on website: seminalsociety.com.